NESTLED INTO A FROTH OF EMERALD GREEN silk sat a clockwork humming bird; the bejeweled and enameled feathers looked real. I touched the long beak. A tiny prick of blood appeared on my fingertip. "Oh!" I jerked my hand away, finally feeling the tiny bit of pain after the fact.

"Let me show you," Drew laughed as he touched a long bit of green enamel at the base of the tail. A spring whirred, the bird chirped, and the back opened to reveal a tiny clock face, and a compass.

And beneath the compass, a little well for . . . a small thimbleful of poison?

"I can always tell the time and know where I'm going, even without your guidance," I said, amazed at the delicate detail.

I could also use it as a weapon to ward off pickpockets and unwanted admirers.

Or to draw blood for arcane magic rituals.

THE TRANSFERENCE ENGINE

Julia Verne St. John

THE
TRANSFERENCE
ENGINE

DAW BOOKS, INC.

DONALD A. WOLLHEIM, FOUNDER

375 Hudson Street, New York, NY 10014

ELIZABETH R. WOLLHEIM
SHEILA E. GILBERT
PUBLISHERS

www.dawbooks.com

First Printing, July 2016
1 2 3 4 5 6 7 8 9

This book and all the stories that go with it are dedicated to Augusta Ada Byron King, Countess of Lovelace, credited with being the first female computer programmer and an incredible forward thinker.

 Prologue

Burgage Manor, Southwell,
Nottinghamshire, Autumn, 1824

IN 1802, LORD GEORGE Gordon Byron came to live there with his mother, but he disliked the provincial village intensely, describing it as the resort of "old Parsons and old Maids."

It looked damp, dark, and dismal. If ever a place was haunted, it was this moldering country house. Maybe that was why Byron disliked the place so intensely; the ghosts of his experiments with necromancy followed him around even as a child.

Of all the properties associated with Byron, this is where his widow chose to live. Because he hated it.

Did she believe he would avoid haunting her here? Or did she hope he would?

I had to find out before I revealed how much I truly knew about the poet king and his . . . obsessions.

"Miss Elise Vollans," Lady Anna Isabella Byron read aloud the last item on my letter of reference. She held a title of her own as Baroness Wentworth, and need not rely on her notorious husband for her honors and income, and yet she clung to his name and title.

"Governess and nursemaid for three children in the household of Baroness Von Gutenberg . . ."

She didn't need to know that I had left the Von Gutenberg household after three weeks when I'd learned what I needed to from her husband's aetheric powered Leyden jar experiments. Lord Byron's soul—if he ever had one—wasn't in one of them.

"Your credentials are interesting, Miss Elise." Lady Byron looked down her long nose and formed her mouth into a prim moue.

Those references should be interesting, if not impressive. I'd created them specifically to . . . intrigue her. If not the whole truth, they did brush facts occasionally.

I stood before her, tall and straight, blonde hair braided and twisted into a stylish chignon, my dress and jacket suitably modest, and as severe a cut as I could manage, though I hated the tiny pin tucks down the blouse because they looked so prim and proper and never lay flat even after heavy ironing. They were considered right and proper for a woman of my station, or the station I aspired to. I preferred silk for my blouse instead of the new cotton from Egypt, made cheap by the advances in steam power to the separating gin. No governess applying for a new position would wear my preferred white Chantilly lace and vivid red silk roses.

(Don't rail at me. Of course Chantilly is supposed to be black silk, but some aristocratic bride in Paris had requested white lace from the makers in Chantille and now it was all the rage. No black to be had, anywhere, except Spain.)

The poet's widow had to look up, way up to engage my gaze, from her perch on the edge of the threadbare satin sofa in her second best parlor.

Today I needed her aware of just how formidable my raw-boned Teutonic frame could be. I stood half a head taller than many men and could lift my own weight when I had to.

"I have never met this woman who pens this letter, Mary Godwin Dessins," she said, not at all intimidated. She'd survived Byron; why should I intimidate her? She snapped the paper of my carefully constructed resume with disdain. She didn't need to know of my talent at imitating another's voice, walk, and laugh, as well as their penmanship.

"You have heard of Mme. Dessins, though." I kept my gaze firmly planted on hers. Neither of us flinched. This could be an ... interesting relationship, if word of her charitable good works was true.

She nodded briskly, once. "I know her father preached free love ..." Lady Byron swallowed deeply as if acid had attacked her mouth. "And my *deceased* husband and his comrades followed his ... philosophy."

"You also know that my previous mistress repented her *affaire de coeur* with one of those comrades and escaped him. I helped her and her infant son flee the Villa Diodati. We spent ten years together before I put her on a ship headed west from Liverpool."

Again she nodded and drew her knitted lace shawl tighter around her shoulders. Good black wool, as light as a cobweb and expensive ten years ago, but scant protection from the autumnal chill creeping through the ancient walls.

She had not indulged in steam heat or gaslights in this shabby and isolated home. She must know the dangers as well as the benefits of the new sciences. Or she couldn't afford them. Rumor had it she was still paying off her husband's debts with her own money, some months after his supposed death.

At least with a body buried at the entailed estate of Southwell Abbey and the title passed to a distant cousin, George Gordon, Lord Byron, couldn't lay claim to any of his, or his wife's, income. Nor could he publish under his real name and reputation without revealing his sacrilegious secrets of rising from the dead. He'd have to earn a living by his wits. Unless he stole cunning along with his new body, which I knew him perfectly capable of.

I also knew he still collected followers through his secret books on the topic of necromancy. Newly penned works, as well as older ones, were still available if you knew which booksellers to approach.

His followers tended to be fanatical about their lord and master. Willing to die for him. Literally.

My mistress Mary Godwin and I had escaped them a time or two. We both knew too much.

"Lady Byron, you will have heard that Mistress Dessins and I spent the last eight years escaping from both Mr. Shelley and Lord Byron." I didn't mention the disgraced Dr. John Polidari. His name was even less respectable than those of the poets. Shelley and Byron at least could claim artistic sensibility for their perfidy. Polidari could claim only negligence and unbridled curiosity that had cost at least two patients their lives.

I suspected he'd murdered them in his own quest for immortality through necromantic experiments. He was Byron's personal physician and constant shadow, hoping to learn from a truly formidable necromancer.

Lady Byron opened her heavily lidded eyes and stared into mine, challenging me with her silence.

"I protected Miss Mary, her children, and her new husband more than once. I know what to look for in a man to know if he is an agent of your husband."

"My husband died. He is no longer a threat to me or my daughter."

This time, I held her gaze, forcing her to think about the unspoken truth. She didn't back down, but she did speak. "My daughter, Augusta Ada, is in need of tutors in mathematics and the sciences. Firm men who will drive any shadow of artistic nonsense from her. They will make sure that she never succumbs to her father's poetic spells or evildoing."

I continued my silence. I knew this. I also knew that

before his "death" Lord Byron had sought out some of those same mathematicians and scientists to help him rebuild his transference engine. They could still work for him and corrupt his daughter—or trick her into redesigning the engine. I wished, not for the first time, I'd done a more thorough job of smashing the original into oblivion back in that fateful and desolate summer of '16 at the Villa Diodati.

"What do you know?" Lady Byron blurted out, almost angrily. But I knew her anger was not directed at me.

"I know how to keep secrets." Secrets of how Lord Byron was obsessed with immortality. He and the incompetent Dr. Polidari had tried more than once to transfer his soul into a different body, more perfect than his own malformed one. He preferred drowning victims—less damage to the external features. Percy Shelley reportedly drowned two years ago in a boating accident in Italy. He was a very handsome man with an exquisite body. He was also reputed to have been seen in Greece a month later. His beauty I knew from firsthand experience. He practiced Godwin's *free love* philosophy with less … discrimination than Lord Byron. Shelley merely liked his paramours young—his first wife and Mary Godwin had both been fifteen when he seduced them. I was sixteen. Byron insisted they be petite and dark-haired as well as young. I didn't qualify as female in his opinion.

"Secrets? You will have no secrets from me. If I employ you."

I arched my left eyebrow in reply.

"I have no doubt that you can protect my daughter, physically. In that we are in agreement. But what can you teach her? She has had the finest tutors."

"I speak and read four languages fluently." What child of Switzerland didn't? Five languages if you counted Romany. I needed to know more about Lady Byron before admitting I was friends with a tribe of "gypsies."

"I have read history extensively," I continued. "I have

observed politics across Europe. I know the social graces acceptable in Geneva, Paris, Rome, and Copenhagen. They differ, if only slightly. Knowing that difference when dealing with international personalities in London will be an asset to you and your daughter." I had more arguments in my favor. Lady Byron dismissed them with a tired wave of her hand.

My stomach bounced and wriggled uncomfortably. My vision narrowed. I needed . . . The blackness crowding into my peripheral vision sparkled brightly around a twirling figure that might be a young girl. Or me. Though I'd never had a vision for myself. Then something dimmed the scintillating lights.

I dove for the floor beside the door, dragging the lady with me.

Anything Lady Byron might have said was lost in a sharp shattering of glass. Sharp shards sprayed across us. I tasted blood before I felt the burn of a slice across my cheek.

A rock bounced from the couch where she'd been sitting, to the floor and across the worn carpet. Such a waste of good Turkish weaving.

I did not pay a ruffian to throw that rock. Honestly, I did not. Though my younger sister Trude, budding pirate that she was, would have gladly done it, if I offered her the last gold crown in my reticule.

"Did . . . did you know of this?" Lady Byron turned a glacial gaze upon me as I heaved myself to my feet and straightened my skirt. I retrieved from my sleeve a gray handkerchief that matched my gown in color and serviceability and pressed it hard against my now burning cheek. I surveyed the side yard from safety behind the heavy draperies rather than glance her way.

I saw no movement or strange shadow that might betray whoever threw the rock. He was probably long gone, having run while we sought shelter.

My belly churned and my vision closed down to a

narrow tunnel. If I had a cup of tea, or even a glass of water, I might see something in the whirlpool as I stirred.

Was that a misshapen lump huddled next to the beech tree?

Only then did the lady notice the crimson stain on my face. "The glass cut you," she said flatly.

"Yes, m'lady," I replied just as flatly. Emotion was wasted on such as she. She wouldn't allow hysterics in herself, let alone her daughter or a staff member. Oh, well, I could save a bout of tears and shakes for another, more receptive audience.

"The rock could have hit me if you had not acted so quickly," Lady Byron said with the slightest edge of panic in her voice.

I shrugged. The obvious needed no answer.

"I owe you thanks." She didn't actually offer them. I could teach her some manners.

I nodded graciously, keeping a keen eye on the grounds visible from the long window in the small room.

The lump at the beech tree had shifted to the opposite side and seemed larger.

A new thought wiggled from the mid-region to my brain. If the target had not actually been Lady Byron, then the missile was merely a ruse to distract from the true purpose.

"Where is your daughter, m'lady?"

"At her studies." She rose anxiously and hastened for the bell. Carrick, the reedy butler of indeterminate years, answered too promptly, obviously expecting the summons to escort me out rather than the anxious query of his mistress. "Send Miss Augusta to me immediately," she demanded, hands reaching out like claws to clutch at his lapels. She restrained her gesture at the last second, not quite touching him.

I surmised they had been together a long time. Just how much familiarity had developed between them?

Wouldn't be the first time a lady had sought comfort

with a trusted servant when she had not seen an estranged and disreputable husband in nigh on ten years.

I wondered if Carrick's eye strayed beyond his mistress while I assessed his long and lean form. We stood nearly eye to eye, he topping me by at least half an inch.

I smiled.

Before the expression had a chance to reach my eyes, a child's scream sent my heart pumping and my mind whirling. Without a thought, I hiked my utilitarian gray serge skirt almost to my knees and quite indelicately dashed up the stairs, shouldering aside both lady and butler.

Damn this corset. I'd laced it tightly this morning to make the ensemble fit properly, not anticipating having to run up stairs and breathe at the same time.

Thank whatever gods might be, Lady Byron kept her child close to her in the family living quarters on the first floor abovestairs rather than in some drafty attic two more stories up. A second scream directed me to the last door on the left, facing the front drive.

I kicked open the door, not caring about splintering the lock. A dark-coated figure with a woolen scarf wrapped around neck and lower face held a knife tightly across the throat of a little girl. A long black, vorpal blade glinted in the lamplight. I noted the girl's dark hair and olive-toned skin—not quite as sunburned and swarthy as her father's—and her huge frightened eyes.

I didn't waste time assessing the danger. I'd done this before.

Three strides in, a kick to the knee, a fist to the side of the head.

A squelched squeal and a grunt. I closed my free hand around a slender wrist and twisted.

Snap. A bone broke. Clatter. The knife fell to the floor. I pushed the girl back toward her mother.

The black-garbed creature scuttled out the open window faster than I could follow. It scampered from ridgeline to chimney pot, then using only the left hand and both feet, it swung down a twist of ivy like a monkey from Gibraltar.

I ran back down the stairs. The grounds were empty as far as I could see. Miss Augusta Ada Byron was safe for now. I decided the name was too big and pretentious for such a fragile child. Ada she would be to me. And to the world, though I didn't know *that* yet.

"Lady Byron, we need to talk," I said. "There are things, unpleasant things, you need to know about Lord Byron."

"I know . . . too much already."

"You need to know more if we are to protect your daughter."

Chapter One

Above London, early June 1838

THE GAS FLAMES HISSED like a malevolent ad-
der as Jimmy Porto, the hot air balloon's pilot,
pushed more gas into the envelope above us. I looked up
and up to the interior of the dull gray silk. Cool dawn air
caressed my cheeks. I marveled that no wind blew my
blonde braids where they dangled down my back. But
we moved at the same speed as the gentle wind, rather
than standing still on the ground, defying it.

"Thank you again, Jimmy, for bringing me up today,"
I said.

"No problem, Miz Elise." He tugged the brim of his
cap once. "We owe you."

Yes, indeed, the Rom did. I thought they'd repaid me
a hundred times over. But the Rom ... carried this debt
through several lifetimes. One lifetime for each of their
lives I had saved back in southern France in 1817.

He met my gaze in gratitude, something Romany men
did not do with a gorgí female, or even one of their own
females unless she was a wife or a sister.

"I know what it is to have violently angry men on my
trail. I could do nothing less." I'd also seen more than
enough needless death. The demise of an entire clan

would have fueled a drunken vicomte's necromancy for a year or more. "I had to warn you. Not one of you would be left alive if I didn't."

"That's a risk you didn't have to take."

Yes, I did. For reasons I'd not tell him. "Still I thank you for letting me observe from your balloon this morning."

Up here, one thousand feet above civilization, the air was fresh and crisp; the golden light of early morning clear and sharp. None of the smells of too many people crowded into too small a space penetrated my sensitized nose. The smoke of tens of thousands of coal fires lay like a pall over the rooftops with only an occasional church spire rising toward heaven, giving a hopeful pathway for all the prayers of people trapped below.

Steam-powered engines lightened the burdens of life, giving us many advances in transportation, communication, and household appliances. But the burning coal needed to convert ordinary water into steam left behind a filthy residue.

Below us, the city sprawled in unruly lines and clumps, blurred by smoke. The dome of St. Paul's stood out from the jumble of London, one of a few distinctive landmarks. But once I'd anchored my sense of direction in the eternal symbol of solidity, permanence, and hope, my eyes pushed aside the pall and found other familiar places. Tower Bridge, Westminster, Piccadilly Circus. The winds pushed us west and north, following the Thames, the heart vein of transportation and commerce of southern England.

"There be Windsor, Miz Elise," Jimmy pointed upriver. Farther than I wanted to go.

I winced at his use of my original name. Jimmy had known me too long. But he was useful as a pilot when I needed one, as a friend and go-between with his family of Romany spread across the entire island and half the continent.

Since Miss Ada Byron had married, I'd transformed

myself into a new personality (not with Lord Byron's dreaded transference engine, merely a new name, a new attitude, and a new wardrobe). No more the drab, respectful governess.

Jimmy's people had helped me protect Miss Ada many times over the last decade—more of their perceived debt to me, which they had extended to my pupil. They also kept me apprised of necromancers taking up residence in ruined castles, and scientists moving their experiments away from the ethical and moral strictures of Oxford and Cambridge.

"Deploy the ailerons, Jimmy. I need to circle the city," I said.

"Be prettier out here," he replied, not moving his hand to the brass lever near the ring joining the firebox to the envelope. He drew in a long breath of the clear country air smelling of freshly tilled fields, trees leafing out, and meadow flowers. I mimicked his inhalation and appreciated why he wanted to linger, drifting aimlessly with the breeze.

"This is important, Jimmy. I love the green land as much as you do. I love the freedom of the roving life that you have transferred to roaming the skies. But I need to see the patterns of movement through the city. I have heard rumors. Possibly of violence at the queen's coronation. My visions have confirmed them. I need to *know* which malevolent force drives those rumors. Or if my visions are failing me."

We spoke in Romany. Most of Jimmy's country accent disappeared in his native language. He even spoke correctly . . . mostly.

"Aye, Miss Elise. I feels it, too. Something wicked stirs the air and the people. I'll get you as low as I dare." He flashed me a cheeky grin as he engaged the lever that sent semi-rigid folds of silk outward and tacked back to the city, much as a sailboat would move against the wind. "Used fog gray for the envelope just so we'd stay invisible a bit longer." A true Romany at heart, flamboyant and audacious when needed, equally quiet and hidden when skirting the law and distrustful *gorgí*.

He really was attractive in his slender, olive-skinned, and dark-eyed way. Alas, he was much too young for me, and though his tribe respected me for my visions and thanked me for my help, I was *gorgí*: an outsider, forbidden to touch.

"Romany know how to hide." I returned his grin, grateful for the lessons they'd taught me.

We drifted back over the city, taking in more of the dark, poverty-stricken jungle of Southwark, south of the river. Evil could hide in the open streets and opulent houses on the north side just as easily as in the tenements. Armed military men were reluctant to enter Southwark. Criminals lived openly there, protected by neighbors who closed in on themselves like any impoverished ghetto. The military might of the country was put to better use protecting our new queen, young and beautiful Victoria. I had my own ways of making sure her upcoming coronation occurred on time, without the blemish of an assassination attempt.

It would be an attempt only. My enemies would use it as a diversion for other nefarious activities.

"There, Jimmy!" I pointed to a dark object hovering in the lee of St. Paul's.

Another balloon. Black envelope, black basket, seemingly empty.

"Hovers, it does," Jimmy said quietly on a long exhale. "Balloons need to move, flow with the air which is never still."

I dropped a single magnifier over my flying goggles. The black basket jumped into sharper detail. Not a lot of room between the rim and the firebox.

Then a long telescope snaked out over the edge and pointed down. Whoever was in there looked at individuals, not large patterns.

"Pointing that thing toward Trafalgar Square, they be," Jimmy muttered.

His young eyes were better than mine. I hated admitting that I needed spectacles.

"What is there? Besides a monument to a beloved but fallen admiral and his mighty victory over the French."

A memorial to the dead. Necromancers needed death to fuel their magic.

And then the light patterns shifted, and I spotted the glint of sunlight on a brass circular opening in the bottom corner of the basket. A musket barrel? Or a small cannon? Aimed directly at Westminster Abbey where the coronation would take place in a matter of three weeks.

We descended rapidly, away from that black monster.

o⚙

By the time I got to the Abbey and the Parliament buildings, all was normal and the black balloon had disappeared. I could neither see nor smell anything out of the ordinary. If Jimmy hadn't corroborated my view of the situation, I might think I'd dreamed it.

So I returned to my home amid the morning bustle along Charing Cross Road.

"That's Madame Magdala," a stout woman dressed in black from bonnet to boots to lace parasol whispered, (a widow of minor means, I guessed from the classic cut of her gown that would take time to go out of style), jabbing her younger companion in the ribs with that wicked parasol. I wondered if she could extend the tip into a knife. I knew I wasn't the only woman in London who'd purchased such an instrument from *Georges' Emporium of Fine Imported Lace*. "She may be a widow and allowed some leeway in propriety, but she takes it too far." The woman in black sniffed in disdain.

"The natural daughter of the Gypsy king?" asked the slight woman in awe. She wore a traveling gown in dark green, a fashion at least two years out of date. Must be the daughter, goddaughter, or niece of the widow, down from the country for the coronation—and the opportunity to meet an eligible man.

The girl continued in a whisper, "I heard that she'd only been married a few weeks when her husband was killed at Waterloo. She never remarried. How romantic." The girl sighed and held her hand to her heart.

At least the myth I'd created to give me license to run my own business and control my own affairs held true.

"I don't know any way to birth a child but the natural way," I muttered. If they wanted to parrot my new name and way of life they should use the appropriate term. Bastard. Yet I was sure they considered themselves upright and faithful daughters of the Church of England, too proper to use such language.

Hastily, I shoved my goggles atop my leather flying helmet and peered at the crowds of people on the walkways and spilling over into the carriage-jammed road. A number of genteel couples adjusted their path around me. My leather jacket atop jodhpurs and high boots couldn't disguise my feminine figure, even if I did stand taller than most of the men. Many of them let their gaze linger while their female companions sniffed in disdain.

"Too damn many people in London these days," I said. The crowd gave me more room to move out of their way as I found the key to my café and reading room in a convenient pocket. The dustmen were late, and the back door was more than a bit noisome in the June heat. Otherwise I'd have used it and avoided the contemptuous crowd.

I sniffed and peered around to see if any of the passersby bore the taint of magic manipulation. Nothing. Whoever spied upon the crowds today had not used magic. One more piece of a giant puzzle of odd bits of information I stored for Ada Byron King, Countess Lovelace. Yes, the dark-haired and frightened little girl I had nurtured through adolescence and taught to appreciate the joys of life as much as the beauty and magic of numbers had grown up and married a wealthy man who adored her. She had helped me purchase the café and left her name off the deed so that our inquiries could not be traced back to her ever-so-proper husband and his titles: the gift of Victoria.

I'd heard rumors that Victoria would return a semblance of propriety to English society after the ... delicious ... scandals of her royal uncles. At least her mother hoped so.

I hoped not. Life would be ever so dull without new scandals every other day.

A "lady" jabbed my knees with her parasol as she passed. "Thank you for reminding me that if I linger gawking I'll be late to my own salon," I whispered just loud enough to make sure she heard me.

The bells inside my door tinkled invitingly as I strode inside with long, mannish strides. I know I should affect a more feminine walk. But why waste the freedom of trousers and boots?

That freedom was short-lived. I needed to bake sweet and savory delicacies for my guests as Violet, my assistant, would not return from her free morning with her mother until the afternoon. Then I would repair to my quarters upstairs to prepare myself so that I could greet my guests properly corseted, beribboned, and draped in fine silk. I wondered if anyone new would grace us with scintillating conversation or controversial issues to debate. Hmm ... I needed to collect the latest newspapers from Hong Kong, New Delhi, Peking, and Tokyo, delivered weekly by dirigible express, so we'd have new information to dissect. Amazing what insights and patterns of unrest or transfer of raw goods to indicate a petty tyrant was building an army of automata I could uncover when I listened while others read aloud interesting tidbits from afar.

Those automata might also serve the purpose of housing the soul of a necromancer after the body had succumbed. I didn't know how or why, but Lord Byron's quest for the perfect body might involve an artificial one. The metal men were still crude devices. Scientists worked hard at making them more human looking.

I kept a neat kitchen, but no order survives the first onslaught of sifted flour and sugar. Butter and cream, cheeses and herbs, fruits and glazes, all my ingredients came readily to hand. I fell into a soothing rhythm combining them in proper ratios, losing myself in recipes based upon my mother's confections that I'd perfected for British tastes. Modern scientists extolled the virtues of coal-fired steam ovens that added moisture and an even baking temperature. While I embraced much of the new technology, properly banked coals from a wood fire still suited my baking best.

When I looked up from removing a fifth batch from the oven, the clock chimed six.

"Six?" I asked aloud, somewhat alarmed.

"Violet?" I called. My assistant should have returned five hours ago. I would have noticed her return no matter how deeply immersed I was in the rituals of baking. Between batches, I had set the wine to breathing and arranged a nice store of hard liquor safely locked into its cupboard in my parlor.

"Violet?"

Silence inside, subdued traffic noise outside.

 Chapter Two

"**V**IOLET!**"** I LET ANGER mask the growing fear in my belly as I ran through the entire building. I started with my assistant's room and the extra cubicles in the attic, then down to my private suite. No sounds, no out-of-place shadows, nothing. The more public parlor and reading room on the first floor abovestairs was equally empty, as was the café, which occupied the entire ground floor, and the kitchen one level lower. That left the hot, moist cellar with the café boiler and the brick walls between the cellar moisture and part of the bookshelves. Violet hated the cellars and refused to enter even with the drayman from the dairy master, whom she fancied, as escort and a brightly lit oil lamp. I didn't find her there either.

So I drew a deep breath for courage and entered the stationers next door from the back courtyard and down to that cellar—I owned it but leased the upper part of the building. The cellar here was filled with boilers, the ones that powered the clockwork book catalog and search engine. The amount of steam they put forth would have ruined my books and periodicals. I had trouble enough keeping the smaller boiler beneath the café from making the entire building too damp for book storage.

No sign of Violet or the coal drayman here either. I made a note to order more coal, having peeked into the bin and finding it half-empty. By the time I could get another delivery, it would be down to less than a quarter.

The only other building on my property was the pump shed that doubled as an icehouse, packed tightly with eggs, milk, and cheese. I'd caught the girl there a time or two with the drayman of her choice. But she wasn't there, nor did it look like she had been.

As I ran down the formal staircase from parlor to café for the third time, a rapid tap on the back door brought me to an abrupt halt beside the circular desk that guarded the steam-and-clockwork–powered library catalog and the empty coffee bar. I did serve tea, but most of my customers preferred to savor the stimulating dark brew recently made popular in Paris by new explorations in Africa. Tea was for ladies and boringly respectable men. My customers sought something bolder, and I embodied that boldness.

A repeat of the knock broke the paralysis from my knees. I hastened down to the kitchen where I cranked open the three locks, and dislodged two chains, hoping desperately that Violet had forgotten her key. A modicum of common sense stilled my hand. Cautiously, I peered through the spy hole beside the door, before opening it. A small ragged silhouette cowered against the building, warily searching the alleyway. Two taller, decidedly feminine figures stood before the peephole.

"Who?" I whispered through the tiny hole covered with a magnifying glass lens before I opened the latch.

The shape against the wall jumped and pressed itself closer to the door. "Charlotte and Addie. We've brought Mickey," came the quiet reply.

I twisted the latch and yanked open the door. My fingers curled around the boy's collar and pulled him inward even as I scanned the alley for any sign that Violet lingered there, perhaps frightened she might lose her job for returning late. Finding no sign of the girl I needed, I made way for the two young women I'd rescued from a life of prostitution at the ages of eleven and twelve and found them places with the milliner down the lane. Then I slammed the door closed again and reengaged the locks. "Mickey, what are you doing out so late of a Monday afternoon? And why couldn't you find your way back here alone?"

Mickey looked scared. Therefore, I needed to be as well.

"We found him huddled in our alley behind the dustbin, crying like the world was ending," Charlotte said. "We brought him to you and now we have to go home before our mistress discovers we aren't crimping blue ribbons and twisting red ones into roses." She and Addie looked to each other as if some silent communication passed between them, then left quickly and quietly together. Arm in arm—more than just friendship between those two, but I'd never say that out loud.

"You be closed 'a Monday. Cain't come sooner, or you'd no be here," Mickey wailed with a trembling lip and a nose just snotty enough to tell me the eight-year-old orphan who knew the back streets and alleyways of London better than I did had cried for a good long time but hadn't cried away all his tears.

"What has happened to upset you so?" I pumped water onto a dishtowel and handed it to him so he could clean his face and hands. Then I used another dry cloth to protect my hands while I drew forth the baking from the oven. Mentally I counted the numbers and hoped this would suffice for my guests.

Mickey rubbed at his embedded grime diligently. He knew the rules of working for me, even if he'd only been tamed a few weeks before. Many of my boys, orphaned guttersnipes, one and all, were like feral cats who had to be tempted back to civilization with tidbits of nourishing food, a discarded blanket, and an occasional foray into the warmth. I pushed them toward a full bath by insisting on clean hands and faces indoors—even if the occasional dishtowel had to be discarded, too grimy to ever come clean. Trust came hard between us, so I let them stay a bit wild. They kept their familiarity with the streets better that way. If they ever showed signs of wanting to stay inside, they lost their usefulness to me. That's when I found them apprenticeships and permanent shelter. No sense littering my nice clean café with muddy boot prints and ragged clothing. Boys were messy and rebellious. Too much trouble past the age of twelve.

Except for . . .

"Cain't find Toby," Mickey said around a sniffle.

I gestured toward the damp and now very hopelessly grimy towel.

"Toby is a big boy." The biggest of my boys, pushing sixteen and all arms and legs and feet. The slight uptilt of his eyes and round face made him an endearing cherub long past needing his first shave. Keeping him in shoes was getting to be a problem, though his castoffs did help the littler ones.

"Toby can find his way home when he wants." I sniffed this time. Lately Toby had shown a streak of dependence and a need to sleep by the fire that indicated I'd have to find him new employment before long. Who else would take on his slow mind? His extreme loyalty to me would be hard to transfer.

"But that's just it, Missus. He gets lost. Cain't read the road markers like I kin. Toby don't know up from down without me tellin' 'im," Mickey protested.

There was that problem. A boy with a body too big for his mind.

"He allus stays real close to me. Holdin' me coattails. Today he just disappeared, cain't find him in any of our usual places."

"Where did you lose him?" I demanded, seriously worried now.

"By the Circus."

Not far from Trafalgar Square where the black balloon hovered.

"Piccadilly," I sighed. For some reason the circular road around a looming statue that connected Regent Street with Shaftesbury always fascinated Mickey but frightened Toby. He saw the winged bronze statue on its tower pedestal with a nocked arrow—often called *The Angel of Christian Charity*, though it was intended to be Anteros, god of requited love—as some kind of vengeful monster about to break free of its bronze casing and devour him.

"What were you doing there, Mickey?" I tapped my toe impatiently, hoping he'd enlighten me to something unusual that the black balloon might spy upon. Maybe Toby was at nearby Trafalgar Square, lost in the open spaces, using the statue of a warrior to protect him from the vengeful angel at Piccadilly.

Inside the darkened café the bronze clock bonged the three-quarter hour. Time was slipping away, and I needed to prepare for tonight's gathering.

Where was Violet?

"We was watchin' t' nobs, like you tell us to." Mickey sounded defensive, building a bit of courage, I hoped. Courage to go back out into the twilight and search for his lost charge and maybe Violet as well.

"Did you see anything interesting? Or useful?"

"Aye, Missus. Aye, that I did. Heard things, too, I did. Seen the beggar with the withered right hand, and heard him say somethin' odd, too." Now his eyes became cunning. I'd have to pay for whatever information littered his brain in scattered fragments. Organization was not Mickey's best talent. He showed signs of needing greater order, like touching his fingers as he recounted things, building lists in his mind, but so far hadn't mastered it.

"There's bread in the pantry, butter and cheese in the stillroom."

"Cream?" His eyes brightened in anticipation.

Did I say he was like a feral cat?

oO

"Tighter, Mickey," I ordered as the little boy tugged fee-bly on my laces. I could manage my corsets most of the time. Tonight I needed to go tighter, almost to not breathing, in order to fit into my gown. Made two years ago, before I began to fill out.

Where the hell was Violet? She'd lose her job the moment she poked her nose in my door. I had to trade Mickey's report on the odd comment about the black balloon by a beggar with a withered hand for assistance in dressing. By the time we finished, Mickey would have forgotten what he heard.

"If'n I pull any tighter, you won't be able to breathe," Mickey protested. Puzzlement colored his voice rather than embarrassment. He was only eight and I showed little more skin in my nether garments than I did fully clothed in evening wear.

"That is rather the point: keeping women from breathing deep enough to speak their minds, or getting up and leaving fast enough to avoid being restrained by a man."

He gave another weak tug and I resigned myself to looking a little stout, with less of a distracting shelf shoved above my corset to hold male eyes this evening. Maybe if I only ate two sugar buns with breakfast instead of four . . .

"You are fed. You are warm. You are clean, and I've given you *three* ha' pennies. Tell me about the black monster in the sky above Trafalgar Square and what the beggar said about it."

"Making me your lady's maid's going to cost you extra, Missus." He looked sullen and embarrassed after all.

"You may have two each of the savory pastries." I'd saved out some of the broken ones just in case.

His smile brightened a bit. "An' you won't go a-tellin' me mates about this? Cain't have 'em thinking I've gone all fancy boy on 'em."

"I won't tell a soul." I had more of a reputation to lose than he. One thing to be bold and flamboyant, quite another to be so penurious I couldn't afford a proper maid who showed up on time. If only Violet had given me some warning that she was about to elope! Or, worse, gossip from the gutter spread faster to the fine houses and salons than butter on hot toast. Rumor would have me the corrupter of young boys. Now if they were older boys. . . .

"Talk, Mickey." I scooped a frothy red gown over my head so I only heard a few muffled words.

"Dragon, it were. All black with one horrible orange eye. An' it spit flame, too."

I didn't correct his redundant language. "A *black* dragon, you say. Flying over the Square." The black balloon could be described as such by the unlearned. The one orange eye: the glow from the firebox. Spitting flame could describe the pushing of hot air into the envelope.

But how did it hover? And what was it looking for?

"Not just the Square. All over t' West End," Mickey insisted. "The beggar said 'e'd seen it spitting flames, green flames, right at Parliament. Toby might 'a run from't." The boy sidled toward the door of my private rooms, aiming for the backstairs. Like any feral cat, the time had come for him to escape comfort for freedom. I'd left the cream out for him along with the pastries.

He fled before I could ask him to fasten the back of my gown. "Keep an eye out for Violet! Check with the drayman at the dairy. And tell him I need an extra gallon of milk," I called after him as soon as my head was free of layers and layers of frothy red silk. Cursed fashions. I said a harsher word, actually, but I don't usually curse, let alone in public. Unless I really, *really* need to.

Twisting and turning, I managed the top two hooks at

my nape and the bottom three up to my waist. After that, the strictures of the corset kept me from stretching further. I almost wished for my boring gray serge costume that fastened in front—or the bulletproof corset that laced up the front. But that one was too heavy and added bulk to my figure rather than compressing it.

Nothing for it but to hope someone "friendly" was the first to arrive. Perhaps Sir Andrew Fitzandrew?

Heavy treads on the outside stairs set my heart pounding. I took up a regal posture along my lounge, disguising the incomplete fastening of my gown from casual view.

Fortunately, Sir Drew was the first to arrive. Taller than me by a full two inches, with trim waist, broad shoulders and long, long legs, he and I had been friends for years.

Five minutes later I was properly laced and fastened into my ensemble for the evening.

"You know I'd rather be taking this gown off of you than fastening it before your audience arrives," he chuckled as his knuckles ran the length of my spine. A frisson of delight followed his touch, even though I knew he merely checked that all the fastenings were in place. "Shall I set my groom to minding your side door and private stair?" he asked, arching one auburn eyebrow. Then he kissed my cheek and lingered long enough I wanted more.

"The assistance of your groom *at the door* would be most helpful. I have no idea why Violet has not returned."

"Or if she will?" he replied more seriously.

"What do you know?" I whirled to face him, needing to read his eyes and posture, not just his voice. The clock bonged a full-throated half hour. I'd run out of time.

"Rumors only. Young women and street boys disappearing in batches of three or four. My sources are not as reliable as yours."

I studied him for a long moment. He hid nothing from me. At least on this subject.

"Are you certain your necromancer friends aren't behind this?" I teased, running a delicate fingernail along his cheek with affection. A second son of a wealthy baron, Drew had too much money with little to occupy his mind or his energy. So he sought thrills, skirting the edges of the law with obsessions such as magic, the occult, and now necromancy.

He grew rigid and cold, face going blank, hiding all emotion. "I have no *friends* who are necromancers."

"Colleagues? Mentors? Teachers?" I offered, on guard as well. If I didn't need to understand every nuance of his posture, I'd turn away and fuss with my accessories. I still needed to affix a gaudy arrangement of red-and-black feathers bound to a ruby-and-jet brooch—a gift from Sir Drew—into my hair and the matching necklace around my throat.

Then he shook himself, and a veil of strong control lifted from his face. "Doubtful. I am but a married dilettante whose wife affects invalidism, so I distract myself with arcane puzzles—and you. Heaven help me if Victoria gives me a baronetcy and I actually have the responsibility of a title beyond the knighthood Father bought for me from King William upon his coronation. Beside, none of *my* colleagues, mentors, or teachers would know what to do with kidnapped street urchins, other than throw them into a bathtub with a bar of soap and orders to scrub." He laughed. It sounded hollow.

Before I could ask him to fasten the necklace, he trooped off down the stairs to set his groom in place.

 **Chapter Three**

L ONDON'S "NOBS" ARE A cautious bunch. They constantly watch the others of their class, making certain that their prestige (within specific parameters of wealth and lineage) is never lessened by the rise of another and that their manners can never, ever be called into question. What they do behind closed doors is another matter.

Therefore, each of them must make an entrance to an assembled crowd. To arrive before a certain quantity of people have already gathered makes them timid and anxious to please, rather than established. To arrive at a salon too late is pompous. Thus, they tend to arrive *en masse* one carefully measured hour after the announced invitation.

When I began hosting a salon and extended invitations to learned scholars in mathematics, science, and language, to budding politicians, and wealthy philanthropists, to artists and performers who could discuss more than their own subject, I knew that if I invited them for eight of the clock, they'd arrive at nine. If I invited them for nine, they'd not show their faces before ten. Since I had to open the café with coffee brewed and sugar buns baked at seven in the morning, I called them all together at seven in the evening, knowing they'd all arrive by eight and depart to more fashionable gatherings before midnight, most by ten.

Oblivious to the perceptions of polite society, my Lady Ada arrived at the stroke of seven thirty. She and her newly belted earl of a husband saw themselves up the grand staircase from the heart of the café—wider and less creaky than the back stairs from the kitchen, and carpeted but otherwise quite ordinary—and greeted me with the affection of long familiarity.

"My Lord and Lady." I dipped a proper curtsy before embracing my girl. "You are still too thin and pale," I whispered as we touched cheeks.

"I agree," Lord William replied. He had extraordinary hearing, honed on the hunting course. "Ada should not have ventured out so soon after rising from her sickbed."

"Nonsense, Billy." She was the only one who got away with using the casual nickname to his face. "I have been stuck in my sickbed for nearly a year." She may have been ensconced in her bed, but she hadn't been idle. Her nimble mind had played mathematical games and come up with new inventions. "'Tis time I saw the world again and the world glimpses the new first Earl and Countess of Lovelace." She squeezed my arms in reassurance as she withdrew.

I bit my tongue, hard, to keep from noting aloud that my Lady Ada had taken ill after the birth of her second child in two years and arisen the day after our new queen had granted the lofty titles—honors granted in return for foiling a kidnapping plot three years ago.

I suspected other reasons for her invalidism. More than the strain of bearing children so close together. After a difficult birth with heavy bleeding she'd taken a full year to recover.

Lady Byron, Ada's mother, and her two special friends had moved into Ada's household to "manage" the servants while Ada recovered. Diligently they used

Romany charms of herbs and incense and something more I could not imitate to protect her from magical attack. We'd nicknamed the companions "The Furies" long ago. For many reasons. The likes of a necromancer, even one as potent as Lord Byron, could not breech a house they protected.

To separate my flamboyant image from Ada's respectability we made choices and saw little of each other in public. Where my gown dipped, hers were restrained and covered. Where my skirts flipped and flirted over three petticoats, her cautious bell with two petticoats swayed in discreet lilts. I wore bright jewel tones with lots of lace and accessories; she kept to more sober and pale earth tones. My sleeves were wispy puffs on the upper arms, leaving my shoulders bare. Hers covered her arms from collarbone to elbow.

Even here in my private parlor, she and I maintained opposite public images.

Drew rejoined the salon hard on the heels of the Lovelace family's arrival. As second son of a minor baron with only two generations of heritage, Drew needed to pay his respects to higher nobility and maintain his unofficial duties as my companion and co-host.

Oh, the public face among the nobs can be a very entertaining dance. And since I lived on the edge of this society, slightly outré, I could do as I pleased, watching them jockey for position. Though I'm not sure this race *could* be won.

"Still no sign of Violet," Drew said under his breath as he placed a tray of delicacies on the sideboard and expertly poured wine for the four of us.

"Violet? Where is Violet?" Ada asked. She flipped and fumbled with her pearls in agitation. "You brought her into my household five years ago. Hopeless in the kitchen but very organized and efficient. She cleaned up the pantry and linen closets, even labeling each shelf so the others could put everything back where it belonged."

"I had errands today away from home. She used her half day off to visit her mother. As she usually does. She has not returned," I replied quietly.

"Her mother lives in Southwark," Lord Billy said blandly. "I'm surprised she has not gone missing before. Robbed and murdered, kidnapped into white slavery are the least of the dangers there. The place should be burned to the ground and rebuilt properly to eliminate the criminal element."

I actually bit my tongue that time. And Drew nearly swallowed his own. New housing would only encourage the criminal element to prey upon a better class of victims.

"We shall be outrageously casual tonight," I pronounced. "We will serve ourselves as and when we wish. We shall laugh and talk and debate with freedom as there are no servants in the room or listening at the door to later spread gossip about us." I flung out my arms in a grand gesture.

"Only you could get away with this," Drew said on a laugh. He took my empty wineglass (how had I drunk it dry without noting?) and filled it nearly to the brim with my favorite Madeira.

"Ah, Charles has come after all," Ada interrupted our exchange, turning to face her business partner and scientific colleague, Charles Babbage. He invented the Difference Engine, proving machines capable of complex mathematical calculations. Lady Ada had corrected his designs and made the machine work.

That invention had led to the Analytical Engine that took the process ten steps further, a machine that could "think" (within the limitations of a stack of thin gold cards punched in precise patterns). My Ada and Mr. Babbage were rapidly becoming extremely wealthy; producing gadgets that performed menial tasks, enhanced factory production, and soon, I was promised, would make a locomotive no longer dependent upon rails to move people and goods about the country.

Something about a special processing of rubber to encapsulate wheels . . .

To my mind, their best project was the steam-and-clockwork–powered book catalog that shifted and rotated, spat out books appropriate to a specific search, and became the heart of the Book View Café.

The day of my grand opening flashed before my memory as if it had happened that morning.

I remembered pacing before the front door for what seemed like hours, the last five minutes before I should officially unlock the doors.

A crowd began gathering in front of the sign that announced free coffee with the purchase of a pastry. Peering through the updated window lights, I recognized a few faces, but only a few. I hoped the others would become familiar and welcome clients.

Behind me, Violet fussed with the steaming coffee maker. She clattered and banged about, unsure of the safety of the loud machine that forced steam through expensive coffee grounds. Coffee she could manage, keeping all the scones together, and the sugar buns on the far side, biscuits in the middle and cream tarts behind the counter, in sight but more expensive and so protected from pilfering. I'd been baking for days.

Finally I could contain my anxiety no more and threw open the latch.

My Ada and her betrothed were first through the door. She wore a lovely sprigged muslin gown that matched her bright smile in spring loveliness. I accepted her hug and Sir William's pressing of my hands. Then I had to smile and greet a dozen others, directing them to tables and the pastries, and suggesting blends of coffee to match their selections. They found their own way to the racks of international newspapers and popular books.

After that first flurry of business, Sir William stood and clapped his hands for attention. When the room quieted, he cleared his throat. "Ladies and gentlemen, you may have noticed the reading material available for your perusal. But what you cannot see is an extensive library of odd, rare, and imaginative books hidden between the walls. I would now like to request a book search of Madame Magdala to show you just what you may find to satisfy every whim of curiosity." He delved a hand into his pocket and brought forth one shilling and two pence. He walked majestically toward the carousel in the middle of the café where he slapped the coins on the curved counter.

"You don't have to pay," I whispered to him as I scooted through the gap in the circular barrier. I closed the solid gate so that it completed the circular counter once more. The newly installed latch clicked into place. No one, except possibly Ada, should follow me into the arcane control center for the machine.

"Madame Magdala, would you find for me any references to King William's first naval battle?"

I had to swallow the lump in my throat and stare at him a moment. This was not the volume I'd instructed him to request. I had to think carefully about the codes to key into the system for this request.

Then Ada whispered to me, "Navy, battles, spell out the name, then a notch at the top to indicate a first."

Right. She'd developed the code to make Mr. Babbage's machine work.

Gears ground, a cutting tool worked upon the large brass key. Noise of metal grinding metal filled the gaps in the pleasant tones of speculative conversation. In moments, I had a shiny, newly minted key as long as my palm. After holding it up for inspection I paraded over to another counter backed by more equipment. The key fit precisely into its designated slot. Then I pulled a lever and twisted the key.

Deep in the bowels of the building, the boiler pushed forth live steam to engage the first of many gears and ratchets and levers; shelves of books rotated up and down, and then it all paused, awaiting more instructions. Another twist of the key while pushing it deeper into its slot. I pulled the lever. It resisted, but I mastered it. More grinding of gears; more shelves slid up and down, across and up again.

My customers gasped.

And then ... and then a slender volume bound in plain beige, heavy paper with a few lines of print on the cover clunked and thunked and whooshed down a chute into my waiting hands.

Gasps all around, then a round of applause as I held up the volume, the title clearly visible: *A Brief History of Naval Skirmishes in the North Sea Against French Revolutionaries*.

Miss Ada clapped the loudest, beaming with pride at the success of her invention. And, I hoped, respectful of me for having thought of the device.

But the device was not perfect. A second volume, bound in black leather had slid down the chute along with the requested book. This one showed up every time I used and tested the machine.

It was a secretly published collection of poems idealizing death, longing for death, fascinated by death—in others, not for the poet himself. The name of the author, Harold Childress, was a *nom de plume* for none other than Lord Byron himself. The book demanded to be read. I presumed the enthralling magic spell woven into the poetry pushed the book into the chute no matter where I shelved it.

I stood in front of the chute so no one else could see that book before I could hide it again.

Maybe I should burn it. But then I'd never have the arcane knowledge Byron hid between the words.

 **Chapter Four**

M Y SALON BUSTLED WITH activity. I dragged
myself back to reality.

"Mr. Babbage, welcome." I lifted my hand for him to
kiss. He stumped across the room without grace. His
waistcoat gaped over his expanding girth and his cravat
really needed the attention of a good valet. His mind
always ran ahead of his manners and grooming. He held
my hand a bit too long while he admired my upthrust
bosom.

I pulled away from him a bit too quickly and avoided
wiping my now clammy palm on the upholstery. Then I
broke eye contact with him and turned my attention to
the shadowy presence behind him. "Please introduce
yourself, sir. We relax formality here in favor of good
discussion."

A tall man made up of sharp planes on his face and
acute angles in his shoulders and elbows, bowed slightly
from the dim recesses close to the door. "Adam Blackwell, Lord Ruthven," he pronounced each word clearly
and distinctly, careful that every syllable reached me
without a trace of slur. His dark hair looked artfully dis-
arranged, much in the affected style of Lord Byron.

I covered my sharp inhalation by pretending to sip my

wine. But this man was too tall, and moved without a limp, to ever be mistaken for the poet king. Of course that did not mean George Gordon Byron's spirit did not inhabit that body.

But his accent denied that. Typical smooth vowels and precise consonants of his class. But the precision . . . as if he had to think each word in a different language and translate. Could English not be his native tongue?

A clever imitation could disguise a voice, but the true accent and combination of words always betrayed the actor. Lord Byron spoke in a lazy drawl with hints of Scotland underlying his excellent education. He spoke Latin and French with that Highland lilt. He probably spoke Greek with the same accent.

Fortunately, Lady Ada had never met her father, indeed had never seen a portrait of him until her twentieth birthday. She merely nodded to acknowledge Ruthven while maintaining a conversation with Charles Babbage about the newest prototype machine. " . . . fires of Vulcan to induce a chemical reaction . . ."

"How do you know Lord Ruthven?" Drew asked Charles. He betrayed nothing from his artful lounge in an armchair. But his fingers curled stiffly around his wineglass and he'd barely looked at the angular man. I wondered if they knew each other already.

Then Madame Pendereé, the current darling of London Opera, arrived in a grand flourish and a bevy of courtiers. I knew most of them. Two men greeted Ruthven and clung to the shadows with him; one of them never took off his black leather gloves and kept both hands behind his back.

I was immediately absorbed into a discussion of the artistic symbolism of the steam-powered horses brought on stage at Madame's latest performance instead of the placid and elderly mares usually employed.

"But all life is a metaphor," she declared in her fake French accent that carried the musicality of fairy bells.

One of the shy men clinging to the walls as if for dear life, stirred himself long enough to bring Madame a glass of sherry and a plate of puff pastries oozing a delicate combination of goat cheeses. His right hand, which held the fine porcelain plate, was twisted at an odd angle, as if it had been broken and not set properly.

I'd seen him before and the circumstances did not carry a pleasant undertaste. Warning bells seemed to clang in the back of my head as I took in his short, lithe figure and keen hooded eyes. I'd been watching for such a man since my first day with Ada, when I'd broken the kidnapper's wrist and watched him damage it further as he scrambled over the roofs with the alacrity of an Italian acrobat.

oO

The next morning found me swathed in a heavy white apron from collarbone to hem instead of layers of red silk. Though the salon passed without further incident and the man with the awkward hand soon left with Lord Ruthven, I hadn't slept well, and arose early to get the baking started.

I hummed a light tune trying to banish the megrims of the previous night as I sprinkled spiced sugar over the tops of hot-from-the-oven buns. Helen, Lady Ada's undercook, kneaded dough for the second batch. The clock chimed half six. I still had to grind the coffee beans and set the grounds brewing. Arabian, Egyptian, and Mexican blends today. I bought the beans already roasted, not having near enough space for the contraption that performed that function. Nor did my nose tolerate the aromas of the process. Grinding and brewing, however, filled the café with an exotic scent that enticed customers to come and linger over a second and third cup while they read newspapers from around the world.

A tap on the back door signaled the arrival of the Paris editions, only one day old thanks to the new dirigible express routes. New Delhi and Peking still took a week, much better than the previous three month shipping time.

I opened the back door ready to tip the delivery boy, only to find Mickey staring up at me with worried and reddened eyes.

One look and I knew he'd not found Toby or Violet. My heart sank. "Come in, boy. Wash your hands and face, with soap." Nothing I could do about his stained shirt and coat except cover them with an apron. "I have work for you today." I grabbed him by the collar and ushered him to the sink.

Helen sniffed in disdain.

I glared at her, a sharp reminder of where she'd come from and might have returned to if her talent with bread dough had not brought her out of a filthy orphanage.

"Yes, Missus," Mickey said, eyes cast down.

"What? No arguments? No delays? No sudden errands to run?"

"Cor, Missus, the sun's only been up two hours. 'T nobs is still snoring," he returned with a more usual defiance.

"Then why the ready compliance? Especially about cleanliness?" I took pains to use proper words with my boys so they'd learn a bit of better language. Sometimes it stuck. Sometimes it didn't. But if they learned the vocabulary from me, they'd at least better understand the same words spoken by others when they spied for me.

"Th . . . the black dragon is back in the sky," he whispered.

"Oh." It frightened Mickey today. Yesterday it had invoked his curiosity. Probably Toby's disappearance had something to do with Mickey's reluctance to confront the monster.

I knelt down in front of him so that I could catch his gaze and hold it. "Mickey, it is not a dragon. There are no such things as dragons, except in fairy tales. What you saw was a hot air balloon, all painted black."

"But it shoots lights in straight lines! Green ones, like magic stuff," he protested.

That was strange. Yesterday it had spit flames—at least I presumed the flickering firebox had suggested the draconic action to the uneducated.

Curses. I whispered a few in the Romany language. It held the best variants in a most satisfying growl. Without Violet to run things at the café, I had to be here. I couldn't afford to lose an entire Tuesday's revenue.

"Mickey, I have a different chore for you today. Do you know where Jimmy Porto houses his hot air balloon?"

"The gray one? Cor, I sure do. Alus wanted to fly w' him."

"Then today you get to fly. Run to Jimmy and tell him I told you to get as close to the black balloon . . ." I barely stopped myself from calling it a dragon. "Spy on the black balloon and see if you can discover who flies it and where it lodges."

"Aye, Missus. But I'll need a copper or two to pay him, won't I?" He held out his surprisingly clean hand.

I found five pennies in my pocket. "One of these is for you, Mickey. The other four are for Jimmy, so he can buy fuel for his balloon."

Mickey grabbed the coins and darted out the door faster than I could grab him for more instructions. He slipped under the raised arm of the newspaper delivery boy where he stood frozen in the act of knocking on the half open door.

Curses! Now I didn't have the coins to tip him. I always tipped well to ensure prompt and polite service.

Helen pounded the dough with indignant fury.

 **Chapter Five**

AS THE HOURS PASSED and the crowd in the café followed its usual patterns, though the numbers were down, I let the tension flow outward from my shoulders, along my arms and out my fingertips. A scholar lecturing at Oxford in ancient languages had visited the reading room last autumn in search of an esoteric tome on Persian necromancy (strangely, I had a copy hidden deep in the dim recesses of the stacks; part of an estate library Lady Ada bought intact without inspecting). His Hindu friend who lectured on esoteric physics had come with him to see what the famous—or infamous—Bookview Café was about. He taught me deep breathing exercises and muscle relaxation. I'd taught him a few things as well.

I needed those exercises today, as I watched the customers come and go from early morning to midafternoon. Most ordered a single cup of coffee, left it untouched as they read their newspaper, then left. Longtime and loyal patrons barely nodded to me today. But strangers paused to chat, asking questions about the upcoming coronation or the country gentry come to town for the season.

I dismissed the extra servers for the afternoon and

began diluting the brews. Why waste good beans on people who didn't drink the stuff? I did keep one pot of fine, dark roast Ethiopian beans at full strength for the table of five gentlemen arguing volubly near the book search carousel.

A young man with the typical out-of-date suit and hopeless cravat of a student who took his studies seriously approached me. He carefully counted out the one shilling and two pence I required for an involved book search. That left about one more shilling in his hand, and I doubted he had more in his pocketbook.

"Excuse me, Madame, but I need a reference regarding Archbishop Howley's arguments against the Great Reform Act." He looked me in the eye, not shy or apologetic. Had I met him before?

I couldn't place his accent or the angles of his face.

Did he want to know if the Church had really decided that people convicted of practicing necromancy would be burned at the stake? That was a last-minute addition to the reform bill. Howley couldn't vote against that part of the massive reformation. Now the punishment for necromancy was the law, but no one yet had come to trial or been convicted.

"Keep your money." I closed his fingers back over the coins. "That one is easy."

He followed me to the front corner beside the window. Who needs to worry about art when you decorate with floor-to-ceiling bookcases on all exposed walls between windows? I studied three tomes of Parliamentary proceedings for the last century and then let my fingers find the gilt lettering on the next slim book spine.

"Archbishop Howley's own treatise on why the bill should be defeated, written before the insertion of the necromancy laws. Read it here, return it properly, and there is no fee." I'd helped Howley write the text when he'd been blackmailed into renouncing the reforms. I had access to historical precedents for and against the act.

"Thank you, Madame Magdala," he sighed in relief and took a seat directly in front of the book's home.

I turned to find Sir Drew leaning against the coffee bar, a wry grin on his tired face. He looked as if he hadn't slept, displaying red-rimmed eyes, gaunt shadows on his cheeks, and a hasty shave that left uneven dark patches in odd places.

"The boy has the look of one of the masses who needed the reform," he muttered half-amused.

"It didn't help you," I replied.

"On the contrary."

I raised an eyebrow in question.

"That drafty and leaking country manor Mum gave me as a wedding present costs more in upkeep than the land is worth. I wanted to let it fall down. But not only did Mum entail it to my son, with the house came the responsibility of two seats in the House of Commons representing about fifty people in the two villages. I had to appoint members or sit in Commons myself. Now I'm rid of the responsibility—except nominal upkeep, so there's something for Andy to inherit. The reeking city of Birmingham takes care of the Parliamentary obligations now. They actually have *elections*, I'm told. What about a cup of coffee?"

"You look as if you need this," I said while I poured and stirred in cream and dark sugar crystals. The whirlpool within the depths taunted me, demanding I look deeper, find answers within the spirals . . .

I yanked my attention away from the cup and handed it to Drew.

He looked at me strangely. I'd never told him the truth about my "Gypsy gift." I'd made my reputation as the bastard daughter of a Gypsy king by reading fortunes within the whirlpools of coffee. Few believed I actually saw things there. Mostly, I didn't. But sometimes . . .

Instead, I directed the conversation back to his rumpled state. "Did you sleep at all after you left last night?"

He hadn't stayed with me, taking his departure before ten, prior to Lady Ada and Charles Babbage leaving.

"A little. I camped in the armchair at my club." He did not expand though I gave him a cautious listening kind of silence to encourage him. Few people can allow a lapse in conversation and will babble anything to fill the gap.

Not Drew. Not this forenoon.

"Madam?" a pompous voice demanded my attention.

"Yes?" I replied, holding up a pot of coffee. I'd met this man before. An investigator of some sort, loosely connected to the Bow Street Runners at Whitehall.

"Nothing more to drink, for now. This worthless rag . . ." He slapped a newspaper from Madras on the bar. "Claims the discovery of a never before seen by humans temple ruin in the mountain forests."

I did not ask, I swear I only thought it: How could it have been never before seen by humans? Someone built it, for a reason. Someone worshipped there.

He frowned at me deeply, as if I'd spoken aloud the heresy of thinking brown denizens of the subcontinent might be human.

"I haven't read the paper yet. It only arrived by express dirigible this morning," I prompted him.

"The reporter goes on to say that the temple was dedicated to some wicked goddess who demanded assassination as a form of worship."

"Kali," I replied, drawing on vague memories imparted by the Hindu scholar. Hmm, that was twice this morning I'd thought of him, and wondered if the vision within the coffee cup was part of that cycle.

"Something like that, yes," the man continued. "Do you have any texts about this goddess and her cult? With the coronation scheduled for just three weeks from now, there are many important people in town. I have heard rumors of . . . I cannot say what just yet. How likely is it that these . . . these . . ." He peered at the paper. "These Thuggees have migrated to England?"

Another connection to death and magic, maybe to a black balloon hovering over the city shooting strange rays of light. Rumors of death at the coronation. He didn't need to say the words. I'd been following my own trail of innuendo and instinct.

"That will require a search," I said, holding out my hand for the one shilling and two pence.

He slapped the coins into my palm, grudgingly.

I led him to the carousel. He tried to follow me into the circular enclosure, but I pushed him out and latched the swinging gate. Then I began the involved process of cutting a key. Following guidelines I'd memorized long ago, I punched codes for India, history, old gods, assassination, Kali, and Thuggees. The last two had to follow an alphabetical code rather than short cuts. Then I pulled a lever.

Everyone in the room looked up as the steam engine in the cellar hissed, gears whirled, and a lathe ground the brass key. An awed silence surrounded the mysteries of the machine. Even the investigator, Inspector Witherspoon (his name tickled my memory like raven feathers brushing by) watched in amazement. Drew had seen this operation many times and still watched in fascination.

After several moments, I took the key, again making certain the inspector didn't enter the carousel, and shoved it into a special lock behind the coffee bar. I twisted it half a turn and pulled a lever. Gears engaged. Another twist and drawing down the lever made steam whistle from the boiler in an adjacent cellar—so the steam wouldn't harm the books—a clang as gear cogs engaged and set levers to pushing bookshelves around. A third time, since this was a rather exotic search. Shelves of books rotated up and sideways, down and sideways again. The aroma of freshly brewed coffee and baking pastries gave way to the acrid scent of burning coal.

More shifts up and around sent my senses spinning. I

had to hold the lever to keep from reeling. Darkness tugged at my vision. This was a giant version of the whirlpool in a cup of coffee. A true maelstrom. This could produce a vision of massive importance.

Shiny jet beads in a long string separated by tarnished silver filigree every tenth bead. The strand circled the room along the top row of shelves, pulling closer and tighter. I thought of a rosary and dismissed it. No one carried rosaries anymore unless they were Catholic, and most of those kept them hidden.

No, this was symbolic. Was the Roman Church behind Witherspoon's conspiracy theories?

I doubted that, too. Part of the Great Reform Act of 1832 brought tolerance to the persecuted religion. Long overdue.

A clunk followed by a thump shattered my vision of choking black-and-silver beads. Two books had slid down the chute in response to the search.

My balance teetered, and I was lost in twirling dancers robed in shimmering black akin to jet beads, carrying silvered vorpal blades tarnished black, closing in on me, my café, and ... and ... Lady Ada.

Senses still reeling, I choked out the urgent words that still swirled around the edges of my vision. "Lady Ada. I have to save my girl."

Sir Drew's strong arms restrained me. I flailed at his grip around my waist with limp hands. "They're coming for her," I wailed.

"Who, Madame?" Inspector Witherspoon demanded, plying me with a cup of black coffee.

The pungent aroma of stale, cold, burnt coffee righted my balance and focus without having to taste the vile dregs. "Your Thuggees, Inspector, or their like." Were the fanatic necromantic followers of Byron any different than Indian assassins? "They are seeking Lady Ada

Byron King, Countess Lovelace." Quickly, I wrenched free of Drew before his bracing grip could turn into an embrace. "I must go to her."

"Magdala, you can't go alone. It's too dangerous," Drew protested, following me toward the kitchen.

Helen sat on a high stool, drinking a cup of tea while she waited for the last batch of fresh cream scones to finish baking. She'd left dirty dishes where she'd discarded them. Sifted flour coated nearly every surface. Batter drips stuck to the floor. Yet her apron looked pristine.

"I don't have time to deal with this!" I screamed, aiming for the back door where my hat and wrap hung on hooks to the side.

"Not my job, Missus," Helen said calmly. "I'm paid to cook, not to clean."

"Violet did everything before she went missing. We ran the entire business together," I mumbled, torn between running to Ada's side and dealing with my business.

"Then she probably found a better job where she didn't have to clean, and got some credit and more than paltry wages for doing *your* work," Helen said, draining her cup. She set it aside and checked the scones in the oven.

While she occupied herself with transferring the pastry to cooling racks, I ripped off my apron and exchanged it for my hat and shawl.

"Magdala, you can't just leave," Drew reminded me. "You have customers."

I gnashed my teeth. He was right. I could not afford to abandon my business even for my girl. A note would have to do.

Before I could find paper, pen, and ink in the key carousel, a liveried servant strode through the café and tipped his hat to me. "Madame, Lady Ada, Countess of Lovelace bids me deliver this note to you directly," he said in a monotone common to those who serve the nobility and are thus superior to those who do not.

"Thank you. Please wait a moment to see if I need to reply."

"Very good, madam." He kept staring at me as if I'd forgotten something . . . like a tip or his right to read the note over my shoulder. I'd used the belowstairs network of observation and gossip for my own purposes. This time I chose not to add to it.

I turned my back and fumbled in a drawer where I should find writing implements and a letter opener. It came readily to hand where a pen would not. Deftly I slid the dull blade beneath the thick wax seal impressed with Lady Ada's personal and secret seal, an eight-pointed star indicative of safe haven in Romany symbolism. Or information.

Inside, Lady Ada had written in her precise printing, all sharp angles with no extra flourishes in keeping with her mathematical mind:

Dearest Elise,

   Violet's mother reports that her daughter never arrived home.

No signature. But then, I did not need one.

Violet missing. Toby missing. A compelling vision of men in black robes wielding blackened vorpal blades endangering Ada. And a café beginning to fill with customers needing a bit of respite from their busy days.

Which needed my attention most?

Time to do what I do best. I turned back to the liveried footman and held three shillings enticingly out of his reach. "I have three serving girls who live nearby. One coin for each of the girls you bring back here ready to work."

His eyes grew big, then cold and calculating.

"And a good word to your mistress, who is wealthier than I, for your assistance."

He nodded sharply. I gave him one of the coins and directions to the flat above the green grocer two blocks over.

"Inspector Witherspoon, if you please, take a note of warning to Lovelace House. While you are there, feel free to engage Lady Byron, the countess' mother, in conversation about black-robed assassins who wield curved blades that might be black, or tarnished silver with vorpal edging." That formidable lady had made a study of the followers of the poet king's work. Some were merely romantically inclined would-be poets. Others embraced his way of life with true fanaticism—free love, sadism, and murder for necromantic experiments. They hailed from all over Europe and spread to India and China. If anyone knew how to thwart the Thuggees better than I, 'twas Lady Byron. I had other things to do.

Witherspoon's eyes lost focus for half a heartbeat and then his gaze sharpened keenly on me. He grabbed the books from the chute. I scribbled a hasty note to Ada that I had received her information and to heed the inspector's warning. He took it and made rapid tracks out the door.

"Magdala, I know that look in your eye. You are about to do something adventurous and probably stupid," Drew said.

"Foolish, perhaps, but never stupid." I set about brewing fresh pots of coffee and bringing pastry from the kitchen to the bar for easier serving, all the while praying that Lucy, Emily, and Jane would welcome the extra wages and return to work swiftly.

"Magdala, I can safely venture where you may not. Let me help you find Violet."

"You might have the right of that. That will leave me free to seek out Toby."

"The moon-faced boy? Magdala, I know you value

your tribe of street urchins, but surely that one is perhaps better off ... He has no hope of a future other than scrubbing your stoop, and I hardly call that satisfying."

"Don't you dare say that!" I rounded on him, raised butter knife in hand. "Toby is special. And he is more useful than you can even imagine. And I'm worried sick about him."

"Then turn the tribe of urchins loose to seek him out. I do not like to think of you endangering yourself for ..." He paused while I glared at him. "For any reason."

"Certainly you may venture where I may not into the kinds of places that see young women as valuable for other than honest work." However, I could easily disguise myself as a man and seek out those establishments.

"There are others than the pimps and brothels of Southwark, who value young women," he returned.

I chilled. "Wh ... what do you mean?"

"Necromancy."

My heart and lungs ceased to work for a long agonizing moment.

"Do ... do you know these people?" I knew he was fascinated with magic and the chemistry of harnessing occult powers to augment new inventions.

"I have heard of a few, and read more." His expression closed down, not allowing me to read his emotions.

"And what do necromancers seek? Death is all around us, from disease, accident, even old age. Why do they have to kill more people?"

"They seek power. Power beyond the ability of normal people to harness."

I gulped, and my fingers itched to find in my library the texts that fascinated him. I knew he'd borrowed some. Had he ever returned them?

Had he found the secret books penned by Byron after his "death"?

"There is a fleeting moment of explosive energy when a person transitions from life to death. That energy encompasses many realms, the mundane one we live in, the heavenly where God awaits us, and many in between where all is possible, requiring only a thought to manifest." His eyes sparkled with enthusiasm. He licked his lips, looking eager to jump to the forefront of these studies.

"What might one do if one can capture that energy, control the moment of death, and trap it?" Now he stared off at something I could not see, his eyes glazed and his lips barely moving.

Did I truly want to know? Had he merely read of this in theory? Or, heaven help me, had he actually participated in this ghastly ritual?

"Light a fire with a snap of your fingers, send objects flying from here to there. *Look upon the face of God and garner the wisdom of the ages.* Imagine if you will, needing a stack of clean plates to serve your confections. With a thought, you can bring them to hand. No need to walk all the way to the kitchen for them."

"Presuming someone has washed them for you," I scoffed. "And right now, no one is washing up in my kitchen." I made to move past him.

He grabbed my arm as if to press home his point of the value of necromancy. "Washing up, another simple chore managed with your thoughts rather than employing people or wasting your own energy on such a demeaning task."

"Honest work is not demeaning. Do what you have to for Violet. I'll take care of Toby." This time I managed to brush him aside and walk down to my kitchen, which was still a mess from Helen's baking.

⚙️

Emily arrived within moments. A robust blonde, as decorative as she was hardworking, she set to cleaning the kitchen. Helen departed the moment the last tray of shortbread biscuits came out of the oven. Breathless and windblown, Lucy slipped through the back door as the grumbling cook departed. Willowy, with the delicate coloring of a strawberry blonde, she donned an apron and began serving the first rush of late afternoon customers.

"Where's Jane?" I asked the girls about my third helper.

"Walked out with her beau, I guess," Emily said with a touch of pride. Apparently, their flatmate had caught the attention of someone of better station or finances than they'd hoped for. A good connection for one of them might bring brighter opportunities to the other two.

Jane's petite frame and ruddy Welsh coloring attracted many men. Violet had similar attractions though she had Irish-pale skin and green eyes.

Violet had worked in the Byron household as a scullery maid before Lady Ada's marriage. That thought reminded me of the near constant fear we lived under that Lord Byron—if he managed to reconstruct his soul transference engine—would return from the dead in a new body. In life, he preferred young, petite women with dark hair.

"If Mickey shows up, or any of the other boys, have them keep an eye out for Jane. We don't want her to get into trouble."

"But her beau is most respectable," Lucy protested. "Son of the barrister that lives two streets over. He's reading over at the Inns of Court."

"A respectable profession. But does the man match his career?"

That left me free to search for Toby. Normally I would change out of serviceable black or dark blue serge to a fashionable gown in a vibrant jewel tone before leaving. Not today. Instead of deep ruches of lace on emerald-green Egyptian cotton and a bonnet decorated with long feathers and broad ribbons, I dug out a threadbare and much mended skirt and jacket meant to fit me during the years of wandering Europe with my first mistress, Mary

Godwin Dessins. Lean years when I went to bed hungry
more often than not. Now I strained to keep buttons
from popping and seams from splitting. I laced my bulletproof corset in the front as tightly as I could. Damn
Violet for leaving without warning. (I still hoped she'd
eloped with her drayman since a different one had delivered supplies this morning) The bloodstain across the
bodice and down one side of the skirt was hopeless. The
Transylvanian Count who'd shed that blood whilst I de-
fended myself from his unwanted advances would still
bear the scar on his face and neck.

His livid curses in an ancient language I barely understood remained in my mind, as insoluble as his blood.

A small chip straw hat trimmed in faded red cloth
daisies and a tattered black shawl completed my ensemble. Twenty steps from my back door I hunched my back,
pushed my right leg inward to affect a limp, and smudged
my clear and pale skin with charcoal dust. Only Lady
Ada, who knew this disguise, would recognize me. I
could pass through any crowd off the main thoroughfares unnoticed or easily ignored. If I had to speak, I had
a dozen uneducated accents at the tip of my tongue.

And I had a cudgel, a stout and twisted tree branch as
tall as I with convenient handholds in the curves. In my
hands, it was as much a weapon as a piece of the disguise.

Slowly, painfully, I limped my way along alleys and
mews. Every time I encountered a group of people, servants mostly, I slowed my pace and held out a tin cup. If
they pointedly looked the other way, I rattled the single
farthing in the cup, like any respectful beggar. A skinny
young groom, probably only recently employed and fed
regularly, parted with a ha' penny and tipped his hat to
me.

"God's blessing on you, boy," I whispered in growly
tones as if I found it painful to speak around a deep ob-
struction. Then I coughed to add credence to my status.
I stood, nearly bent double (damn the tight lacing I

needed just to keep the clothes on) listening to the gossip of the footmen who lounged against the same back wall as my lovely groom.

"No new uniforms for us for the coronation," the tall and muscular man pushing thirty said on a spit.

His gob almost landed on my scuffed boot and I had to back away a bit too quickly for my disguise. The groom looked at me oddly but said nothing.

"Master says Parliamentary reform," he pronounced those words too carefully, like they were a foreign language, "will be the fine-an-cee-al ruin of us all. Lost the three seats in Commons was his due. Can't sell 'em to rich upstarts with more gold than respect for their place in the world, he says."

"Master's uncle also says next the bloody archbishop will say those with land and villages to support cain't sell the living off'n their parishes neither."

This was the second time this day I'd heard Willliam Howley, Archbishop of Canterbury, mentioned in reference to the reform bill of 1832.

Whoever was master of these gossiping footmen was grossly misinformed. Archbishop Howley had publicly argued against reform, until the clause outlawing necromancy was inserted. Only I knew for certain that secretly he applauded reform.

But an indiscretion from his past found its way into the hands of a blackmailer who demanded denouncement of the Act.

"Master says, a good Freemason should'a stood up for t' ancient rights of his brothers and banned the reform as against Church Law," the first man said.

That was a made-up excuse. Many of the reforms had sprung from the Masonic Lodges. Not all Freemasons held ancient or even new titles. Most were ordinary merchants or tradesmen, soldiers, and minor clerics. They had rights, too. And from what I knew about the Lodges, all within had equal rights and opportunity—a servant could become Worshipful Master while a nobleman struggled with the tests in the lower ranks of the organization.

I needed to ask questions of those in the know. So I moved on, looking for more idle gossip that fit into the complex puzzle I perceived.

The next neighborhood took several steps down in wealth and respectability (if title and income automatically resulted in that elusive quality). All the gossip centered on the coronation: could they catch a glimpse of the new queen as her wondrous coach carried her from the Tower to Westminster Abbey and thence to Buckingham Palace? Should they wear their very best while mingling with the crowd as a sign of respect, or make do with second best in case the crowd soiled expensive clothing? Would the queen's mother—the semi-disgraced Duchess of Kent—ride with her daughter, or be relegated to a closed coach in the rear of the procession? That question was followed by much speculation as to whether the Duchess of Kent's lover would sneak into the back of the Abbey or respect the queen's demands that he never be seen in her presence again—she'd bribed him with a title and land far removed from London.

Nothing new or interesting there. I moved on, deeper into the back roads and tenements of the poor. Not a safe neighborhood. I had only the farthing and a ha' penny and my tin cup worth stealing. But I had a few weapons hidden about my person. I'd be safer than Sir Drew.

 **Chapter Six**

D ID I DARE CROSS the bridge into Southwark? The haven for criminals and the desperately poor stirred restlessly as sunset approached. Many denizens ventured abroad only with the cover of darkness.

When I had been with Miss Ada ten years, I knew she'd not need me as a governess much longer. I began to stretch into new acquaintances and after dark became Madame Magdala, the bastard daughter of a Gypsy king. I'd sweep into salons and read the futures of the attendees. My visions came in the swirling whirlpool of any liquid. The hosts of these salons pressed champagne into my hands, hoping the expensive wine would heighten my arcane talent.

Once, after midnight, I was returning home in the carriage of my latest hostess—Madame FitzWilliam of the demimonde. With a name like that, she could allude to royal connections. King William IV, the sailor king, had two-dozen illegitimate children. Who could keep them straight?

The sleepy driver took a short cut near this very neighborhood and did not look smart or control his reins well. The horses slowed to a dreary walk. Without direction, they plodded across Westminster Bridge and came to a halt under a gas streetlight.

"S'cuse me, sir." A girl child approached the carriage. "Got a shillin' t'spare for a girl willing to work for it?"

That brought me out of my wine-induced daze. I dropped the isinglass window and peered through the fog at the youngster. As I expected, her face was smudged with tear-streaked dust.

"Me mum's got the cough, and we ain't got no money for coal to heat the flat." Her voice turned plaintive. "I'd do any as you ask, for a shillin'."

Then she saw me peering out at her. "Sorry, mum. Thought you was a genl'man. No lady drives out a midnight like this."

"I'm not a lady," I informed her. "Are you truly willing to work?"

She gulped and nodded. She wouldn't raise her eyes to mine.

Obviously, she'd been told about women with odd tastes in partners but had never encountered one before. I wondered if this was perhaps her first night on the streets, driven by desperation to help her ailing mother.

"Anything you asks, mum."

"Including sweeping and washing up in the kitchen?"

She raised her head then, eyes wide with hope.

"Three pence a week. Half day off on Sunday and Monday to take your wages to your mother. We'll feed you, give you a place to sleep out of the cold and rain, supply you with a new uniform each year, and insist you stay clean. That means scrubbing your face and hands every day and taking a full bath once a week."

"Thruppence a week!" She looked astonished at the vast sum.

"Yes. But you have to stay clean, and learn to speak properly. Now what's your name child?" I opened the carriage door for her to clamber in.

"Violet, mum. Me mum calls me Violet after her favorite flower. Ain't never seen a real one, but Mum had a picture of one on the wall until we had to sell it to pay the rent. A real pretty flower it was, too."

"Yes, Violet. They are pretty flowers, and come spring I'll show you a real one in my lady's garden." I pounded on the roof of the carriage with my stick to rouse the driver.

And when I left the household the next year, upon Miss Ada's marriage to William King, Violet came with me, the first of my rescued street urchins.

And now she was missing.

As I considered the cheapness of life among the tall and rickety tenements of Southwark, from whence Violet sprang, the open midden in the streets, and those who partied and prowled in search of victims in the gambling dens and brothels, my common sense prevailed. The leaders of whatever conspiracy I searched for would not allow loose tongues to speak in this district. Dressed as I was to appear desperate among the back alleys of London and Westminster, I was too clean and prosperous appearing for Southwark. They'd spot me as an outsider inside of two heartbeats and either silence their own words or eliminate mine with a knife to my throat.

I'd mined as much information as I could for one evening.

Lucy and Emily waited for me in the café, even though they'd closed up hours ago. They sat in the back corner sipping tea and puzzling over a large book from my library.

After I'd made my presence known, I went to the cash box behind the coffee bar and extracted some coins to pay the girls for coming in on short notice. "Any report from Mickey?" I asked as I handed each of them a shilling three pence. Yes, I know I overpay my workers, but they give me good service and loyalty.

"He snatched some shortbread about an hour ago and left again. Said he'd see you in the morning," Emily answered, accepting her coins gratefully.

"Where you been, Missus?" Lucy asked, wrinkling her nose as if I smelled bad. She tucked her own wages into a reticule tied to her waist.

Perhaps I did smell. I usually kept my clandestine observing secret from them. "I've been listening to London, seeing if I can find new information about Toby and Violet."

"No sign of Jane, either," Emily grumbled. "Not like her to stay out after sunset."

I needed to sit down. So I grabbed a cup and saucer and joined them at the table, sincerely hoping the tea was still fresh and not stewed. But I'd drink it any way I could at this moment.

"That sniveling little Oxford don returned this with a nasty note," Lucy said, pushing the book toward me before I could take a sip.

"Skinny fellow, short, wears spectacles, and cannot get his cravat straight or even interesting?" I asked after I'd taken a hearty swallow of tea. Good; it was still hot and fresh.

"That's the one," Lucy said. Her mouth twitched up, and her eyes focused somewhere else. Smitten. With the man or his position?

"He does have an active and keen mind, though," I admitted. The only attractive part of him, to my mind. I glanced at the title of the thick book with its cracked leather binding and yellowing pages. *An Examination of Necromancy and Soul Preservation After Death in the Magic System of Araby.* Then in smaller letters on the title page inside the book: *A Translation from the Latin.* I couldn't read the name of the translator in the dim light, or without my own spectacles which I used only in private when I knew no one would interrupt my study.

"It's an English translation of the Latin which was a translation of the Arabic," Lucy explained. "At least that's what Professor Badenough said in his note. Only he didn't say Arabic. He said ... Persian. The original

was written in Persian, but the translator changed that to
Araby. He was not happy because both the Latin and
English are incomplete and incorrect." She thrust a hastily scrawled note under my nose. The written words
slashed across the page of my own stationery so obliquely
and unevenly I'd have trouble deciphering them in good
light with magnification.

"Angry a bit?" I laid the note flat on top of the book.
"I'll examine this later to see if I need to remove it from
the library catalog. If it truly is inaccurate, then it is
worthless."

With that, I dismissed the girls, wishing Toby was
around to walk them home. I didn't like my girls out
alone after dark. But they would walk together and
knew to keep to lighted streets and familiar neighborhoods.

And neither of them fit Lord Byron's requirements of
being petite and dark.

Sleep eluded me that night. Drew did not knock upon
my door, or use his key, to help ward off the vision of
dark despair and fear I had touched at the edges of
Southwark. Nor could I banish my worry about people
going missing. I wondered how many more than just the
ones close to me had left home never to return.

Rather than fight the clinging shrouds of nightmares,
I settled in my big armchair in the study and took up the
book that Professor Badenough had returned. With
abundant gaslight from my lamp and my wire-rimmed
spectacles, I puzzled out the Oxford don's note and
found his signature almost legible. Jeremy Badenough.
A pleasant mouthful in the right accent. Lucy's shop girl
intonations would make it sound pretentious when it
was probably meant to honor respected relatives.

Most of my linguistic skills came from modern spoken
languages in the lands I'd traveled through. Latin and

Greek, let alone Arabic or Persian made no sense to me.
So I could not determine if Professor Badenough's assessment was valid. I did find most of the translation
twisted into pompously archaic sentences that wandered
through six subjects and eighteen predicates before coming to a conclusion totally removed from the opening. If
the text did not improve drastically further in, I agreed
with Badenough. The book was worthless. I should probably seek the original and have it properly translated if I
wanted to keep the subject matter in the library noted
for esoteric publications.

Five pages in and I drifted off to sleep, the book in my
lap and my spectacles dangling on the end of my nose.

Mickey showed up on my doorstep at dawn the next
morning. His eyes remained red-rimmed and his nose
damp from another night of tears. He shook his head the
moment I opened the door to him.

What could I say? What could I do to ease his misery
and my own worry over Toby?

"Wash your hands and face. Then after breakfast you
can sweep the front walkway and the café for a penny."

"Them's Toby's jobs," he said sullenly. But he eyed
with hunger the sugar buns just coming out of the oven.

"Wash first." I slapped his hand away from the treats.
"And you'll have the cheese yeast rolls first."

"Does I have t' sweep? Shouldn't we save it for
Toby?"

I had to bite my lip to hold back the tears. "Toby takes
pride in how well he sweeps." I would not, not, NOT, use
the past tense. "We need to do his jobs well so that he
knows how much we love him when he returns."

"That one won't get un-lost without me." Mickey
stuck out his lower lip in pouty protest. "I should be out
on the streets looking for him. And them other girls you
ain't seen nothing of in nigh on two days. And the black

dragon was flying yesterday, low and circling Westminster. But we lost 'im in the clouds when he left. Flew higher than Jimmy could."

"Mickey, I want you to stay close. I need to know you are safe." I knelt on the floor to bring our eyes level. I fussed with his ragged coat and straightened his shirt. "Almost time for new clothes for you. You're growing fast now."

"If you got shoes that fit better, I'd be mighty grateful. I'll sweep for you for a week to pay for 'em." He sniffled as he stared at the broken toes of his too tight footwear. He'd come to me barefoot, with an even smaller set of clothes.

"Deal. Now wash up so you can eat. I'll root around in the cellar closet to see what I have that might fit you."

The rest of the day progressed as usual. Except Violet and Jane and Toby remained missing. My customers reflected the mood of my employees: more subdued in conversation, fewer arguments over the newspaper reports, and no requests for book searches, mundane or esoteric.

One quiet conversation caught my interest.

"There's a petition going round," a man of middling years said to his companion, an older man. They came to my café for coffee and foreign newspapers about once a month. I couldn't say I truly knew them, only recognized them.

"The one that's going to be handed to Archbishop Howley when he comes to town for the coronation?"

"Aye, that one. The people want to make necromancy illegal."

"Not only illegal but a higher crime than murder, a crime akin to both treason and heresy."

But necromancy is already illegal, via the Great Reform, I thought.

A chill wind blasted in from the door, banishing any heat from the boilers that leaked up from the cellars.

The archbishop again. A pattern was developing. I needed to stir a cup of coffee or tea into a whirlpool and consult the images I conjured.

But the world remained firmly fixed in place.

I couldn't go out to listen to the city or gather my tribe of childish spies for consultation that night. I'd promised to join Drew in his box at the opera to hear Madame Pendereé perform.

Perhaps Howley would attend the gala performance, and I could watch the dance of those seeking to court his patronage.

Drew sent his carriage for me. And he sat within rather than wait for me at the theater in his box, as discretion would have suggested.

Within the shadowy privacy of the closed carriage, he kissed me thoroughly—without mussing the braids encircling my head or the bobbing feathers on my turban. "Later?" he asked, his hand lingering in delicious places.

"Of course."

 **Chapter Seven**

ANY BOX AT THE THEATER gave only illusions of privacy, as I knew all too well. The opera was a place to see and be seen, as well as a stage for enthralling music. Usually the upper tiers provided open balcony seating for less elite performances. For audiences at a special gala opera mere weeks prior to the coronation when *everyone* was in town, folding doors secreted in thick pillars—the new alloys allowed a hollow column big enough to hold the hinged wall sections—slid out of their pockets to form side walls that connected with the flimsy barrier between the seating and the corridor. A lockable door in that wall was only an illusion. A hatpin could defeat the latch in a matter of moments.

Gaslights, painted wooden sets, and steam boilers all make for a magnificent recipe for fire. This theater had burned and been rebuilt many times in the last century, most recently seven years before when William IV was newly king. The owners kept to a naval theme in honor of our sailor king. Dark blue curtains with gold fringe and tie ropes enclosed the stage. Rich looking veneer paneling in exotic woods covered the box's interior walls and the corridors behind the boxes. The carpeting had been updated more recently but still reflected the blue-and-gold color scheme in the feather-and-fan design.

Three tiers of boxes/balconies encircled the floor seating in a giant horseshoe. The lowest, and most prestigious tier contained only eight boxes, including a permanent one on each end. These had more substantial walls and doors with limited access from the rest of the theater. Ten boxes filled the second level, and twelve on our level. Before the performance, people mingled and shifted up and down, back and forth, exchanging greetings, and enjoying light hors d'oeuvres and champagne toasts. The Royal Box, the largest of all, closest to stage left on the first tier, remained determinedly closed. Brightly uniformed members of the Bow Street Runners stood staunchly in the way in the corridor behind The Box, and the private entrance stair. We all surmised that Her Majesty was most likely to appear at some point in the evening.

Don Giovanni was on the playlist. I had not seen it produced in many years and looked forward to the breathtaking music.

All of London seemed to be here, major and minor nobility and their favored retainers filled every box, often two or three groups crowding together. Lord William and Lady Ada had their own box above the royal enclosure and hosted Charles Babbage as well as Lady Byron and her two friends; women Ada had grown up with, and from whom she had learned caution and self-defense. Lady Byron was never seen in public without them.

If Archbishop Howley was here, I could not find him in the crush.

Even Sir Drew's minor box needed to host his friends and relatives. At nearly the last moment Charles Babbage's mysterious guest from the salon slipped through the door to our box. A footman brought one additional chair and we all had to shuffle closer together to accommodate him. As he pushed himself next to me, I leaned away from his sour, wine-soaked breath. I didn't need more light to see that his closely set, nearly color-less eyes did not focus easily. When I moved closer to Drew, keeping him from sitting between us, he frowned, bringing his narrow features into a foxlike pinch.

His retainer, the man with the perpetual black gloves, stationed himself against the wall in the back right cor-ner, out of my line of sight. I could not politely catch his eye or engage him in conversation. In my mind I imme-diately labeled him a bodyguard, higher than a footman, lower than a companion.

Queen Victoria's mother, the Duchess of Kent and her lover . . . er, officially her comptroller and private secretary, John Conroy, seemed the only people missing. Our attention remained on the Royal Box where blue curtains remained closed, shielding the occupants from view. While the orchestra tuned instruments in the pit, a flutter of the blue curtains across from us, two tiers down, and two rooms closer to the stage arrested all attention in the packed house. Even the timpani and cello silenced. The actors lined up on stage and the director took the center. "Ladies and gentlemen, Her Majesty, Queen Vic-toria," he pronounced in tones meant to reach the far-thest corners.

We all stood. Unseen hands drew the elegant curtains aside. A delighted gasp rippled around the theater as our young queen stood before us, short, slim, with dark hair neatly parted at the center and drawn up in a simple chignon. She wore a crown made up of fresh spring flow-ers in shades of white and pale blue to match her simple gown with delicate Nottingham lace and tiny blue glass bead accents.

As one, all attendees curtsied or bowed to her.

I had met her before, but only briefly at an intimate musicale evening when I still chaperoned Lady Ada. Most of England had seen very little of Victoria until the death of her uncle William IV last year. Her mother had raised her more strictly than a nun—actually, some of the nuns I knew on the continent lived lazy and pampered lives in comparison. Her efforts and her attempts to get Victoria to sign a regency agreement until she turned twenty-five had cost her; she was now *persona non grata* at court.

On this night, the queen smiled graciously at the audience, waved politely to the performers, and sat regally, surrounded by her Prime Minister and other political dignitaries. Obediently and respectfully, we remained standing until she settled in her chair and nodded to the director to begin.

"I'd heard she might come," Drew whispered under the sounds of people shifting and fluttering printed programs. "Always a nice surprise for our monarch to venture out among her people."

"I wonder if she needs a translator," I mused, trying to figure a polite way to offer my services and thus join her in her box. Then I noticed a tall woman of proud carriage and Mediterranean coloring perched on the edge of a seat directly behind the thronelike chair. Victoria had brought her own linguist.

My gaze continued to rove from box to box, high and low. I couldn't retain any respectability if I leaned out to observe the adjacent seating, but those across the theater offered many opportunities to collect information. I noted various royal and semi-royal (i.e. multiple illegitimate children of Victoria's uncles) cousins with wives or mistresses. Politicians preened and the nobility looked bored. A few had set their chairs back from the openings where shadows masked their faces, but they could still see out.

Then, as the gaslights came up and the conductor raised his baton to begin the overture, a darkly swathed figure directly across from me leaned forward. My attention riveted on the black veil and loose black clothing.

Hard to determine build, size, or gender at this distance or in this lighting.

"Drew?" I whispered leaning close to him as if to exchange an intimate comment about the performance.

"Hmm?" His gaze shifted to the same direction as mine. He stilled. "Should I send a message to Inspector Witherspoon?"

"Not yet. I need to watch more closely."

But so did Lord Ruthven. He did not bow to propriety and leaned over the balcony, calmly assessing the dark figure. He licked his lips in anticipation of . . . something.

But watch the crowd I could not. Mozart's masterpiece of opera entranced me. The staging and music flowed in a seamless event. Advances in mechanical sets and backdrop changes looked more real than any theatrical performance I'd seen. I hardly noticed the steam and clanking noise of their movements. That had become so much a part of everyday life, it faded into the background, unless it was timed to punctuate the music. That wonderful glorious music! Madame Penderée as Elvira, and Antonio Valdez as Leporello, her tenor, drew me into the action and emotion as if I participated in the complicated lives, deceptions, and revenge plots of the characters.

"Makes you wonder if Mozart knew in advance that his life would be short," Lord Ruthven said on a long, awestruck exhale at the end of the first act. "I saw a similar production in Rome last year. His depictions of Hell are inspired. The moment of death and descent near prescient."

Despite the heat from the constantly working steam and the early June evening, I grew cold at his avid licking of lips and narrow-eyed focus upon the closed curtain and the turn of his thoughts. He had much the same expression as Drew had when he described his fascination with necromancy.

Drew touched my hand to capture my attention. Gratefully, I turned to him, away from the pinched-face baron. A single thrust of Drew's chin to the box directly across from us and below one tier, above and to the side of the Royal Box. The figure heavily swathed in black had moved and looked to be working closer to the queen. If it leaned over the rail, it could shoot the queen, where she laughed gaily and flirted with the politicians surrounding her.

As if our minds were linked, Drew and I excused ourselves. Once in the long corridor behind the boxes, we set our strides to the same rapid pace, working our way relentlessly through the throngs. He touched the inside pocket of his coat to indicate he carried a pistol, but I already knew that from our lingering grope and kiss in his carriage. I touched my skirt about mid-thigh to let him know I carried a tiny pistol in my garter. He probably knew that as well. He didn't need to know about the Chinese throwing stars in my other garter, the long and sharp hatpin that could double as a dagger holding my turban in place, or the long, thin blade inserted in the busk of my corset, which for once was not laced too tightly. Then, too, my corded petticoat could be dismembered to produce yards and yards of rope to restrain someone.

We rounded the corner and hastened down the stairs to the more elite level. I was tempted to slide down the banister for greater speed, but too many people milled about for me to make that big a spectacle of myself. Then around to the other side of the theater. On this level, the nobility entertained inside their roomier boxes rather than in the corridor. We had a clear view and empty path to our destination. I lengthened my stride in my haste to assure myself of the queen's safety.

As we approached our goal, we slowed our pace,

peering at closed doors and tight paneling for signs of intrusion, overt or clandestine. At the next to last of the boxes before we encountered a locked private stair, a door opened a crack and no more, as if someone peered out cautiously. I dropped my heels to slow my speed and nearly toppled over at the shift in momentum. We halted directly in front of the opening door. Drew placed himself with legs braced and gun in hand as I yanked the door open wide and out of the clasp of a delicate hand covered in lace gloves.

"What is the meaning of this!" a feminine voice hissed. Traces of a German accent left behind long ago, identified the lady as much as her face would, if she'd revealed it.

"Your Grace." I dipped a curtsy, a convention not true respect.

Drew pocketed his weapon and bowed shortly and sharply.

"Out of my way," the Duchess of Kent ordered. But she kept her voice low. A remnant of hesitancy told me all I needed to know.

"You will not be welcome in the Royal Box," I said calmly, almost pitying the woman. Almost. I knew too much of the cruel strictures she'd placed on her daughter's life in order to keep her naïve and helpless, opening the door for Her Grace to become regent of England in Victoria's name long after the queen had reached adulthood.

Much as Lady Byron tried to rule Ada's household. Different methods, similar object, control and power over the daughters in order to protect them. Prestige? Maybe, more likely control. Both women might say they did what they did for love of their offspring. I knew Lady Byron loved Ada, and needed to protect her. I wasn't so sure about the duchess.

"Welcome or not, I must see my daughter. I must separate her from those greedy men who want nothing but to suck away her power and then discard her. As all men do."

That explained much. Lady Byron had the same opinion of men and had forsaken their company for her female Furies. That didn't explain why the queen's mother had fallen under the spell of her . . . comptroller.

I'd been betrayed by men. Starting with my father, followed shortly thereafter by Percy Shelley. But I'd learned to control my life and take pleasure from men, but never allow them to take more than that from me.

She tried to sidle toward the private stair, leading to the Royal Box and nowhere else.

Drew stepped in her way.

"As you would have done," I accused the duchess. I could say such things. I had no place in her society, and therefore nothing to lose by insulting a royal.

She gasped and her posture stiffened. "I must see my daughter. I must warn her . . ."

"She is well protected, Your Grace," Drew said.

"By such immoral riffraff as you two?" She tried to sound outraged, but I suspected much of her energy dissipated in the face of opposition.

"Yes," I replied, as if proud of being immoral riffraff. "And others who are loyal to the crown. Now may we escort you to your carriage?"

She stalked toward the theater front, shaking off the supporting hand on her elbow that Drew offered.

"Speaking of carriages, should I summon mine as well?" he asked with an arched eyebrow.

"Not yet. I wish to see the end of the performance." And observe Ruthven's obsession.

The second act lived up to the expectations of the first. Vivid sets, gorgeous costumes, and voices so well-tuned to the orchestra as to make my heart ache and my lungs tremble. Each exquisite note that lingered and faded to nothing kept the audience on the edges of their seats. Ruthven pushed himself so far forward as to lean over the rail, still crouched as if sitting but with no chair beneath him.

Not a single sound wafted from the audience, not a whisper or rustle. More than one jaw gaped. Her Majesty's eyes grew wide and round above the lace fan she held before her face.

Then the horrific and yet mesmerizing climax when death and hell consumed Don Giovanni in dark flames.

I could smell the brimstone. The actor's screams lingered in my ear long after his "death."

I shivered in fear.

Finally, the audience gasped as one when the fire ceased abruptly to reveal a pile of ashes where the actor had writhed moments before.

"I have to know how they do that," Ruthven whispered.

I wondered if he meant anyone to hear his utterance.

When the actor reappeared to take his bow, the audience applauded with extra enthusiasm—for his performance or the fact that he survived, I couldn't tell.

"That was dramatic. And exhausting," Drew said as he slumped in his seat, gaze still fixed upon the closed curtains after the cast, director, and conductor had all taken their bows. Flowers still littered the stage apron, far too many bouquets for the performers to gather.

I nodded agreement, too drained to speak.

The others of our party prepared to leave, many of the ladies still fanning flushed faces. Then they had all departed with thank yous for sharing the box and reassurances they would reciprocate, etc. etc. etc.

I heard little of the ritual phrases; my attention lingered on the breathtaking opera, and Lord Ruthven leaning over the railing, a puzzled frown on his face.

"Ruthven, there are ladies present." Drew looked pointedly at me. Then he relaxed into his chair as if he had made his point and no longer needed to reinforce it. "And if you must learn the secrets of stage effects, I suggest you become a patron of the arts and thus gain a detailed tour of the entire theater." Drew affected a lazy drawl. His clenched hands belied his lack of interest. "All tricks and sleight of hand. Distraction and misdirection."

"That I may do. I may have to forgo a few little luxuries to afford a large donation, but the knowledge gained should be worth it." He bowed abruptly to us and strode out of the box with new purpose and energy. His bodyguard lingered a moment, briefly scanning the box and the theater beyond before he clicked his heels, bowed shortly and abruptly, and left. I hadn't seen his gloved hands leave their clasped position behind his back.

Drew and I stared at each other. "What was that about?" I finally asked.

"I do not want to know. Ruthven's esoteric hobbies range widely." Drew dismissed my question with a flip of his fingers. But he broke eye contact and turned his gaze toward the stage and the emptying theater.

"Is he a necromancer, enthralled with death and its imitations?"

"Leave it, madam. Do not ask questions if the answers will frighten you." Abruptly he stood and offered his hand to assist me.

I wouldn't learn anything by angering him. So I placed my hand in his open palm. But I stood on my own power, not leaning into him, or taxing the strength of his arm.

 **Chapter Eight**

A RIPPLE OF CONTENTMENT sent languid warmth through my arms as I tried to finger comb the mass of tangles in my hip-length hair. Drew had tousled it lovingly, and I could not regret that. But the rats' nest of the aftermath defied every brush stroke. Static electricity only made it worse.

The sounds of gentle splashing in my dressing room alerted me that Drew had almost finished cleaning up. I hated that he'd see the mess of my hair.

"Let me do that," he said softly, padding up behind me on bare feet, wearing only his silk undergarment. He took the boar's hair bristle brush from my hands and began applying it judiciously at the tips of my hair where the tresses curled around his fingers.

I swiveled on the low stool before my dressing table to give him better access.

"Such a luxury to have someone else deal with this," I said. "I could get used to having you around."

"Nonsense." He kissed the top of my head. "Neither of us wishes to give up a mote of independence. You will not let me set you up in a home of my choosing and I will not give up the freedom to come and go as I please without requesting permission from anyone."

Like his wife.

The argument was an old one, rehashed at regular intervals. He wanted me in an establishment of his choosing. I wanted to build a life for myself to have a living when he left me. As I knew he would eventually.

Men always left.

For now, however, I'd enjoy his company.

I handed him my comb as he worked his way upward with the brush.

"I will be gone for a few days," he said hesitantly, tugging gently and therefore ineffectively at the mat of hair near my crown.

"Oh?" He often left to deal with business at his country home, or to visit relatives. He never sought out political allies on these ramblings. He hadn't a political bone in his body.

Other bones, yes. Very lovely bones.

"Ruthven has invited me to his estate to consult on some of his inventions."

His eyes would not meet mine in the mirror.

"Is that wise?"

"He's a friend. We have much in common." He set the comb and brush on the table and turned me to face him. "Why don't you trust him?" he asked kissing my nose.

"I . . . I'm not certain why." I *would not* bring up his fascination with death, so similar to Drew's. They both frightened me as they licked their lips in anticipation when they talked about death, almost as if the biological function was a person. A person they wished to know intimately.

"To make up for my absence, I made you something special," he said, almost without pause. He rummaged through his clothes for a midnight-blue velvet box. Too big for a ring, too small for a necklace. He had, upon occasion, fashioned lovely jewelry for me. Usually he gave it to me before we left for a social engagement so that I might wear it for others to admire and envy.

"What's this?" I stroked the soft covering, sleeker than a kitten's fur.

"A memento, to remember me by. Fondly I hope."

"Just how long do you expect to be gone?"

"Long enough for you to count the hours of missing me." Impatiently, he flicked up the hinged box top.

Nestled into a froth of emerald-green silk sat a clockwork hummingbird; the bejeweled and enameled feathers looked real. I touched the long beak. A tiny prick of blood appeared on my fingertip. "Oh!" I jerked my hand away, finally feeling the tiny bit of pain after the fact.

"Let me show you," Drew laughed as he touched a long bit of green enamel at the base of the tail. A spring whirred, the bird chirped, and the back opened to reveal a tiny clock face and a compass.

And beneath the compass, a little well for . . . a small thimbleful of poison?

"I can always tell the time and know where I'm going, even without your guidance," I said amazed at the delicate detail.

I could also use it as a weapon to ward off pickpockets and unwanted admirers.

Or to draw blood for arcane magic rituals.

⚙️⚙️

Drew was gone when I awoke at dawn. The little hummingbird sat on my dressing table, bright and cheerful, a lovely reminder of the previous evening. I tucked it into my pocket, mindful of the sharp beak, and let its slight weight remind me of the man who had crafted it.

Helen worked in the kitchen, preparing the first batch of pastries. Mickey swept the front stoop diligently, with determination if not expertise. I patted his shoulder, then indulged in a brief hug. He flung both arms around my waist. His fingers clutched at my skirt fiercely. Certainly, I'd have to find him an apprenticeship soon if he'd tamed enough to return affection.

Maybe I'd keep him close and teach him the fine art of brewing coffee. He was brighter than most of my boys, and I liked him.

Decision made, I set about filling crumpets and scones with fresh strawberry preserves. Some of my customers liked brandied raisins. Others liked caramelized walnuts. In companionable silence, we worked side by side, filling the building with the fragrance of baking treats.

At half seven I fed Mickey a cheese roll and showed him how to grind roasted coffee beans into a coarse powder. He sniffed the grounds appreciatively.

"We'll need more before we open, and then several times during the day," I said around a grin. "Try it on your own while I brew the first pot."

He climbed up on a stool to reach the counter that had been designed for my height. Tongue peeking between his lips and eyes narrowed in deep concentration, he followed my instructions slowly and carefully until the beans reached a good imitation of the perfect texture. While he worked, I forced steam through the earlier batch and then whipped milk into a lovely froth to top the brew. The first cup went to Mickey as a reward. He took one tentative sip, mindful of the heat. His eyes grew wide and a smile nearly split his face in two. "'Cor that's loverly," he said on a long exhale. "Better'n tea any day."

I'd make a domesticated cat of him yet. Maybe a baker as well. Though he'd have to accept a full soaking bath to scrub away all the ingrained dirt on his hands and neck before I'd let him near fine white flour and sugar.

Inspector Witherspoon rapped upon the front door. I checked the clock over the coffee bar. Still five minutes to opening. Normally, I held fast to the posted times of opening and closing, not making exceptions for even a belted earl. Well, maybe for William King, Earl Lovelace and husband of my Lady Ada. I couldn't remember ever having a duke in the place—just the illegitimate son of one at my salon.

I unlatched the door and then relocked it the moment the policeman stepped through. No sense giving anyone else ideas about me loosening my rules. The inspector thrust the two tomes on exotic beliefs in India into my hands.

"Did you find anything useful?" I asked, placing them carefully into the bin that would reshelve the books.

"Partly. I know how to set my men to watch for the illusive shadows. But I have dismissed the possibility that Thuggees from the subcontinent have reason to assassinate Her Majesty at the coronation. No. We must look closer to home for the disaffected."

"May I be of assistance?" I led him to a small table at the center of the open café, then hurried to fetch him coffee without waiting for him to order. I knew how he liked it, two lumps of sugar, thick cream fresh from the dairy. No steam whipping or expressing for him. "Fetch two of the cream cheese and puff pastries and two savory scones with cheddar," I whispered to Mickey.

"I ain't no serving wench." He scrunched his face in his offended rebellion expression.

"And you will not be a serving lad until you learn to speak properly. If you do as I say, you may have one sugar bun." I flipped my hand to shoo him down the stairs to the kitchen.

He slumped off, trying to tell me how insulted he felt, but there was just enough lightness in his step that I knew he considered the sugar bun an almost adequate bribe.

"What brought you to the conclusion that any danger will not come from India?" I asked, placing the pastries and coffee in front of the Inspector.

He jerked his chin toward the chair across the table from him, and I sat there, leaning forward to catch every nuance of his voice and posture.

"These Thuggees are extremely loyal to their cult. Will only take orders from one they know, respect, and revere. William Sleeman is doing a good job of rooting out this pervasive cult. It is everywhere in India, hidden among respectable merchants and professionals, even the nobility. There are religious prohibitions against spilling blood, so they strangle with a ritual yellow kerchief, or poison if they have no other means. But he says they have strict rules against attacking women, fakirs, musicians, lepers, and Europeans. No telling what they may think next week."

"They will not spill blood, so they will not shoot or use explosives," I mused. "Would a cannon that shoots light spill blood?" My own veins felt icy at the thought. "It might burn through flesh, cauterizing as it goes and kill the heart." The black balloon hovered over the West End for a reason.

"No such weapon exits. No. I believe we can dismiss the Thuggees for now." Inspector Witherspoon settled back in his chair to sip his coffee and chew his pastry.

"Her Majesty is young." My thoughts took a different turn. "She hasn't been out in public enough to offend anyone. And there are precious few legitimate heirs left. Remove Victoria, and quite likely England would dissolve into chaos and civil war. Only a dedicated anarchist would want . . ."

"Got most of those rounded up and held in Newgate," Witherspoon said around a mouth full of cream cheese. "As well as a few foreign spies who'd like to weaken our resolve to resist invasion. If a plot still exists, and rumors say it does, I have to look farther afield."

"Perhaps the whispers of danger at the coronation targets someone else," I thought aloud, remembering the black dragon of a balloon and its shafts of searing light.

"Who else is important enough?"

"Nearly all our nobility and lords of the Church, Members of Parliament, ambassadors, and foreign dignitaries will all be gathered in one building."

"A single explosion could eliminate our entire government and . . . and likely bring down the Church as well," he gasped. He finished his coffee in one gulp, scooped up the remaining pastry, and tossed three crowns on the table on his way out the door. "Gunpowder. Damme, everyone has stores of gunpowder for hunting and discouraging outlaws and miscreants." The door slammed behind him, but three customers slipped in for their morning coffee.

"'Cor, are all them coins just for treats and coffee?" Mickey asked, sticking his head out from around the coffee bar.

I nodded without really thinking about the words.

"If you make that much money, how come you only pay me a penny to sweep?" He came closer, fingers inching toward the table, making little grasping movements. He had yet to learn all the fine nuances of becoming an adept pickpocket. Others of my tribe of urchins did it better when I asked them to steal letters and notes. Another reason to keep him close and let him be tamed.

I slapped my hand flat atop the coins. "Sweeping is only worth a penny. Serving, brewing, baking, and keeping the library require better manners, cleaner hands, and an education. Therefore, those tasks are worth more."

"Oh." His mouth made a near perfect O and he retreated toward the kitchen. I hoped I'd given him something to think about.

I opened the front door and welcomed the rest of my customers, wishing Drew were here to discuss Inspector Witherspoon's ideas.

Lacking Drew, I had access to someone else with knowledge of machines that performed near impossible tasks.

"Mickey, I need you to take a note to Lovelace House! After you've scrubbed your hands and face."

"What do you think of this, Elise?" Lady Ada asked the moment my foot crossed the threshold of her workroom.

She didn't bother looking up from a mass of gears and gyroscopes. She'd appropriated the big family parlor adjacent to the servant stair on the first floor above ground. Normally this room would make an admirable morning room, with good light from the east and south.

I watched as she pressed a spring and a thin metal sheet slid down over an opening and then slid back up into place. Upon more careful examination, I determined there were two such openings in the area that approximated the head of her machine.

"Are you trying to make the automaton blink?" I shuffled my feet so that I could see the length of the machine well enough to know what most of the parts represented, without coming close enough to actually touch, or be touched, by the artificial person. I had read too much, seen too much, to ever be truly comfortable around these machines.

When my lady was but a tiny babe, her father, the infamous Lord Byron and his physician Dr. Polidari, had invented a machine to transfer a man's soul from a damaged but living body into an undamaged but dead body. He was still out there waiting for ... the perfect body, mechanical or real, to accept his soul, personality, and poetic genius, as well as his perfidy.

Tapping his daughter's mathematical genius to accomplish his nefarious schemes had always been a worrisome probability. Possessing her body while she still lived, so that he could share her genius bothered me more. He'd tried that once and failed. Would he try again next time she fell ill and vulnerable?

"Oh, come closer, Elise. It won't hurt you. It doesn't have its thinking cards installed," Ada said, dismissing my misgivings. "I've been studying Henri Maillardet's theories of automation for his puppets—parlor tricks and games only; he never went beyond to something useful. Still, his work is amazing and set me to thinking what else I can do with his methods."

"Might it be taught to harm?" I asked, still not coming closer.

A mischievous smile creased her too thin face. I hadn't seen much of that smile of late. She touched another spring, and a skeletal arm made of metal and leather, gears and hinges, jerked outward, fingers grasping toward me.

"Eeeek!" I jumped back, hand to chest, trying to still my heart that suddenly beat so hard and fast I thought it might burst through my ribs.

"You!" Ada laughed, long and loud, the delightful sound rippling up from her toes and making her eyes dance with mirth. "You are so funny."

"Enough of your pranks, my lady," I admonished, returning to my governess voice and tone.

"Why is 25.807 banned from usage?" she asked, her face a mask of false innocence.

"I don't know. Why?" I knew better, truly I did. But how can one resist harmless if incomprehensible jokes from the child one has raised?

"It is the root of all evil!" she chortled.

"Huh?"

"The square root! 25.807^2 equals 666."

"The root of all evil." I kept my face bland, not truly understanding why she nearly doubled over with laughter. Her mirth warmed my heart. That was enough.

She'd long outgrown fear of me. Her lingering respect for our former closeness made her gulp air.

Useless. She burst out with more peals of laughter. Her hand brushed another control and the machine leg, just as skeletal, jerked and kicked from the knee.

I restrained my instinct to jump farther away from that bobbing leg.

Ada turned her back and drew in several long breaths. Jaw still working to contain her mirth, she faced me once more. "So what do you think? Does the blinking eye make it appear more friendly?"

"Too much so." I shuddered with atavistic revulsion. "I do not like the idea of machines indistinguishable from humans." My gaze kept returning to the skull-like head in fascinated horror.

"Oh, dear. Mr. Babbage and I had hoped that making it more like a pet and less of a machine would allow people to identify with them and accept them into their households and factories." Ada frowned at her creation. One hand hovered too close to the spring controlling the arm.

I looked elsewhere, not willing to become a victim of her pranks again. Various gears and wires, sheets of metal, and other arcane paraphernalia littered another long table to Ada's left.

A brighter patch of wallpaper in the center indicated the place her father's portrait used to hang. She'd removed it, thank heavens. One less place for him to invade.

To her right, a smaller table contained stacks of gold sheets, uniform rectangles, three inches by four, and less than one sixteenth of an inch thick—the all-important codex cards that determined mechanical actions. A punch press with thirty-two calibration dials sat in pride of place at the center of the table. It was a more complicated variation on the key cutter of my book catalog search engine. There were large sheets of paper, covered in mathematical equations that Ada, and no one else, could translate into the codes she punched into those gold cards.

"What are these?" I asked, holding up the top sheet of paper.

"Oh, factorials," she said on a delighted exhale.

"Oh, ducklings," I replied in the same tone.

She looked at me quizzically.

"You said that with the same delight as someone who has just come across a parade of ducklings in Regent's Park."

"Well, they are certainly cute." She studied the page

with a cocked head and carefully returned the sheet of paper to its proper place. Then she took up the pen from the stand and made a hasty note on one of the clumps of arcane symbols.

The gold cards were still blank and the mathematics unfinished. Ada had not yet completed the internal working of the automaton on the table. The mechanical man remained inert, incapable of independent movements. Technically.

No. I would not think about the possibility that some poor soul, having lost its body, and not yet moved on to whatever fate God determined, might take up lodgings in the machine.

No. No. No.

Although, wasn't that one of the purposes of necromancy? To achieve with magic what Lord Byron had tried with machines and bodies, moving a soul from one to another. And Lord Archbishop Howley of Canterbury would not need to outlaw necromancy if someone, multiple someones, weren't already practicing it.

"Enough of your games, Lady Ada. I need information. Like how someone would contrive a cannon that shoots deadly light and mounts the weapon inside the basket of a hot air balloon?" I looked her straight in the eye, avoiding the creepy imitation person on the table.

Her gaze kept drifting downward to the place where the machine should have eyes. She'd contrived devices to make it blink. But what kind of machine would make the automaton "see?" Her face took on the slack-jawed expression common to her when in deep thought.

"Light as a weapon?" she murmured. "Electricity can set glass and copper to glowing. Light can blind. Light can illuminate. Light . . . I know of no property of light or any method to turn it into a weapon." She shook her head to jerk herself out of her trance, just as she had at the age of twelve when she'd solved or failed to solve an advanced equation.

"Do you know of someone who perhaps has studied light more extensively than you have?"

She tapped her fingers on the table edge, one of her tricks to sort the massive amounts of information stored in her brain. She never forgot anything because she organized her thoughts as well as she did her work.

"Perhaps. There is an Oxford scholar who has tried repeatedly to work out the equation for the speed of light. He's from India originally. A convoluted name, I never bothered to learn how to pronounce it. Let me write his address for you." She wiped her hands on her dark leather apron. The color masked any new stains she might affix there. She tore a corner off one page only partially filled with numbers and symbols, then hastily wrote the name I half expected her to—Ishwardas Chaturvedi, *Ish* the Hindu scholar who had taught me special deep breathing and relaxing exercises between lectures at Oxford—he'd been lecturing on the physical properties of solids, liquids, and gas. Could the right light agitate gas into a weapon?

Only one way to find out.

 Chapter Nine

THE ADDRESS ADA HAD given me was not the same as I remembered. Should I write to Dr. Chaturvedi directly at the new address? Where he had lodged three years ago? Or should I apply to someone else for information? Oxford scholars were notorious for changing rooms frequently unless they had quarters within one college where they taught. As far as I knew, Dr. Chaturvedi lectured at several colleges and kept rooms separate from all.

I had to think about my plans, so I spent the next happy half hour playing with Lady Ada's children. Tiny mites as they were, simple things delighted them, like dust motes in a sunbeam, and tickles from my bonnet feathers.

"We play numbers games in the nursery," Lady Byron said sternly, from the doorway. Heaven forbid she step any closer to her grandchildren except at a formal two-minute greeting at a designated time in the comfort of her own parlor. The children would, of course, be fresh from their bath, fed, and sleepy enough to not interfere with the lady's schedule.

"I want to thank you, my lady, for your contribution to Bedlam Hospital. They can now hire three charwomen to keep the place, and the patients, clean. A small step toward helping them, but a necessary one."

"Next you'll be asking for better food for the poor souls, too." She tried to sound indignant, but I knew her well enough to know that her anonymous donations gave her a source of pride.

"Better food would help. But at least they have food now. There are a number of war widows who have nothing . . ."

"Ah, yes. Always the war widows, and orphans. A never-ending supply of them. Leave a note with Little Miss Doyle. She'll see that we send something. Perhaps we should organize a jumble sale at the church . . ." Her eyes glazed over as she thought of things to donate. "Now about your being here; why must I always remind you of what games we allow in the nursery?"

"Number games. Of course," I replied. Then I grabbed the baby's bare foot and began counting toes, complete with tickles and giggles.

And an inspection of the skin on those toes for any abrasion or puncture that could indicate tampering by someone in search of a way in.

When this little one was but a few days old, I had visited her mother. Ada did not fare well after the difficult birth. I'd told the midwife and the physician which herbs to pack into the bandages to stop the bleeding. They ignored my advice. Home remedies—especially those that originated with the Rom—were not considered clean or approved by the Church.

So I'd gone myself and taken care of the chore. Afterward, I sat beside her, holding the baby while she slept. Ada's eyes were heavy and her face pale. Her left hand lay listlessly beside her, not stirring even to stroke her baby's hair.

"Ada, what ails you?" I asked.

"Two difficult births in two years," William King replied from the doorway. He shuffled his feet and looked up and down the hallway as if he'd rather be anywhere else, and yet could not pry himself away from his ailing wife.

Ada barely lifted her fingers, and he dashed to the other side of the bed. Deep lines of worry drew his mouth down and furrowed his brow so deeply the skin looked like a recently plowed field. He turned her hand over and kissed the palm, holding it in both of his.

"I told you we should wait," he said. "It's all my fault. I should have made you wait, but I love you so much . . ." He dropped his head to the sheets. "Don't leave me, Ada. I couldn't go on without you."

"Hush, Billy. Don't invite Death when I'm not ready for him yet."

"I think, Ada, that you will live. But you do need time. And rest. I should give the baby to her wet nurse and go myself."

"No, Elise. Stay a bit more. I . . . I want my baby close."

I settled back into my chair and rocked the tiny child. She opened her big blue eyes and stared at me, puckering her rosebud mouth. Then she let out a wail. Probably demanding food and a change of nappy.

Ada sighed her consent. The effort of staying awake for ten minutes had exhausted her.

I rose, still cuddling the child and turned to find the wet nurse. Just then, I smelled sulfur. Rancid, hot, and the tingle of electricity, like the first second after a lightning strike.

I knew that smell. The one time I had used Lord Byron's transference engine, the process smelled like this; a soul hovering between two bodies smelled like this.

Ada had nearly bled to death. She'd need months to recover any vitality. She was vulnerable. A greedy soul that needed a new body waited for her.

I whipped off my shawl and threw it over Ada's face and upper body. William lifted his head, instantly alert, and added his own body as protection to cover his wife from invasion. The baby willingly pressed her face against my chest, rooting for the food she craved, but would not find. I held her for several long, breathless moments. I thought I saw a dark mist swirling around and around us. It sent long stabbing tendrils toward Ada, and then the baby. William and I kept our vigil. With a snap and a cold breeze that came from nowhere, the mist was gone. In the far distance, perhaps only in my mind, I heard a howl of disappointed rage.

We relaxed and checked baby and mother. Other than gasping for air, Ada seemed untouched by the invader. The baby howled for food.

Ada kept to her bed for over a year after that. The baby grew naturally with fine dark curls like her mother and a sunny disposition.

Ever after, I checked Ada's babies every time I saw them. They were both free of any blemish. Feet and hands were clean, devoid of evidence of a puncture, and deliciously ticklish.

Lady Byron sighed. "I forgot how good you are with children. Perhaps we should hire you as nanny for these two."

"I am too old," I said firmly.

"Did you never wish for children of your own?" A personal question from the great lady herself! Was the world coming to an end?

Thirty-eight might not be too old to bear children, but my mind and life were no longer young enough to cope with the demands of motherhood. I replied to Lady Byron, "Only occasionally and briefly. I had eight younger brothers and sisters that I helped raise. Then, at the age of sixteen, I went to work as a nurserymaid to Mary Godwin and Percy Shelley at Villa Diodati to earn enough money to send my younger brother to school. I don't need any more children of my own."

Something pungent wafted to my nose from the region of a nappy. "One of the advantages of visiting other people's children is that I can play, delight, and be delighted. And then I can give them back when they need changing." I rose with the child in my arms and handed her to the nurserymaid who hovered protectively just behind my shoulder. She had watched diligently all the while that I had sat in the rocking chair with children climbing over me.

"Now if you will excuse me, Lady Byron." I bobbed a sketchy curtsy and sidled past her to the top of the stairway. "I have letters to write and a business to run. I'm training new employees and dare not leave them more than a half hour. I'll let Little Miss Doyle know where you should send your contribution to the war widows."

"Do you have any *special* news to impart?"

"Nothing for certain. A few rumors suggesting we be wary and extra diligent throughout the coronation celebrations."

She nodded curtly.

Without a backward glance, I departed Lovelace House, hailed a hansom cab, and returned to the Book View Café where light from the new windows brought life to an otherwise dreary hole of a building. Light, the giver of life. So how did one use it to take a life?

When in doubt, duplicate. I sent notes to Dr. Ishwardas Chaturvedi at both the new address and the old. Then I wrote to the Oxford scholar who had returned the bad translation tome, apologizing for my error in purchasing the book or offering it up in the search engine. I never offered Byron's last book of poetry, but it slid down the chute at regular intervals. Then I asked if he knew of a better translation that I might acquire on the subject, and—by the by—did he know a better address for Dr. Chaturvedi.

"Mickey!" I called from the center carousel of the library.

"Aye, Missus?" He poked his head through the open front door, a fierce grip on his broom.

When I'd returned from Lovelace House, I'd noted that the front stoop looked spotless and scrubbed.

"Mickey, I have a chore for you." I held up my letters and a tuppence.

His eyes grew wide at the size of the coin.

My boy was growing up, equating money with success, security. Safety.

But giving employment to Toby, Violet, and Jane hadn't kept them safe. "When you have delivered the letters to the post, I need you to spread the word that Toby, Violet, and Jane must be found, alive, if at all possible."

His chin trembled and he looked away from the enticement of the coin. But his focus came back to the shiny round of copper. I added a second tuppence to the first. "This one is yours if you spread the word that I need another girl to serve coffee and pastry and bring one back here."

"What happens when Violet and Jane come back?" Lucy asked. She stood straight with shoulders thrown back and defiance in her level chin.

"If the new girls work out, I'll keep them on. We need the extra hands."

Both Emily and Lucy breathed easier. They had known the tantalizing hope of permanent employment and a chance at a better life dangled in front of them, only to have it yanked out from under them, throwing them back onto the street. I'd faced that fate a time or two.

"I like to reward hard work and loyalty. Would either of you consider moving into the attic and taking on the chores of assisting me, both personally and professionally?"

Violet was hopeless in the kitchen but extremely organized and insistent upon cleanliness. I baked; she cleaned my utensils and made sure they were always close to my hand.

The girls exchanged silent glances. "Only one of us?" Lucy asked. They'd been friends and flatmates for a long time, companions and protectors of each other on the street before that.

"I can use you both if you can squeeze yourselves and your things into the attic." They'd be safer there, neither had family to entice them to walk alone through London.

"We're paid through the end of the month at the flat," Lucy said. "If you hire new girls and vouch for them, they can stay there."

"Thank you. That's a good enticement to get girls off the street." I smiled widely at them. "Mickey, spread the word. I need servers in the front of the café, a dishwasher, too."

"If . . . if you bring in extra hands, may I learn to bake and stay in the kitchen?" Emily asked shyly. She twisted her hands into her apron and kept her eyes on the floor.

"That sounds like a marvelous idea!" I nearly crowed. "Tonight, after we close, I'll start teaching you both the fine art of baking." And then I could send the sullen Helen back to Lady Ada's household.

"Me, too?" Mickey asked. He plastered a look of bland innocence on his face. But he couldn't hide the light sparkling in his eyes, brighter than when he'd spied the second tuppence.

"Cooking school starts tonight. I host salon tomorrow night, so we'll need both sweet and savory prepared before then. Now, back to work, all of you." I swept upstairs to my private sitting room and the ledgers, inventories, and new book acquisitions that badly needed my attention.

 Chapter Ten

DREW DID NOT RETURN in time to attend my salon. He said he'd be gone for a few days. I shouldn't expect word from him yet. He sometimes retreated to his country home for weeks to attend to business or see to his son's education. Friends invited him to house parties for his wit and charm.

So why did I fret about his absence while Lucy tightened my laces to make my old sapphire gown fit properly. The last time I'd dressed for salon Drew had performed this chore. Because Violet had gone missing. She had not returned yet. The chances of finding her or Jane or Toby alive diminished with each passing day.

Enough worrying about things I could not change. I needed to host the intellectual elite and gather information, the two things I did best.

The first guest, much earlier than fashionable, through my door surprised me. "Ish!" I squealed the moment I spied Dr. Chaturvedi standing awkwardly in the doorway to my parlor. I threw my arms around him and held him tightly. He returned my embrace with equal fervor and kissed my chin. He stood half a hand shorter than myself with a slight frame and the vague myopic expression of a man who truly needed spectacles but refused to wear them in public.

"My dear, it is good to see you again," he whispered in my ear in that lovely singsong accent. "I am most satisfied that you went to such lengths to find me." His fingers dug into my back fiercely, then released me, and he stepped aside to reveal an even shorter man standing hesitantly behind him.

The newcomer ran a finger around his tight collar while studying the door lintel. He wore little round spectacles with a silvery wire frame that slid down his nose. His tweed coat had seen better days, revealing fraying threads at the lapel edges and sleeve ends. His nose looked raw and damp. I wanted to hand him a clean handkerchief, but had to remind myself that he was a grown man, unlike Mickey.

"Madame Magdala, may I present my colleague Dr. Jeremy Badenough." Ish bowed slightly, tugging on his companion's sleeve to indicate he should imitate the action.

Ah, scholars! So intent on their studies they had trouble remembering etiquette. I loved them for their brilliant minds and loved them when I taught them what they needed to know about life and they remembered it afterward.

"Jeremy Badenough, you borrowed the book of bad translations," I said, holding out my fingertips to him.

He clasped my hand, as a man would shake another man's. That intrigued me. He hadn't bothered with the etiquette of greeting a ... mature woman of casual acquaintance. Instead, he treated me with the respect he'd accord a man he admired and considered an equal.

I liked him immediately.

"It wasn't all bad," he said, blinking rapidly. I wondered if that was an indication of embarrassment or a need to replace shyness with intellectual zeal.

"Did you learn anything of use?" I gestured them to proceed me into the parlor. Trays of pastries lined the sideboard, wine breathed in its decanter, and a coffee urn simmered over a candle burner, all waiting for my guests to serve themselves.

The men gathered refreshments and settled on the settee while I perched on the wing-backed chair as if on a throne. Ish preferred the cheese and savory delicacies with coffee—I had no tea prepared, which was his preference. Dr. Badenough loaded his plate with sweets and filled his glass to the brim with wine, most of which he drank in one long gulp, then topped off the glass.

"So what nugget of information did you glean from the bad translation of Persian into Latin and then a worse translation into English? I must admit that I had a great deal of difficulty parsing anything sensible from the twisted sentence structure."

"Actually, the most useful bit was that the Oriental magicians cling fiercely to the notion of cleanliness. They insist their laboratories must be completely whitewashed: walls, floors, and ceilings. Not a single dust mote must enter the equation," Dr. Badenough said, leaning forward in his enthusiasm until his hopeless cravat nearly dangled in his wine and his spectacles slid farther down his nose.

"Whitewash," Ish mused. "The lime in the compound has proved effective in preventing certain molds from growing."

"Did I read somewhere recently that some physicians are expounding the value of washing hands and . . . disinfecting surgeries?" I interjected, trying to remember where I had read that, or overheard a conversation. I knew that farmers, such as my father, frequently whitewashed both interior and exterior walls of a dairy. They said that the brighter atmosphere kept the cows happier and the milk sweeter. But there might be a more scientific explanation behind the old folk wisdom.

"Yes." Ish leaned forward, nearly dropping his tray. "I

have heard of this obscure theory of cleanliness. Some cultures value scrubbed hands and thus suffer fewer contagious illnesses. In Calcutta, for instance . . ."

A knock on the door interrupted us.

I excused myself and rose to open the door at the top of the private stair. "Hold that thought, Ish. We will talk more, later." My two guests looked to each other and nodded.

Three esteemed, if not well-selling, artists descended upon us along with a sprinkling of minor nobility. Coronation parties and special performances at theaters about town drew many of my usual guests. Well enough, this smaller group suited my mood admirably. And they were all young enough and hungry enough not to complain if my pastries were less than perfect, baked by my new apprentices.

Quickly the conversation turned to the way Vernon St. George used light in his paintings of the Madonna.

Surprisingly, Ish contributed to the sprightly conversation with his scientific observations of the properties of light. He even recommended a chemical wash to layer on top of oils to give the illusion of glowing in dim light.

The technical terminology meant nothing to me.

Dr. Badenough, Jeremy, looked as bewildered as I. When Ish shifted to a straight chair beside a painter and his . . . er . . . model, I took his place on the settee.

"What intrigued you about the book?" I asked, transferring one of my jam scones from my plate to his and topping off his glass of wine. His eyes looked a bit heavy, but his nose had dried in the cozy warmth of my parlor.

"The book?" he asked blearily.

"*An Examination of Necromancy and Soul Preservation After Death in the Magic System of Persia*," I reminded him, deliberately correcting the title.

He opened his mouth to protest, but I cut him off. "The book you borrowed and returned to my library. Why did you borrow it in the first place?"

"Lord Ruthven requested my analysis of the text."

"Lord Ruthven." The fine hairs along my spine stood up straight.

"Yes. He attended school with my older half brother. He took advantage of the family connection. My brother begged me to assist Ruthven so *he* wouldn't have to. Ruthven's always been fascinated with necromancy. I don't know why. Rather repulsive if you ask me. He quotes Lord Byron at length, giving the poet king's melancholy as evidence of a need to study death in all its phases."

I sighed in relief. Badenough wasn't a practitioner. But Lord Byron reared his ugly head once again.

"Why you?"

"I have studied many obscure religions as part of my ancient language studies, and their inherent magic in foreign realms. He thought there might be spells encrypted in the text and that was why it was so difficult to understand. Once I discerned the Latinate grammar beneath the English and a foreign subtext, I knew there were no true secrets, just bad scholarship." He bit deeply into the rich cinnamon bun, strewing spiced sugar across his beleaguered cravat. I wanted to brush it clean and launder it for him.

But I needed one more piece of information from him first. "Is Adam Lord Ruthven a practitioner?"

He paused with the remnants of his sweet halfway to his mouth. His mouth twisted in distaste and he set the bun back on his plate, then put it all aside on the end table. "He never said so. My brother was most anxious to prevent him from pressing his cause at the family manor."

"You believe he does more than study and observe."

"His fascination with death is untoward. When he visited my brother some twenty years ago—I was but six or seven—he spent nearly the entire two weeks in the parish cemetery or the manor crypt—it's very old, from the days of its original abbey foundations, and not altogether sound. He liked the crypt best. My brother discovered him trying to open one of the tombs and terminated the visit. We believe he made off with the skull of one of our Crusader ancestors. He left under protest, spouting nonsense about the magical powers contained in the bones of a true believer."

$$\infty$$

"I will not go to Mass this morning!" Augusta Ada Byron stamped her foot as she screamed at Mrs. Carr, one of Lady Byron's "friends."

"You have no choice, child. 'Tis the law," the Fury replied.

"Well, it shouldn't be. The requirement of attending Church of England services weekly outlived its usefulness with the defeat of the Spanish Armada in 1588 and the crushing of invasion plans from Catholic monarchs in Europe."

"Don't you dare preach to me, young lady!" Mrs. Carr quivered in indignation. If she'd had an ounce of fat on her tall and spare frame, it would surely flap and wave as if a flag in a strong wind. "Constant diligence in faith and repentant prayer are the only defenses against demonic powers. You must go to Mass to have the purity to fight off the minions of yo . . . of the Devil."

She'd been about to say "your father," meaning Lord Byron, a demon of a necromancer.

"Religion is nothing more than superstitious nonsense that appeals to the emotional excess of poets and dreamers with nothing better to do with their lives." Oh, my girl knew the right words to make her mother see her point of view. At the age of twelve she knew how to manipulate and maneuver her mother as well as her tutors. She and I had no need for such histrionics.

But Mrs. Carr had a point. I just had never seen proof that piety could fend off a necromancer.

However, she had no authority in this household to order me, or Miss Ada, to go anywhere or do anything.

But Lady Byron had taken to her bed last night with a slight sniffle. She declared she needed a week of solitude and bland food.

I thought she needed less wine and heavy sweets with her dinner and then more of the same upon retiring for the night. But 'twasn't my place to criticize the woman.

"Miss Ada, please keep your voice down," I admonished her. I'd dressed soberly for the ritual of walking in the family procession to the tiny chapel between the manor and the village.

"Christianity is little more than death worship designed to control the masses out of fear."

Mrs. Carr froze.

And so did I. Was organized religion any different from necromancy? Yes, it had to be different. Our priests didn't demand human sacrifice. Now.

The Crusades came to mind.

"Blasphemy," Mrs. Carr gasped as she waved her handkerchief in front of her face. "Next you will imitate your father by taking a lov . . ."

"She will not!" I stepped between my charge and her erstwhile protector. "Miss Ada is much too logical to consider anything but the most practical and sensible course. I believe her time today will best be spent reading inspirational sermons to her mother." I grasped Ada's shoulders, turned her around, and marched her up the stairs to her own rooms on the third floor. The Furies had usurped her suite on the second.

"I think I should like to open my father's tomb and study his skull. Do you think, Miss Elise, that it will differ greatly from, say the skull of the gardener who died last year?"

Mrs. Carr staggered into the parlor, commanding tea from the servants.

"You didn't really have to say that," I whispered to

Ada as we retreated upstairs. "It will upset your mother terribly. Not to mention bringing down the wrath of Father Huntley."

"I know." Ada sighed and looked chagrined. For about three heartbeats. "Do you suppose a study of skulls might reveal differences in intelligence and creative genius?"

"I have no idea. But such study is best left to medical scientists."

"None of my tutors are well versed in medicine. Perhaps we should expand my education."

"Something to discuss with your mother, after she rises from her sickbed."

"In the meantime, I presume I do not have to attend Mass?"

"Not today. Today, after you read a sermon to your mother, you shall write an essay on the necessity of mandatory attendance at Church of England services. This essay will be at least five pages long and must meet approval from both your mother and Father Huntley."

"I'd rather calculate logarithms."

"I'm sure you would."

 **Chapter Eleven**

"I SAY, there's been this curious black hot air balloon hovering over the West End of late," one of the artists said, by way of nothing.

"Yes, yes, I've seen it. The children say it's a dragon that spits green flames," another chimed in.

"And I'd swear that when it dipped low, as if checking something on the ground, I saw Sir Andrew at the controls and Ruthven guiding him," the first artist continued.

Chills ran through me at the thought of Drew spending time with Lord Ruthven who was even more fascinated with skulls than Ada was. She at least gave up the idea as soon as she realized that her mother and friends were shocked. She wanted to shock, not study at that point.

How deeply involved in the hideous cult of necromancy had Drew become? Maybe he only wanted the adventure of flying the balloon himself.

A part of me truly wanted to believe that, but I knew him. He'd done that already. He sought a different adventure this time.

My desire for Drew's return to my life and my bed waned. Not if he had blood on his soul from nefarious attempts at powerful magic. Not if he lightly took the lives of innocents to fuel that magic.

I had more questions for Jeremy. Before I could voice them, his face turned ghostly pale and he swallowed convulsively. "I must go. I regret troubling you with my sordid activities with Dr. Ruthven." He almost bolted from his chair and raced for the door to the back stair.

Ish looked up from his conversation with the painters. He looked to me for explanation. I shook my head, not truly knowing if a discussion of necromancy had upset our young friend, or if it had to do with too many sweets and wine on an empty stomach.

The party lost some of its vivacity with Jeremy's departure. I did not encourage the others to linger as, one by one, they finished their wine and departed, seeking other salons with more life than mine. Not unusual for salon participants to wander from gathering to gathering over the course of the evening. I did not regret their leaving.

"I should go as well," Ish said quietly, as he leaned toward me, taking my hand in departure. He glanced around the room at the few lingerers and whispered, "May I return later, my dear? Not too late, though."

"Of course."

He exited as hastily as his colleague had.

The last artist had just descended the stairs when Ish returned, interrupting my quiet contemplation of whitewash and cleanliness in dairies as well as magical workshops.

Hours later, with the languor of sleep tugging at my limbs, I forced myself to ask the questions of him I'd been seeking answers to for days. "I took a ride in a hot air balloon."

"A marvelous trip, I hope?" he asked while tirelessly nibbling my ear and cheek down to my shoulder.

Marvelous and indefatigable. But I needed answers and then sleep.

"While hovering over London I saw another balloon all in black. The pilot had a small cannon that shot light from the bottom corner of the black-painted wicker basket. Had the conveyance been left its natural color, I might not have seen the light."

Ish sat up in bed, revealing his honed torso. Alas, I was too tired to indulge myself in more than looking. I began breathing deeply, as he had taught me. The influx of air postponed my need to close my eyes and drift into pleasurable dreams.

"Purpose?" Ish asked, staring into the darkness, as if seeing the ominous contraption.

"I do not know. It looked as if he aimed for the statue above Trafalgar Square. However, Inspector Witherspoon of the Bow Street Runners is chasing rumors of an assassination attempt at the coronation."

"Practicing his aim?"

I shrugged.

"Color?"

"Of the light?"

He nodded as he threw off the sheet and fumbled for his hastily discarded clothing. A pleasant enough view, but clearly he had other things on his mind than a return to our earlier activities.

"Yes, yes. He'd need concentrated fuel and a focus. Did the light burn anything? What was the color?" he demanded, turning back to me wearing only his trousers.

"Green light, I think. But the next day I heard a report of red light. He had a burner to refresh the balloon; that could account for the giant red eye of the black dragon. I saw only a circular hole in the basket near the bottom, about this big." I held up my two hands, making a circle of both thumbs and middle fingers. About eight inches. "All the workings were hidden, only the tip of the muzzle fit up against the hole." Any smaller and I'd not have seen the hole at all from the distance between us, even with magnification.

"The muzzle could have been thick—to prevent light dissipation—leaving an actual opening of only an inch or two. That would be best. Yes, a tight focus. But it must be magnified . . ." He continued with his musings in terms I did not understand. Waves and prisms and such. More than a few Hindi words crept into his verbal thoughts.

"Can you explain in normal English?"

"Have you ever held a magnifying glass over a piece of dried grass on a sunny day?"

"I watched the Romany light a fire that way when they had no lucifers to strike."

"The glass focused and concentrated the broad swath of sunlight into a tiny pinpoint of light, hot enough to ignite a fire."

I nodded, beginning to see where his thoughts led him.

"To make a weapon, your villain would need a bright light source—say the fire within his burner—the blue-white light at the core, not the dissipated red flames. He'd have to open a window within the fire box and set a glass . . . or a crystal before it. As the light passes through the crystal, it would refract into the barrel of his gun. All in close proximity. But a normal fire and fuel source would not be bright enough to keep the shaft of light closely concentrated once it leaves the barrel."

"It is possible, then? Given the right fuel, crystal, and light source? I didn't imagine it?"

"Possible, not probable according to accepted science. I have seen many stranger things. I must think on this." He dropped a light kiss on my cheek and let himself out.

∞⚙

Morning came too early. I awoke to the smell of baking flour and sugar, and freshly brewed coffee.

Ah, Lucy and Emily had begun my work for me. Briefly, I wondered if Mickey was still about, or if he had gone back to his feral ways. I didn't think he would once he discovered the enticement of money, and warmth, and a regularly full tummy. Best he stayed close and away from kidnappers who walked the streets.

The only way to find out, and make sure my girls got their recipes correct was to climb out of my comfortable bed that stilled smelled deliciously of Ish.

"It be wicked out there," a ragged girl of about fourteen with lank and tangled hair that might have been auburn but was too dirty to be certain, said quietly. She hung her head over the fragrant cup of coffee Mickey placed before her.

Something about the uptilt of the end of her nose looked remarkably like Mickey's. They might be related.

His hands were cleaner than I'd ever seen them. So was his face. And I swear he'd grown another inch just this last week. Time to either accept him as part of the household or find him an apprenticeship.

As things were going, he seemed to have slid into place as *my* apprentice without me noticing.

But the girl was new. One way to start the cleanup process was to assign her the chores of washing dishes.

"What is your name, dear?" I asked kindly, accepting my own coffee and a flakey puff pastry filled with marmalade from Lucy. And, wonder of wonders, a rasher of bacon appeared on a plate in the center of the table. I grabbed a piece before the others could devour the rare treat.

Emily took the plate of pastry from my hand and thrust a bowl of oatmeal into my grasping fingers. "Me mum always said, best to start the day with something that will stick to your ribs." She flounced back to the oven and peered in to watch a batch of scones turn a delicate brown.

What was happening? The kitchen wasn't mine anymore!

Part of me smiled in satisfaction at how well my girls, and Mickey, had flourished under my tutelage. Part of me screamed defiance that the kitchen was mine and only I could dictate who ate what and when.

"Philippa," the lump of rags at the counter mumbled.

"That's a nice name," I said. "I think we had a queen with that name in olden times."

No response. She didn't even sip her coffee. From the limpness of her arms and the sag of her neck, I had the impression that she was too tired—or too frightened—to eat.

Mickey hovered nearby, twisting his fingers in anxiety.

"Philippa, what is so wicked out there, on the streets?" I prodded.

"More girls gone missing, Missus," Mickey answered for her. "Found this one hiding in the shadows of a dust-bin, shaking all over, like. Heard some noises down the alley—thumps and bumps and squelched screams—I did."

"Street girls that have no home and no one will miss," Emily said. A cloud of indignation seemed to set her hair to frizzing. I'd seen the like once at a lecture of a philosophical society in Germany. The showman—I wouldn't grace him with the title of scientist, not like Ish, or even Drew, for lack of education at school or through his own resources—had rubbed a chunk of amber with raw wool and touched the stone to his own hair making it stand on end. In the dim light he'd actually glowed a bit. I'd seen a tiny spark leap from the amber to his hair. Electricity. The spark of life. Each of us held some of the ethereal substance within our bodies.

Dr. Polidari, for all of his negligent worthlessness, had proved that to me.

Call it a soul if you like. Lights and souls. The two were aligned. I just did not know how yet.

"Any reports of boys or men gone missing?" I asked. If the kidnappers continued to take new victims, then hope of recovering Violet and Toby alive dimmed.

Philippa shook her head. Mickey shrugged. "Only Toby," he said.

I had to shake my head and body to rid myself of the glum mood.

"Well, then, Philippa, what do you want from me?"

"To be safe," she whispered, finally slurping a big drink of her cooling coffee.

"And what are you willing to do in exchange for safety?" I sat at the worktable and sampled a tiny morsel of oatmeal from the tip of my spoon. It instantly brought back memories of my childhood home, on the farm near Lake Geneva. Home had always been safe, if boring. Not like my life at the villa rented by Lord Byron that year without a summer.

"I'll . . . I'll work for my keep, Missus. Work hard so's I don't have to sleep out there alone. I'll work so's I don't have to favor men for a bit o' coin just to buy enough food to survive."

She looked as if a strong wind would blow her away, thin sticks for arms and big hollows in her cheeks.

"Then work you will. After you eat some of this excellent oatmeal and clean up a bit. Emily, help her find something less dirty to wear and show her how to wash pots and the cutlery." I'd not trust her with breakable china until she'd proven she could handle it. "I'll be out front if you need me."

 **Chapter Twelve**

A LOUD RAP ON the window beside the front door startled me out of sorting clean cutlery and counting serviettes. The wavy glass revealed a bulky gentleman pacing impatiently on the stoop an hour before official opening. Something about the set of the shoulders and slapping a riding crop across his hand shouted military. The shape of the hat looked familiar.

I unlatched the door, leaving the chain on. "Inspector Witherspoon, how can I help you?" I peered out, noting two uniformed men behind him. Caution stiffened my posture and set one of my large feet against the door panel to block any untoward push.

"Madame Magdala, I must speak to you immediately. A situation of utmost urgency has come to my attention."

"And how does that concern me?" Out of the corner of my eye, I saw Mickey slip from the kitchen, my stout walking stick in his hand. I usually only carried the device when I patrolled the city in my old woman disguise. As good a weapon as any sword or pistol in the right hands.

Frantically, I gestured for Mickey to hand me the stick. He slapped it into my hand and melted into the nearest shadow as if he'd never been there.

"Just open the dam . . . the door so we don't have to inform the entire neighborhood." The inspector scanned right and left and behind him. His two soldiers—enlisted men by the lack of ornamentation on their uniforms—stood at parade rest, equally vigilant.

"Very well. A moment." Slowly and making as much clumsy noise as I could, I released the chain and stood back, leaning heavily on the stick.

"Are you injured?" Inspector Witherspoon asked, pausing just inside the door.

"A trifle," I dismissed his concern while keeping the stick close. I limped a bit as I moved back into the café. "Mickey, will you bring the inspector a cup of coffee? Or would you prefer tea, Inspector?"

"Nothing." He stayed close behind me. Too close for politeness.

"Madame Magdala, if that is your real name . . ."

I whirled to face him, too fast for the injury I mimicked. But I managed to shift my grip on the stick to defend myself.

"No defense?" he asked with an ugly sneer on his lips.

I met him with silence.

"Madame Magdala, you have Gypsy friends." An accusation more than a statement.

"We no longer live in medieval times when being Romany was illegal."

"True. But they are not welcome or trusted anywhere."

"Make your point, Inspector."

"I could arrest you and hold you in Newgate for your association with criminal elements."

"Many of the Rom walk a narrow path of acceptability on the edges of society," I hedged rather than reveal my outrage. And fear. Newgate prison was not a place to take lightly. Even if innocent, people had disappeared into the depths of that dungeon of horrors and never returned. Or never returned to their right mind.

"Few of the Rom that I know openly commit crimes." They might pilfer and steal small items. They might overcharge for repairing pots and tools. But they never hurt women, children, or horses, often proving better doctors for the latter than educated men.

"And yet they were camping near Norwynd Manor last week when the baron's fifteen-year-old daughter went missing. She is quite fair and I am told that Gypsies prize blondes." He gazed pointedly at the heavy braids wound around my head, pale gold in color. When I reinvented myself to become the owner of the Book View Café, I had supported the rumor that I was the bastard daughter of a Gypsy king as well as the widow of a war hero. Neither true, but people believe what they want to believe when seeking explanations for things outside the ordinary.

"Another girl gone missing? This one of quality rather than a nameless street girl no one would miss or report missing. The culprit has changed patterns. I must investigate this." I hastened toward the kitchen, needing to ask more detailed questions of Philippa.

"No so fast, Madame."

I froze in place barely two paces away from him. "Yes, Inspector?" I asked with my back to him.

"You have no authority to investigate anything. I know you have an amazing ability to gather information, often faster and more complete than I can." The inspector held up his hand to stall any protests I might make. "And who is to say the same person, or persons are responsible for Miss Abigail's disappearance as for your street urchins? I have heard nothing out of the ordinary of street girls going missing. They disappear every day. Their disappearance has nothing to do with Miss Abigail Norwynd."

"They might. Three of my employees are among the missing. I believe your authority extends only as far as events that might disrupt the coronation."

"Lord Norwynd is well respected in the royal household. Miss Abigail was scheduled to help carry Her Majesty's train."

"The Rom have rules—religious beliefs—that prevent them from harming women, children, and horses. None of my acquaintances could possibly be involved." In for a pence, in for a pound. "My *friends* are very respectful of women, virgins in particular. Whoever is behind these kidnappings has no respect for anyone."

"I have only your word on that."

"In many circles my word is respected. Especially at Lovelace House."

"Do I need to remind you of Lady Lovelace's origins? Seducing virgins, including his own sister, was Lord Byron's specialty, if I remember correctly."

"You do not need to remind me. I have spent the last fourteen years protecting Lady Ada from her father's reputation and his active perfidy."

Inspector Witherspoon gasped. "He wouldn't . . ."

"There is nothing I believe Lord Byron would *not* do in his quest for immortality in a perfect body."

"Are you saying that he lives, that his death in Greece fourteen years ago was a false report?"

"I have no evidence one way or the other." The coffin beneath the grave marker at the Church of St. Mary Magdalene in Hucknall, Nottinghamshire, could lie empty. We never opened it to study the skull. With the slowness of travel from Greece to England, the body would have been too much decayed for anyone to willingly check the coffin upon arrival.

"But you believe he lives."

"I have no proof." Except a few books of necromantic poetry published after his death. "And Lord Byron's life or death has little, that I can see, to connect him or his fanatical followers to an assassination attempt at the coronation."

"I have to take your word on that. The Gypsies are

still my prime suspects. Be just like them to try to throw the kingdom into chaos by assassinating our queen on her coronation day. Miss Abigail knows details of the procession and ritual that have not been made public. They will torture her for information about the best time and place . . ."

I gritted my teeth. "The *Rom* will not. But someone else might. Someone with a greater grievance and more resources." My mind went back to the black balloon shooting green light and my discussion with Ish this morning. I would not think about Drew piloting that balloon, even just for practice. "Look to the skies, Inspector Witherspoon. Look for a midnight-black balloon with a matching wicker basket, not a cloud-gray one."

"What do you know!" He grabbed my arm.

"Inspector?" I stared at his offending hand.

He separated from me but remained close enough to grab me again should he deem it necessary. "Madame Magdala, what do you know about black balloons with black wicker baskets?"

"Not enough. But I saw one hovering over London when I took a . . . pleasure trip with one of my Romany friends in his cloud-gray balloon."

"Hovering? Balloons must ride the winds . . ."

"Unless they have the new ailerons that allow them to tack against the wind like a sailing ship. *Expensive* ailerons. I believe a Hussar regiment in the east is experimenting with them." I didn't add that Jimmy Porto had designed and built his own.

"The deuce they are. How did you know? That information has not been made public."

"I listen and observe all classes of society, as should you. There is more afoot than you want to believe. Now, if you will excuse me, I must prepare my business for the line of customers outside the door." I curtsied in dismissal, barely deep enough for politeness.

The inspector nodded, bending his back in a perfunctory bow almost as polite as my own.

I threw the door open wide in welcome as he tipped his hat and stalked down the street in the direction of Piccadilly.

Piccadilly, with its avenging angel statue that frightened Toby so badly he sought refuge with the war hero Nelson in Trafalgar Square.

The black balloon had shot its green light in the direction of Trafalgar.

Somehow it was all connected. I just could not find the pattern yet.

∞O

Several of my street waifs reported in that day. All with the same story. Fear rode on the wind, driving all sensible people to walk the back streets only in groups or to hide indoors. The major thoroughfares seemed safe enough with the obvious patrols of Bow Street Runners, Horse Guards, and at least three other regiments. The military pretense of casual strolls through the city didn't fool many. The soldiers' eyes moved too warily, their posture remained too alert. Their hands hovered over weapons too readily. My customers reflected the same mood, cautious but determined to enjoy the rare festivities surrounding the upcoming grand ritual that defined Englishmen—the peaceful transition of power from one monarch to the next.

Since Henry VII, only once had we succumbed to civil war. But when the war was over and Charles I lost his head, we remained peaceful under Cromwell. And his son had transferred power willingly to Charles II. Even his brother James II had slunk away without a shot when he proved himself unworthy and we'd suppressed the Jacobite rebellion twice—well over three hundred years.

But someone wanted to disrupt this most sacred of traditions.

"Who?" I asked myself several times during the day when a pause in business allowed me to think.

Then the impoverished student returned Archbishop Howley's dissertation on the reform act.

"Excuse me, Madame Magdala, may I borrow that book?" another student asked within five minutes of the book's return.

His tailor seemed a little more expensive and more talented than the previous student's. But he, too, bore the unmistakable signs of attempted scholarship: ink-stained hands, a hopeless cravat, and stooped shoulders from too many hours spent peering at fine print in poor lighting.

"Do you have a professor requiring a thesis upon this subject?" I asked casually, trying to disguise a tremor in my hands and chin. A pattern had begun to form: a request for the book on the recent reform laws, an overheard conversation among footmen in an alley about those reforms, and now a second request for the book.

The young man blushed and stammered something that might have been a yes, but might also have said "For my own amusement."

The lingering color in his cheeks and his furtive glances everywhere but into my own eyes, told me that neither statement was true.

"Feel free to peruse the book here in the café." I smiled as sweetly as I could while sorting thoughts and information.

"But ... but that other fellow ..."

"My book, my rules. The topic has become too popular to let the book leave my library."

His expression turned stone still, frozen in politeness while his eyes blazed in indignation. "Do you know who I am?"

"Doesn't matter." I took the book off the counter.

"My father is Sir Winston Chemworth, second son of Earl ..."

I kept my own firm gaze on his, not caring who paid his tailor.

"Very well. Where may I sit with it? I do not wish to be disturbed."

I pointed to a back table where I could keep an eye on him. He'd not leave with the book without me or one of my employees seeing him.

Five minutes later, a young cleric with a snowy cravat, a properly brushed beaver flat-crowned hat, and a fine-fitting suit approached the center carousel requesting the same book.

I'd seen him before, I knew it, but could not place his eyes or his accent.

"You'll have to wait for it," I replied. "I'm surprised your church library does not contain a copy."

He looked right and left as if expecting eavesdroppers. "Madame, may I suggest that it would not be politic for me to be seen reading my lord archbishop's questions on the validity of the reforms . . ." False questions, logical questions, written to appease a blackmailer rather than solidify the archbishop's stance.

I knew too much and not enough.

"I see." But I didn't. "While you await the availability of the book, perhaps a different account of the reforms might interest you." I led him to where Archbishop Howley's account usually resided. On the same shelf I found a compilation of the newspaper accounts on the debate in the House of Lords, much cleansed and edited, though.

The cleric raised an eyebrow at the title. "Is this accurate?"

"Perhaps less biased," I murmured.

He raised his eyebrow again, but he took possession of the book and retreated to the same table as the scholar. At the last moment before seating himself, he turned back to me. "Perhaps a cup of tea and a scone?"

"Lucy will serve you in just a moment." I half smiled

at the idea of Lucy turning her flirtatious nature upon the young man. Unless he was a truly committed celibate priest—and those were rare in modern times, even those who preferred male company usually married to avoid scandal—he'd not think too hard about his reading material. With a few whispered words, I suggested she question him about why he needed to read about the reform acts.

 **Chapter Thirteen**

TWO DAYS LATER, I still had not heard from Drew. For reasons I could not fully define, his absence left me uneasy.

Ish reported from his lodgings in Oxford that he had begun experiments with light passing through crystals and the resulting strength of the prisms. He said nothing about his companion Dr. Jeremy Badenough. Neither did Dr. Jeremy Badenough have the courtesy to write a thank you note for my hospitality at my salon.

I fretted over Badenough's silence almost as much as I did Drew's. We had discussed many important aspects of necromancy that touched upon my concerns about Lord Byron and Lord Ruthven. I could well imagine Lord Ruthven digging up Byron's bones (if his bones did indeed reside beneath his gravestone) and building an arcane spell around them. Either lord seemed capable of kidnapping young women for either bizarre sexual rituals or ... horrors ... to fuel a different kind of magic spell: one that required the power of death.

Inspector Witherspoon visited the café twice daily. He ordered coffee only and sipped it cautiously.

"Do you fear I will poison you?" I asked him on the third morning.

"I did threaten to arrest you and throw you into Newgate," he replied, setting aside his cup and making a grimace.

"But you did not." I glared at the discarded cup as if it offended me. "Is the brew not satisfactory? Perhaps too much cream? Or is the turibano sugar not to your liking?"

"The plots I chase offend my stomach. I have drunk far too much of the brew of late. No, I came to quiz you about your network of guttersnipe spies and what they report."

"Nothing for certain, only tales of two men dressed all in black, wearing black masks beneath hooded black cloaks. They take young girls who work the streets by force, into a black coach pulled by two black mechanical beasts wearing the black feathered head stall of hearse horses."

"Funereal," he muttered staring at his undrunk coffee.

The golden-brown mixture drew my attention as well. It nearly begged me to stir it out of its sluggish stillness into the life of a whirlpool. The compulsion grew stronger. For once, I indulged my need to heed the maelstrom of sights.

I drew a circle inside the discarded cup with a silver spoon. My vision centered on the swirls of coffee and cream, here and there, now and then, probable and impossible. Another flick of the spoon and another.

The room closed in on my peripheral vision. Sounds faded from my awareness. The word "funereal" echoed over and over inside my head.

The whirlpool deepened, sending its vortex well beyond the confines of a small china cup. The darkness of the abyss swarmed up. Black on red, red on black. Flames that shed no light in a dark cavern. But whitewash brightened the scene without strong light.

Cavern. A whitewashed cave where the screams of the dying burst forth with extreme anger but were swallowed by unforgiving stone walls.

Then a blaze of white nearly blinded me—physically and metaphorically.

I had to sit, groping blindly for the nearest chair.

Gentle hands guided me. "Nice performance, Madame Magdala. Care to share what your urchins have reported? Without the dramatic fainting spell," Inspector Witherspoon said blandly before I could think on my own.

I repeated my vision, not caring if he believed the source. The information was more important than the source. I found no new details in the memory. Then my eyes cleared, but my hands shook and my stomach trembled.

"Here, drink this," the inspector said reaching for his nearly untouched cup of coffee. "A frightening scenario. I wonder which of your spies followed the abductors and reported back to you."

"Not that cup. 'Tis tainted now." I could still taste the ashes of death in my vision.

He raised a hand and summoned Lucy. The girl, my good girl, assessed my situation in one glance and promptly returned with hot, barely-brewed tea, sweetened heavily.

My head cleared and my hands steadied, but my belly still quivered in fear of what was to come.

"So you seek a cavern. A deep one. You'll not find it locally," Inspector Witherspoon said. "But not too far away or your informant would not have been able to travel there and back without assistance. One of the Gypsies perhaps? The one who flies a cloud-gray hot air balloon?"

"More likely the black balloon," I insisted.

We stared at each other a long moment, both insisting on our own point of view. I broke the standoff. "A crypt, perhaps. An ancient one." I swallowed back my revulsion at the protests of the dead and dying. Let Witherspoon believe what he wanted; I *knew* what we sought. "Death feeds on death."

"Do you think I might find the Norwynd girl there?" Witherspoon mused.

"More than likely. And many more. Many, many more." The dying screams of thousands of victims still echoed in my mind.

"Let me ponder this over maps." The inspector stepped away from the table.

"A moment, sir." Witherspoon paused while I gathered my thoughts into coherence once more. "You did not question the source of my information."

"You are the bastard daughter of a Gypsy king. You made your reputation with such performances. I have my informants. You have a wider and more accurate network. Dispense the clues as you must to preserve what you have built."

I nodded graciously and gulped my tea. "If I were known to be merely a farmer's daughter from the shores of Lake Geneva, no one would believe me and seek my counsel."

"True. Nor would they attend your salons and consider an invitation a privilege. You are what you are, no matter your origins. If anyone asks, to me you are indeed a widow with shadowy beginnings among your friends the Romany." He bowed respectfully and exited.

"Look for a recently whitewashed building with very old cellars. Ancientness need not be a church crypt in the heart of the old city." Where had that detail come from?

The blinding white light.

Jeremy had said the Persian book on necromancy had insisted upon meticulous cleanliness from whitewash in the work area. I pondered that for many long moments in absolute stillness.

I had resources. Possibly better resources than Inspector Witherspoon. I performed a search on the library engine. The few customers—including a new scholar perusing the reform act literature, original and derivative—who remained during the noon lull, watched with avid enthusiasm. The shelves shifted and rotated, clanging gears and levers—must remember to oil them soon—moved noisily through their dance, pushing books and shelves about. At last, sound and movement ceased with a jerk, then a whoosh of compressed air exited the chute just before an oversized tome of ancient maps thunked into my hands. Applause erupted all around me. I curtsied in acknowledgment of the machine's ability to find and select the right book based upon my calculations encoded into the brass key.

I dropped the key into a basket—once a week a foundry worker collected the used ones and recast them for new cuttings—and I swept up the broad staircase to my private parlor.

The first page was a redrawing of a map of London from Roman times. My eyes nearly crossed trying to read the antique script. While not part of my linguistic repertoire, Latin bore enough resemblance to French and Italian to be discernible. I found seven landmarks where I knew more modern buildings now rested upon original foundations. I marked them on a separate sheet of paper and moved on.

The next five maps showed other parts of Britain during the same period. The sixth brought me back to London at the time of the Normans. Three of the buildings I'd marked remained unchanged on this chart, but I noted several newer ones built at that time, beyond the ancient city walls, that held possibilities.

At each successive stage, my list of buildings both expanded and shrank until the most modern, charted ten years before. One of the original seven, a church dedicated to an obscure saint of Turkish descent was now a warehouse near the Strand, its sidewall might have been part of the city defenses at the time of the Magna Carta. It had gone through many changes of purpose and ownerships, but it looked to have original cellars with possible access to the Thames through a water gate similar to the one at the Tower.

Time for an investigative journey. What disguise was best for this expedition? Did the owner operate the warehouse for a legitimate business, or did he lease the place? Much property in London belonged to landlords who kept to their fine houses outside the city and never set foot on their other properties. A woman alone, no matter how fashionable, could not approach the place.

I needed help. Or a better disguise than the old beggar woman.

To Ada, Lady Lovelace,

   Please accept my regrets that I cannot attend your most excellent dinner party this evening at eight of the clock. Other business requires my urgent attention. If you would be so kind as to lend me the services of a stout footman of the utmost discretion, loyalty, and bravery, I would be most grateful.

Your most obedient servant,
Madame Magdala.

Eight of the clock that evening and the sun dropped beneath the smoky cloud cover long enough to send long, distorting shadows and bright streaks of gold, orange, and crimson light along the Thames. A stout country lad, broad of shoulder and long of leg, from Lord William of Lovelace's stable steadily rowed a small, hired boat downstream beyond the Tower. He and I wore similar garb of black knee breeches, tall boots, and dark jerseys beneath our short coats. His two-day stubble darkened his face naturally. I'd resorted to soot from my coal fire to keep any light from reflecting off my fair skin.

We skimmed along close to the embankment. I hoped that the side light from the westering sun would reveal any imperfections in the seawall. We passed several rusty iron gates with solid barriers of bricks behind them. The mortar looked reasonably old with brighter patches in odd places. Clearly, new work shoring up the old.

"There! Angle in close," I instructed my coconspirator.

He obeyed wordlessly, expertly handling the oars. When the hull brushed against the stonework, I grabbed the iron bars. Thankfully, I wore sturdy leather work gloves, for the rust broke off in large flakes. New iron, smooth and recently from the foundry, showed beneath the cloak of false rust, more like ruddy paint sloppily applied. Behind the bars, my fingers brushed against a wooden panel, cunningly painted to look like old brick, match to so many of the previous outlets. A wonderful triumph of *trompe l'oeil*. I wanted to salute the artist for his mastery. At the same time, I cursed the evil it might hide.

"Can you see what building sits above us?" I whispered to the nameless lad.

He shook his head.

Frustrated, I pushed hard against the barrier. It gave a bit, but remained firmly latched from the other side. Forcing it would alert any watchmen here or in adjacent facilities to our illicit entry. The gate held firm on well-oiled hinges and a stout padlock, also inside. I hadn't enough light or leverage to pick the lock.

"Can you move toward the center of the river without drifting too far downstream?"

The lad nodded and did so. In the last of the glaring red light from the sun, I marked the location of the Tower to our left and the squat shape of the warehouse above.

Good enough. Time to return the boat upstream. From there, I must venture on my own. Something about the rounded shape of the gate I sought reminded me of the Romany Bardo, their homes on four wheels pulled by sturdy ponies.

It also appeared larger than normal, of a size to ease a body through and into an awaiting boat—or to be washed out to sea with an outgoing tide.

Jimmy Porto and his family made locks and knew how to work around any one of them in absolute silence while leaving no trace of their manipulations.

I wondered if I had time enough on this night to find my friends, return to the warehouse, and scout the interior before dawn in the scant hours of darkness this close to the solstice.

Chapter Fourteen

A S I MADE MY WAY back to my home, I stopped
at a tavern and left a whispered word in the ear of
the barmaid. At an inn on the edges of the old city, I
suggested to the stableboy that a traveling person might
earn a bright coin for some assistance. Three of my guttersnipes took the same message farther afield.

The oldest of my army of street urchins, Kit Doyle, a
boy of fourteen who was nearly ready to settle down to
real work and respectability, took a note to Inspector
Witherspoon. I said only that I'd found something old he
might find interesting.

Then I retired to my bed, too fatigued to stand upright any longer and too heartsick to sleep.

Dawn found me kneading bread dough and roasting
in the special oven enough raw coffee beans from Africa
to serve the café for a full week. By the time Emily and
Lucy stumbled down the stairs from the attic, sleepy-
eyed and grumbling, I was able to hand them freshly
brewed drinks and the first scones out of the oven.

"That's our work, Missus," Emily protested when half
a cup of coffee had roused her sensibilities.

I shrugged and returned to shaping the bread dough
into loaves of several sizes, from tiny single-person

servings to long rolls that would fill the tummies of a family at their dinner.

"What troubles you, Missus?" Lucy asked.

"I fear that Toby, Violet, and Jane are lost to us. They've been gone too long."

"Don't fret for Jane just yet," Emily said around a mouthful of pastry.

I frowned at her to remember her manners and not speak with her mouth full. She gulped down the last swallow and repeated her statement more clearly.

"Why should I hope that our Jane thrives when so many others have also gone missing?"

"Because her young man is also missing," Emily said softly.

I raised my eyebrows in question, prodding her to fill the silence with more information.

"His da, the barrister, came round yesterday to ask if we'd seen him. He's livid that his son has not been home studying to finish his exams. Wants the boy to join him in his law offices."

"Did you tell him that we have not seen Jane?"

"Yes, Missus. He did not like that at all."

"But he understood," Lucy chimed in. "He's not so old as he's forgotten what it is like to be young and in love. He wanted them to wait until after finishing exams and working, earning some money."

"Then he admitted that Jane is right pretty with decent manners and might become an asset to the boy. The barrister's missus likes Jane and says she has polite conversation," Lucy added.

"That's all thanks to you, Missus," Emily reminded me.

I preened a bit under the praise. If indeed Jane had eloped with her love and made a decent marriage above her station in life, then I could claim a bit of her success. Without me, she'd still likely be walking the streets and selling herself for barely enough coin to eat.

"We'll see about this. I'll not hope that she lives until she returns and apologizes for leaving without a word." But I did hope. Perhaps one of the missing might not be a victim.

Moments after I unlocked the front door for customers, a tall grim-faced Runner appeared in my café with a note from Inspector Witherspoon. In response, I merely wrote down an address in the old city and sent the uniformed man on his way before he frightened my customers with his frowns and keen gaze.

We settled into a normal day of serving coffee and pastry, searching for books, and perusing the newspapers, domestic and foreign. Eavesdropping on political conversations suggested no new patterns of unrest or amassing of resources that could fuel a new military campaign, or trigger a major industrial advancement. But I did hear a wild-eyed young man read a few lines of poetry, strongly imitative of Lord Byron's style.

I'd read everything Lady Ada's father had written in his official life and knew most of it by heart. He was a genius. This poetry was more than derivative and lacked the horrific undertones, if you knew what to listen for. I could almost hear the lord's affected drawl reciting this poetry with drama and flourish to a fascinated audience.

The fine hairs on my spine stood on end in atavistic dread that Byron really did live in a different body from the one that "drowned" fourteen years ago.

I knew he continued to write esoteric books, not all poetry, that glorified death. The arousal of intense pain, flashes of light, drifting between this world and the next . . . I thought that only one who had experienced death and come back could have written those words.

The noon lull came and I took a few moments to survey the café. A few spills needed scrubbing, newspapers folded neatly and replaced on their rack. Books needed to be coded and returned to the engine that near miraculously "knew" where it should be stored with similar volumes. After the debacle with Jeremy's bad translation book, I feared that I relied too much on the machine. I did not personally know every one of the twenty thousand volumes I stored. But the machine did. Was my trust well-founded as Lady Ada and her partner Charles Babbage said? Or was that trust dulling my own senses and intelligence by doing so much work for me?

A hesitant knock on the kitchen door interrupted my survey of the café and the new wave of customers. I nodded to regulars and introduced myself to newcomers, always checking their fashion choices and how closely they followed mine as I wended my way toward the stairs.

Mickey had assumed the job of transporting plates filled with pastry from kitchen to the shelf beside the coffee bar. He bit his lip in concentration and walked slowly with careful steps. I mentally applauded his new determination to better himself. I just hoped he kept his ears open among the customers as he did on the streets.

"Ya'know, Missus, if we left the plates beneath the coffee bar and carried trays of pastry up from the kitchen, t'would be faster for t' customers," he whispered as we passed.

"Figure it all out and talk to me tonight," I told him and moved on.

With my mind half on the organized but frantic pace of my business, I opened the kitchen door and had to look down to find a blob of wriggling damp rags and a mop of unrestrained black curls that fell below shoulders hunched against a chill wind that preceded a brief shower. Female, I decided.

"Yes?" I asked, wondering if I should kneel to look the creature in the eye.

She bit her lip and looked up at me with dark brown eyes wide with wonder. I expected a request for food, or money, or even work to earn said food or money. She lisped out some words I could barely understand.

So I did kneel and asked her again what she needed. I think she said in Romany "Me da says to come." Her accent was strange and thick, not one of the local tribes.

"And who be your da?" I asked in Romany, hoping she'd understand my accent with an over-layer of gorgí intonation.

She thought for a moment, still biting her lip. It must be important for the Rom to trust a girl child with this errand. They usually kept them close to home and very well protected. The words that tumbled out sounded like chief and da to the one who flies. I couldn't be certain but the "one who flies" sounded right. Then she put her hands up encircling her head, mimicking a balloon.

"Ah, your da is also da to Jimmy Porto."

She nodded vigorously, beckoning me to follow. A strange response to my messages of the night before. But then I could never be quite certain of tribal politics and concerns. Coming to me might not be safe for Jimmy. So I must go to him.

An expected routine if not completely within the usual protocol.

"Go," Emily said, her arms elbow-deep in dishwater with the china and fine cutlery. "We can manage a while longer on our own now that Mickey is helping and Philippa scrubs the pots and linens. She has a good eye for faint stains that require additional attention."

"Show her how to apply lemon juice to the stains," I said.

"Lemons be expensive," Lucy reminded me.

"Less so than new linen."

Mickey looked up with one of his charming grins as he deposited an empty plate on the counter stacked with other used service ware. "If t' toffs wants a book, they kin wait until you return or I learn how to run the bloody machine," he said.

"Don't curse, Mickey," I reprimanded him automatically. "Very well, I trust you all to do me proud." With that, I swept out the kitchen door and followed the urchin through the alleys and backyard paths north toward the open heath.

My toes cramped in the light indoor shoes—red leather with black painted dots—I'd chosen to wear with my red dress and bonnet with the black ribbon and lace trim. I should have known that any trek with a Romany would involve mud paths as well as cobbled streets. But the nameless child seemed in a desperate hurry. She did not touch me—forbidden among her kind—to tug at my hand. Mostly she dashed ahead a few yards with a peculiar rolling gait and beckoned me forward.

The moment we cleared the maze of houses and lanes and set foot on the barely discernible trail through the wild grasses and shrubs of the heath, I knew where she headed. I hung back in caution. No ordinary cutthroat or outlaw would know enough of the Romany language to coach a small child to speak the proper words. But her alien accent—closer to the mountains of Transylvania than generations of English born or even Irish tinkers— and her lack of names of the people who had sent for me, made me think twice now that we were away from the protection of an audience within the city. I should have thought of this before.

If the child's mission was not honest, then those who sent her knew me very well and had traveled far to understand the mostly secret language.

"I know you are watching. Come to me or I go no farther." I spoke Romany as I stopped and crossed my arms at hip level. My Rom would know I reached for weapons secreted among the folds of my skirt. They'd show themselves as harmless before I had a chance to throw sharp metal stars or shoot a gun. They knew my aim to be true and my distance eyesight keen.

"'Twill do no good to summon them," the little person said in heavily accented English and straightened up from a stooped posture. While still short—no taller than my breastbone, the aspect of a small child wearing rags too big for it disappeared. With a shake of the head, the tangle of dark curls flew back to reveal a masculine dwarf. The dirt on his face turned out to be two days' worth of beard stubble. The voice I noted was still high-pitched but no longer childlike.

"You are not Rom," I said, fingering my weapons.

"No. I am not." The accent lingered. It carried no hints of the languages I spoke. Dark hair and olive-toned skin hinted of the Mediterranean.

Greek. *Greek!*

"Where did you learn the language of the Rom? They do not share it willingly with *gorgí*." I needed time to stall. Time to think.

"No, they do not share it *willingly*. But it is ingrained in their blood from birth. Drain the blood, bathe in the blood, and the rudiments become clear. A little observation and the rest becomes understandable." The creature shrugged and a layer of dust shifted off his rags. "We knew that a child who speaks the Rom was the only way to lure you away from the protection of your friends and of the city."

"Why did you bring me here?" Long ago, I'd learned the trick of appearing to maintain eye contact while searching the environs for signs of danger. The wild grasses of the heath shifted slightly in the opposite direction to the constant breeze. To my right and left and two more directly ahead. Behind?

My summoner did not focus on anything on the path he'd led me along. Unless he'd learned the same trick I used. I'd learned it from the Rom. He may have as well when he indulged in his gory blood sacrifice.

"We have need of your expertise and that of Lady Lovelace."

"Does Lord Byron, Lady Lovelace's father, still live?"

"Define living."

Trouble. This was the nightmare that had haunted me

for over twenty years. I frequently dreamed/remembered the night Mary Godwin, her infant son, and I had fled the villa on the shores of Lake Geneva. Percy Shelley and Lord Byron followed in outraged pursuit. "Your master managed to capture his soul into a vessel, awaiting an appropriate body to house him," I said on a deep exhale.

The little man nodded.

"We have a body. We need a machine."

"I cannot help you."

"Cannot or will not?"

I had no true answer for that.

"We hold you here while my helpers send a ransom note to Lady Lovelace."

A chill ran through me and dried my throat. "My lady places no value on me."

The dwarf threw back his head and laughed long and hard until he gulped for air. "You underestimate her."

"Do I?" I raised an eyebrow, seeking calm in my demeanor if not in actuality. "She never forgave me for leaving her household when she married," I lied.

I knew I should have just taken my chances and shot him, then run all the way back to London proper.

However, he'd thrown out the possibility that somehow, Lord Byron had found a way to transfer his soul out of a body into some kind of storage vessel, or a temporary and imperfect body. He wanted Lady Ada and me to rebuild his transference engine; the one I had destroyed. I knew it worked. Mary Godwin and I had used it to save the soul of her new lover before breaking the gears and steam pipes and electrical connections into hundreds of pieces and pieces of pieces.

I needed to learn all I could to keep Lord Byron from coming back to life and corrupting more innocents. Was his spirit, or his fanatical followers, behind the disappearance of so many innocents in the last week?

This dwarf seemed the only tutor in the vicinity. And

he appeared to be Greek. Lord Byron had died in Greece assisting freedom fighters against the Turks.

Not that he cared for the Greeks' freedom. He cared only for glory. And got the reverence he desired, but in my mind never deserved.

"What are you intending to do with the transference engine, if you can replicate it?"

"The master is a genius, a master of arcane arts, and deserving of a new body. However, my need for one is more critical," the man said. He squinted his eyes as he surveyed my form. "Yours will do for now if I cannot find another."

"No way in hell!" I drew and loosed both weapons as I dove for the ground.

"That can be arranged," the dwarf ground out through clenched teeth. He drew the metal star from his shoulder.

A gush of blood followed. I stared in fascinated horror at the brightness of the red, so much brighter than the crimson of my gown. My mind wandered wondering why modern dyes could never quite match . . .

My mind snapped into focus again as pain lanced my side. I grabbed the offended area, not truly surprised to find it warm and sticky with my own blood, contained only by the tightness of my stays. Damnation! I hadn't thought to change into the bulletproof corset as well as stouter shoes. Chill coursed through my veins like electricity, followed by debilitating heat to my face.

I heard shouts, then more yelling in a language that brushed past my understanding. Darkness pushed inward from my periphery.

Then a snort of disgust (my own?) and I lost my fragile grasp on consciousness.

 Chapter Fifteen

A GREAT ROARING in my ears that pulsed with the rhythm of a heart. My heart, perhaps. It faded enough for me to realize I hurt. All over. More so on my right side. My gown tangled with my body, binding tightly and restricting. I needed to move, to straighten myself and my garments. But I couldn't quite figure out how.

Voices intruded on my pointless ruminations that looped and swirled like a tangle of ribbons. Rough voices that sounded like a person with a sore throat gargling. Not quite Germanic. Not quite anything familiar.

Then I remembered the dwarf pretending to be Romany who practiced necromancy. Greek.

Were the male and female voices around me speaking Greek?

Possibly. I kept my eyes closed as my awareness increased and listened intently to tone, striving for something that sounded familiar. Something, anything, to cling to and set to rights in my scrambled mind.

No words, just garbled sounds. But the tone ... urgency, anger, fear. The sound of sorting and discarding metal tools. Fine metal clattering into a metal bowl and resonating. My eyes snapped open. I'd heard steel on steel.

Suddenly the constrictions made sense. Not a tangle of garments. The secure binding of heavy leather at wrist, ankle, and brow. I lay spread-eagle and naked upon a hard bed. Not a favorite position even with a skilled lover. A light sheet covered me from chin to toe.

I shivered in the warm room. A fire behind me seemed to be the heat source. It roared and crackled as someone threw new fuel into it with a thud and crunch. The smell of alcohol, lots of it and not good Scotch or fine wine either. A raw grain distillation that had become popular in some schools of medicine for cleaning a wound or a room.

Absolute cleanliness is a must for working any kind of necromantic spell . . . A quote from the book on Persian necromancy. Had every soul-stealing necromancer in Europe read the damn book?

My eyes were open but not focusing well. Was the thickness at the back of my throat a residue from my wound—I don't think it still bled—or from dousing me with strong drink to reduce pain? Or worse, drugs on the blade that had penetrated my corset?

I couldn't turn my head, only blink rapidly to force my eyes to add to my information gathering.

Then a face loomed into the center of my field of vision. Female, olive-skinned, with hair like fine jet reflecting light in silver shafts. She appeared middle-aged with refined features and smelled of exotic flowers beneath the nearly overwhelming odor of the alcohol. A white smock covered a simple black dress that matched the plain chignon in color and style. No ornamentation, not even jet beads. A governess or a widow?

"You must tell me how," she demanded in excellent, but accented English.

"How to do what?" I choked around a thick tongue and still muddled thoughts.

"To put a soul into another body."

Oh, God!

"We know how to capture a departing soul and store it. But it diminishes when stored. I need to transfer one soul directly to a new body. That requires the machine you demolished."

Oh, that again.

"Tell me! Or I put you in a jar to wane and ponder your stupidity." She shook her right fist at me. A curious scar ran from the base of the thumb to disappear into her sleeve. An old wound. I wondered about the nature of her injury.

"Who will you push into my body against my will?" Those words came a little easier, a little less slurred. My hands and feet ached from the restrictions. If I could stall just a bit longer, I might regain the use of my faculties. I had to think and think fast.

"Not important. You will be beyond caring."

"I will care. This body is mine. Not yours. Not Lord Byron's. And certainly not the ugly dwarf's."

I tested my restraints for any weakness I could exploit. Useless. The leather bindings while soft and supple with raw wool padding, were also thick and strong.

"He is more than a dwarf!" the woman protested angrily. "He was not always ugly."

Emotions I understood and could manipulate. Sometimes. Strong emotions could rob a person of logic and sense. "I take it his body is dying."

If she honestly thought I'd willingly die to allow another soul to inhabit my body, she was either stupid or a true fanatic. Only one person I knew of could inspire that kind of loyalty. Lord Byron.

Maybe Napoleon Bonaparte, but I doubted he had enough drive left to seize a new body and raise an army to conquer Europe again. He had no other purpose.

"I need your name before I attempt to rebuild the machine," I said around a lump of trepidation. Would she buy my cooperation long enough to let me escape? "And the name of the man I allow to replace me? For you know the transfer must be voluntary on my part, or it will not work. Insanity for certain, in both. At best, you will wind up having two warring souls in the same body who will fight each other until both die. In that case you will have lost everything to haste and desperation." I made that up. No one truly knew what happened during this arcane process. I knew of only one instance where it had worked. Just before I destroyed the machine.

"I . . . I am Stamata." She looked elsewhere as if in shame.

"A Greek name."

She nodded.

Petite and dark, she was of an age and type to have been one of Byron's last mistresses before he died the first time.

Circumstantial evidence at best. But I had learned over the years of wanderings that circumstances form patterns and the pattern will lead to true evidence.

"And the person I give my body to?"

"You know."

"The dwarf said that Lord Byron's genius deserved a new body, but he has greater need."

"Yes, he is the poet Percy Bysshe Shelley. We do not know how he managed a transfer into that body. Probably the first one handy when he drowned but refused to die. We know there must be a connection between the two souls for the transfer to last. You were intimate with Shelley. Your body will accept his soul as once it accepted his manhood."

Accepted is not the word I'd use. I was too frightened of losing my place in the villa, and the money they paid me. Money that I must take to my father every week or face a beating.

"We know you have worked long and hard to foil my

lord's plans. The dwarf is only a temporary housing for Shelley. And now that body dies. My lord must wait and rest, for not much longer. Time in the jars is limited."

"Why should I cooperate now?" Was that a little bit of wiggle in the leather around my left wrist? I flexed my hand muscles and tugged. *Yes!* The buckle shifted a tiny bit. Not enough to free myself, but a step forward. I rested my arm a bit so Madam Stamata would not notice and grow suspicious.

"Quickly. You must help me save him." Stamata looked anxiously over her shoulder. "Shelley is important. If necessary, a test case for my lord. The poet king is the love of my life. The only man I can love unconditionally, as he loves me. We will be together again."

Not likely. From what I knew of George Gordon Byron, she'd passed being attractive the day she hit her eighteenth birthday. He'd lived with and lusted after older women, true, but only loved the very young while they were still young. The same with Shelley.

The leather strap across my forehead prevented me from seeing the source of her anxiety, or anything else but the whitewashed rough timber ceiling.

Whitewash again.

"Did I shoot the dwarf?" The throwing star he yanked out of his shoulder wouldn't inflict a mortal injury.

"Yes, you have nearly killed him. You will pay for that with your life. Now tell me the secret. What must I do to force his soul into your body and yours out! How does the crystal work? Tell me!"

"No." Crystal? That was a new wrinkle in this game.

"Then you will die without hope of transferring to a new body." She showed me a wicked double-edged knife of blued steel, at least a foot long. She demonstrated by pricking the inside of my left arm just above the elbow. Hardly any sensation, but warm blood trickled from the tiny cut.

As she bent over me, I noted a huge purple crystal pendant set onto a thick gold chain that dangled between her breasts. It scintillated in the light, sending prisms against the white surroundings.

"One eighth of an inch lower and to the right and I will slice the vein. You will feel the life draining from you. I have no Leyden jar ready to receive your spirit."

I licked dry lips and thought hard. My only tool was to stall.

"Electricity," I mumbled.

"What was that?" She leaned closer to hear. I wanted to spit in her face but couldn't rouse enough moisture around my fear.

"Electricity," I repeated a little clearer. "Giovanni Aldini reanimated the corpse of an executed prisoner . . ."

"Electricity? Of course!" she nearly sprang away from me, taking the wicked knife with her. A snap of her fingers brought the sound of shuffling feet across the floor. "My lord never said anything about electricity. How do I know I can trust you?" Her face loomed over mine once more with the knife held much too close to my neck.

"If you bleed me dry, then the new resident in this shell cannot live," I reminded her.

More footsteps and the suggestion of shadows moving around the room, quietly, without words, back and forth between Stamata and the dwarf.

Damn the restraints! How could I plot anything without information?

Use your other senses, the voice of Dr. Ishwardas Chaturvedi whispered through my memory. *The eyes can be deceived. Add sound and scent, the taste of the air, and the feel of it against your skin. Know your surroundings through your entire being.*

I took a deep lungful of air and exhaled slowly, closing my eyes and absorbing information through my pores as he'd taught me. Five sets of feet, each tread slightly different. The smell of unwashed male. Garlic. Horse. Woodsmoke. Wind through the pines.

They reminded me of the open road.

My eyes flew open. I scanned as far right and left as my restraints allowed.

"How do I create a generator for the electricity?" Stamata demanded.

"A stick of amber rubbed with wool felt," a familiar male voice said from right behind her. She whirled to face the speaker. "Who dares invade my laboratory?"

Other hands worked on my wrist restraints.

"The corpses of your death-loving minions litter the path to this basement room," said Jimmy Porto, my rescuer. "It seems they only lust after the death of others, not themselves."

One hand loose, I attacked the buckle close to my left temple while the unseen hands worked upon my ankle straps.

Fumble. Fumble. My fingers didn't want to move after being idle for so long. They didn't like to work on their own without the guidance of my eyes. I'd learned my lesson in observing through other senses. Slow down, concentrate, feel the shape of the buckle, the metal tang, the holes in the strap, the leverage point. *Yes.* I yanked my wrist to loosen the tang's grip on the hole and pulled it free.

I turned my head toward Stamata too quickly and lost focus to sudden dizziness. *Breathe,* I reminded myself. I could do most anything if I just breathed.

Jimmy stood eye to eye with my captor, preventing her from reaching the shrouded figure of the dwarf on a table similar to my own resting place, though without restraints. A maze of different colored wires was attached to a metal band that encircled his head. The wires connected to a large ceramic pot with white glaze and the distinctively Greek keyhole design worked in purple around the shoulder and base. I had no doubt the jar contained the proper fluids and thin copper sheets. With a steady pulse of electrical sparks from the chemicals reacting with the copper, it contained and preserved the essence of whoever resided in the dwarf's body. The linen-covered chest did not rise and fall with breath.

"Let me pass!" Stamata demanded. "He's dying." She pushed at Jimmy.

He held out his arms to keep her away from the dwarf. I knew he'd never strike her. Abuse toward women—the bearers of life—was against everything the Rom believed. Of course they did confine and keep their women illiterate and naïve—as much for control as protection.

With my feet and arms finally free, I sat up, dragging my shroud with me.

I did not have the same constraints about protecting women as Jimmy and his fellow rescuers. With all my might, I balled my right fist and slammed it into Stamata's temple.

She reeled. The knife clattered against the floor. Jimmy's little brother, who had worked so well at releasing my restraints, leaped to encase her right hand in the leather strap that had recently captured mine. Her head lolled as she sank to the floor.

"We must hurry," Jimmy said, averting his eyes from where the sheet slipped away from my bosom.

I hastily draped it around me, toga style, and flung the loose end over my left shoulder. Not secure, but it would do until I found my clothes.

"The household servants of this vile woman are dealt with. There are others, armed men with dogs, patrolling the grounds. We must leave now and move stealthily." He eyed my scant garment. "The white in the darkness will reveal us to the enemy."

Another of Jimmy's brothers came through the

doorway—the whitewashed planks of the portal sagged on their hinges—carrying a pile of dark cloth.

He handed me shirt and trousers, then turned his back, as did his brothers.

"Smash the jars. All of them," I ordered. "How did you find me?" I had wriggled the trousers over my hips. My bosom strained the buttons, but they held. It would have to do for now.

"Mickey sent word. He did not trust the dwarf, or that you followed him so willingly." The sound of breaking crockery followed his words. One down. Fifteen to go.

"I should have peered closer at the dwarf, but he spoke a flavor of Romany, so I assumed wrongly that you had sent her—or rather him." Shame at my own gullibility heated my face.

"Your trail was not hard to follow to the heath. From there we knew of only one abandoned home where they could have taken you with any stealth. This place has been empty for years and is slowly falling down. But the cellars are sound. We have camped here occasionally."

Another jar broke as I tucked in the shirt and fastened the trousers.

We were not in the cellars of the warehouse by the river. Of course not, I detected no odor from the rotting garbage that filled the Thames.

I knew of this place, though. An impoverished baronet owned it. He could not afford to keep it up, but he could not sell the house or the lands due to an inconvenient entail. The estate must pass to his next male heir. But since he was an only child and too committed to gambling, drink, and male lovers to ever attract a wife and beget legitimate sons, I suspected the crown would confiscate the place soon.

Another jar broke.

"Shoes?" I asked, not liking the idea of walking miles across rough ground in my bare feet.

The youngest brother, the one who had brought the

clothing, handed me my own worn and uncomfortable red shoes. They would have to do.

"You found my shoes, but not my gown?" With proper stays and underthings.

"Shredded to less than rags. By a vengeful woman, I suspect," Jimmy said, turning to face me at last.

Thank heavens she hadn't had access to the bullet-proof corset. As uncomfortable as it was, covering me from above breasts to below hip, the crossed layers of spider silk and fine wire mesh—as delicate as a cobweb, but able to resist projectiles—had cost the earth.

His brother touched a fourth jar almost reverently, pausing to murmur a prayer. It contained the essence of death. Their religion was cautious about dealing with the dead in any form after the soul had left the body.

"Then we must be going. The vengeful woman rouses." I took the jar from the boy, held it over my head, and threw it to the floor. It shattered with a most satisfactory sound, followed by the slurping of leaking liquids.

"You should kill her, Miss Elise," the middle brother said.

"Her worst crime was loving too well, if not wisely." The dwarf who might be Shelley or Lord Byron was another issue.

I stepped toward the dwarf, intent on disconnecting him from the soul-preserving jar.

Jimmy grabbed my arm as my fingers clasped around the wires. I yanked all the connections free, then traced them to the proper jar—there were at least a dozen left stored on shelves along one wall. One swift kick sent the pottery clanging to the whitewashed floor. It cracked raggedly along the middle. Fluid leaked out. Whoever was in there died as the chemicals spread across the floor.

I stepped into the thin puddle and ground my heel through it. One of my enemies would trouble us no more.

"We are out of time," Jimmy said.

"There are still . . ."

"We have to go now, before the dogs sniff us out."

"Wait. We need the crystal!"

"Dawn approaches, and my sister Reva is missing. We need your help to find her." He dragged me away with some urgency.

 **Chapter Sixteen**

W E MOVED SILENTLY AND CAUTIOUSLY up the exterior stair to the nicely proportioned kitchen courtyard. Jimmy paused for many long moments listening to the night. Then, satisfied the armed guards and their vicious dogs were not near, he motioned us across the open space to an archway in the brick walls. Rusty but empty hinges on one side and a broken lock on the other told me a gate had once protected the yard, but no longer. Most likely, the wooden planks had fueled someone's fire. Or if it had been made of intricate wrought iron, it had been sold to cover gambling debts.

I thought about the intact jars in the cellar. As I hesitated, debating about turning back, Jimmy grabbed my arm and dragged me through the ragged opening in the brick-and-hedge wall of the courtyard.

In the near distance a dog yipped, followed by a man's curse. Then the dog bayed. He'd caught our scent.

We ran.

Once free of the immediate manor grounds, we moved more swiftly toward the encroaching wilds of the heath. When the Rom wish to move unseen, ordinary men cannot find them. No one spoke until we passed into a copse between the manor and the city that crept closer every year. Soon there would be no heath at all.

"When did anyone in the family last see your sister Reva?" I broke the silence the moment Jimmy's shoulders and arms relaxed into a normal swing and he lengthened his stride beyond carefully placed steps.

"Noon."

"Which noon?"

"Yesterday."

"When did you notice she was not there?"

"Supper." Which meant sundown close to half eight in the evening. A long time for a Romany girl to slip beyond notice or control by a male.

"Why did no one look for her sooner?" A note of anger crept into my voice. The Rom protected their females well. Too well. To the point of allowing them no skills to interact with the outside world. We *gorgí* tainted them to the point of *marimé*. Men could overcome the uncleanliness or withstand it. Women could not. I appeared to be the exception, but then I was never Rom, only a friend to them.

"Reva has . . . has been difficult of late," Jimmy admitted. Without a torch or lantern, I could not see his face to know if he was embarrassed for his sister or for himself. Angry at her? Or at himself?

"Define 'difficult.'"

"She requested several times an introduction to you so that you might teach her to read." He stepped further into the copse and kept his back to me. Probably so he would not have to witness my outrage.

"And since you and your father deemed that impossible and just requesting such a forbidden action drew her close to *marimé*, you ceased to pay attention to her until her mother or aunts cleansed her."

He chose silence.

I sighed, knowing I'd get no more information from him on the subject.

"There was an incident, about a year ago."

I listened more closely.

"My youngest brother, little more than a toddler, fell into a pond. The moon-faced boy who sweeps for you pulled him free before he drowned."

"Toby?"

Jimmy nodded. The faintest lessening of the dark allowed me see his silhouette. Dawn approached. Half four in the morning. I should be at my baking within the hour.

"Why was Toby away from the city?"

Jimmy shrugged. "There were other boys about. Teasing and taunting him."

"He ran away."

"Yet he stopped when he saw my brother in trouble, and helped him."

"Toby didn't know enough to fear drowning," I said. "He had . . . has a big heart and it hurts him to see another distressed."

"The other boys ran from the water. They shouted something about monsters living in the murky depths."

"What has this to do with your sister, Reva?"

"From the safety of her bardo, she witnessed our father honoring Toby, giving him food and hospitality. She wanted to thank him herself, but speaking to a stranger, and a male stranger, is forbidden. She spoke often of the moon-faced boy who risked sticks and stones from bullies to save her brother. But Toby's impurity as well as being a man not of our family meant she must not approach him. Ever."

I had to think a moment while I gained control of my temper. Toby could not help his damaged mind and unusual body. He'd proven he could not hurt anyone, nor willingly taint them.

"Has Reva been going off on her own for longer and longer periods of time since then?" I asked.

"Yes," responded one of the nameless younger

brothers. He must view Reva's return as more important than her taint.

"But she always returned in time to help prepare meals, as is her duty," another brother added.

"Who did she meet while off on her own? Could it be a man? Possibly an educated man who fell in love with her exotic beauty and promised to teach her to read in return for ... favors, or possibly marriage." The last was my own musing out loud rather than a true question.

Silence.

"If you will not tell me everything, then I can do nothing more for you than to have my urchins question others." I firmed my shoulders and my steps as I headed back toward the lights of the city as the first streaks of a fiery dawn shot beneath the smoky cloud cover.

"Miss Elise, we came to you because you can ask questions and get answers where we may not," Jimmy finally said. "We do not know who she met or where she went. Perhaps she headed for your café to meet the moon-faced boy. The Rom have learned well how to keep secrets. She kept hers from us as well as the *gorgi*."

"Will you still love her, even if she is *marimé*?"

"We will still love her, but we may not welcome her back into the tribe. She will be as dead to us."

"Then I need nothing more from you." I abandoned my plan to have him help me pick the locks of a certain warehouse with ancient cellars and a disguised exit to the river. The Rom must find another solution for their errant daughter.

Inspector Witherspoon didn't need a lockpick or secrecy. Even before he returned to the café with his report, I heard through my web of contacts about the squad of Bow Street Runners who stormed the warehouse and smashed the locks.

"We found little," Inspector Witherspoon said as he

downed three cups of milky, sweet tea and half a loaf of bread and butter. "As you predicted, the cellars are ancient, but the mortar is still tight. And all had been recently whitewashed, including the passage to the river gate. Cunning disguise on that. We've torn down the painted wooden wall. There is now normal access from the river through that gate."

"What was in the warehouse?" I prodded him as I wrapped my cobwebby knitted lace shawl of fine Highland wool more tightly around me, still chilled from my adventures the previous night in a whitewashed cellar on the opposite end of town.

"Not much. In one room there were some new shelves lining the walls with some pottery jars, some short strands of wire, two thin sheets of copper. And some curious metal tables. Otherwise empty from floor to ceiling." The inspector sighed and slathered butter on another piece of bread.

"The cellars where I was imprisoned?"

"Cleaned out, in a hurry. We found a tangle of copper wires and glass tubing. Shards of pottery, and foul smelling puddles of liquid. The shelves were old but showed clean rounds in the dust, where pottery might have rested. Scrapes on the floor where something heavy, maybe one of those metal tables, was dragged away."

"Could the people at the warehouse have somehow heard we were looking for them and moved to the house on the heath?"

"Timing is wrong. The empty laboratory on the heath my men searched had been there a long time. The place had been whitewashed several times and they left some equipment. I think we are dealing with two necromancers."

"One connected to Lord Byron, the other not," I mused.

A new thought bothered me. If Percy Shelley had managed to get into the dwarf, why couldn't Stamata get either him or Lord Byron into me? She'd said that storage in the Leyden jars had a finite duration before the soul diminished. The dwarf was a sloppy and inadequate job, perhaps only accidental success—a weak will due to a damaged body overcome by a stronger personality in desperate straits? Perhaps he'd ended up in the wrong body because Stamata did not fully understand the process, and neither did Byron or Shelley.

I could not dismiss the idea that they would eventually approach an educated and determined necromancer to complete the process properly.

Necromancy had been specifically defined and illegal for four years now. The practice did not conform to practices within the Church of England in any way, shape, or form. Any deaths occurring during the illegal rituals were murder and blasphemy, punishable by hanging by the neck until dead or burning alive. Howley wanted the latter punishment. He'd told me burning and then scattering the ashes in the river was the only way to be certain a necromancer died. Hanging might allow the body to revive as Aldini had tried with executed George Foster in 1803. The House of Lords had not granted Howley the right to burn anyone unless the necromancer profaned a church in their rituals.

I'd read that clause a dozen or more times—every time a different student or cleric asked to read the archbishop's treatise. He had allowed the entire act to pass, because he needed to take a stand against necromancy. Blackmailers be damned.

Whoever had found out about his wife's youthful indiscretion had agreed. Ridding the land of necromancers was important enough to allow a few reforms. Those could be changed by legislation later.

I had no idea the hideous cult had enough practitioners to warrant laws aimed specifically at them. They must if the archbishop's blackmailers gave way for that one issue.

"Inspector Witherspoon, is it possible that Archbishop Howley is the target of the assassination plot and not the queen?"

He sat in silence for many long moments. "I must ask many more questions in different quarters before I answer that. I doubt it, though. Killing him, while heinous, would not bring down the government, not like the loss of our queen to violence."

But it would give a necromancer revenge, possibly beget enough fear among the clergy to recant on the laws against the hideous cult.

"Did you at least discover who owns the warehouse?"

"Some country lord who never shows his face in London. Forgot his name. Someone said he has to be in his nineties if he still lives. I've got a man chasing him down. Local constables haven't had time to reply to our messages. Leased it to a shipping company that went out of business twenty years ago."

If he still lives. That phrase sent chills up and down my spine.

"That's a valuable property to leave empty, seemingly abandoned for so long."

"Aye. Who knows how and why country lords, or city lords for that matter, do anything." He left abruptly without excusing himself.

I wished Drew would come home. I needed to talk to him, mine his extensive knowledge of the peerage, hear him support or tear down my arguments. I always thought more keenly when I discussed things with Drew.

Where was he?

He was with Lord Ruthven, recently come to town from an obscure country estate, who exhibited a fascination with death. As did Drew.

I grew hot and cold. A great buzzing in my ears presaged a closing of my peripheral vision. My knees trembled so badly I doubted I could walk across the room.

Drew was in league with Ruthven, and they both practiced necromancy. I knew it deep in my soul and hated the knowledge.

Hated him for hiding his practice beneath a guise of charming indolence.

Hated myself for loving Sir Andrew Fitzandrew.

 Chapter Seventeen

"MISSUS," MICKEY WHISPERED from behind me. He sounded hesitant. "There be a messenger at the kitchen door. Won't talk to no one but you. I told him you was busy, but he insisted."

"You do not trust him?" I asked, gathering my senses so that I might stand without pitching forward into the remnants of Inspector Witherspoon's tea.

"Nay, Missus. Seen him before I 'ave. That night I acted your lady's maid. He come to the salon." He paused over the word alien to his uneducated life. But he got the essence if not the proper pronunciation. "Came late with one of the gentlemen he did. Hung back, keeping to the shadow and never truly showing his face."

"And does he reveal his countenance now?"

Mickey had to think about my words. I watched understanding dawn in his eyes. "Barely, Missus. Won't come in, stays on the back stoop, half turned away from the light coming down the outside stair."

I checked the amount of light coming in through the café windows. Still full daylight at a time of year when sunset came very late. Time meant little to the sun. From the scarcity of customers, I suspected the early afternoon when we frequently had a lull in business. The clock that would verify this needed winding, something I would have to do since none of the others were tall enough to reach it. "If you did not see him clearly before, or now, how did you recognize him?"

"I know people and I know how they hide behind changing shoulders and neck, different clothes and hat. It's him. And I seen 'im afore, dressed as 'e is now."

"Who did he come with to the salon?"

Mickey shrugged and backed away. "Not one of the toffs I usually watch about town. Not seen him before that night or since."

"Very well, I will take the message from this person."

I had to unlatch and open the kitchen door. During business, we left it open for deliveries and taking trash up to the dustbin in the back courtyard. Mickey *really* did not trust the messenger if he locked the door. On the back stoop, a short, wiry man stood with his back to me. He cradled his right wrist within his left hand as if it hurt. Or had little strength. Considering the paleness of his skin below the wrist and the withered skin, I suspected that even though it hurt, he had little use of the limb.

Mickey had said once or twice that he'd seen a beggar with a withered hand. That he should recognize him as one of the extra men at my salon made me nervous. I'd seen no one recently with a withered arm. But I had seen a man who never removed his gloves, both at the salon and at the opera, in the company of Lord Ruthven.

"You have a message for me?"

"Man from Oxford said to give it to you. Said you'd thank me for the delivery," he mumbled. He used his good left hand to fumble inside his ratty greatcoat that had seen better days when the Duke of Wellington defeated Napoleon Bonaparte at Waterloo. Eventually he found a folded page much besmudged with dirt from his hands . . . and elsewhere. Or did the new filth cover old stains?

I didn't trust anything anymore.

"Said you'd thank me." He held the document protectively against his chest.

Quickly I assessed his need against the value of his offering. "A farthing when I know that the note is from the man who claims to have signed it." I wasn't about to be fooled again by unlikely messengers delivering notes I half-expected.

For the first time, he lifted his face and his eyes to look at me directly. His mouth opened slightly in surprise, revealing broken and blackened teeth that distorted the shape of his lips.

I knew those eyes. I knew I'd seen him before.

"The farthing will do," he said, returning his gaze and his countenance to the ground once more.

I snatched the letter before he could hide it again, replaced it with the tiny coin, then slammed the door in his face. The snick of the locks engaging did not reassure me that he'd leave and not return.

Madame,

Please accept my apologies for not thanking you in person for partaking of your excellent hospitality. I find I must return to Oxford forthwith and consult with my colleagues.

Respectfully yours,
Dr. Jeremy Badenough,
Professor of Ancient Studies

Studiously polite and correct, as expected. Despite the neatness and precision of the document, Oxford dons were notorious for their illegible scrawling signatures. This letter matched the norm.

But I had a sample of Jeremy's handwriting. I dashed up to my study and dug his previous note about the inaccuracy of the translation of the volume I now thought of as "The Book."

As I remembered, even in haste, Jeremy was incapable of anything but a neat signature. Part of his need to make certain the reader knew who he was and his qualifications.

I did not believe he had penned this note. Not only was the signature different, the formation of his letters was at the wrong slant and the "R" lacked a peculiar loop at top left and bottom right.

"Damnation! I should not have dismissed the messenger so readily." I needed to know who had sent him. And where he'd met the sender.

The withered hand could be encased in a padded leather glove. Lord Ruthven's aide had reached for a wineglass with his left hand. The unnamed servant (more than a footman, or valet, less than an equal or favorite companion) had hung back and kept his gloved hands behind him while Ruthven and Drew practically panted and drooled over the scene depicting death and hell for Don Giovanni. He'd maintained a passive face, betraying neither disgust nor enjoyment of Lord Ruthven's reaction.

If he were the trusted companion of a lord with an adequate wardrobe, why had he disguised himself as a beggar?

So I would not recognize him, or connect him to his master.

A small and wiry man who, except for the damaged hand, might have been quite nimble and acrobatic. Like the kidnapper I'd confronted that first day in Lady Ada's household; the person in black who had scampered over the roof despite the broken wrist I'd inflicted upon him.

I presumed him male. I'd been wrong before. But who . . . ?

"Damnation, who is he working for?" Lord Byron, I'd assumed at the time. Now, Lord Ruthven. Was *he* the connection between the two sources of necromancy that now haunted London?

And was he behind the kidnapping of several girls? Other than Toby, all of the missing people I'd heard about had been young girls, guttersnipes, shop girls, and now a noble offspring.

I needed more information. The kind of information I'd likely find only on the streets. Beggars with missing limbs and injuries were quite common. A beggar with a withered hand would not attract much notice. A well-dressed man with a withered hand, even if he did wear a black leather glove to hide it, would be noticed.

Was I dealing with one man or two? Who was he?

I needed information and I knew how to get it.

"Mickey, summon the troops!"

Nothing. My army of listeners had heard absolutely nothing. No rumors and no reports of more missing girls, highborn or low.

And no word from Drew.

I started into the downward spiral of gloom and doom. So I did what I always did when I could not make a decision or find a course of action to get me the information I needed. I baked.

Emily became quite disgruntled that I sent her upstairs to help run the café. I needed my kitchen to myself.

And then Mickey came crashing down the stairs late in the afternoon three days later. "Look who we found!" he chortled. He clung tightly to the arm of a young blonde woman with a new bonnet slightly askew and wisps of hair creeping forward around her face. A familiar and welcome face.

"Jane!" I grasped her by both upper arms, heedless of the flour I strewed in my wake and upon her, and dragged her down the last three steps into the kitchen. Off-center her bonnet might be, but it was new, chip straw with lovely crimson velvet roses and blue ribbons sewn to the brim at the crown. Her summer gown of blue and red with a short coat of blue with red lapels—similar to the uniform of the Bow Street Runners—was much finer than her shop girl salary could purchase.

Hastily I grabbed her left hand, not at all startled to find a wedding ring on her fourth finger. A slim gold band suitable for the wife of an up-and-coming barrister.

"So he made an honest woman of you," I said evenly, belying the warring relief and disappointment that she had eloped without a word to me, or either of her flatmates.

"Yes, Missus," she said quietly. She looked all around the kitchen, noticing the changes we'd made in the last week. "We took the new train to Gretna Green."

I humphed. "A proper wedding, I hope, and not just a declaration in front of the local blacksmith." The Scots had a rather loose definition of marriage, and all a couple had to do was declare themselves husband and wife before witnesses. Even my Romany friends made more of a ceremony and ritual binding than that.

Of course in the wild Highlands with more sheep than people and settlements few and far between, a couple might have to wait a year or more for an itinerant priest to reach them, so a simple declaration made sense. Unfortunately, couples from all over the island, not just Scotland, in a hurry to marry used the system to bypass church regulations.

"We found a church and a proper clergyman, if you can call the Presbyters proper priests," Jane said, lifting her chin in righteous determination. She tidied her bonnet, retied the ribbons and tucked escaping tendrils behind her ears, restoring her dignity with her proper grooming.

"Do you know how worried we were about you?" I asked, angry now that I'd assured myself of her well-being and her virtue.

"But why? We were only gone a few days."

"More than a week while girls are being abducted off

the streets nearly every night, including Violet and the daughter of a baron. We feared for your life, and your soul, as well as your virtue."

"I'm sorry, Missus. We had no time to prepare. My Freddy's da said we had to stop keeping company until Freddy passed the bar, and Freddy wouldn't hear of it. So he proposed right then and there, and his da went storming off threatening to throw him out on the street. He . . . he accused me of only wanting his money and not loving him. When I do love him. I really and truly do." She looked right and left rather frantically, as if needing us to believe her. As if she needed our approval to convince herself her emotions were real.

"We had to leave. We couldn't wait." Jane fished in her reticule for a hankie to dab her eyes.

Her tears looked genuine.

Emily gave me a sidelong glance that told me she didn't believe a word of it. "His father," she mouthed. "He approved." Then she deliberately took up my rolling pin and rolled out the pastry dough I had just abandoned, removing herself from the conversation.

Maybe the father had a change of heart. Maybe Freddy lied.

"Wait a moment," Jane looked up, clear-eyed and without the blotchy skin that follows copious tears. "You said Violet is missing? But I saw her the morning that Freddy and I left. She was boarding a train for Devon. We were headed north and had no time to talk to her."

"Devon? Why would she go to Devon? She said she needed to visit her mother in Southwark on her half day." Without thinking, I headed upstairs to my office. I knew I had a map. In fact, I had a detailed map of southern England dating back to Roman times, and others covering many eras including modern times. I had not returned the tome to the library.

I loved maps. They held more information than most people thought to look for.

Jane and Mickey trailed after me.

"Toby's gone, too," Mickey whispered to Jane, none too subtly. "Went missing the same day."

"Devon. What's in Devon besides the best cream in the world?" I opened the atlas to the first map of the southern coastline.

"The end of the railway line," Jane offered.

"Did Violet say anything else?" My head came up so fast my neck cricked.

Jane pursed her lips into a pretty pout. I wondered if she'd practiced the expression. "She . . . she wished me luck and said she wouldn't be a shop girl much longer. I thought at the time she'd found the same luck as me, a man to marry and take her away from . . ." She blushed, also prettily. "I'm sorry, Missus. You gave us all wonderful opportunities to better ourselves. Without you and this café, we'd all be nothing better than slatterns with no hope. If we still lived. Life is short and brutal on the streets. Even with the Bow Street Runners doing their best to catch criminals."

"Running away for a better life . . ." I mused. "Was she lured away with false promises?" I didn't think so. Violet had been loyal to me from the first day. The first of my rescued children. She often hugged me with utterances of gratitude and hopes she could always work with me.

My fingers flipped pages to the most recent map of the southern coastline. It showed the ancient Roman roads as well as the newest addition of rails for the iron horse steam engines. Beyond the crossed hatch marks indicating the rails, another fainter line extended toward the rocky and broken coast of Cornwall.

I checked the date on the map. Charted in 1832, printed in 1834. Four or five years for the rails to expand toward the mines of Cornwall to fuel modern industries.

Cornwall, land's end.

Cornwall.

A haven for smugglers. The place was riddled with

tiny coves surrounded by tall cliffs. I hadn't spent much time in the area, but the one time I'd stood on a tall promontory, I'd spotted caves in the cliff below. Caves to hide French brandy and silk during the recent war and embargoes.

Caves that could harbor a necromancer's secret laboratory when London's Bow Street Runners became too curious about an abandoned warehouse on the river.

A cavern like the one in my vision.

"Congratulations on your marriage, Jane. Please know that if life sours for you, you are always welcome here. Now, Mickey, you and I need to discover who owns that warehouse." I grabbed a bonnet and shawl, oblivious to Jane's protests that her life would not sour; she and Freddy loved each other too much.

"Just make sure you and Freddy register your marriage here in London to make certain it is legal and his father can't have it annulled." I swept away, preoccupied with the people still missing, not with the one prodigal who had returned.

Some of the girls might have followed the lure of a brighter future. Toby wouldn't. Toby liked routine. Routine was safe. My Book View Café was his safe haven. He hadn't left voluntarily.

Chapter Eighteen

A DRIZZLING MONDAY MORNING, June 22, 1837. King William IV had died a few days before. Victoria had already distanced herself from her mother and her mother's lover. She'd gathered her Prime Minister and other advisers she trusted—meaning her mother didn't trust them—about her like a tight cloak of protection.

I did what I always did on Monday mornings. I scrubbed my stoop. Violet was off to see her mother and hated getting her hands wet and dirty. So I did it myself, while I thought through the last week and what I needed to do to improve my business, to watch over the ailing Lady Ada, to observe patterns in the news both at home and abroad.

Already, after only a few days, I sensed the shifting of the power players in Parliament, and the money men. Caution all around as they weighed and assessed the nature of the new power on the throne. Would young Victoria become an independent thinker? Or would she become a puppet of the Prime Minister?

The sound of weeping, quiet like the crying child was afraid of being kicked in the ribs for the crime of hopelessness, off to my left, around the corner in the narrow alley, kept me on my knees and moving my scrub brush long after the slates were clean.

Patience, I told myself. Feral children were very much like cats, skittish and untrusting. They could lash out with flying fists or thrown stones in their hunger and desperation.

Slowly, I dropped my brush and drying cloths into the bucket of soapy water and levered myself up to my feet, moving as if stiff and sore. Well, I was; crouching on my knees and washing the grime of hundreds of muddy boots and shoes off of slate isn't easy. But I still had enough ease in my joints to run, or fight if I had to.

The crying became muffled sobs. I suspected the lost one was aware of my movements and watched carefully, face covered by an arm, while trying to stop the tears that still controlled him.

Did I know for sure it was a boy? No. But I suspected. Girls learned early on that tears and wide-open eyes softened the heart of those who could take care of them. Boys hid their uncontrolled emotions as if they were a sign of weakness.

A lump of rags huddled in the dim alley—only wide enough to admit one person at a time. A big lump of rags that nearly filled the passage. One slow step at a time I edged up to him.

He dropped his face between his bent knees. *I can't see you, so you can't see me.* Very catlike.

With my back against the brick wall of my shop, I slid down to sit beside the lump.

He froze in fear.

"I won't hurt you," I said quietly.

"Yes, y' will," he mumbled.

"I have no reason to hurt you."

"Yes y' do."

"What have you done?"

"No'what."

"Then why should I hurt you?"

"'Cause."

"Because what?"

"Old man give me somewhat for y' and t'others stole it. Said it was too good for the likes o' me."

That sounded interesting. An old man had given this big boy something for me. A message perhaps? "Which old man?" I coaxed, edging close enough to put my arm around his thin shoulders. His shoulder blades felt prominent and his arms too thin.

He froze again. But as I tugged him in invitation to put his heavy head on my shoulder, he gradually unstiffened, then gave in to the force of my grip. A new spate of tears followed, and he succumbed to place his head in my lap.

In that moment I caught a glimpse of his round face with poorly defined features and up-tilted eyes, cheeks slightly darkened with the downy beginnings of a fair beard. A child of low intelligence probably. He'd always be a child. If born into a poor family, his parents would kick him out of the household as soon as he demonstrated an inability to learn. With any luck, his mum might continue to feed him for several years if she could. Not recently, though.

I hugged him tightly, sad for his condition, and sadder for the mother who had to give him up when he became a drain on the family, both financially and emotionally.

"What old man?" I asked again.

"T' one in the woods."

That could be anyone, homeless outlaws, highwayman or Romany. I hoped for Romany. "Where in the woods?"

"By t' pond."

More likely Romany. "Did he have horses?"

"Lots. Pretty little things. Sturdy, too." He let go of the sobs as he lost himself in the memory of pretty Romany ponies.

"What did the old man say to you?"

"He . . ." hiccup . . . "he said I was to take his gold coin and give it t' you. Said you'd know it, and help me. But t' others, the bully boys, threw stones at me and stole the coin. Said it was too good for me. But they didn't know about you. They didn't hear what t' old man said."

Of course it didn't all come out in a gush like that. He had to pause and think between phrases, and to choke back more tears as he remembered the cruelty of those who didn't understand his weakness. Bullies who thought themselves better than him. But they were no better off, and no better in my mind because they had no heart or compassion.

"I know the old man in the woods," I reassured the boy. "I know what he wanted me to do."

"You do?" He lifted his head and smiled at me with hope.

That smile transformed him. He looked more cherub than lost idiot. I wondered if the sun had finally penetrated this dark and dirty alleyway.

"Do you have a name?" I asked, still holding him close.

"Aye." He answered my question, not realizing I needed more information.

"And what is your name?"

"Toby."

"Toby," I affirmed. I didn't elaborate on the origin of the name: Tobias, meaning The Lord is Good. Sometimes He was. He brought me this child in a man's body when we both needed something to cherish.

"Well, Toby, I have chores to do and you could be a big help to me if you'll fetch and carry for me."

"But I lost t' coin!"

"Never mind about the coin. It was only a token to tell me I should help you. But I'll help you. I promise. You'll help me enough to earn a good breakfast. And I'll watch over you, make sure the bully boys don't come back."

"I . . . I smelled fresh bread."

"Yes, you did. And fresh bread you shall have. With

butter and jam. Now come along, there's trash to carry to the dustbin, and floors to sweep." I stood and walked to the back of the alley and thus into my courtyard and the back stairs down to the kitchen, where we both belonged.

"Missus," Mickey whispered at my elbow. I held up one finger to suggest he pause while I finished counting and sorting the keys in the discard basket behind the carousel. Fifteen in the last three days, only two large, deep search keys, but five were medium and the remainder quick and easy. Quite a few, all told. My library was gaining in popularity. Fortunately, not all of them were queries into Archbishop Howley's treatise. I'd left those books on a shelf behind the carousel.

The upcoming coronation had brought many folk to town. They added more than a bit of chaos to my relaxed and genteel café.

"Yes, Mickey?"

"Robbie an' Joe an' Kit Doyle just reported, they did, t' beggar with t' . . . weak 'and was seen down on t'docks, he was, three days a-running. Always about tea time." He gulped for air after the headlong spate of half-formed words.

"Slow down, Mickey, and tell me proper." Already my mind spun around ways to trap the man.

Mickey repeated his report, this time pausing for breath and finishing most of each word.

"Tea time," I cursed. My busiest time of day and short staffed. Jane was a properly married woman now and wouldn't return to work, though I suspected her young husband had little income as a barrister yet and they could use the cash she'd earn. The new girls couldn't yet be trusted working out front and Emily knew only a few recipes, though she showed quite a talent for baking. This morning she and I had started making bread and pastries before the sun came up. We should be well stocked for the day. She could fill in with sugar buns, and jam biscuits if things got too busy. That would free Emily to help Lucy maintain order out front. And Mickey was proving a dab hand at grinding and brewing the coffee beans. The few orders for tea Lucy could handle well.

Nothing for it. "Mickey, where on the docks?"

"Where no lady ought'nt to go. No nobs neither, with or without a carriage and stout footmen."

"Typical. A place where beggars walk with impunity but civilized folk can't." I wondered if the Rom could explore there and be overlooked or run off like everywhere else. Prejudice knew no boundaries or class lines.

"What you goin' t' do?" Mickey asked, wide-eyed with curiosity.

"What I should have done days ago. I'm going to ask direct questions of the one person I know is involved in more than one side of whatever conspiracy surrounds us." Decisively, I withdrew to my private parlor.

Mickey followed me. "Remember last time you run off on your own? I'm going with you."

"I need you here to protect the girls." I proceeded into my more private bedroom and closed the door, only to find Mickey's foot in the way. His boots were still a bit big for him, so even if I slammed the door, I'd likely only hurt the leather, not his toes.

"Protect them from what? You taught us all how to kick and scream and scratch where it'd do most good. Now if I had a pistol and knife and some of those little metal stars, I could do a proper job beating off robbers and such." He was careful to speak properly now that he needed to argue with me.

I couldn't think of a single thing that would keep the boy here, safe. I'd grown to depend on him too much. Maybe I should have cut him off and left him feral rather than bring him inside as my own apprentice, where he'd become a target for anyone out to hurt me.

"Two's safer than one. You always taught us that when I was running the streets with the rest of your crew. Three's better so's one can run for help—meaning you. But what if you's the one needin' help? Inspector Witherspoon would come with me, but I don't always know how to find him quick. I'm going after Kit Doyle. Don't you go nowheres without us." He stomped out of my quarters and back down to the café.

He acted like we all owned each other. That's not how my life was supposed to work.

I'd best hurry if I wanted to slip away while Mickey sought his companions.

What was this? Emily had tied my laces in the back in a complex knot I couldn't hope to unravel myself; not without time and a sharp pick to loosen the knots. I stamped my foot in frustration, ready to cut the cords with my embroidery scissors.

"Mickey says you might need some help," Lucy said from the doorway that Mickey had left open.

"He does, does he?" I fumed as I tore at the knot and only made it worse. Did the girls know I'd need to leave abruptly in the middle of the day so they conspired to keep me home long enough to summon reinforcements?

"Mickey also said not to let you leave until he returns even if we have to tie you up. I doubt it will take that to make you see the sense of exploring the docks with silent companions who slink from shadow to shadow and don't appear to be with you." She applied nimble fingers to the massive knot and had it unraveled in only a few breaths.

"I deal with enough conspiracies in London's shadows. I don't need my own apprentices and helpers forming another." My wardrobe revealed only clean and ordinary day gowns. "Where are my . . . ?"

"Hidden in the back of the upper shelf behind your bonnet boxes. Right where you left them."

"I used to like living on my own with only Violet to help."

"And she didn't help much, a little here, a little there, never finishing anything because you gave her too much to do, taking care of you and running the café as well. Good that you've hired more help if you intend to spend so much time investigating 'London's shadows.'" She hung back while I reached down the noisome pile in the back corner of the top shelf. I could easily stretch to pull them down. She'd need a stool or small ladder to even see the shelf, let alone the back of it.

"You've been afraid that you'd grow to love us and you'd lose us, like Jane running off to get married. I saw how you worried over her until she got back, then you dismissed her as if she'd never belonged here," Lucy grumbled as she picked up my discarded garments and laid them out neatly, along with the bulletproof corset. "She broke your heart, so you had to throw her out 'cause she might do it again."

I stood rigid, trying to deny it. Desperately, I fought to regain control of the tears that pricked my eyes. Yet she had hit the truth more soundly than I expected.

"I don't have a heart to break," I affirmed to myself, as much as to her.

She snorted, rather indelicately. I turned to reprimand her. She flashed me a cheeky grin, as if she had done it deliberately to break me out of my gloomy outlook on my life and future. A lonely outlook.

"Go back to work," I ordered, not ungently. "And tell Mickey when he returns that I don't want him getting into any trouble so that I have to rescue *him*. My mind will be full enough keeping myself whole and hale in that district. Even Inspector Witherspoon's Runners won't go there with less than an army." I'd be safer in my rags, part of the background rather than wearing an easily identifiable uniform.

Life wasn't safe. Not for me or for any of the young people gone missing. Not even a baron's daughter or a Romany girl of intelligence and independent mind.

 **Chapter Nineteen**

"SPARE A H'PENNY for tea?" I asked a man of substantial girth and middling means judging by the brocade of his waistcoat. He stood at the edge of a long dock surveying the loading of a tall ship with a supplementary steam paddle wheel. The short smokestack suggested that he still relied more on the canvas to sail across the deep ocean and used steam only when wind failed completely, or navigating inland rivers to the ports, like the Thames downriver from the Tower.

"Get away with you," he snarled, kicking at my dirty skirts.

I jerked my outstretched palm back into my pocket, just in case I needed more defense than scuttling away with bowed back and using the stout walking stick as a crutch.

"Won't never get nothing from the likes o' 'im," a gravelly voice muttered from the shadow cast by an old warehouse that seemed a bit too clean and well-kept for the neighborhood. The doors and window frames just under the eaves sported new paint, and the gutters looked solid.

I surveyed the man in a filthy greatcoat and wilted wide-brimmed hat that hid much. After three hours of prowling through the relentless drizzle, I'd finally found the man I sought. Mickey and Kit Doyle lounged against a tumble of crates off to my left. To the right, another small, shadowy form sat atop a coil of rope, dangling short legs over the rim.

"Do I know you?" I asked the man.

"No," he replied emphatically and turned to flee.

"Your accent slipped," I said, straightening from my hunch and easing the unnatural strain on my back and the unforgiving corset. I'd never have achieved this disguise if I'd worn a normal one.

He paused, mid-step.

"You accompany Lord Ruthven about town, yet disguise yourself as a beggar to deliver his messages. I wonder why Inspector Witherspoon hasn't taken you to the Yard for questioning in regard to the disappearance of Miss Abigail Norwynd."

"Witherspoon's shortsighted and won't see the obvious even when it's pointed out to him." His voice returned to the normal drawl with a bit of a clip in some words of a man who had grown up with one accent and worked hard to obscure it. I guessed he'd been educated in the south.

"Perhaps," I admitted. "The inspector is quite class conscious but very thorough when his intellect is engaged."

The man whirled to face me, eyes bright and curious. Those familiar eyes . . . Pale brown, almost hazel, eager and yet world-weary at the same time. Not the eyes of the man I'd deflected from kidnapping Miss Ada long ago. That man had been darker, possibly only dirtier, and his eyes hooded and shadowed by a cap brim so that I couldn't determine their exact color. I'd only presumed them darker because of his skin tones.

The image of a curved scar disappearing up a sleeve flashed before me. *Stamata!* She'd been the nimble kidnapper, determined to force Ada to rebuild the transference engine. The scar showed where a surgeon—possibly Polidari himself—had repaired the broken wrist.

I remained wary as I dragged yet another memory out of many. I'd seen this man more recently, and not just with Lord Ruthven or in his beggar disguise.

I cocked my head, trying for a different angle to shake loose the right memory.

"Allow me to introduce myself, Madame Magdala." He bowed properly for a man approaching an older woman of equal status if not rank. "Right Reverend Morten Rigby, at your service."

The young cleric in search of the treatise on the Reform Act!

I wiggled my fingers to signal my young helpers to move closer. This man would not escape me.

"This conversation needs to take place more privately." I eyed the merchant on the dock. He seemed intent on the handling of his cargo coming off the ship. Still he could listen, if he chose to.

"You might be interested to know that yon merchant rented this place not two days ago, after the Bow Street Runners invaded and found it empty. It has no use to the owner now."

"Oh?" I asked. "And who would the owner be?"

"No one I can tell you about."

That said a lot and not enough.

"Shall we meet back at the café in an hour?" he asked, sidling away an inch at a time.

"No, you will accompany me back to the café, with my escort." I gestured to the two boys and a mop-haired girl of six who had the most nimble fingers for pickpocketing in the entire city. I had future plans for her. Might be time to bring her in and complete her training under close supervision so that she didn't get caught and lose those fingers in punishment for her crimes.

Father Rigby heaved a great whoosh of air and then in again, as if he'd forgotten to breathe. "Very well. Though I'd like to shed this garb and be clean again."

"Time enough for that, after we discover more about

each other's observations and plans." I resumed my hunch from mid back to shoulder and leaned on the stick as I led the strange parade back toward Charing Cross Road.

A gesture sent one of the younger boys in my entourage off to Lambeth Palace to check Father Rigby's credentials.

o⚙

"May I have my rosary back?" Father Rigby asked as he settled into the wing-backed chair beside my hearth. He'd shed the greatcoat and hat to reveal a normal cleric's black trousers and shirt, minus the white ascot. The fine weave of his clothing looked a bit shiny and threadbare with age, but still respectable. He held out his left hand.

Ruefully, I handed over the strand of black-and-silver beads with a rather plain silver crucifix dangling from one end. "Raggedy Maggedity must be losing her touch if you noticed," I said, glad I'd banished my companions to the scullery for tea and buttered bread while I interviewed the reverend in my semiprivate parlor reserved for special customers or as extra space when my salon overflowed my rooms. We'd entered by the stair at the back so as not to arouse suspicion among the last, lingering customers before closing.

"She's very good. I doubt anyone but me would have felt her tiny fingers filching the smallest coin out of my *inside* pocket." Rigby ran his fingers along the strand of black-and-silver beads before replacing it in his trouser pocket. Had he checked to see if any were missing?

A vision of a black-and-silver strand of beads choking the life out of me and my café flashed before my inner vision. His silver decade beads were neither filigree nor tarnished. The vision must mean something else.

"I used to be as good or better than she, but I'm a bit out of practice." He held up both hands and examined the long fingers.

"The withered hand?" I glanced at the greatcoat hanging on the rack beside the door. A black glove hung from the right sleeve as if a small hand still filled it. A clever prosthetic. Actually a marvel of clockwork and puppetry.

"A useful disguise. Everyone notices it while pretending they don't, so they won't have to be disgusted. The fascination of horror. They dwell so long on imagining how they might feel if it happened to them, that they forget to notice anything else. The military greatcoat and hat give me a bit of credence and authenticity as a wounded war hero. I learn a lot from retired soldiers also living on the street."

I poured tea for him, and he lifted the cup with his left hand.

"Naturally left-handed?" I asked. "Or a great deal of practice?"

"Bit of both. The world is not kind to left-handers—going back to old heraldry terminology, left is the sinister side, so a left-handed person is also sinister, black-hearted, in league with the Devil. I trained to use the right as much as possible. But when I must go about the streets in disguise for His Grace the Archbishop, my left hand is just as dexterous as ever."

"Except when picking pockets."

He laughed long and loud, resting his head against the chair back. "Oh, I still have my hidden right hand for that. I just don't have to use that skill as often as I did before His Grace—merely Bishop of London then—took me in and educated me."

"Winchester? His Grace's *alma mater*?"

He nodded.

"Rosaries are out of fashion these days."

"And His Grace does not fully approve of a public display, though he keeps one by his *prie-dieu*. Old Church and all. He's the one who sent me to Rome for a year to study ancient rituals of the Church. I picked up the habit there. Useful for meditation and penitentiary prayer. Also useful in sorting my thoughts or the pieces of a complex and puzzling conspiracy."

Lucy came in with a tray of substantial cheese and plain scones with jam and Devonshire cream. She curtsied deeply, never letting her eyes stray long from Father Rigby's thin face with the high cheekbones and a slightly receding chin. He looked a bit rabbity with an overbite. That didn't deter my Lucy.

Father Rigby returned her gaze with equal admiration.

"What did you learn about ancient rituals in Rome?" I pointedly admired the lovely scones rather than peer any closer into the attraction between these two young people. Eventually they might make a match. Unlikely since she had no dowry, and I wouldn't approve until he gave up his clandestine jobs and settled into a parish or administrative work for the archbishop.

"I learned that the claim by necromancers that Christianity in and of itself is the worship of death with the promise of resurrection is entirely false. I learned that Archbishop Howley did not betray his brother Freemasons by declaring necromancy not only a crime of murder but blasphemy as well. The Freemasons have not endorsed that portion of the Reform Act because they feel that addressing necromancy as a crime against man and God shouldn't be necessary. The death cult goes against everything Freemasonry stands for. It is obviously a crime—the crime of murder—and should be dealt with as such."

"Interesting. And yet His Grace opposed the reforms in the House of Lords."

"You know why."

I nodded.

"Traditionists feel that those who own land should determine our government and not the masses of industrial workers who own nothing but their lives and souls.

They found something in his past, painful enough that he felt better served to vote against the bill than have a scandal exposed. The only way he could get his laws against necromancy passed was to stand down from his arguments against reform. He convinced his blackmailers of the same, but had to write his treatise against the act to please them."

"I know. I helped write that treatise based on research from my library," I said quietly.

"You did! I thought the phrasing was off from his usual style when he gave it to me to add a few Biblical quotes to give it authenticity."

"Did he ever tell you what scandal would be loosed on the public if he did not comply?"

A moment of stony silence. "No."

I couldn't tell if he lied or not. So I smiled at him, and suddenly I knew where he'd come from. But I needed to change the subject rather than reveal that I knew the archbishop's deepest secret.

"I had not realized the cult of necromancy had grown so large and powerful as to require additional laws." I jerked my head at Lucy so she'd leave. She'd indulged her fancy for Father Rigby long enough. I was certain they would flirt later and perhaps begin a courting dance.

I'd lost one helper to a hasty marriage. I did not want to lose another. Time enough for that later, when they both had a bit of money to ease their way through society.

"So what is your position with the archbishop that you must disguise yourself as a civilian with a withered hand?"

"When escorting Lord Ruthven about town, I claim it as a war wound." Reluctantly, he watched Lucy leave and then returned his attention to me.

"How do you manage that? You can't be old enough to have served even as late as Waterloo." Nearly twenty years ago.

"Again, I use distraction. Amazing how old a weary face can make one appear." He frowned, squinted near-sightedly, then dropped his chin and shoulders. The vibrant young man in his mid-twenties suddenly aged another two decades. I could hone my own skills observing him.

"Your purpose?"

"I search out practitioners of necromancy and bring them to His Grace's attention, *with proof*, undeniable proof of their perfidy. To that end, I understand you possess a certain book that has been badly translated."

"I do."

"Might I have a glance at it?"

"Why?"

"To see if I can glean anything from it."

"It is so badly translated it is unreadable."

"But it might have information added to it beyond the original. Which I have read. Necromancers are notorious for feeling superior to their predecessors and inserting their own theories each time they republish. I might discover something about the latest batch of practitioners." He sighed as if all of his troubles stemmed from bad translations and self-indulgent practitioners.

"Practitioners like Lord Ruthven," he added.

"I have it on good authority that the translation is so inaccurate it could lead the inexperienced or unwary into even greater perfidy than they think possible," I said.

"I understand." He nodded, eyes closed in deep thought. Or deep fatigue. His life could not be easy or safe. Another reason to delay any courtship of Lucy.

I fetched the book from my rooms. When I returned, Rigby appeared almost asleep, but three more scones and half the pot of tea had disappeared.

He started as I placed the book in his hands. But his eyes went wide in surprise as he flipped through several pages. "Oh, my. Oh, my," he muttered as he paused to read a passage.

"Not exactly easy reading," I said, resuming my seat, never taking my eyes off him, or those ever so nimble fingers that were accustomed to removing items from their rightful owners and secreting them away.

"This passage that reads . . . I won't bother reading it, one sentence goes on for five pages with multiple colons and semicolons, all improperly used. But it should define the necessity of prayers offered for the soul of the victim before his life is stolen and in the victim's own language to the god of his choice. Instead, it implies that the practitioner's god is superior to all others and thus prayers should be offered *after* the death of the victim in the practitioner's original language."

"Oh, my. That is dangerous." What else could I say? Though not overly spiritual, I do believe and attend Anglican Mass most every Sunday morning, usually early. To die as a sacrifice to an alien god without opportunity to petition my own made me squirm.

Would Lord Ruthven adhere to the original or the mistranslation? Or would he disdain any prayers at all?

"Anyone else of note I should be aware of?" I asked to change the looping thread of my thoughts.

"Some. Without proof, I will not say."

I nodded my acceptance. For now, anyway, I could pretend that Sir Andrew Fitzandrew hovered on the fringes of evil with the fascination of horror, but not the moral breakdown to actually join them. He'd said that he planned to spend some time with Ruthven in the country. Weeks ago.

Rigby made uneasy movements as if needing to leave but too tired to rise.

"Before you go, I must know if Lord Ruthven is behind the kidnapping of so many young people."

"I do not know. I suspect him. But without knowing the purpose I have no way to trace the victims. I can understand the taking of the street girls. Who of consequence would miss them, and who would demand restitution, pay ransom, or even try to track them? But Baron Norwynd's daughter? That was bold."

"Audacious," I said. "Something about the street girls failed to fill our villain's purpose. So he goes after bigger game, takes more risks for grander results."

We let that rest for a long moment of silence. Then I offered him another scone and refilled his cup. "Tell me what brought you to the docks?"

A tiny smile quirked the corners of his mouth. "Partly to watch if a black balloon with a black wicker basket would be loaded onto any vessel headed upriver."

"Yes, the notorious black balloon that has the facilities to house a cannon that shoots searing green light instead of gunpowder and lead balls."

He suddenly sat up straight and leaned forward with renewed energy and interest.

I related my tale of observing the craft and having turned the problem of recreating the weapon over to Dr. Chaturvedi.

"Good. Good. May I have the professor's address? I must speak with him right away."

The writing desk customers sometimes used provided me with proper pen, ink, and paper. But I held onto the address a moment.

Rigby raised his eyebrows in question.

"The other reason you lingered on the docks?"

"I knew if I frequented the same place often enough, word would reach you and you'd come looking for me. Or one of your army of urchins would. And I needed to make certain the new tenant of the warehouse is not connected to the previous occupants."

"You could have just come to the café and requested an interview. You've been here before, requesting books."

"Ah, but would you have believed my tale without you discovering my disguise for yourself?"

 **Chapter Twenty**

FATHER RIGBY DEPARTED the same way we had come in, a nearly invisible shadow. He planned to ride to Oxford that very night. I'd asked him to keep a lookout for Jeremy Badenough as well.

The long case clock in the corner chimed half seven. I had invitations to three parties, a musicale, and late supper *en famille* with Lady Ada and her husband. They planned to attend the last party of the evening, and so offered me a place in their carriage. The musicale enticed me more than parties, but I hadn't talked directly to Lady Ada in many days. I missed her sorely.

All I really wanted was a bath and bed. But I could not ask the girls to draw water off the boiler and haul it up here after a long day at work. My cash reserves were building. When I had enough, I'd have pumps and pipes installed to bring the hot water from the boiler directly to my private washroom.

And even if I washed up at the basin, I doubted I'd sleep. My mind was too full of patterns that tried to fit together but kept drifting apart as different information added new pieces to the puzzle, filling in some blanks but tearing apart others.

I'd only met Mrs. Howley twice and not recently. Still

a trick of the light had revealed something in the cast of Rigby's eyes and the set of his chin that looked enough like her that I knew she had birthed him. The daughter of respectable gentry, she'd been seduced by her father's guest (a man too important and wealthy to force into marriage), then abandoned.

Her parents had arranged for her to "visit relatives abroad." Then she'd given up the baby to a childless, older merchant and his wife. They welcomed and cherished the child until their deaths eight years later in a carriage accident.

Greedy relatives had found something irregular in the adoption, ignored the merchant's last will and testament, confiscated his estate, and finally cast the child into an orphanage.

No one knew to notify the Bishop of London of the accident.

By that time, the young mother had married Reverend Howley and used her dowry to help him on the political path to the bishopric.

Three months after the death of the merchant and his wife, the nephew who had confiscated much of the estate found some of the correspondence from Bishop Howley. Thinking to exploit the advantageous connection, he finally wrote to inform the bishop of the death of his "friend."

Mrs. Howley drove immediately to the orphanage only to find the child had run away, willing to take his chances on the streets rather than endure abuse and near starvation.

It took them a year to find her son. Unable to acknowledge him and still hope to continue the bishop's career in the Church, they took responsibility for Rigby's education and career path.

I now knew that knowledge of this scandal had forced Howley to reconsider his vote on the Reform Act. And that the Right Reverend Morten Rigby was the child.

His Grace the Archbishop had told me the story, but never the name of the child or his adoptive parents.

If Howley himself had been threatened by scandal he'd have stood firm. But he bowed to something that endangered his wife and family.

I needed the distraction of people. I needed gossip. I needed to encourage my public image of a slightly outré trendsetter. Some customers flocked to my café simply to risk being seen with me.

So to the one party and supper I would go.

Then the age-old question of what to wear. Not the ruby, too recently seen at my salon and the matching turban needed a new feather and some trim. The sapphire? That simple gown with my lapis lazuli necklace and earbobs suited my mood. Then I spotted the dark green gown, not bright enough to be called emerald, more like jade. The décolletage dipped enticingly with a faint sparkle of iridescent beads along the edge. I had jade jewelry. Thankfully, the ensemble fit loosely enough that I could manage my own laces and have room to breathe freely.

And I had Drew's delightful mechanical hummingbird I could fasten to a plain gold band for the middle finger of my left hand. I looked impressive and flamboyant even when I fought mental exhaustion with every eye blink.

The hummingbird could cure that. I kept on hand a measure of condensed coffee for emergencies when I was too tired to think but had to force my body to move. Carefully, I decanted a thimbleful of liquid, thick and dark and similar to the sludge at the bottom of a steam-expressed pot of coffee at the end of the day, into the poison chamber in the body of the bird. Easy enough to dilute it in a glass of water and quaff in a discreet and empty alcove. I had to make certain that if I set the bird fluttering and chirping to amuse my companions that I flicked the wings and did not depress the tail.

Something about bright sconces newly adapted to gas fuel, lively music, free flowing laughter, and effervescent wine revived me better than a bath and bed. The moment the footman announced me at the top of the stairs to the ballroom, I drew the attention of three ranks of guests. Their stillness alerted the rest of the room to my presence.

When all eyes turned to me, and the music paused, along with the chatter and laughter, I curtsied lightly and descended the four steps to greet Sir Michael and Lady Bramhurst, my hosts. The fact that I arrived alone made almost as much a stir as the expanse of bosom I revealed above the neckline of my gown.

Drew would have approved. If he were here. If he still lived. If he hadn't succumbed to the lure of necromantic power.

I lifted my chin in defiance of my negative thoughts and passed among an eclectic crowd, many of them regular customers at the Book View Café. Plenty of minor titles dominated the group, but two greater ones took precedence. Fat merchants and industrialists showed off their doweried daughters in search of titled husbands who'd gladly marry new money *sans titles* to preserve the family estate.

"Oh, let me show you the newest invention from Babbage and Lovelace!" Lady Bramhurst enthused as I passed a series of small round shelves on pedestals above the light buffet. Carefully she placed a wineglass in the precise center of one burnished copper disk. A mechanical arm extruded from the pedestal, holding a bottle of wine. In smooth movements, it tipped and poured a precise amount of wine into the glass. Much more useful and less intimidating than the full automaton my Ada had worked on the other day.

I took the glass and sipped. "Excellent vintage, my lady. How does the arm work?"

"I'm not exactly sure, but placing the glass on the

copper triggers the arm. We purchased three of them especially for tonight. We hope to show them off to Her Majesty next month, after the coronation, of course. She's much too busy to attend our little gathering tonight."

I nodded.

"Much more useful than my little toy," I said as I flicked the clockwork hummingbird into life. The wings flapped so quickly they set up a hum of displaced air, much as a real bird would. Then it tipped back its head and chirped.

"Oh, how delightful!" Lady Bramhurst enthused. "You simply *must* show that to his lordship. He likes mechanical toys." She moved off to show another guest how *her* device worked.

I drifted toward the musicians performing on a dais in the back corner. Much to my surprise Inspector Witherspoon basked in the harmonies, eyes half-closed and swaying lightly to the lilting waltz.

"Oh, Madame Magdala, I didn't know you'd be here. Would have offered to share a hansom if I'd known." He bowed, keeping his head up and his eyes moving.

"Thank you for the offer. I didn't know until the last moment that I'd be able to attend. Too many commitments," I explained. "I'm surprised to see you here, what with your obligations to Bow Street. This must be a very busy time for you as well."

"Oh, I've retrieved a fair bit of stolen property for this lot. They thank me by inviting me to hobnob with a bit of society, knowing I'll keep a watchful eye out for any blighters who might sneak in as uninvited guests, or even extra servants. A most pleasurable part of my job." He winked at me and returned his gaze to a servant removing empty glasses from various perches. I saw a bit of glitter slip into his pocket.

Before I could remark upon it, Inspector Witherspoon had his hand clamped onto the offender's wrist and was escorting him elsewhere.

"Neat bit, that. A clumsy effort by a recognized pick-pocket who should know better than to try such a trick in the presence of the good inspector," a cultured voice said just behind my left shoulder.

"Reverend Rigby? I thought you'd be in Oxford by now." I replaced the inspector with my own surveillance of the crowd.

"I had hoped to be there. His Grace sent someone else to summon the professor to Lambeth Palace tomorrow. He bade me attend this gathering in his stead while he dances with the queen elsewhere." He nodded to a passing acquaintance. His black evening clothes and snowy linen were perfect attire for the gathering. Not a bit of threadbare shine anywhere on him. Or a black glove to hide a nimble-fingered pickpocket. He held a wineglass in his good right hand. "I believe I am also to attend a late supper with the Earl and Lady Lovelace."

"As am I," I replied as I kept an eye on another foot-man who seemed to hover behind a lady with an expensive diamond brooch on her feathered headpiece.

Rigby nodded that he'd seen it, too. We drifted in that direction. The footman backed off.

"Are we dealing with a ring of thieves, controlled by a single mastermind?"

"Probably. But why here tonight?" Rigby looked around a bit confused.

"More money than titles." I nodded to an acquaintance and smiled brilliantly. *Nothing to worry about, nothing out of the ordinary in this corner.* "Now, why are you attending the Lovelace supper party? I was told it would be *en famille*."

"We like to keep an eye on Lady Lovelace," Rigby continued. "Lord William claims close friendship with His Grace of Canterbury. Therefore, his invitation becomes mine upon occasion. You know how important she is to all of England as an inventor and mathematical genius."

"Actually, Sir Charles Babbage is the inventor. Lady Lovelace is the mathematician who makes it all work properly."

"So I understand. Which actually makes her the more important partner. And the object of much envy to those who need new or reconstructed inventions but don't have the mechanical knowledge, or the genius to make them themselves."

"I am aware of that. I had not known that His Grace also sees the value in keeping her safe."

"And since her father's cult is so closely aligned with my . . . other duties, I find it useful to attend her little gatherings now that she has returned to health."

I debated telling him about my brush with Lord Byron's cult, or why Ada had remained invalid so long.

A bustle of movement at the doorway to the grand salon precluded my statement. Lady Ada and her tall, handsome husband—strong jaw, thinning fair hair, and a proud carriage which would stand out in any crowd— waited patiently, framed by the white-and-gilt doorjamb as if posing for a portrait painter. The footman cleared his throat. A semblance of quiet and attention rippled among the crowd closest to the entry. I raised my glass, catching my girl's eye. I dipped my chin a fraction in salute to her choice of a mint green gown of fine organza over shot silk, appropriate for a young matron. Was that a hint of electricity scattered through the organza?

Ada gestured with her lace fan to the artistic array of beads that near-filled her décolletage. Glass strung with copper wire, more wires and tiny glass beads woven into the organza. And hidden in the folds of her neckline, I knew a tiny Leyden jar anchored the copper and generated a mild electrical current. An untoward touch on her gown would trigger a shock to bare skin. Not much protection, but a first line of defense against potential kidnappers. Also an eye-catching fashion trend soon to be mimicked about town. We'd played this game before.

"Why is her gown glowing?" Reverend Rigby asked so quietly I had to strain to hear. "Not a fashion statement, I gather."

"You said yourself that she is both valuable and vulnerable. I raised her to be less vulnerable than many think. The glow only looks like a new fashion statement, while actually creating an illusion and blurred afterimages. You can't tell precisely where she is at any given moment."

⚙⚙

"What happened when the chemist told a joke?" Reverend Rigby asked Lady Ada. He sat to her immediate left and I sat next to him at the long formal dining table at Lovelace House. Since becoming a belted earl, William King's idea of *en famille* had expanded greatly.

Ada returned an almost blank face toward her newest admirer. But the corner of her mouth twitched as she resisted a smile. "He got no reaction," she said quietly.

Then the two of them burst into laughter, much too loud and uninhibited to be acceptable at a formal dinner, or even an informal one—which this one had ceased to be.

Lord William rolled his eyes at me. We knew this game. He'd initiated it during his courtship of Ada. He had a fine mind but rarely turned it to mathematics anymore. He used it to craft logical, compelling speeches in the House of Lords and among the queen's advisers. The few other guests at the table were a Cabinet minister, his wife, and a country baron and his lady with an estate near Lord William's. The confusion in their eyes told me that they had no inkling what the joke meant. I didn't feel obliged to explain.

Reverend Rigby continued to ingratiate himself while Lord William entertained the country lady who looked as if her fingers itched to examine the lace on my sleeve more closely. Her pale cream-colored gown with champagne lace from Nottingham was well made and quite fashionable. I thought I recognized the modiste's styling in the ruching. She'd begrudged not a penny on the ensemble.

"Are the seating arrangements inside the Abbey complete?" the Cabinet minister's wife asked her husband, an interesting ploy to change the conversation back to something we all understood and appreciated.

As footmen served and removed each course, I realized that here, in the home of the greatest innovator of serving machines, Lady Ada preferred human servants. Unless . . . No I detected no sign that any of them were less than human or even partially machines.

Ada and Rigby smothered smiles and joined in.

We lingered over an excellent pudding glazed with marzipan until the clock struck midnight. I'd been thinking longingly of my bed for over an hour, wondering how to extricate myself gracefully from excellent company and good food.

"My dear Madame Magdala, let me call the carriage for you. I know you have obligations quite early in the morning," Lord William said quietly.

I smiled my appreciation to him just as the door opened and an agitated butler made hasty steps to the earl.

"Excuse me, m' lord. An urgent message from the Prime Minister."

Lord William's face paled and his hands shook so violently he had to put down his coffee cup lest he spill the remaining dregs at the bottom. He shoved back his chair quite violently in his haste to meet the messenger elsewhere.

The dinner party began shifting, making noises and motions toward departure.

"I can offer you a seat in His Grace's carriage," Rigby said quietly taking my elbow and steering me toward the exit.

"Thank you. I fear his lordship will require the use of his own carriage," I whispered back.

The butler returned and made haste to my side. "Madame, my lord requests your immediate assistance in a matter of some delicacy."

Rigby and I exchanged glances. "Perhaps my assistance can be of value as well," the reverend said.

The butler nodded and led us toward the earl's private office on the other side of the house. We found Lord William leaning heavily against the mantel, gripping it fiercely with both hands. A shorter man would not appear so cowed, but his back was nearly bent double in despair.

"Magdala, thank God you are here tonight. We must go at once." He gathered himself upright once more tall and decisive. "You, too, Rigby. Your expertise will be most welcome."

"What has happened, my lord?" I asked from the doorway.

"Miss Abigail Norwynd has returned to her parents' home."

"That is good news," Rigby said. But joy did not color his voice.

"Not if she left her soul behind when she escaped her captors," William ground out.

 **Chapter Twenty-One**

"**YOU'RE A GYPSY!**" Lady Norwynd screeched as she clung to her limp and bedraggled daughter. They sat on a settee upholstered in fine French brocade. The cream and gold matched the lady's coloring, as well as her daughter's. They seemed to blend in with it, becoming almost unnoticeable, and I had to wonder if she'd chosen it for that purpose. A wonder that she'd allow the daughter's damp and stained day dress to touch the upholstery. "Surely you know a spell to break this Gypsy curse."

I swallowed my outrage as all eyes in the small family parlor abovestairs turned to me.

Lord William stiffened in his perch upon a spindly chair much too delicate for his height and form.

Reverend Rigby frowned from his study of the mantelpiece—carved and painted to resemble Italian marble—then resumed his compassionate priestly demeanor. I'd seen him change appearance and identity so often that day, beggar, spy, social dandy, experienced pickpocket, and crime fighter, I had no idea which one exemplified the man. "My lady, may we examine the girl?" He held out a long-fingered hand that had proved adept at picking pockets and piously counting rosary beads.

Reluctantly, the lady released her fierce grip on the blonde teenager. The girl flopped back against the back of their seat, eyes blank and staring. Unblinking. Messy golden curls dangled in her eyes and down her back, hairpins long lost. Her once-pretty day gown of white and light blue muslin was stained with blood and dirt in random splotches. The bruising on her face and upper arms matched. Odd patterns I could not puzzle through. Which had come from a slap and which from a fierce grip? The edges had begun to blur and shift from dark purple to ugly greenish yellow. A week's worth of healing, at least, not hours or days.

Had she disappeared long before her parents reported her missing? Had she run away from physical punishment rather than been abducted?

Rigby knelt before the girl, running his fine hands from her crown, down her shoulders and arms, not touching. I wondered if he felt her life energy as Ish had tried to teach me to do, to feel a person's health in ways my other senses could not assess. He could detect lies within that energy. Could Rigby?

Then the priest held up his black-and-silver rosary before the girl's eyes. She couldn't help but see it, even if her eyes remained unfocused.

Nothing. No flicker in her eyes, no flinch away from the potent symbol of faith.

Rigby swung the crucifix back and forth with the slightest tremble of his fingers. Still no reaction. Like the chemist who told a joke.

I bit back the laughter of hysteria.

Tears streamed down Lady Norwynd's face. She could not have yet reached her thirty-fifth birthday, younger than me, and much less worldly wise.

Lord William and the girl's father turned away.

"I have no tricks up my sleeve. Madame Magdala, do you have any ideas?" Rigby asked, rising stiffly to his feet and pocketing the rosary.

"I need a cup of coffee." I blurted out the first words that came to mind.

Everyone in the room gasped at my audacity.

"Not to drink, or restore me. To *see*."

"Then it's true? You do have Gypsy magic?" Lady Norwynd whispered, hope coloring her words.

"A cup of water will do. Anything liquid."

Lord Norwynd strode to the door to summon a servant, his pudgy frame shifting side to side with each stride.

The movement captured my straining gaze, side to side, side to side. My peripheral vision began to close in; darkness crouched ready to pounce inward like a leopard awaiting prey. Side to side, back and forth.

The silver crucifix replaced the image of the girl's father. Side to side, around and around and around again, creating a swirling vortex of sparkling silver. I focused on the glitter and gleam as gaslight caught the precious metal, fixing my gaze on the dying Christ, sacrificing himself for all mankind. Sacrifice. Death that is not death. Resurrection.

The silver crucifix became a light beckoning through a tunnel, reflecting off whitewashed walls. Darkness banished to the far depths of ... a cave. A cave where steam engines chugged and whistled, where metal laboratory tables awaited victims, scrubbed clean and polished to a high sheen, filling the floor space, and Leyden jars stacked neatly on a wall. Copper wires everywhere. Ghosts wandered aimlessly about, restrained by the wires that connected them to the jars.

Blue-and-red electrical jolts sparked along those wires—as they had with the dwarf in Stamata's cellar laboratory.

Only one body remained unconnected. One sheet-draped body remained on a table pushed into the corner, useless, forgotten.

A black-and-silver strand of beads encircled it all, choking the life from the ghosts, from the victims, from me ...

A sob convulsed in my chest, breaking the trance.

I blinked rapidly, trying to sort the rapid change of scene and lighting, live companions replaced numerous ghosts, all girls, all angry. All lost.

Father Rigby crossed himself, murmuring a prayer. Then he kissed and pocketed the rosary. Head bowed, he touched my hand.

An electrical jolt from his skin to mine finished my transition to reality. I had to shake my head vigorously to clear it of the ghastly images.

"We have true necromancy at work," Rigby said quietly.

Lady Norwynd reared back, hand to chest, eyes wide and jaw moving wordlessly.

"Popish nonsense." Lord Norwynd spoke for the first time, his voice pushed higher than his normal tenor by anxiety.

"Gypsy curses," Lady Norwynd countered, finally finding a voice, though she kept her hand over her heart as if to still its too rapid beat. "Can we trust Gypsies any more than we can Roman Catholics? They are both aligned with the Devil."

I bit my lip to keep acidic words from leaking out.

Miss Abigail remained motionless, eyes closed, no longer staring. Yet she breathed. A pulse beat strongly on her neck just below her ear.

How?

"Did I speak?" I whispered to Rigby, hoping the others could not hear.

Did I speak of the black-and-silver beads that could either choke the life from the hideous experiments with death, or choke the life from those who sought to end it?

He jerked a quick nod and turned away from me. His shoulders trembled slightly as he fought for control.

"What can we do for her?" Lord Norwynd took up a protective stance behind the settee, one hand on his wife's shoulder, the other on the furniture, close to his daughter but not touching her.

"I saw this happen in Rome," Rigby said, staring at the fire, or into his past. "The female victims were sent to a convent. The sisters were dedicated to nursing the sick and caring for the feeble ... of mind as well as body. The church leaders hoped that cloistered in a community of deep faith, the stray souls would find their bodies again."

"We do not hold with Popish ways," Norwynd replied. "I could not vote for the Reform Act because it granted freedom and tolerance to Roman Catholics." Implying that he agreed with everything else.

"I will speak with His Grace tonight, late as it is," Rigby said, taking a firmer, more decisive stance. "By morning, we will have made arrangements for placing your daughter in an *Anglican* convent in the north. In the meantime, bathe her and put her to bed. Try to give her water or broth, a sip at a time so she does not choke. And now we must take our leave." He turned to face the door, keeping his glance averted from Lord Norwynd and his wife.

As I rose to follow him, the exotic clockwork hummingbird snagged on my skirts. I stared at it a long moment trying to remember why I'd worn the thing, other than to delight and amuse at the party. I was too tired to think straight. . . .

The bird contained condensed coffee to boost my body and mind when I fell to this depth of fatigue. I looked back at the girl. Her eyes blinked once. An automatic response that needed no thought or will to control it. What if she was merely in shock from the trauma of a kidnap? What if she had escaped before Ruthven had a chance to drain her soul from her?

She still faced the ruin of her reputation. But perchance she could testify against her captor. Perhaps the Norwynds could have their daughter back.

Before anyone had the opportunity or wits to stop me, I shoved the sharp bird beak, as fine as a stout needle, between her lips. Her mouth opened a fraction in response to my prod. The beak slid along the top of her tongue. With eyes glued to her face for any flicker of awareness, I depressed the bird's tail with my thumb. A thick sludge of coffee, boiled down to its stimulating essence, shot into the back of her throat.

Her neck muscles remained still, so I clamped the fingers of my other hand over her nose, forcing her body to gulp so she could breathe.

"What are you doing?" Lady Norwynd protested, fluttering her hands and looking more pallid than before. Like a properly trained lady, she did not rush to stop me, politely leaving that chore to the men in the room. "Gypsy poison!"

"Nay, my lady. Simply a common remedy," Reverend Rigby spoke in my defense. He shifted to stand between me and the others.

Miss Abigail choked, swallowed, and blinked again, three times in rapid succession.

Then, disappointingly, she dropped back into her catatonic state.

"I think the good sisters will have something to work with," I said, hiding my minor triumph. "I have roused her to the point she will accept her soul, should it choose to return to her." Graciously I stepped back and gestured Rigby to exit. Hastily if possible.

Lord William made polite leave-taking gestures.

"I presume this means our daughter will not have the honor of carrying Her Majesty's train at the coronation?" Lady Norwynd looked up with hopeful eyes.

"No, she will not," Lord William pronounced resolutely, no room for compromise.

"Perhaps her younger sister?"

"No. The honor will go to another family."

We left, each of us collapsing into the carriage pulled by mechanical horses powered by steam. The groom had kept the boiler stoked so that the beasts trotted off smartly with no delay.

 Chapter Twenty-Two

I HAD TO SIT up straight in the carriage, every muscle rigid and my bones perfectly centered. Too much had happened. Too much to think about.

I could not separate my outrage at the necromancy from my disgust at the Norwynd family's prejudice and insults.

Taking the soul from a living body, but leaving the body alive, just empty. That was a new puzzle piece. What did the necromancer hope to achieve by this new method of chaos?

Chaos. As good an answer as any.

I choked. My lungs fought for air, but my throat refused to work. I felt as if burning iron bands caged my chest, growing tighter by the second.

Through a red haze, I saw Reverend Rigby draw out his rosary and begin sliding the beads through his fingers.

At last, I forced myself to breathe and gasp, "Ideas? Solutions? Plans?"

"The girl will be cared for. Beyond that?" The earl shrugged his shoulders in the dim light from the carriage lanterns hung from the four outside corners of our conveyance.

Rigby nodded, gulped, and finally spoke. "I cannot predict the outcome. But . . ."

"What . . . what happened in Rome?" I asked. The

carriage increased speed in the deserted streets of early morning London. I doubted I'd sleep tonight since I had to rise in a few hours to begin the bread rising.

"We never knew for certain." Rigby blinked rapidly, as if fighting tears. "But one of the victims woke up one morning, fully restored. Or so her caretakers thought."

"Until?"

"Until she spoke with the accent, education, wisdom, and memories of the Reverend Mother who had died from a tragic accident on the same day the girl arrived at the convent." He let that statement rest among us for a long moment.

"Not her own soul," Lord William gasped. "The ghost of one who was not ready to pass took possession of her body?"

Rigby nodded.

Was possession a worse fate than to have one's soul stolen? To merely exist without mind or will? Or to speak and think with another's voice?

"How did this happen?" Lord William logically came back to the core of the problem.

"As best I could piece together, each of the victims had encountered a known sorcerer from Persia. A necromancer. We had no proof to bring him down. His Holiness Pope Pius VIII managed to have him exiled."

"Are we dealing with the same sorcerer?" I asked. Stamata and the dwarf hailed from Greece, much closer to Persia than we were, but still far removed in geography, culture, religion, and language. So I dismissed them from my list of suspects. Dr. Jeremy Badenough would know more.

But he, too, numbered among the missing.

"I doubt it. The Persian was an old man at the time, over eighty. From the transcript of interviews with him, I gathered that he saw the end of his life looming and hoped to reinvigorate himself with the stolen souls of young people, preferably virgins, both male and female."

"Our victims are young..." I couldn't vouch for

virginity since I knew most of the girls had been street walkers, the girls I sought to help with real jobs and a modicum of education and manners.

We all bowed our heads a moment, each seeking solace in our own way.

My mind jerked back to the ill-translated book about necromancy in Persia. Could the original have been written by *the* Persian?

A connection? Jeremy had said that Lord Ruthven— a decidedly English lord but with ties to India—had asked him to decode the tome. A bad translation of a bad translation did not lend itself to decoding. One would have to go back to the original.

"Rejuvenation? Seeking eternal life? That has been a source of evil in the name of science, and of religion for time out of mind. And no one has succeeded." Lord William pounded his thigh with an emphatic fist.

A vision of how Drew explained the awesome wonder of necromancy flashed before my memory with a painful jolt. "Power. If not endless youthful vigor, there is power in the ritual taking of a life."

Lord Byron had said the same, oh, those many years ago. He'd begun torturing cats and dogs, and elevated to people while still in his teens. I'd never witnessed it, but I heard his speeches to Shelley, my Miss Mary, and Byron's *inamorata*, Mary's stepsister Claire Clairmont.

"But the taking of the soul? Not the life, just the God-given unique and wonderful soul?" Rigby said.

Power. Life. Soul. Not the death of the body, the death of the soul.

Another vision of the Greek dwarf attached to wires and crystals and other arcane paraphernalia that transferred the soul of Percy Shelley, and possibly Lord Byron, from a body to a Leyden jar for storage.

Then to another body until they found one with a connection to the original. I'd be willing to bet a year's profits that Byron had been in and out of the jars dozens of times, waiting to get his tendrils into Ada, or one of her children.

"Why preserve the soul without the body?" I gasped at the horrible thought. "The necromancer wants to use the soul for something else. Maybe not to practice transference to another body, heaven forbid, but for power . . . power. What purpose is power except . . . as fuel for something that gains more power?"

"The light weapon," Rigby said, eyes wide with new understanding. "An angry soul—and a soul stolen from a living person rather than a dead one would be much more angry—could fuel a light."

"Enough angry souls could wreak havoc," Lord William added.

My thoughts twisted through my own anger and outrage. Toby and Violet stolen off the street. Toby didn't have an angry bone in his body, except when frustrated that he couldn't *do* something he felt important, or find the right words, or please me the way he thought he should.

But Violet did. She'd worked hard to overcome the stigma of poverty and prostitution as her only option to earn enough money to survive. I'd helped give her a future, but she'd fought hard to gain that possible future. Her angry soul would fuel a dozen torches.

What of the other girls stolen from the streets—ladies of the night who had lost everything, dignity, family, honor . . . They were more victims to despair than anger. Miss Abigail was a young virgin from a noble family with prospects of a brilliant marriage. Now, even if her soul returned to her, she was ruined. At best, if she healed, she would find herself a spinster aunt, merely tolerated by her respectable family and locked in an attic or tower room when "good" society came calling. Her anger would fuel two dozen torches.

"Lord William, I believe our villain has failed in finding power in the souls and deaths of the street girls. He has had to step up the quality of his victims."

"That makes sense. Miss Abigail was not the only gently bred girl to disappear in the past few days. She was the first, and the first to return."

"Why have I not heard of this?" Reverend Rigby nearly shouted before I could.

"The Cabinet ministers and senior nobility thought it best to prevent panic. Can you imagine the chaos if every well-born daughter was whisked away from London to the safety of country houses mere days before the coronation?"

"Chaos indeed. Possibly a postponement. Does our villain wish the postponement? Or does he wish it to go forward with every important personage in the nation gathered into one building at a specific hour?" I asked.

The black balloon had hovered over Westminster Abbey and shot its light cannon. Practicing? Finding its aim? With the new railroads bringing in spectators from far and wide, an assassin could easily escape merely by blending in with the crowds.

News of an assassination would spread quickly, deepening the chaos, and further inhibiting investigation. Inspector Witherspoon was right to be worried.

"What are the arguments for murdering our queen at her coronation?" Lord William asked. He progressed from pounding his thigh to drumming his fingers on it. I knew him well enough to know that his mind whirled almost as rapidly as his wife's. But while she worked with the precision of theoretical mathematics, he sought logical solutions to imprecise politics and history.

Reverend Rigby fingered his beads, also thinking deeply.

"Who is to say she is the target?" I asked the most illogical question of all, but in a strange way it made much more sense.

Rigby froze, his forefinger poised over one of the big decade beads. "Many people packed together. Few isolated enough to target. Except at the altar, at the moment of crowning. The archbishop!"

"That explains why so many young men, students and clerics, are immersing themselves in the literature and legal reports on the Great Reform Act. Her Majesty is not the target. The man who did not condemn the reforms is." The blackmailers knew why and accepted his reasons for silence rather than a resounding no vote.

So the current necromancer was not privy to the scandal, and why the archbishop had not voted no.

"I petitioned copies of the work from you, Madame Magdala, because so many other clerics wanted Church library copies that I could not commandeer one. Research to help defend His Grace. The students, though . . . could they be recruits of our master criminal? Doing his research for him?" Rigby mused aloud.

"I don't understand," Lord William said.

As quickly as I could, I explained the provision against necromancy in the act. Howley couldn't condemn the entire act, or he'd lose the provision against necromancy.

The issue of the archbishop secretly supporting the act to avoid revelation of a scandal I kept to myself. Rigby and I exchanged agreeing nods to keep that part quiet.

Rigby jumped in to mention how a few tried to argue that Howley had betrayed his Freemason brothers by *not* denouncing the reforms and that since the Freemasons had not come out for or against the new laws they must therefore condemn the archbishop.

The carriage slowed, and I heard a snort of released steam from the horses.

"Flawed logic," Lord William said. But he leaned forward with interest even as he checked outside the window to see how close we were to his home. Or to see if anyone listened to our conversation.

"We are dealing with a flawed man," I said with contempt. "Anyone who embraces necromancy is deeply flawed in mind and soul. Logic does not enter into the equation."

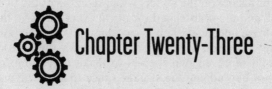 Chapter Twenty-Three

INSTEAD OF RETIRING TO my bed when Lord William's carriage finally took me home, I changed to a threadbare day dress and engulfing apron, then set about kneading the dough the girls had mixed the night before and set to rise. By the time Lucy and Emma descended from the attic room, I'd given it a second kneading and shaping.

Lucy had taken extra time to coil her hair in a complex knot at the back of her head with enticing tendrils curling down to her jaw in front of her ears. The height of fashion. I didn't have to wonder who she had primped and primed herself for.

"I doubt Father Rigby will grace us with his presence today," I whispered to her as I passed up the stairs to the café. He probably had no more sleep than I did and faced an equally grueling day.

As the kitchen filled with the enticing aroma of baking, I carefully wrote down a new recipe for Emma, down to how the dough should feel beneath the fingers before baking and the tint of the pastry when it was done.

Mickey wandered in from his adjacent cubbyhole. He didn't like the feeling of a lot of open space around him when he slept, (and who could blame him after living most of his life on the streets with predators of the two-legged and the four-legged variety at every turn). So the tiny alcove lined with shelves gave him just enough room to stretch out on a thin mattress beneath the bottom shelf. I'd removed two shelves to make that room for him, not begrudging the storage space to know he was safe at night.

"Did you sleep at all?" he asked me, feet spread and hands on hips in an authoritative stance.

"No. I spent most of the night in service to Her Majesty on a matter that I will not discuss." I returned to dusting some French puff pastry with powdered sugar and cocoa.

"Well, then, shouldn't you take yourself off to bed and let us run the shop in your place. As you trained us?"

Oh, my. I'd created a bit of monster in the eight-going-on-thirty-year-old tyrant. I'd tamed him of his feral ways, brought him indoors, and started teaching him. I should have known better. I usually found apprenticeships for the boys *elsewhere* when they reached this stage. Kit Doyle would never be ready, and I expected him to run afoul of Inspector Witherspoon any day now. Then he'd either face a judge and transportation for his crimes, or become an informant for the inspector.

I didn't like the thought of Mickey facing those alternatives. And he'd shown no talent for any craft, other than grinding coffee beans and ordering me about.

"Well, Mickey, since you seem to have settled in and made this your permanent home, I have a better idea."

"Don't know as I like the sounds of that," he said suspiciously, backing toward his own private space.

I'd have a devil of a time getting him out of that cubbyhole if he wedged himself in.

"I am going to teach you the fine art of bathing." I grabbed his shirt collar and held on for dear life.

Fortunately, the cloth was relatively new and still strong. His struggles didn't tear it.

"You . . . you mean get everything wet. At once?" He sounded terrified.

"Don't worry. I won't let you drown."

"With all me clothes off at once? 'Tis indecent."

"Not indecent. Healthy. You know the rules. If you stay, you have to be clean. All over. Every inch of you."

Behind me, the girls giggled at his discomfiture.

"Seems to me 'twasn't too long ago, you girls gave me the same arguments. Now back to work. I expect everything ready for opening before we finish."

I dragged the boy down another level toward the bathtub beside the boiler. Nice hot water right to hand. Soon I'd have the money to install the pipes to take the same hot water up to my own bathing chamber.

Much screaming and a few attempted kicks ensued. "I am bigger, stronger, and smarter than you, young Mickey. You will do this, or you're back out on the streets and out of my employ forever." I foiled his plot to escape this cruel and unusual punishment by grabbing his bare foot and tipping him backward into the tub. He came up spluttering, but quieter.

Then I handed him a cake of soap and a washrag. "You know how to use them. Do it, or I will. Your choice." Politely, I turned my back on him, arms crossed and stance wide enough to shift my balance to any direction should he choose to run. I doubted he'd do that since I'd confiscated his clothes and thrown them into the laundry on the other side of the boiler, beneath the chute from the upper levels.

I had a woman come in once a week who washed and pressed the clothes. I don't know how she did it, but my petticoats always came away from her hands, crisp and sparkling clean without damage to the '*Broidery Anglais* and less sturdy lace. And the hems of my gowns never showed traces of the mud and dirt one was forced to march through on the streets of London.

When the sounds of splashing and dipping became more playful than angry, I reminded him, "Hair, neck, and behind your ears."

"My hair? Water will ruin it!"

"But soap will restore it. Now wash, and make sure you don't get any suds in your eyes. You'll cry the whole day through if you do." Mickey thought himself too big and grown up to cry anymore.

More splashes and splutters. I counted to twenty, slowly, and handed Mickey a bath sheet. "Dry off every inch of you. Even cracks and crevices you don't normally think about. Those are the worst if left wet and chafed by clean nether garments."

A mumbled mutter came from the depths of the towel. Then a prolonged silence. Very unlike Mickey. I risked a peek over my shoulder. His head emerged from the enveloping folds of white cotton. I opened my eyes in wonder at the cherubic white skin with pink cheeks. Water had darkened his hair, but I thought it might dry to a comfortable dark blond with auburn lights. A handsome child after all, now that I could see the real Mickey beneath the dirt and grime.

Then his nose started wrinkling in puzzled sniffing.

"What?"

"I don't smell like me," he said.

I couldn't tell if he was disappointed, pleased, or just surprised. "Actually, now you do smell like you rather than dirt and sewage."

"All I can smell is soap."

"Which is what polite folk smell of." I started rummaging through the clean clothing on shelves behind the tub and came up with suitable linen and outer clothing. He'd have to make do with the shoes he'd been wearing until I found or bought another pair for him. Now that he was eating properly and regularly, he'd start growing more rapidly than I could keep up.

He leaned forward and took a long smell of me. "That is very impolite, Mickey."

"How else are we supposed to tell who's really who beneath the soap and smelly flower stuff?" He shrugged. "You smell like you. Lucy and Emma smell like the café, baking and spices and sugar and coffee. Me, I'm not sure. But I guess I can get used to it."

"Um . . . in polite society we rely on appearance and voice."

"Easy to lie that way."

"Of course it is. So we become very observant to how they hold their body, blink their eyes, or touch their ear, and listen to the undertones of the words."

"But we still need to smell people to know where they've been, what they've eaten, and maybe what they are trying to hide. Like that toff what come the night of your salon."

"Which toff? Many came."

"The slimy man what brung the man with the withered hand."

My blood froze and every muscle stilled in preparation to flee or fight. "Lord Ruthven."

"Yeah, him. Only he didn't smell like a regular toff. The bloke pretending to have a withered hand smelled like normal people: soap and food and horse and stuff."

"What did Lord Ruthven smell like?"

"Whitewash."

Immediately I was back in my father's dairy before I turned sixteen and was sent off to serve at the big villa rented by Lord Byron that year without a summer. Cold. Whitewash always smelled cold, with an undertone of damp earth; even on days with blistering heat, whitewash smelled cold.

The book on Persian necromancy insisted the

workspace must be kept clean and the floors, walls, and
ceilings whitewashed to keep them so. Stamata had
whitewashed the cellar she used as a laboratory.

The warehouse where Lord Ruthven had temporarily
hidden his captives had been whitewashed.

What was he whitewashing now?

Was Drew with him? Helping in the nefarious rituals?

I shuddered and left Mickey to drain the tub of grimy
water and dress in privacy.

Questions about Drew burned in my belly without relief.
Food, even my finest French puff, tasted like sawdust. I
went about my duties as proprietor of the Book View
Café by rote, as if one of Lady Ada's automatons.

Drew had been my lover for many years now. Everyone expected a comely and vigorous young man of title
and wealth to take a mistress. His wife had not welcomed
him in her bed since they had conceived their son,
shortly after their marriage. Indeed, she'd suffered hor-
ribly during pregnancy and labor and now lived the life
of an invalid. I asked my network of spies, and three servants who befriended Fitzandrew's servants confirmed
that Lady F never left the house, accepted few visitors
other than the parish priest and her family, and only
moved about when she could lean on the stout arm of
the housekeeper. Her son had turned seven last month.

Many times Drew had asked me to become his true
mistress, dependent upon him for income, and living in
one of his houses. I'd fiercely clung to my ability to support myself with my café and my salon. I had purpose
and reasons for living on the fringes of society, outré
enough to appear flamboyant and attract the adventurous to my side. People confided in me and didn't ask
questions when I associated with the Rom or rescued
guttersnipes. They welcomed me at the opera and ballet
and accepted my fashions with a lower neckline, deeper

lace, higher hems, brighter color, and more feathers and gems in my bonnets and hairpieces.

I liked my life.

But I loved Drew. There. I admitted it. I loved him and would have married him if his inconvenient wife ever succumbed to her illnesses—real or feigned.

Was it my fault that he dabbled in unpleasant hobbies like necromancy because I refused to always be at his beck and call?

Polite society might blame me in this. I could not take responsibility for his actions. I encouraged his jewelry designs and clockwork toys. I did not push him into necromancy.

He was a younger son with too much money and not enough responsibility. He found adventure where he could, pushing ethics, morality, and legality a bit further every year.

I was not responsible for his behavior.

And yet I loved him.

So if he were not Lord Ruthven's partner or apprentice, then where was he?

He had not appeared at my salon, nor had he been seen at the opera or theater, or any of the parties, galas, or musicales we frequented together or apart.

Where was he?

My answer came five days before the coronation. The sun had not yet set, but teatime had passed and the dinner hour approached. I'd ushered the last customer out the door and locked up. While Mickey and Philippa cleaned up (she succumbed to her first bath the day after Mickey told her she'd be safe in the tub), I showed Emma how to garnish and carve a haunch of mutton that had been roasting in the back of the oven all day with potatoes and carrots and new spring peas. She needed to learn to cook more than just biscuits and scones.

I looked up sharply as a tap on the back door barely reached my hearing. My legion of urchins reported in at odd times, frequently when they knew I had a meal ready to set out. Maybe one of them had spotted Drew.

Drew himself slithered through the barely opened door, looking back up the steps to the courtyard and alley. Fatigue lines deepened the hollows beneath his cheekbones, sagged beneath his eyes, and drew his mouth into a dark frown.

"I haven't much time," he whispered quietly, eyes darting anxiously right and left, never settling on anything. Or anyone. Not on me.

He hadn't shaved in several days and his frock coat looked rumpled, as if he'd slept in his clothes.

My helpers all withdrew, deeper into the kitchen so as not to appear to eavesdrop. But I knew they would. I'd taught them to do that.

"What?" I asked quietly, keeping my distance when all I wanted was to throw my arms around him and kiss away his distress, to offer him the bath and bed he obviously sorely needed.

"No matter what you hear or see, don't believe all of it. Nothing is as it seems right now." He kissed my cheek and darted back out the way he'd come.

He smelled of whitewash.

 Chapter Twenty-Four

THOUGH MY HEART GREW heavy and sank toward my gut, I turned a blank face back to my helpers who all leaned slightly forward as if to capture every last nuance of my conversation with Sir Andrew Fitzandrew.

"I see you have begun carving the roast. Let me show you how to angle around the bone for the most tender meat," I said, anxious to divert attention away from me and my recent visitor.

"What's you going to do, Missus?" Mickey asked, tugging on my skirt. He let his fingers entwine with my apron, clinging to me as he never had before.

My heart stuttered and swelled with long suppressed emotions. I gulped and swallowed, then ruffled his silkily clean light auburn curls.

"In the morning I shall send a note to the archbishop to see if he learned anything useful from his interview with Dr. Chaturvedi."

"What . . . what about Father Rigby?" Lucy asked. Her eyes grew wide and her chin trembled.

"If he is still resident with the archbishop, I suspect he will deliver the reply." I bent my head to the roast and proceeded to serve up dinner for my family.

The scent of whitewash lingered.

When the kitchen was clean and tomorrow's bread mixed and set to rise slowly overnight, I excused myself from the others and retired with a glass or two of wine intent upon trying to read once again The Book. I desperately needed to know to what depths Sir Andrew might have fallen.

Search as I might I could not find it. Not on my nightstand, not in my private parlor, not in the semiprivate parlor or anywhere else above- or belowstairs. I even went so far as to let the machine search among its shelves for the tome. Perhaps I'd absently returned the book to the chute when tidying. Or one of the girls had.

Nothing. The machine clacked and rotated and circled for many long moments before sending only a whoosh of hot air down the chute.

The book had gone missing.

When had I seen it last?

In Father Rigby's hands the night I first met him.

I tried to remember if he'd returned it to me or laid it on the side table. The wine clouding my brain held the exact memory hostage.

"Lucy?" I called up the stairs to the attic rooms.

"Yes, ma'am?" She appeared at the head of the steep steps, still fully clothed and hair still tidy. Did she have a clandestine rendezvous?

I shook off that thought. I would not suspect her of anything until I had more proof.

"Have you seen the big book with the blood-red leather cover? The one Dr. Badenough returned as unreadable?"

"No. You had it last." Her color remained neutral and her eyes stayed fixed on my own. She did not lie. I knew my girls and could tell when they did. "Did you look behind the cushions of the settee? You sometimes put a book down and it slips down when you change positions."

"Not this book. It is much too fat for that." I had to pause a moment to measure the next words I knew I must speak. "Has anyone been abovestairs of late?" Meaning, had she brought Father Rigby up here secretly to continue their courtship?

"No, ma'am," she replied just a little too hastily and firmly, as if she'd rehearsed the line until she considered it true and I could not detect, for certain, the lie behind it.

I dismissed her and returned to my search. Just in case, I did search between cushions and behind furniture.

The book had completely disappeared, and Father Rigby, special agent for the archbishop, had been the last one to touch it. If, indeed, he truly was an agent for God's representative in our Church, and not a consummate liar pretending to work for the archbishop. A year on the streets between cosseted home and expensive schools instilled a lot of survival skills and bad habits.

I wished I could ask the archbishop directly if Rigby were indeed the illegitimate child of his wife. I couldn't. We'd trusted each other for a brief time while we worked on his treatise. Since then, we'd rarely seen each other and never spoken. I did not number him among my acquaintances.

I shivered and wrapped my arms tightly around myself. My confidence in judging character slid into the ether. I couldn't trust anyone anymore.

⚙️

Dr. Ishwardas Chaturvedi replied to my query about his discoveries himself the next morning. "I need a crystal," he said, leaning on the carousel of the café.

"What kind of crystal?" I asked, already thinking of the codes necessary to find a book on the subject.

"A special crystal that I do not know if it exists anywhere but mythology. The ancients claimed it rested in the center of the forehead on the statue of Kali to hold the souls of those killed in her honor." He pointed to the place on his brow where a caste mark might reside, if he still held to that rigid system. He then went on to describe density and refraction as well as the number and placements of facets.

Facets I knew about. The angle and number of them could enhance or ruin the value of a precious gem. The rest meant nothing to me, but I'm sure explained a lot to him. A flash of purple in the black satin gown of a new customer just entering the café sent my memory reeling back to the whitewashed basement of a house on the edge of the heath. A purple crystal the size of a large hen's egg dangling between the breasts of Stamata and reflecting prismatic light in all directions.

"If Kali's third eye exists, where would it be now?" I asked. Hot and cold flashed through my veins.

Ish shrugged. "I study physics, not folklore. I know more about the properties and the mineral content of the crystal I need than half-remembered tales from my childhood. I left India before I was ten to attend school in England and have not returned." There was a story there I needed to explore, but not now. Later, in privacy, when he was less obsessed with this cutting light.

"Would the minerals turn the crystal purple and be about this big?" I circled thumb and middle finger to describe the size, as best I could remember.

"Yes!"

Blood left my head in a rush. "I think I know who has it. How she came by it and where she is now I do not know."

"Then we must find her. Quickly. It is the only way I can replicate the searing light cannon."

"But that light was green."

"The operator was using a different chemical base, possibly a liquid to conduct electricity into a clear crystal. Not a pure Yuenite and unless he has discovered some new combination or alloy, I do not think his weapon will work as he planned."

"I don't know that name, Yuenite." I tasted the word, testing nuances and sources. Something Asian and beyond my experience.

"A newly discovered mineral in the mountains of northern China, near the boundary with Korea. It crystallizes quite nicely, though the raw crystals grow in awkward columns. A cultured crystal grown with clean facets is quite useful in magnifying light for close work in dark rooms. I believe lacemakers and clockmakers find it useful, better than passing light through a clear bowl of water."

"Is it becoming common?"

"Unfortunately, no. It is quite rare in pure form. Mostly it is blended with and tainted by other minerals and chemicals. The lesser, blue Kenjite is more common, but not as powerful in its magnification properties."

He gathered his hat and gloves from the sill of the carousel, very much the proper Englishman in all but the color of his skin and the exotic shape of his eyes. "Now we must find this woman with the crystal. You're certain it was a crystal and not an amethyst?"

"She referred to it as a crystal ... and she thought it might be useful in a necromantic procedure." Relief lightened the restrictions around my lungs. I had not told her to channel the electricity through the crystal. Was she intelligent enough—desperate enough—to think of that on her own? She knew how to force a soul from body to jar and jar to body—both only temporarily. But from body to body—I guessed a stronger and more permanent transfer—eluded her. She'd said there had to be a connection between the two bodies. A connection ... Oh, God, I had to warn Ada to be more vigilant and to be extra vigilant in guarding herself and her children against ephemeral invasion by her father. She knew to fear her father, but now he was closer than ever. Was he in the crystal? Perhaps it preserved the soul more completely than the jars.

"How do we find this woman with the crystal?" Ish asked, suddenly eager again.

"I doubt she resides in the house where I last saw her. She and her minions would need a safer place to hide."

"Oh." Disappointment seemed to deflate him, and he sank onto a high stool.

"But I know some people who may have kept watch, possibly followed her."

"Then let us go. Now." Energy nearly vibrated out of him.

If the crystal was necessary for Ruthven's necromancy, then I needed to make certain he and Stamata did not meet and transfer possession of that crystal.

If we weren't too late.

Chapter Twenty-Five

ISH AND I HIRED horses and rode west, much as Miss Ada and I had done a decade ago. Only that time, Ada and I rode the fine horses from her mother's stable.

Romany camps are not hard to find, if you know what to look for.

I followed the signs, much as I had the first time I tried to introduce Ada to the Romany.

An eight-pointed star above the stable door at an inn read hospitality and warm welcome then and now. I asked the right questions of a dark-haired man with gnarled hands who shoveled soiled straw from stall to wheelbarrow. A younger, and different man had worked there seven years before.

Farther along, other symbols scratched into fence posts or the way a hedgerow had been trimmed at ditch level told me whom to pass by, and who might part with information.

oO

Ever the good student, Ada made careful note of where I looked for signs. By the time we left the main road and urged our mounts onto barely visible tracks, I felt certain that my girl would be able to find the signs anywhere. Would she find refuge there, as I had? On that day, just before her fifteenth birthday, I needed to make certain the Rom knew her, and would value her.

Her mother allowed the Rom to camp on her lands and made certain they had food and medical care when needed. But she did not pass among them as I did. She stayed safely indoors, and kept Ada with her when they were near.

"This branch has been bent, by a hand," Ada said, cupping her own hand around the tip of a hawthorn in full bloom. She had to stand in her stirrups and reach higher than where a mounted man might casually brush his hand against the flowers.

"Very good, my girl." I hadn't seen that but was too embarrassed to admit it. "What does it tell you?"

"The hawthorn is a puzzling tree; while very beautiful in bloom, it hides wicked thorns that can take out the eye of the unwary. I suspect this is a warning of a trap."

Patrins.

I hadn't told her that! She'd puzzled it out herself like any logic problem presented her. Only Rom logic is different from the other kinds of logic.

"We need to ask who laid the trap and who is the intended victim," I said, trying to think in the convoluted twists and turns that made sense only to the Rom.

I scrutinized the ground for other signs, the *patrins*. We both spotted a pile of five stones atop a nearly flat and overgrown boulder. We spotted it at the same moment. Nestled amongst the ivy vines the stones remained almost invisible, especially the arrangement of twigs and bird feathers. She would have exclaimed aloud in triumph. Instead, I gestured her to silence.

Eyes wide and alarmed, she nodded slightly. "Outlaws," I mouthed.

She paled.

The *patrins* did not specify what kind of outlaws. But the symbolism was slightly off, not a band of normal criminals that plagued our highways and byways. The trap indicated someone organized enough to lay a trap. Someone organized enough to expect me to bring Ada in this direction. Someone who'd been watching the manor for more than a few days.

While dangerous enough, homeless ruffians were not the ones who sought Miss Ada and launched a kidnap attempt every year or so. I backed my horse toward a slightly wider spot on the track and turned it around. Ada mimicked my movements.

The beasts made an enormous amount of noise.

I looked around sharply, not at all surprised to see a man in a broad-brimmed hat from a century ago blocking our way. He drew a pistol from the depths of his greatcoat. Disguised as he was by the bulk and shadows of his garments I had no idea of his true size, age, or fitness. But he was tall; hunching his upper back couldn't disguise its length or how well he fit a large horse.

I cursed volubly in a mixture of Romany and German. A touch of my heel to the horse's flank sent him sidling restlessly, straining at the reins and stamping his heavy, shod feet. A big horse to fit my stature, and intact for breeding.

The best kind of horse. He'd trained easily and protected me as fiercely as he did his mares.

Ada used the distraction of my horse's movements to back hers away from the highwayman.

A second and third man appeared out of nowhere, unmounted, but brandishing old-fashioned muskets. Five stones. I was certain two more lurked in the shadows, ready to rush in and help if needed.

Miss Ada stayed in place, calming her horse with a balanced seat and quiet hand to the mane.

"I'll take the girl. You'll live if you do not interfere," the mounted man said in surprisingly educated tones.

I couldn't place his accent—which meant good schools and many years of them. Nor did his voice sound familiar. Lady Byron frequented the salons and parties of London, ever hopeful of finding a highly placed protector for Ada, royal interest if possible. I kept Miss Ada in isolation, as was expected of a girl not yet out in society. So I'd little chance to know if this man supplemented a bankrupt estate with outlawry, or was a younger son not suited for either the military or Church who'd taken to the road as his only income.

"Why?" I asked, keeping my horse restless and unpredictable.

"I'm to be paid a great deal of money to deliver her to interested parties." He chuckled.

"Enough money to overlook any sense of morality?" I asked.

This time he laughed out loud. "And how moral is it to keep a father from his daughter?" His attention on his pistol did not waver.

"You have not the accent or mannerisms of her father," I said plainly. "Lord Byron has been dead five years and more, so I can only presume you will deliver her to her grave."

"There you are mistaken, Miss Elise. Lord Byron did not die as reported."

I thought as much. His body may have died, or may not have. Either way, his spirit and his fanatical followers kept alive his memory and the hope of resurrecting him. How many had died for that? How many had become ensorcelled by the codes in his poetry?

Miss Ada declared her mathematical formulae as beautiful as poetry. Her arcane symbols might be as much magical code as her father's words.

His I could decipher. Hers I couldn't.

I shook my head free of such nonsense. Miss Ada would never misuse her math. She loved it too much.

Suddenly, with the lightest of commands, my horse reared, slashing those wicked iron-shod hooves in the face of the gelding in front of us. He snorted and squealed a dramatic challenge. Ada sent her mare prancing in a tight circle, also lifting hooves menacingly.

The outlaws backed up, too shocked to fire their weapons straight. But fire they did, in the air, into the ground, at each other.

Ada needed no other encouragement. She dug in her heel and galloped away, past the mounted man, using the horse's shoulder to push him back.

I followed, lashing out with my crop toward the eyes of the enemy horse.

We raced, dodging under branches, and jumping small obstacles. As wild a run as any fox hunt.

And then we burst free into the wide lane where it opened onto the highway little more than two miles from the manor. I turned us toward home and kept running until I judged it safe. No matter how much money he was promised, the highwayman would not dare to follow. We dropped to a walk that would give the horses a chance to breathe.

My stallion tossed his head, thankful for the gallop, and equally grateful for the easier road.

"Are we abandoning the rendezvous?" Ada asked quietly as we dismounted in front of our own stable.

"For today. My friends will have moved their camp away from the intruders."

"But I thought they were expecting us. Wouldn't they place new directions for us?"

"No. Not until the outlaws have shown their hand to either settle in or move on in a day or so." I urged my girl into the house, needing to put stout walls between us and the unwanted. Only this time the unwanted were *gorgí* and not the Rom.

○○

Ish and I traveled quickly. Within an hour, perhaps a little longer—hard to tell time by the sun this close to the solstice when daylight stretched to past eight of the clock in the evening—we turned off the road onto a narrow path that quickly became overgrown, nearly impassable atop a horse. I silently signaled Ish to dismount and maintain quiet.

I led the way, holding back drooping branches and kicking aside dead underbrush piled alongside the narrow track and spilled over to inhibit or deter casual inspection. Not *patrins*, just enough deadfall to make the path look undisturbed. For about the thousandth time I thanked my practical sense that sometimes overrode fashion. I felt safer riding astride and wore knee breeches and tall boots as part of my riding habit—less fabric to get in the way or catch on reaching brambles.

Then suddenly the overgrowth retreated, and the path became more a lane.

"I come in peace," I said, a little too loudly for casual conversation, but in a tone that would carry far in this green glade. Useless to proceed at this point. I spotted no clear path except back the way we'd come.

A giggle high among the branches off to my left alerted me to the presence of young watchers.

"Are you not afraid?" Ish asked, turning around and around, searching every shadow.

"No. If they'd wanted to harm us, they would have ambushed us back in the overgrowth where we had no maneuvering room."

"You know these people well?"

"I have helped them many times in the past." The smell of gunpowder and strong drink on men who blindly followed a French vicomte to murder an entire tribe of Rom filled my senses. I shuddered in remembered fear. I had to warn the innocent. I had to get them out of their sheltered glade and over the treacherous pass into Italy. Away from the French. Away from the Swiss, too.

Then I shook myself back into the present. "The Rom in turn have helped me more times than I can count."

Like that time with Ada. If they hadn't warned us with their *patrins*, we might have fallen prey to the highway-man and Ada's enemies.

"The Rom consider me among their wise elders and do not enforce upon me the restrictions they require of their own women. They have given me a secret Romany name, a masculinized version of one of their distant an-cestors. I may not tell it to you, or anyone, except an-other Rom. And they do not use names much."

Ah, a tiny shift of movement straight ahead. I led my horse in that direction. Ish stayed behind me, so close a less well-behaved mount would kick back at him and his own gelding.

A few yards beyond the next line of trees, the forest opened into a larger clearing that rose toward a knoll. A chuckling brook divided the open ground into neat halves. Our side of the running water sheltered horses and a few goats in a makeshift corral constructed of dead brush and brambles. The goats ate the brambles while the horses grazed the lush grass. Convenient rocks pro-vided a ford across the creek, natural or placed, I could not tell. We left our mounts with a tall young man who hid his eyes beneath a snap-brim cap and balanced our way across fast running water toward the central camp-fire.

My trusted balloon pilot Jimmy Porto sat atop a flat rock nursing a cup of hot liquid. Other rocks and stumps provided seating for a dozen men in a circle facing the fire—the coals banked against the summer warmth, but ready to burst into flame when they needed it to cook or warm them. Their coats and trousers may have grown threadbare, but they were meticulously clean.

All of the women and children had retreated along the slope of the knoll into the bardos, their curious round-topped and gaily painted wagons that were both home and transportation.

Jimmy nodded toward an older gentleman, perhaps in

his fifties, judging by his grizzled hair and the lines around his dark eyes. I nodded to him with proper respect for an elder and a leader. He alone would decree if I stayed or left immediately.

"Old friend, you may join us," he said in Romany.

Ish cocked his head in puzzlement. "Some of those words sound familiar, but his accent is strange," he said in English.

The Rom all smiled in a knowing way.

"Perhaps because we share distant ancestors," Jimmy said in his perfect English with only a hint of an exotic accent.

"But I'd heard you hailed from Egypt. I am not Egyptian," Ish protested.

"And neither are we. But the popular belief serves us as well. We remain mysterious and apart to suit their prejudices. This allows us to retain our culture and language." The elder pulled out a pipe and fragrant tobacco. So did the other men.

As part of the ritual of joining, I sat next to my friend Jimmy, with Ish to my left, and accepted a puff from his pipe. My breeches allowed me to associate with men where Romany women were excluded. In their eyes, I was female and yet not. I was a friend and a visionary. A savior and hero.

Back in 1818, I worked in the kitchen of a French vicomte while Miss Mary and her son stayed in a slovenly inn in the village. I listened more than I worked and found evidence of a loose association between the local lord and Lord Byron. The vicomte owned *all* of Byron's books, even the secret ones. I learned much, including plans to murder an entire tribe of Rom gathered for a reunion. The vicomte had gloried in his plans to watch the light of life leave the eyes of small children.

Half a mile ahead of the marauding necromancer, I'd urged the Rom to flee in a mixture of French, Italian, German, and English, not yet having learned their language. In the organized chaos of women throwing things into the bardos while men caught and hitched the horses, I'd taken one of their sturdy little mountain ponies and ridden back toward the enemy. The moment I caught sight of the wavering torches and shouting men, I showed myself and headed north and west, away from the mountain pass. The necromancer led his besotted army in pursuit of me.

I led them a merry chase, the pony sure-footed with a smooth gait, through forests and up rocky hills. When I guessed that the Rom had enough time to flee into obscurity, I abandoned the pony, slapping his rump into a frightened run, and hid in a crevice of tumbled boulders.

The marauders stomped right passed me three times as the sharp rocks pressed into my back and my legs where I crouched, twisted, with muscles screaming for release. They'd lost much of their drunkenness, but still smelled as if they'd swum in vats of liquor. Eventually, they gave up. The pony was long gone.

At dawn, I walked back to the village and took Miss Mary, her baby, and her new husband to safety, elsewhere.

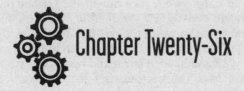 **Chapter Twenty-Six**

ISH LOOKED LIKE HE'D reject the pipe offering of his left-hand neighbor.

"Do it," I muttered to him. "One puff only. It makes you part of the group, temporarily."

Looking askance, Ish pretended to take a deep inhale and then immediately released a tiny stream of smoke on a series of hacking coughs.

Laughter rippled around the circle. When it died down, the elder—he would not part with his name easily and would not appreciate me using it—held up a crockery jug. "Perhaps this will soothe your throat."

Ish's eyes opened wide in horror.

"It won't kill you," I said and took a long gulp from the jug, then passed it to Ish. "You need only sip. But it is important to them that you do."

"I only do this for access to that crystal," he replied before tipping the jug up and pouring a little into his mouth. He sloshed it around his teeth and tongue a bit before swallowing. Then he gasped, mouth agape on a long exhale. "That is marvelous! Better than twenty-year-old scotch whiskey."

"Magic," I replied.

The men all smiled and relaxed. "What is this crystal the distant cousin speaks of?" Jimmy asked.

"The woman who held me captive and tried to drain the life out of me wore it on a fine gold chain."

Jimmy nodded in acknowledgment. "It looked valuable. I regret that we did not relieve her of the weight of it in recompense for the crime against you."

Ish blanched that we had been so close to his prize and not taken it.

"It is very valuable to one who knows its purpose and how to use it," I said.

"How much value?" the elder asked, eyes bright with greed.

"I would pay a year's salary for it," Ish said.

Raised eyebrows and whispered comments passed around the circle.

"It has mystical properties that are beyond value," I interjected lest these men get ideas of stealing it—if they could find it—and selling it to someone else with more money. Like Lord Ruthven.

Or Father Rigby.

The reverend surely would want to keep the crystal out of Ruthven's hands. If he were indeed an agent of the archbishop and had not fallen into the traps of power promised by necromancy—a year on the streets could do that to a young man. I feared Drew had fallen into those traps out of boredom.

"What is its purpose?" Jimmy brought the speculation back to where it belonged.

"It is said that the ancient goddess Kali stores the souls of those who have been murdered in her honor in the depths of that crystal," Ish said flatly. "I am a scientist and do not believe this. But others do and wish to capture souls for themselves. The crystal would aid them well in this horrible practice."

The Rom, one and all, made warding gestures

against the evil lurking within and around those words.

"Please reassure me that you are not a Thuggee," I whispered in Latin, a language I knew Ish used in his work but I doubted the Rom understood.

"Thuggee!" the elder pounced on the one word he knew. "What does this have to do with the cabal of death? What evil have you brought among us?" He half stood in outrage, ready to ban us from the fire circle. Or stone us.

"We seek to end the murderous cult that enthralls too many who seek magical power in taking lives," I said firmly.

The elder sat down. "Then we will assist you. This death cult defiles this land. If you cannot root it out and destroy them, we must leave England. All the Rom must leave England."

More than a few would have no problem with this. But I did.

"Jimmy, when we left the house with the whitewashed basement, did you leave a watcher behind?" I turned my attention on the young man.

He smiled with a flash of teeth and then quickly hid it. "You know me well, Madame Magdala. Your enemy is our enemy. Of course we watch." He paused a long moment, staring into the depths of his cup. Long enough that I wondered if he used the swirling liquid to induce a trance as I did. "We followed her as well."

I sighed in relief. "And where is she now?"

"Her creaking wagon is overloaded and ill constructed. She makes her slow way toward Nottinghamshire."

"Lord Byron's grave is in Nottinghamshire." I did not realize I'd spoken aloud until I heard my own words.

"Can we intercept her?" Ish demanded.

"We need to ride now to do so," Jimmy said, standing and looking across the brook toward the corral. "But your horses are old and too slow for such a journey."

"We hired them since we do not own beasts of the magnificence of yours," I said.

Jimmy shouted orders in Romany to the young man tending the livestock. With a curled upper lip, he replied that, yes, he'd return the horses to their owner, if they lived long enough to make the journey, and that they were not much good for anything but glue.

"You, Madame Magdala, may ride my horse," the elder said. He gazed fondly at a tall white stallion who snorted and stomped at the prospect of a good run.

"Oh, my. He is awesome. I fear my skills are not up to managing him."

"He will not throw you. As long as you hold on tightly," Jimmy replied on a grin. "As for your friend, we have an aging mare who has speed, but she is lazy and used to teaching youngsters how to sit on her back with and without a saddle."

"I beg your pardon," Ish retorted. "I ride quite well and own a decent steed, but I keep the gelding in a stable near Oxford where I live." Something I did not know about him. "I come from a long line of noble Hindi who live a-horseback."

"We'll see about that. You will ride the mare anyway as we have few extra horses with the stamina to make this journey." Jimmy stalked off toward the corral.

"Wouldn't your balloon be a better and faster conveyance?" I really did not trust that stallion to not throw me into the first ditch.

"My father does not approve of my balloon," Jimmy said softly. "And the basket has little room for extra people to help us at the other end of the journey."

"You know me, Jimmy Porto." By invoking his name, I gave myself a level of power over him. "We need only you, me, and the scientist. I will not be fooled by her tricks again. I hold a grudge against her and her purpose. That grudge fuels my strength and purpose."

"Balloons are expensive," the old man said sternly. "We have no extra coin to buy fuel."

Jimmy's shoulders slumped. He would not defy his father.

"I can pay for the fuel," Ish said.

Jimmy straightened with hope. The leader narrowed his eyes, assessing what else might be gained from this deal.

"He'll pay a crown for the fuel and Jimmy's time. No more," I insisted. If Ish wasn't careful, he might find himself "adopted" and responsible for the upkeep of the entire clan.

The old man eyed me keenly. I stood firm, holding his gaze as an equal.

He backed down just before I blinked.

Jimmy bowed to me. "As you decree. Hurry, we must fly now, while the wind is in our favor." This time he held his huge smile, revealing all of his teeth, including the gold one I'd bought for him to replace a rotten and aching one. He still owed me for that favor.

∞

We had to walk a mile to a clearing large enough for the balloon to escape through an opening in the canopy of deeply green branches. The contraption looked strange, the cloud-gray envelope neatly folded over the equally drab wicker basket. I'd flown with Jimmy several times, but always, I met him in an open field with the balloon fully operational. This collapsed monstrosity looked devoid of function, or functionality.

Fortunately, six men had followed us and set about unfolding the cloud-gray envelope and laying it flat on the ground, stretching it to its full dimensions, and setting up a burning brazier to force hot air into it.

Ish seemed to know the principles of the thing and helped the men sort ropes and fix sandbags to the basket.

I did what I do best: stood by and watched, making careful note of each step so that I could remember most of it.

In a short amount of time, the balloon had risen, like a misty ghost reaching through the canopy toward the stars. It strained against the ground ropes, anxious to loose itself from the bonds of the earth.

"Everybody in!" Jimmy shouted, gesturing me forward.

Ish bounded into the basket with a huge grin on his face. "I've always wanted to do this."

"Men were not meant to fly with the birds, only shoot them down," the elder warned. I hadn't noticed him within the shadows of the first line of trees.

A shiver ran through me at the portent in his tone. He had the gift of sight. I'd known it for as long as I'd befriended this clan. They knew I had the sight. That common bond had forged early acceptance between us. Mutual respect and genuine affection had nurtured acceptance to grow into true friendship.

"Come, Magdala," Ish called. "We need to hurry. She has a week's head start on us."

"He is one of us, yet not one of us," the elder said directly to me. "He suits you better than one of my boys. Keep him safe." Then he faded into the forest like a wood sprite or a gnome from ancient fairy tales.

Jimmy had joined Ish in the basket. They both offered me a hand to help me clamber over the high wicker walls.

"Cut her loose," Jimmy called to the men scattered around the clearing. As one, they pulled the lines from their stakes and cast them free.

The basket rose willingly, following the straining need of the balloon. We drifted away from the earth in an easy glide. The first branches of the surrounding trees passed beneath us, then the swaying treetops. I looked up and over the obscuring forest. The Thames sparkled in the afternoon sunshine, a silvery road through the heart of England. A southerly breeze pushed us northward, away from the dark smudge of coal smoke that cloaked the city on all but the windiest days.

Ish opened four sandbags, one from each corner, letting the contents dribble downward to balance our weight. We shot higher, faster than our first casual drift upward. The world grew smaller and smaller; it was like looking at a terrain map of a battlefield with all the miniature soldiers ready for a great hand to push them into place.

The wind blew stronger at these levels, but we felt none of it as we flew at the same speed. We moved faster and faster toward our destination. I turned to look where we headed, leaving behind where we'd been.

"What do you hear from Dr. Badenough?" I asked Ish, to fill the time. Even at the speed of the wind, we could only travel the distance to Nottinghamshire over the course of several hours.

"Jeremy? Why nothing. He stayed in London." He sounded as alarmed as I felt.

"I received a note that I do not think he actually wrote, saying he regretted not seeing me again before returning to Oxford."

"Does this have something to do with that blasted Persian book?"

"Possibly. The man who delivered the note has ties to the man Jeremy read the book for. It is indecipherable, too many bad translations." I began to consider the many roles Reverend Morton Rigby played in this little adventure.

Nor did I mention that the book had gone missing, much as Jeremy and Violet and Toby had.

I had checked Father Rigby's credentials both with one of my guttersnipes who had begged a slice of bread from the scullery maid at Lambeth Palace, and with my own contact within the home reserved for the archbishop. Not all of my spies are street urchins and guttersnipes. The undercook in the archbishop's kitchen (a former orphan I had trained as a spy as well as a baker) assured me that Reverend Rigby was special assistant to Howley. He matched the description of the man I knew, but he seemed to have no specific duties and was absent from the palace as much as attending the archbishop. All of that fit.

But, could that be just one of his disguises? Which was the real man and where were his true loyalties?

He knew too much about the Persian sorcerer and the book about Persian necromancy. He had handled the book last before I noticed it missing. I'd expect him to know about those since he investigated the cult for the archbishop. But he'd quoted a passage from the book *correctly*, as if translating from the original, not the Latin or English mangling of the text.

I wondered if he'd done those translations himself, deliberately distorting the words to keep European practitioners from using the book, or possibly to set himself up as the *only* authority on the subject for his own purposes: to recruit warped or bored young men with a fascination for death and magic.

"I can see your mind spinning, Madame Magdala," Ish said quietly. "What plots do you weave?" He placed his warm hand atop mine, comforting and comfortable. We'd been good friends as well as lovers for several years.

Was I ever this comfortable with Drew? Not really. Intimate yes, but the spark and sizzle of our bodies always kept us from settling into familiar routines that worked well together without making demands upon each other.

"No plots, just trying to make sense of puzzle pieces." I smiled at him, grateful for his concern.

"Do any of the pieces fit together better for the deep mulling you do?"

"Some. Others keep flying off into other puzzles that don't belong, and yet I know they would fall into a proper place if I could find the missing pieces."

"Perhaps when we find the crystal, more will make sense."

"Perhaps. But it also opens the question of where Stamata found it and whether she knows how to use it as either a weapon or an artifact of necromancy." A chilling thought—colder than the wind at this elevation—almost buckled my knees as I gazed far into the distance seeking answers. "What if Lord Byron found the crystal and used it upon himself? What if he inhabits the crystal?"

"You said she needed the Leyden jars for that," Jimmy added.

"The wires led from the dwarf to the jars and they sparkled blue with electricity. But she claimed the dwarf contained the soul of Percy Shelley, not Lord Byron. And she clutched the crystal most possessively. Proof to me that Lord Byron's soul had never resided in the dwarf. So many of her actions were merely a ruse to frighten me into revealing the design for the original transference engine, the only certain way to keep a soul in another body without a blood connection."

"From what I know of the poet king, he would die once and for all rather than accept the imperfect body of a dwarf," Ish snorted in disgust.

"My thoughts exactly."

"Miss Elise?" Jimmy said hesitantly, pointing toward a flurry of movement on a bit of open road below us. "Looks like we've been spotted. I'm taking her up!"

He pulled on the lever to send more hot air into the balloon. At the same time, Ish released more sand from the bags.

"More!" Jimmy said as misty clouds enveloped us.

A musket ball whizzed past my ear at the same time the cracks of several high-powered guns exploded beneath us. I ducked to a crouch within the basket.

Ish followed me, clutching his upper left arm. Blood oozed through his coat sleeve and between his fingers. His dusky skin grew pallid, and his eyes rolled up.

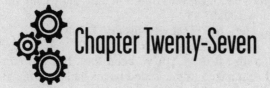 **Chapter Twenty-Seven**

"**D**ON'T YOU DARE COLLAPSE on me. There's no room!" I shouted to Ish, forcing my voice to penetrate his instinctive retreat from the unexpected that brought pain and an unbalance to his logical life.

"Them were no muskets, Miss Elise," Jimmy muttered, frantically working the ailerons and the burner.

"A lucky shot?"

"Aye. Fired from one of them new American guns. A long barrel with rifling for accuracy and smokeless powder."

Six more shots followed in a rapid barrage.

I crouched lower, ducking my head between my knees. Ish's head lolled right and left.

"Damme! A repeater. Heard about experiments with them," Jimmy said. His body stretched to peer over the side of the basket without loosing his hold on the now flapping and out-of-control ailerons.

"Curiosity killed the cat," I reminded him.

"Aye." He twisted ropes and pulled levers. The burner flared, and we rose higher into the obscuring clouds.

But we didn't rise as rapidly as I expected from the height of the flame.

Then I heard it. A low-pitched hiss buried beneath the sound of the hot air rising into the balloon.

"Three holes from big bullets," Jimmy muttered. "We'll fly a bit longer on a different tack. They'll not find us when we land."

"Stay alert, Ish." I slapped his face lightly.

"It . . . it hurts," he moaned.

"Of course it does. You've been shot. But not mortally." I rummaged in the lidded boxes built into the insides of the basket. In the third one I found whiskey and bandages that looked like they might have started life as a lady's fine petticoat. I folded one into a tight square, soaked it with the whiskey—took a sip for myself—and tied the makeshift bandage over his coat so that it applied pressure to the wound. I'd not get the garment off him in the tight confines of the basket. The pressure would have to slow the bleeding.

"Looks like a flesh wound. The bleeding is already slowing." I looked at the flask, took another sip, and forced a few drops of precious amber liquid between Ish's now chattering teeth.

"Cold," he said. Then his eyes opened wide and the pain glaze faded.

"Another sip and you're good to face dragons or Thuggees, or whatever awaits us on the ground."

He took that mouthful more readily.

"Did you see who they were?" I asked Jimmy as I ministered to Ish.

"Red uniforms around a cart. Possibly smugglers. They probably thought we were part of the ring come to take the goods elsewhere."

Jimmy's eyes were sharp. That was a lot more information than I thought possible from a thousand feet up, even for him. I suspected he or his kin did their part to aid that bit of smuggling.

We lost altitude with a jerk. I gasped. Ish groaned and clutched his wound. The shrouding clouds lost density.

"Sorry 'bout that, Miss Elise." Jimmy didn't sound sorry at all. At least not on my account.

I glared at him. His attention fixed on the circle of small holes in the silk balloon.

Was the hiss of escaping air stronger than the burner's ability to push more into the silk?

"I'm going to believe that you are shedding altitude quite rapidly because we have reached our destination." Ish looked a little less pale. Maybe the thicker air below the clouds was easier for him to breathe.

"Close enough." Jimmy continued to play with his controls, sensing the mood of the wind before the wind knew what it wanted to do.

And then the sun burst through, shredding the clouds like a cheese grater taken to a fine round of cheddar. Warmth caressed my face. I drew a long lungful of air in and out.

Ish mimicked my reaction to sunlight. "Is that a promise of a happier ending than the beginning?" he quipped, the corners of his mouth tugging upward.

I peeked over the edge of the basket and wished I hadn't. The ground rushed toward us at an alarming rate. Copses dotted a broad meadow full of grazing horses. The stallion looked up as we flew past his curious nose. Bare inches above his nose by my reckoning.

A bump, a drag, a bounce. Then another bump and drag. No bounce. We careened right and left, then settled squarely on the lush pasture. Mr. Stallion meandered over, curious and alert but not menacing. This was, after all, his pasture full of lush grass and his harem of mares.

"Out we go," Jimmy ordered. He grabbed my upper arm and heaved until I tumbled half out with the basket rim pressing hard on my belly.

Indelicately, I swung a leg up and managed to land with both feet flat and my balance swaying only a little. I grabbed the basket to steady myself even as I looked around to pinpoint our location.

The stallion sniffed and then lipped my coat pocket.

"And here ye be, Master Thor," Jimmy said holding an

apple in the palm of his hand. "Sorry 'tis only one of last year's that lasted through the winter. A small and pitiful offering it be, I know, to the god of thunder. Next time I'll bring you a carrot." The horse chomped down on the dried and withered fruit, nearly taking a finger with it. Satisfied with the offering, he strutted off, bragging in horse language that he'd gotten a treat and the others hadn't.

"Out now, afore the mares decide we are their missing snack." Jimmy helped Ish to his feet and over the barrier of the basket with more gentleness and care than he had shown me. But then, Jimmy knew I could take care of myself and Ish couldn't.

"Where are we?" I asked, helping hold Ish upright until his head and feet started talking to each other again.

Jimmy reached back to turn off the burner before speaking. The balloon slowly collapsed in on itself. "Road's about one hundred yards to the west. From the latest reports, I expect you'll find your Greek lady within a mile or so." He went about his chores, tending to his balloon with the same care as a well-paid groom gave to a hard-ridden horse.

I scanned the line of trees that marked the edge of the road and the hilltops for sign of a house. "Whose land do we trespass upon?" I urged Ish into movement toward our destination. He stumbled on an imperfection in the grass but righted himself without assistance.

"Someone who turns a blind eye while he be in London. Done a bit of outlawry in his day, knows the rigors of the road." Jimmy fingered the bullet holes in the balloon. "I need to patch this and then keep the burner simmering in case we need to fire up in a hurry to leave ahead of yon redcoats."

I wondered briefly if the absent lord was the same outlaw who'd tried to kidnap Miss Ada near a Rom campground ten or more years ago. A lot can change in a man's circumstances and title in that amount of time. Did I know him in this life?

I didn't think so.

Still, I kept a wary eye on all of our surroundings.

By my reckoning, the soldiers with the smugglers were miles behind us. But they had horses and accurate repeating rifles.

Unless the smugglers were actually Stamata and her cohorts and their cargo was Leyden jars filled with souls stolen from innocents, all in a vain attempt to keep alive the genius—and perversions—of George, Lord Byron, sixth baron of that title.

Ish appeared a little steadier on his feet, now that the shock and pain of his first bullet wound wore thin. I wondered briefly that his life had been so free of violence that this was his first encounter. I hadn't time to dwell on it.

Stamata and that all-important crystal demanded our attention.

"Catch up if you can. Keep the burner going and the balloon ready if you can't," I called back to Jimmy. Checking to make certain I had weapons about my person—including the tightness and fit of the bullet-proof corset—I tromped toward the road.

When we reached the tree line, I paused and peered along the road, north and south. Sure enough, I heard shouts around the next bend in the road to the north. Then came the sound of someone kicking wood, thumps and bumps of moving crates or barrels. And the grunts of men lifting something heavy. A piercing descant of a female voice rose above all that.

Jimmy must have circled south while we were in the clouds, to avoid the skirmish.

We approached cautiously, keeping just inside the line of trees where we could see the road, but the shadows obscured us. Unless our clomping feet in the underbrush and our movement attracted attention, I doubted the army men or the smugglers would notice us. Few military enlisted men, in my experience, were that observant.

Before I could formulate a plan for getting the crystal

away from Stamata, we caught sight of the red-and-white uniforms. We crept through the woods until we stood level with the wagon.

Half a dozen enlisted men pawed through trunks of clothing and laboratory equipment, ripping and smashing it all. Broken crates and traveling trunks lay scattered across the road, the pieces of one mixed liberally with another.

As I watched, a corporal used the butt end of his firearm to break a crate into even smaller pieces so that it might kindle a fire but would never protect and contain scientific instruments again.

As I expected, Stamata huddled on the bench, shoulders folded down, all the while she clutched at the gold chain around her neck. She kept her back to the sergeant who stood beside a civilian clad in fine hunting clothes, tweed knee breeches, tall boots, leather patches on the elbows of his matching tweed coat. He reached with his left hand to yank the gold chain until it broke, near strangling the woman in the process. He came up with a fine deep purple crystal held aloft for the summer sun to penetrate and send intense prisms arcing over the man's head to land just short of my feet.

His right hand remained cradled against his chest, encased in a black leather glove.

Now that I knew what to look for, I saw the lump of his right arm beneath the coat where the fine tailoring could not hide it.

"You can come out now, Madame Magdala," he said, not looking toward me.

Since he hadn't mentioned my companion, I gestured Ish to retreat toward Jimmy and the balloon before stepping onto the sunlit road.

"What are you calling yourself today?" I asked.

Three long rifles—modified from the American design that had cost Britain two wars—turned away from Stamata and aimed for my heart.

Chapter Twenty-Eight

"WHATEVER YOU WISH to call me, my dear," Rigby replied, still holding the crystal aloft.

"You must be on a mission from your primary employer," I said, trying desperately to figure out if I should trust him or not. The archbishop's name would gain him command of a military patrol. But if he truly worked for Archbishop Howley, why did he need the guise of the withered hand?

He threw back his head and laughed. "As if I would stoop to truly working for anyone but myself." Finally, he turned to face me, his visage bland.

I could determine nothing from his expression or body language.

A snapping twig deeper in the forest sent the aim of the menacing rifles toward the sound.

Silently I cursed inept Ish. Inside his laboratory with books, and arcane equipment and mathematical formulas scrawled on every viable surface he was a genius. Out in the real world he was more helpless than the youngest of my guttersnipe army of spies.

"Sorry I can't stick around to help, Mags. I have an appointment that can't wait." Rigby palmed the crystal and marched up the road to where a black lumpy shadow resolved itself into a black wicker basket straining at the ropes of a huge, black, hot air balloon.

I hadn't noticed it. I hadn't even looked for it!

I should have known better. But, like most people, I focused on the action on the ground, not the hovering presence above.

Instead of uselessly kicking myself, I dashed after the chameleon. He heard my footsteps and increased his pace, diving into the basket as Sir Andrew Fitzandrew stood up from the depths of the basket and loosed the ropes. He worked hard at keeping his face turned away, never meeting my gaze.

I knew him too well.

I leaped to follow. My fingernails scraped the side of the basket as it rose quickly. The brittle reeds embedded sharp splinters deep into the quick. I squelched a squeak of pain. I'd endured worse and would again to prevent that crystal from being used in a light-cannon, no matter the target.

Ish screamed.

The basket rose higher, beyond my reach.

I had to help Ish, a babe in the woods with no defenses.

I picked myself off the road where the basket had dumped me and ran toward Ish. The patrol of six enlisted men surrounded my poor friend, their red coats appearing dull and dirty in this light. Ish cowered on the ground, raising one hand above him to ward off another blow. The sergeant raised his rifle to slam the butt into Ish's head.

Without thinking, I drew my pistol and a throwing star, shot both guards and tackled the sergeant. My claw-like fingers yanked off his poorly sewn-on stripes. His weapon fired as we landed heavily on the ground.

"Get out of here!" I called to Ish as I slammed my fist into the jaw of the false soldier.

Three down, three to go. I jumped up and whirled to face my next opponent.

They grabbed their comrades and dragged them off, deeper into the woods to the south of us. Not true soldiers. Probably hired bullies outfitted with used and hastily dyed clothing.

Ish staggered upward, clutching his injured arm and his ribs. A dirty boot print marred his side beneath his uninjured arm. Leaf litter and twigs stuck out of his tangled hair. A bruise reddened and darkened on his left cheek.

His grimace turned to sneering outrage and he lashed out with his own foot into the sergeant's ribs. The man on the ground groaned and rolled, flailing in his stupor to prevent another attack.

I inserted myself between Ish and his target.

"Don't stop me Magdala. Don't keep me from giving this dog the punishment he deserves." He tried to sidle around me.

"No. Ish, think. Do what you do best, think, damn you. He's down, damaged, and deserted. What more can you do to him?"

"Kill him." He turned fever bright eyes on me.

Then I noticed the blood trickling from his right temple and the way his pupils dilated. He swayed and nearly dropped to his knees.

I caught him as best I could and steered him back toward the meadow. "We need to get you to a doctor," I said quietly.

"That man . . ." He waved vaguely toward the road.

"Too far to follow now. And the sun is headed toward setting. We'll catch him. Not today."

"He's got Jeremy, you know," Ish said. He stumbled against me, barely able to lift and aim his feet.

"I guessed as much. Now we need to get you back to the balloon. Jimmy will take you to a doctor."

In the background, I noted the sounds of reins slapping against horseflesh and the creak of wheels turning on weakened axles. Stamata made her own escape. Without the crystal and laboratory supplies, she could not do much to restore her lost love. She presented no threat to us. For now.

The bruises blooming on Ish's face and the flow of blood welling up from his vulnerable temple did. I checked his arm. He'd knocked the bandage loose and it was bleeding freely again. He was in trouble, despite the new bandages I applied once we were aloft.

"There," Jimmy said, pointing to a cluster of thatched cottages about twenty miles south of Windsor. The only word he'd said since we tumbled Ish into the basket and lifted off from the field with the watching horses.

Ish groaned but didn't open his eyes. He sat, slumped against a corner of the basket, head lolling.

I straddled him, one foot on either side of his knees. We just did not have room for him to sprawl his legs and leave space for Jimmy to move about as he needed, adjusting the flame and tilting the ailerons.

"Is there a doctor in that village?" I asked, more to hear the sound of my own voice than to confirm what I guessed.

Jimmy nodded.

"I'm sorry they damaged your balloon." I offered my friend the only apology I could, along with a few pennies for repairs.

He shrugged, but only with his shoulders, not his full body, and he didn't look me in the eye.

"I don't know what else to say, Jimmy. We've helped each other many times over the years. I thank you for taking us to find Madame Stamata."

"Sorry we failed," he grunted and dropped us lower. The coins disappeared into a pocket. "This is for fuel.

The crown he gave me earlier will cover the repairs." He gestured with his shoulder toward Ish in silent thanks for the money.

"I'll figure out something to stop that madman."

Jimmy grunted again, still angry about his precious balloon, but we were friends again. Then he busied himself with getting us back on the ground, aiming for a clear stretch of road just west of the cottages. He'd not willingly damage ripening grain in the fields on either side of that narrow dirt track.

Workers in those fields spotted us, paused in their weeding, and pointed at the strange contraption. This close to London, about thirty miles south by southwest, they must have seen steam devices traveling through the area. But they were some distance from the main road. I'd seen many such villages, isolated by choice as much as distance.

The smoke from the coal fires of the cities did not spread this far. Yet. It was only a matter of time.

We landed with a bump and a drag, precisely on target. The light breeze from the north threatened to dump us into a field. The curious workers leaped to steady the basket as Jimmy deflated the balloon enough to keep us in place, but not enough to ground him for any length of time. I watched the gray silk sag, much as my own tension did.

"Please, is there a doctor about?" I asked the villagers as they peered into the basket and spotted Ish, still dripping blood from head and arm. He managed to open his eyes a bit. They looked as glassy as they were bloodshot.

"Aye, Missus." One man tugged on his forelock, unable to take his eyes off the fascinating horror of so much blood.

Four other men rushed to the nearest fence and unhinged the gate. They ran back with the makeshift litter much as they'd do for a rider thrown in a foxhunt or a man accidentally shot while bird hunting.

Jimmy stamped his feet impatiently while we hoisted Ish carefully out of the basket and onto the flat boards. The men arranged his legs and feet carefully; they'd done this often. I sincerely hoped that thoughtless horsemen waited until after harvest to careen madly through the fields in pursuit of their nasty prey.

Once Ish was settled, I slung my legs over the rim and jumped clear. Seconds later Jimmy cranked up the burner. A whoosh of hot air brought refreshed rigidity to the silk. As I balanced against the wicker, it rocked and lifted. I stumbled away and nearly kicked the gate where Ish lay breathing shallowly.

Jimmy departed without a wave of farewell.

The local men each took a corner of the gate and trotted toward the jumble of rooflines in the near distance. I followed as best I could. Men started moving closer to us from the far fields. The women and merchants of the village moved into the street, more curious than wary. The jabber of their questions, and speculations, grated on my ears. All I wanted was for Ish to open his eyes and give me one of his endearing smiles.

We came to an easy halt before a cottage door that overlooked the town square—a meadow more than a village common, bigger than most with signs that sheep had recently grazed there before moving them to summer pasture closer to the river.

Alerted by the noise of conversation the door in front of us opened with a hard jerk at the same time a youngish priest made haste to join us from the tiny stone church on the opposite side of the green. He carried a Bible under one arm, his stole draped over the other and a small black box in his hands—the kind men of the cloth used to hold already blessed Eucharist wafers, wine, and holy oil. Emergency tools for any serious injury or illness.

The man of middling years who stood in the doorway assessed the situation with keen eyes and a straightening of his slouched posture. His frock coat had seen better days, but once was of fine cloth and tailoring. The same for his boots and trousers. I guessed he'd once thrived in a city and moved here to finish out his years in relative peace. And boredom. Ish presented him with an interesting challenge.

With sharp gestures, the physician waved us all in. He and I both assisted the four farmers in transferring Ish from the gate to a long metal table, akin to the ones in Stamata's laboratory. There the resemblance ended. Tools and equipment, as well as books, filled the built-in bookcases. Though scrupulously clean, not a bit of white-wash alarmed my sense of smell or my eyes.

When the farmers left with their gate and nods of respect to the doctor, Ish opened his eyes fully for the first time. He flapped his hand for me to move closer. I clasped his fingers tightly.

"Magdala," he whispered.

The doctor looked at me sharply while he felt his patient's scalp gently for evidence of his wounds and clucked his tongue at my clumsy bandages. "Magdala? The bastard daughter of a Gypsy king?" he asked in cultured tones with hints of Edinburgh behind the lilt. The Scottish school of medicine was the finest in the western world. That affirmed my guess of earlier prosperity and significant education. I felt easier about leaving Ish in his care.

"Yes. One and the same," I admitted.

"Mags. You must go, pursue the crystal. I need that crystal," Ish said, as if we hadn't interrupted the flow of his thought. "Leave me. Now. I will return to Oxford when I can."

Gently I kissed his brow. "Good-bye, Dr. Ishwardas Chaturvedi. You have been a great help and a good friend."

With that, I left—slapping all the shillings I had with me into the doctor's hand for his care of Ish and for his silence.

As I trudged out into the street, I wiped away a single tear, knowing that while Ish and I would always be friends, he was not cut out for my adventurous existence, and I couldn't allow his hesitations to hold me back. Some things I had to do, no matter how dangerous.

In that arcane manner I could never quite grasp, Jimmy had communicated with his tribe. The young groom from the camp met me on the village green with two horses and a crowd of villagers eyeing the fine horseflesh. He escorted me back to London. Jimmy and his balloon were long gone and I wondered if I'd see him any time soon. My life felt rather empty and devoid of friends at the moment.

I'd no sooner dismounted than the groom gathered up my reins and headed out of town. The horses' hooves made no sound on the cobbles. Of course they didn't. They were Romany horses and knew the value of muffling stealth.

Shaking my head to clear it of a thousand images and details, I descended the back stairs to the kitchen and let myself in with my key. Emma and Philippa were cleaning the kitchen. Mickey supervised Lucy as she counted the day's take.

Everything looked normal.

And yet it wasn't.

"Mickey, please send for Inspector Witherspoon. Tell him I need some additional information regarding a man with a withered hand." I stared down the interior stair toward the bathtub.

"I knew it!" Mickey chortled. "He's up to no good, ain't he?"

"Probably. Emma, when you finish, would you bring me clean clothes and a cup of hot tea."

"Aye, Missus. We had a good day. The shortbread biscuits with icing and a half cherry sold out twice," Lucy said.

"Good thing you taught me to make a decent short-bread," Emma said. She pulled the plug on the washbasin and toweled her hands dry. "Philippa, you be careful putting away the china," she called to the girl.

Philippa frowned deeply. "I knows. I knows. No need to keep reminding me." As she spoke, a crockery bowl slipped from her hands to crash against the tiles.

I sighed and retreated to the bathtub before Emma could take a rolling pin to the girl. They'd work it out.

For the first time in many years I found the problems of the kingdom more important than running my own tiny kingdom. Crisis loomed, and I had run out of ideas.

 Chapter Twenty-Nine

"ARE YOU CERTAIN THAT Lord Ruthven is at the center of the plot and his target is the archbishop?" Witherspoon asked as he sipped milky tea and wolfed down three jam scones as if he hadn't eaten in days.

For that matter, the dark circles of exhaustion around his eyes suggested he hadn't slept in that long either.

"I'm not certain of anything. But I followed the logic." Rigby had pushed me through to that logic. Did I trust him to lead me down the proper path?

"Well Ruthven has gone to ground, that's for certain. I've had my boys out looking for the lord and his amanuensis with the black leather gloves that never come off. Nowhere in London. Nor the beggar with the withered hand."

"Does Lord Ruthven maintain a house in London?"

"Don't think so." Witherspoon looked longingly at the empty plate in front of him.

I ignored his silent suggestion. Then my own stomach growled from lack of sustenance. "Oh, well, we might as well both eat. We'll find something in the kitchen."

"You asked for a private consultation, Madame

Magdala," he reminded me. Still, he got to his feet and held the door of my parlor open for me.

"My employees have access to more information than your entire army of runners," I said blithely and led the way down the broad staircase to the center of the café.

"And so does that library of yours."

"The most obvious place to start is the most obvious." I reached down a battered copy of Debrett's *Peerage* as we passed and continued down the stairs to the kitchen.

While Witherspoon thumbed through the pages of the thick book, I put together a tray of cold meats, cheeses, the last of this morning's bread, and some sticks of vegetables. The aroma of new bread rising in the brick cubby beside the oven that stayed warm long after the oven fires died away sharpened my appetite.

"Are you certain he's a peer?" Witherspoon asked. He shoved the open book toward me as he took possession of the cold collation. "If he's not well known in London, he could easily invent a country title and few would suspect. Except those with an up-to-date copy of Debrett's."

Before I even glanced at the page, I repossessed some of the food. "Tea will be along in a minute," I said around a mouthful of sliced mutton, cheese, and bread.

Then I looked. Backward and forward. I checked indexes and cross references.

No mention of Ruthven at all. Not a past title or a current one. No record of the name or place at all.

"This can't be," I muttered. "He was introduced to me by . . . a dear friend. And confirmed by a respected Oxford don." I flipped to the page showing Sir Andrew Fitzandrew as the first baronet of Fitzandrew with a home seat in Lancashire. I'd viewed that page many times over the years, wishing I'd taken the opportunity to visit his home, even if I had to go clandestinely and view it only from the outside.

Finally, I drew out my reading glasses and donned

them. Details jumped out at me. Details I didn't want to see.

Witherspoon didn't bat an eye at the unflattering addition to my accessories.

"Someone has removed that page with a very sharp blade. I have no way to determine if Ruthven is the family name or the name of the estate, or if they are one and the same. I have no geographical references to even find the estate." I thrust the book away and attacked my food.

"Got another copy of that book hidden below in your fancy library?" Witherspoon raised his tufted eyebrows and bit into his bread, now spread liberally with butter and jam.

I stilled a moment. "This is the most recent. Debrett's is updated frequently to mark the changes as old men die and younger men assume the titles, or everything reverts to the crown."

Therefore, I must have older copies stashed away in the stacks of books in the basement, the walls, the attics, in the next building connected by cellars, and anywhere else the great machine knew about. I took my food with me back up the shallow stairs to the café proper. After a few minutes of fiddling with the keys I had a search working for the three previous versions of Debrett's.

The machine barely hissed or rotated at all before sending three books down the chute.

"That's one good thing about having the majority of books hidden away," I said. "Only the most current and popular books remain available to anyone wandering the café. Destructive hands can't get to the older versions. Even I don't know where to find most of the volumes I own."

The oldest of the previous versions revealed only the name Ruthven as both family and title. Estate not mentioned. But the title had reverted to the crown after a seven-year search because Adam Blackwell, heir presumptive to his great uncle the eighth baron, had gone to India and not returned.

India, the home of the Thuggees and their death cult honoring Kali. The purple crystal known as the Eye of Kali. India was also a place where a man of small income might make a large fortune. Ruthven seemed to have a great deal of money if he purchased an oversized black hot air balloon and outfitted it with a cannon that shot green light.

Coincidences began to fall into place.

The next volume said that Adam Blackwell-Ruthven, ninth baron, had returned from India and reclaimed the title and the estate. Not much of an estate—three hundred impoverished acres of land, a house built upon older foundations during the Restoration, and a seat in the House of Lords. Income estimated from the land was only about one thousand pounds a year—mostly from sheep—hardly enough to keep the roof from leaking and the servants fed. One shouldn't expect more after being abandoned and neglected for seven years.

Then I noticed in the older version that the land and title came with an endowed curacy and a seat in the House of Commons. Both of those positions could be sold outside the parish for more than they were worth. But the Reform Act would have moved both positions elsewhere and out of Ruthven's hands.

"Where is the manor?" Witherspoon asked as I read.

"Devonshire. Hard upon the coast." Jane had said that Violet was headed toward Devonshire when they saw each other at the train station.

"Smugglers' caves," Witherspoon said on a nod.

"A proposed rail line through the village," I mused. Then I went in search of a map.

Fortunately, I have a bad habit of not returning books to the stacks or even the shelves in the café. My atlas of historic maps still rested on my reading table. I fetched it forthwith.

Old maps of Devonshire showed the Ruthven estate before Cromwell, and the rebuilt manor as mere dots near a no-name village. Only the most recent map showed the proposed railroad running north of the village and a wagon track—a thin squiggly line—connecting the two. This map was five years old. More and more rail lines were constructed every year.

"We need a newer map," I said.

"I'll be back here tomorrow morning at opening with the latest. We at Bow Street need to keep these things on hand."

"Best we both get some rest." I showed him out by the back stair. Then I lay down on my bed for just a moment before changing into one of my beggar disguises to prowl the streets.

The next thing I knew, Emma was creeping down the stairs to set the bread to baking at dawn.

Curiously, the new maps showed the rail line had diverted south to run through the village now named Ruthven Abbey Downs.

Abbey?

That sent me looking for listings of abbeys and other church properties dissolved during the early reformation.

It took some time and three books until I found a line drawing of a small square building from about 1500. The travel guide mentioned the three hundred acres supporting the Dominican chapter in residence. I surmised that inside the square two-story building lay an open courtyard with a covered, possibly partially enclosed, walkway—the cloister. A square Norman tower dominated one corner, the chapel. Standard. Nothing unusual. The new manor was reported to be built on the same square, but rose three stories plus attics and a modern tiled roof. No open cloister.

But the foundations were original. Ancient churches, monasteries, convents, and *abbeys* always included a crypt to bury their own dead and possibly those of local nobility and donors of large sums of money to the order.

The Ruthven family or whoever bought the property from Henry VIII after the dissolution might have been burying their own dead in the same crypt.

A crypt in an area with a lot of natural caves and cliffs on the coast. The builders would not have to dig deep before stumbling on a natural hollow within the rock.

A crypt. Jeremy had mentioned Ruthven's fascination with Crusader bones. How much more power would he attribute to centuries' worth of bones of people who lived day in and day out with a deep and abiding faith?

"I have to go there," I told Inspector Witherspoon when my brain had run through to the conclusion.

"I can't protect you there. I have no jurisdiction," he replied.

"I have my own cohorts to take with me."

Which of my information gatherers? The constantly changing list ran past my inner eye. Young faces. Clean faces. Filthy faces. The littlest ones, like nimble-fingered Maggie, might be useful wiggling into tiny places, like hidden entrances to caves, or trapdoors in and out of wine cellars. Mickey would eagerly go with me. But I'd come to value the boy more than he knew—or I'd summon him right now. The older girls needed to stay here, protected by the law as well as the constant stream of customers guaranteeing they were never alone.

That left middling boys, those who had learned discretion and invisibility on the street.

Kit Doyle, the orphaned son of a longtime servant of Lady Byron. She'd taken him on as one of her charities, but he rebelled, blaming the lady for his mother's death. So he ran wild. His loyalty to me existed only as far as the coins and food I gave him. He drifted away from me as he learned the value of violence while living on the street. I had only a narrow window of time when I must either break him of these tendencies and find him an apprenticeship, or cut him loose. I doubted I'd tame him.

Today I would use him. Tomorrow I'd let him decide if he stayed in my service or he made his own way.

"I have my resources, Inspector. I promise to share whatever information I gather." I excused myself from our table by the window and went about serving the growing line of customers. What I needed to do, I would do best toward the end of the day, when shadows crept long and no one looked too closely at an old beggar woman walking alleys in parts of town polite society ignored.

 **Chapter Thirty**

FOUR DAYS BEFORE THE coronation. London was crowded beyond reason with people from the provinces come to see their beautiful young queen, full of promise and hope, officially assume her responsibilities. Not a single room to let in the entire city and beyond. I fielded three requests from potential boarders before noon.

Customers old and new filled my café from opening to long past closing without a lull. Emma baked fresh batches of everything three times during the day. By half seven in the evening we were reduced to serving hunks of hard cheese with bread and butter. Gratefully I latched the door and put the closed sign in the window. Still three people knocked tentatively to see if I'd reopen for them. I had to turn my back and breathe deeply. I don't think we had even a hard husk of day-old bread or a rind of cheese left, and there were no coffee beans to grind or tea leaves to steep.

In four days, all of the gaiety and hope for the future could end if Ruthven and his helpers pulled off their assassination.

Time to find Kit Doyle and take him with me to seek out Ruthven's lair. I'd given up the notion of a headquarters close to London. With that big, black, hot air balloon with wide and nimble ailerons, he could fly the distance from Devonshire in only an hour or two.

Jimmy had taken his balloon elsewhere. He didn't mind spying on my enemies. Engaging them, as we had in Nottinghamshire, was something else entirely. I was on my own.

So, dressed in near rags and hunched over the bullet-proof corset—as much as I could with layers of cross warped spider silk and fine meshed electrum wire laced tight around me—with a stout stick to support (and defend) me, I made my way toward the docks Kit Doyle was wont to frequent. I rattled my tin cup—properly primed with a farthing and a ha'penny. A large party of tipsy celebrants dropped a few more coins into the cup. I made a show of biting two of the coins to make sure they hadn't passed on counterfeit. Seemingly satisfied, I moved on.

Kit Doyle remained elusive.

Anywhere I might expect a ring of pickpockets I found them. But not Kit.

I moved deeper into the slums. Victims of the kidnappers had come from this district. Some of them. Then Ruthven had lifted his sights to girls from better neighborhoods, girls with more to lose and a higher degree of anger.

A clump of dirty teens lingered in a recessed doorway. I counted noses. None of them were mine. But two of them had been Kit's companions upon occasion. I approached them with shuffling steps, leaning more heavily against my stick.

"Good hunting to you," I murmured as I passed them.

They sneered as they inspected the contents of my cup. I'd pocketed all but the original coins—no sense in tempting thieves.

"Seen Kit Doyle?" I asked, straightening my back a little. Oh, how I longed to stretch and shed the artificial hump. Instead, I clutched at the muscles above my waist, easing the cramp a bit, but enhancing my appearance of helplessness.

"Why's y' asking?" A spindly boy of about thirteen stepped away from his companions, brandishing his belligerence.

"Need his help," I replied. "Seen him?"

"Not since yesterday," a smaller boy squeaked. He hung back, pressing his spine against the building stones as if he could melt and merge with his own shadow.

The rest of the pack clamped their mouths shut.

"Where?" I asked, hoping against hope that one among them would speak up.

More silence as one of the bigger boys rammed his elbow into the gut of the one who'd dared speak.

I stumbled away, making sure my stick pounded loudly against the cobbles; signaling to them that I was not prey.

A broader avenue beckoned me. Tonight was the kind of night that bold denizens of the slums risked the light among laughing crowds of the unwary. Kit should be out there, moving from shadow to shadow cast by the gas lamps on every street corner.

A carriage rumbled past me, tilting dangerously as the mechanical horses careened around a corner. I dismissed it as unimportant. The driver was probably as drunk as the occupants, and artificial beasts had not the sense of real ones to slow down or shift their footing.

Then the bobbing black feathers of the horse's headstall caught my attention. Funereal headstalls on steam-powered mechanical horses.

Expensive.

They didn't belong in this part of town.

I hurried my steps a bit to follow. The whistling blow of steam through the tight confines of nostril tunnels didn't sound right. Just as I rounded the corner, the left-hand door of the closed carriage opened a crack and a limp form spilled out.

Macabre laughter followed the body.

One look and I knew I could not help the ragged victim. Kit Doyle's dead eyes seemed to stare at me accusingly.

I could do nothing for him, except to pay the local parish for a decent burial with a marker instead of the anonymous Potters Field. Tomorrow. In my heart I murmured nearly forgotten ritual prayers for the dead, hoping fervently that he had not suffered too much pain.

Guessing at his murderers, I knew such hope was useless. Kit was gone, and I'd never have the chance to tame him nor help him make a better life.

I gulped back a sob and leaped to cling to the back bumper of the carriage. With the footman's handhold barely within my grasp, it lurched forward. With a long blast of steam and prancing metal hooves it gained speed as it swayed around another corner.

A few awkward scrambles and I gained a better purchase, crouched on the back bumper. But I lost my stick and my tin cup in the process. Then I risked a peek into the interior through the small, round, rear window.

Adam Blackwell, Lord Ruthven, lit a cigar from the flame of a small oil lamp. Beside him, Sir Andrew Fitzandrew drank long and deep from a silver flask.

I didn't need to look further to know that the Right Reverend Morten Rigby drove the steam horses.

Knowing that these men—I wouldn't grace them with the title of gentlemen—would take me where I needed to go to thwart their plans, helped me cling to the boxy carriage. The wheels rumbled and bounced so hard on the cobbles that I could hear nothing else; could concentrate on nothing else.

After a time that felt like a month, we broke free of city streets onto dirt roads. The noise abated enough I could listen when the men deigned to talk. They didn't speak much or often. When I peeked through the window again, the oil lamp had burned too low for me to see anything but dim profiles, one on either side of the carriage, both looking straight ahead, or out the window, a good six inches between their shoulders.

We'd passed beyond the city lamps. An occasional light glowed through the window of a dwelling set back from the road. The carriage lanterns on either side of the driver's feet illuminated the road a short distance ahead. The driver would have to keep a sharp eye and firm hand on the mechanical horses. These beasts might move faster than ordinary animals, but they had no sense of their own. They didn't know road from ditch or open field. They ran straight ahead unless directed elsewhere.

"Is this enough?" Drew asked his companion. His low voice startled me out of a semi-doze.

"It has to be. We are nearly out of time," Ruthven replied.

"Who knows how much soul energy was in the Eye of Kali before Lord Byron stole it. He and Stamata added quite a bit more. Surely we've reached the one hundred deaths your instructions demand." Drew sounded weary. Or was that disgusted? No. Just tired. He didn't seem to have the energy behind his words for disgust.

"I can feel the way the crystal vibrates. We have enough. All we need is one clear shot, possibly two, not highly taxing to Kali's strength."

"What about the souls you have locked up in Leyden jars? Surely you have more than enough of those to recharge the crystal." Now Drew sounded agitated. My anger toward him abated a tiny bit. I wanted to believe his parting remark to me that not all was as it seemed. I truly did. But he'd betrayed my trust in being with Ruthven, in laughing as he dumped dead Kit Doyle in a filthy back alley. I couldn't give it back lightly.

His shadowed profile, as he turned his head to stare out the window jolted another memory. A highwayman wearing a broad-brimmed hat, sitting astride his horse with an easy seat, pointing a pistol at my heart as he demanded I turn over Miss Ada to him.

My lungs felt as if I'd pulled my laces tighter and tighter again. I nearly lost my grip on the carriage. He'd whispered hoarsely then, disguising his voice so I didn't recognize him when we met again in London at Ada's coming out.

Had he turned adventurer because of boredom? Or had he been building his fortune to live beyond the generous allowance provided by his father?

I wanted to cry.

But I couldn't. For Kit and Violet and Toby I had to follow through with this and bring down Sir Andrew Fitzandrew along with his friend Adam Blackwell, Lord Ruthven.

"Those very angry young women must fuel the kinetic galvatron. The souls stored in the crystal will focus the death ray." Ruthven sounded smug. "I'd feel safer with a few more young women. The Gypsy girl, though, shows promise of more anger energy than five of the others. She shall incite those gone dormant and lead them in a bolt of electric power." He chuckled.

His laughter masked the sound of my gasp. Reva. Jimmy's missing sister.

Ruthven had lured the girl away from the protection of her family, probably with the promise to teach her to read, the one thing her father and brothers had denied her in a culture that honored their women by protecting them from outsiders—controlled them to the point of suffocation of intellect.

"Archbishop Howley doesn't stand a chance of surviving," Drew said flatly.

The carriage jolted and tilted slightly. A wheel had gone through a pothole, hard and fast. I wondered if the driver reacted to the conversation inside. He slowed, for whatever reason.

"Rigby, are we there yet?" Ruthven called, leaning out the window.

"Nearly, sir," came the muffled reply.

Firming my grip on the footman's handle, I leaned out as well. Ahead, lights glittered and a hot fire glowed eerily red. I heard the chug of an idling steam engine and smelled the acrid stench of burning coal.

Rigby slowed the steam horses to a walk, then turned the carriage so that the doors faced the engine—a tidy little beast with a coal car, a passenger lounge, and a baggage car. The shed that served as a station looked dark and abandoned.

Rigby turned the carriage over to a silent groom in dark livery, then clambered aboard the engine. As I watched, he twisted and shifted his shoulder, hiding his good right hand and extending the prosthetic. His sinister left hand remained dexterous and strong.

Drew and Ruthven ignored him while they boarded the lounge. The moment the door closed behind them, I scooted from my hiding place onto the landing behind the baggage car. I had to cling tightly to the iron railing when the engine jerked us forward into the dark night, without even a glimmer of moonlight peeking through the clouds to light our way.

 **Chapter Thirty-One**

THIS LATE IN JUNE, we had very few hours of darkness. The little engine chugged through the night taking us farther and farther away from the lights of London. I began to wonder if Ruthven had allowed himself enough time to perform his last hideous ritual, assemble his equipment, and fly the black balloon back to the city on schedule for the coronation.

I also began to shiver. My ragged clothing was just that, ragged. A cold moist wind off the south coast cut through threadbare cotton like a knife left in the ice-house. It found every rend and split seam, worming its way inward until it touched my skin.

I pondered the warm glow of the firebox next to the engine. Even Rigby with his extra hand would be hard put to keep the fire burning hot enough to maintain this speed and drive. Who assisted him? I couldn't imagine either Sir Andrew or Lord Ruthven getting their hands dirty shoveling coal, or even throwing firewood. I dared not climb to the roof and thus make my way to the front, even for the reviving heat.

When my teeth began to chatter, I pressed myself against the door to the baggage car out of the wind on the platform. Much to my surprise, the latch jiggled invitingly.

A little extra pressure and it swung inward. I paused, listening before crossing the threshold. If anyone waited inside, I could not hear voices, breathing, or shuffling over the sounds of the steam engine or clicking rail noise.

The train lurched as it took a curve too fast. I stumbled backward, into the car and bounced from one crate to another that caught me across the middle. Air whooshed out of me as explosively as the steam whistle. I ricocheted in another direction and landed on my behind. The next crate slid toward the wall with me following.

Someone cursed inside the lounge, a low grumble of words just barely discernible over the click of metal wheels on the rails. Then the rattle of one door opening that also released a bar of light across the platforms and around the adjoining door. The light crossed my boot toes.

I scrunched my body as small as I could manage, knees to chin, arms wrapped around them, head down. The back of my thighs ached from the unnatural stretch. My heart beat faster, sounding as loud as the chug of the engine.

The inside door rattled and screeched as it slid inward, bringing with it more light and the sound of approaching footsteps.

All the while, the car rocked back and forth, as if still recovering from the too rapid curve.

My stomach rebelled.

But I held on, wrapping shadows around me as if they were a thick blanket on a cold night.

The man retreated. I didn't need to hear his voice or see his face. He had the stance and posture and breadth of shoulders of Sir Andrew. Ruthven could never aspire to that magnificent body. My Drew. No, not my Drew, never again my Drew. I had to lose any sense of intimacy with him.

And never would I share that body again. Drew had chosen to side with the most heinous of villains imaginable.

The light disappeared as the door closed. I heard a

rumble that might have been voices, but I couldn't be certain.

A better hiding place seemed my next move. Fighting back panic and grief, I resolved to finish this adventure. The little bit of light had revealed two rows of wooden crates, now partially scrambled, with an aisle down the middle of the car. Some of those crates had shifted, but they hadn't crashed into each other or the walls of the car. I could navigate if I moved slowly and felt with toes and hands before taking each step.

Carefully I inched my way upward, using the crate behind me for leverage and balance. Another tilt and surge of speed sent me sprawling across the aisle. Sharp pain stabbed my left elbow, turning it numb. I nursed the hurt with pressure while I bit my lower lip to keep from crying out.

The train slowed and the whistle screeched. By my jumbled sense of time and a glimmer of light around the edges of the doors, forward and aft, I guessed that our destination neared as early dawn approached, roughly half four in the morning.

Frantically I searched for a place to hide. The back corner behind a jumble of tools and tarps looked promising. Moving cautiously with arms stretched for balance—and the better to grab something should I topple again—I took one step, two, then three and ...

Stumbled over an imperfection in the floor. My toes didn't recognize the shape or purpose. I crouched and then dropped onto my knees that still stung from the last abrupt collision with the floor.

The train slowed even more, smoothing out the ride. I didn't have long.

My fingers found the shape of the imperfection. Cold, smooth, metal caressed my fingertips. I traced out the shape of a handle. Then I found the crack outlining a trapdoor. I grasped the brass and heaved upward. It didn't budge. Locked.

But if a door, or escape hatch could be locked, then it

could be unlocked. No keyhole presented itself to my examination. But I found a longer, wider crack than the trap. I barely had room to reach my fingers in, but once past the initial blockage, the space opened up enough that I could feel underneath. This time I lifted a short lever, and the trap swung downward to reveal some kind of platform. Not much room for me to hide. I swung my legs into the opening and dropped down.

The dawn grew brighter, red light beneath the retreating clouds, promising a sunny day with a warm breeze.

I had enough light to examine my new hiding place. Metal cross bar, a folded support post. And the platform was nearly as wide as the train car. With wheels!

The floor of the baggage car reverberated with heavy footsteps. I pushed the trapdoor back into place, feeling it click shut. Something else whirred and my "jitter" dropped down to the rails as the train rushed over the top of us.

I held my breath and counted to one hundred.

o⚙️

As much as I had traveled around Europe on trains and by carriage pulled by steam horses, I had never encountered a jitter I had to propel myself. I'd seen railway crews pump the handles up and down—usually one fore and the other aft—to propel them from one bit of maintenance to another. This one was folded in on itself and the wheels tucked flat over the top of the platform.

Not operational. I searched for a lever or something that might open a box with tools.

I needn't have worried. After a full minute, an unwinding spring whirred. Slowly the wheels stretched out and down, coming to rest upon the rails themselves. Sensible. It had to remain flat and within the rail bed until the mother train passed. Once settled on the rails, the crossbar and support column unfolded. Only one crossbar, so this must be intended for a single operator.

And I was the single operator. Someone had kept the jitter well oiled and maintained. The bar pumped easily after the initial attempts to persuade the vehicle to move out of its sleeping state. Up down, up down. I fell into the rhythm despite protesting arm and shoulder muscles. Soon my lower back and thighs began protesting the unaccustomed movement.

I'd been awake most of the night and worked a long day in the café before that. But I had to see this through. No one else was available to thwart Ruthven's plans. He might only be interested in exacting revenge against the archbishop for some perceived slight. I had to look further and know that if Howley died before the conclusion of the coronation, then Victoria would not legitimately be queen. Distant relatives and older nobility of the realm could easily step in and demand she step down. The Duchess of Kent and her lover could demand a regency. Chaos would ensue. Possibly civil war. Probably the end of Britain as we knew it.

I pumped harder.

The train had been slowing when I escaped. Presumably, we neared our destination.

Up down. Up down. I ignored my aches and pains and kept going. For once I appreciated the confines of my corset. The tightly woven layers of silk and wire mesh supported my aching muscles. If a bullet or blade should manage to penetrate, the compression would also reduce bleeding and swelling. Mostly I'd bruise badly at the point of impact as the cross-warp layers absorbed and dissipated the energy of the projectile. Covering me from mid-breast to below the hip, it protected all my internal organs.

How would it perform if Ruthven unleashed his weapon of searing light?

I didn't like the name he'd given the weapon, kinetic galvatron. It sounded doubly ominous.

I pumped the jitter harder. Someone had to stop him.

The sun came up in a glorious riot of pinks and oranges. Dew sparkled on every blade of grass and branch of gorse. Tiny flowers in yellow, pink, blue, and multiple shades in between winked at me. Wild roses tangling with themselves on the berm released their heady perfume, inviting bees and such to share their nectar.

I kept pumping. Nothing mattered but the constant up and down motion.

My vision began to narrow as it did when a trance enticed me inward. I let the otherworldly images flow through me. This might be important. Knowing some symbolic piece of the near future could save my life, and that of England.

A slender figure in white, crowned in gold and diamonds marched solemnly around and around the circle that my inner eye perceived. She lifted her chin with pride, nodding and smiling to those who greeted her. Muffled bells sang a joyous litany of celebration. A smile spread through me. I was on the right course to ensure the successful crowning of our queen.

Other figures, dark and angry, skipped asymmetrically out of synchronization and out of harmony with the proud queen. Slowly they made inroads on the queen's path, forcing her to walk in ever narrowing circles. They pulled light away from her, snuffing the aurora of her magnificent crown.

Then, with a snap, my vision cleared and returned me to the jitter and the monotonous pumping action.

The rail line curved inland and disappeared into the dark maw of a looming hill that rose high and plunged low down a cliff to the waves that lapped a narrow beach. A square building sat atop the hill.

I had to hurry.

But I had to proceed with caution. Reluctantly, I slowed my pumping, letting the jitter's momentum carry me forward. As I cleared the arching cave entrance, I pulled up on the brake lever. The jitter slowed noiselessly until it slid to a stop within inches of the back landing of the baggage car I'd abandoned.

The growing daylight outside had veiled my perceptions. I noticed little change in the amount of light from outside to in. Then it hit me. The cave should be dim, even if the four oil lamps I counted had been placed right in front of me instead of against the far wall where the steam engine's nose nearly touched the rock.

The smell of damp earth struck me before realization. The entire cave had been whitewashed, including the rails, ties, and gravel bed. The paint reflected and compounded the little bit of artificial light.

I stepped off the jitter and it immediately began winding its spring, folding in on itself. Once the wheels were in place, a magnet beneath the baggage car drew it inward. With a click and a snap, the cart nestled into its normal place attached to the struts.

A brief touch of the cool cave walls, rough and irregular, told me that much of this opening beneath the mountain was natural. But not all of it. Someone had enlarged the natural hole with tools, smoothing the walls so that the whitewash adhered more evenly.

Some of the white paint rubbed off on my dark rags. The work had been completed recently.

A natural cave beneath an ancient abbey that had become a more modern manor.

I heard no voices or movement within the cave, only the slow tick of the boiler cooling and the steam chambers emptying.

Why whitewash this engine barn if the only exit was back the way the train had entered? I searched for an opening that led elsewhere. Whitewashed wooden stairs, complete with handrail blended into the white on white background. My eyes slid over them twice before I noticed that the sharp angles didn't quite fit into the natural curves.

I crept up the eight steps, cautious of creaking wood

that might betray me. The carpentry was new and solid, taking my weight easily. At the landing—long and wide built to maneuver large equipment—an arched opening, without a door, led inward. More whitewash and oil lamps placed at odd intervals.

The tunnel curved right and then left, inclining slightly upward as it wound into the heart of the mountain.

Low voices, in deep male tones drew me on. I pressed myself against the wall so that I'd cast no shadow in the uncertain light. This section had been plastered long enough ago that little of it transferred to my skirts.

I thought a long moment about how the steps had been hidden in plain sight by the illusion of the same color. My outer rags and boots might be mostly black and dark forest green, but my petticoats, corset, and stockings—my own normal underthings—were bleached and starched white.

Quickly I shed the top layers and shivered a bit in the cool damp. My pale hair, face and arms still held too much color. The ruffles of my topmost petticoat provided a sheer veil I could see through. I wound the long strips around my head and draped them artfully over my shoulders and arms, like an elegant shawl. I hoped this was enough obfuscation for my purposes.

Sidestepping carefully, I pressed my back against the wall and crept forward at an upward angle until the tunnel suddenly opened into a wide room, also whitewashed. On all sides, the walls were lined with niches, each about six feet long and three high. Five in each tier. Four across on each wall.

Skulls and bones lay jumbled together on the lowest rows of funereal resting places. Five or six skulls to each. The upper levels had been cleared to make room for row upon row of clear glass Leyden jars. Hundreds of them. Colored clouds in angry red hues roiled within each.

I'd found Ruthven's crypt.

 Chapter Thirty-Two

I DREW SEVERAL shallow breaths, not daring to take more of the damp-tasting air, lest the slight sound and movement of my lungs alert the enemy arrayed around the room. Three men only. No fourth groom to stoke the firebox of the engine.

In the center of the domed room, where a funeral altar should stand on a slight dais, three metal tables on wheels sat in a neat row. The one closest to me contained a sheet-draped body. The far one was empty but for a shrouded lump that contained no human shapes, or pieces thereof. I did detect a long rounded shape that could have been a skinny arm. I suspected more likely the barrel of a weapon.

In the center lay a naked girl with masses of dark hair, struggling against wrist and ankle restraints. A metal band attached to long copper wires waited to encircle her brow.

Reva. Jimmy's beloved sister.

I'd been in her position and seethed at the indignity as well as her potential demise. Not even a sheet to cover her, a small grace Stamata had granted me. She needed only my body, not my anger and humiliation.

Drew and Rigby faced the necromancer where he

presided at the head of Reva's table. Ruthven's back was to me. I prayed that if either Drew or Rigby noticed me, they would make no sound or expression of recognition.

Ruthven concentrated on the dark flush of anger on Reva's face. "Ah, my beauty, you shall enhance my army of tainted women in powering my lovely gonne."

Cautiously I took one side step into the cavern, keeping my back as close to the wall as possible. Silently, I slithered closer and closer to the array of Leyden jars and the red sparking along the copper wires.

A rustle of my skirts, or a brush of my arms against a wire, I'm not certain what caused Ruthven to look up.

With a lifted eyebrow and a cruel smile he greeted me. "Ah, Madame Magdala. I'd hoped you would join us. You shall complete my triumvirate of anger to fuel the kinetic galvatron."

oO

Just because I shed my outer garments didn't mean I shed my weapons as well. Before I could think about it, a throwing star flew from my hand and landed precisely in Ruthven's right shoulder.

He screamed as he yanked it free along with a well of blood. "You shall pay for that," he sneered. Then he righted himself, absorbing the pain as fuel. "Blood for blood. The Persian promised that the necromancer's own blood triggers the spell much more efficiently than all the angry emotions of the victims. The spell will be stronger for my blood mingled with yours." He flung the sharp metal back at me.

I grunted with the impact of metal against metal. I felt as if he'd jammed his fist into my gut. I bent double expecting a warm trickle of blood. But the star dangled uselessly from where a point snagged on the wire mesh embedded in my corset.

"You need to put more strength into it," I taunted him, still bent double, as if he'd truly hurt me.

He didn't pause to gloat but leveled a small pocket pistol at me. I had to stand to make certain the corset did its job in protecting my vulnerable torso. But, oh, Hades, it hurt to do anything but curl around the bruise in the region of my belly.

Ruthven pulled the trigger before I completed my shift in posture.

I screamed from the sharp slash to my chest. Impact spun me backward, around, and down. I let the bullet's momentum take me to my knees. Then I fell forward in a controlled slump. Gasping against the pain.

"Magdala!" Drew screamed.

Dimly I heard him thrash.

"Leave her. She's dead meat. Unless you care to join her and fuel the gonne with your outrage?" Ruthven said calmly.

I crawled beneath the foot of Reva's bier, keeping three pairs of legs in view. Drew and Rigby shifted uncomfortably from foot to foot. Ruthven remained hideously calm.

Reva grew still, no more weak thumps and bangs against the metal table as she thrashed against her restraints. But I heard her rasping breath. She lived. From beneath the table, I yanked on the straps binding her feet.

The star dropped free with a gentle ripping of fine cloth and clanked on the floor, chipping the whitewash.

"You've contaminated the whole process!" Ruthven yelled in outrage at the marring of his perfectly clean and bright floor. He bent to watch me as I reached to free Reva's other foot. "You're supposed to be dead or dying. What an amazing creature you are. Your soul will strengthen my spell beyond the addition of my own blood."

I grabbed the table legs and shook them. Ruthven jerked up and banged his head. Hard.

He withdrew with a grunt, hands clasped to the top his head.

Rigby used the distraction to dive for the shrouded object resting at the head of the empty bed. He grabbed it with his left hand, still not revealing the mechanical nature of his hidden right limb.

And Drew, bless his heart, *my* Drew yanked all the copper wires and glass tubes free of some infernal machine—also whitewashed—that pumped and groaned in the corner.

Ruthven pulled another gun. A revolver fully loaded. We froze in place. My fingers worked anxiously at Reva's wrist restraints while I assessed Ruthven's intentions. He waved his pistol with the huge bore at each of us in turn and back again. His eyes narrowed and his lips thinned. An ugly sneer of disdain crossed his face.

"Do you honestly believe you can thwart me?" he asked. Too calm. Too focused.

I watched his eyes for clues. They'd tell me when he meant to pull the trigger before his hands did.

Not a flicker. I don't think he even blinked. Slowly he moved the gun back and forth until the barrel pointed at Reva. Shivering, naked, and tied down, she was vulnerable. An innocent girl with everything to lose.

Anger flashed in her eyes as she set her chin and twisted her wrists. If only I could get her free . . .

Then I spotted it. A simple button on the side of the table. I stretched the middle finger of my right hand as far as I could. Not far enough. Was I quick enough.

"Don't even think about it," Rigby said.

I looked up with a lie on my lips and determination in my heart.

But he had his strange weapon, a collection of bulbs and crystals and barrels pointed at Ruthven's heart. Not mine.

Ruthven turned his head and his gun at Rigby.

Then, and only then, did Rigby thrust his undamaged right hand out, through a slit in his greatcoat. He held the magnificent purple crystal. The eye of Kali that held the captive souls of those sacrificed to the goddess.

Possibly the soul of Lord Byron, the poet king, as well.

Ruthven gasped and made half a step toward his foe. All the while patting his pockets for that crystal. "How did you . . . ? You gave it to me days ago."

"And stole it back an hour later," Rigby smiled without mirth. Slowly, deliberately he seated the crystal between the fuel bulb and the head of the barrel.

That must be the kinetic galvatron, the monstrous weapon that shot searing light at great distances.

With Ruthven's attention elsewhere, I slammed my hand against the button. Reva's headband snapped free with a clang as it bounced against the far side of the table.

Ruthven lunged at Rigby, taking him to the floor where they wrestled and rolled for control of the gonne.

Drew clattered with the connections and machine behind me. I hadn't time or attention to spare him.

I grabbed the sheet from the dead body on the other side of Reva and threw it over her. She had one hand, her head and feet free. I trusted her to help herself.

But my eyes sought the face on the body.

Toby!

My precious moon-faced boy who performed every task I asked of him without question. The small boy inside a man's body who loved cleaning my stoop because it pleased me. His innocent blue eyes stared sightlessly at the white ceiling, mouth agape with his last scream of pain and frustration. I knew that scream. I knew his anger, blind rage when frustration and his own limitations kept him from doing what he wanted to do.

Toby.

More clatters and clangs behind me. I had to turn away from my grief for now, as I had with Kit Doyle, though this gaping hole in my gut felt larger, like my very being seeped out of me.

Toby's death damaged me more than a throwing star and a bullet ever could.

With renewed resolution and determination, I turned back to face Ruthven. I had to stop him from murdering more innocents for his own senseless revenge. For his own perverted, selfish, vile, sense of justice.

My own anger roiled and I whirled to face him, a scream on my lips, my hands curled into claws.

The light in the room changed. I saw red everywhere, swirling and stabbing. I winced against the fiery glare but felt no heat.

Drew backed away from the machine toward the obscured white stairs that spiraled upward toward a white trapdoor.

Rigby and Ruthven rolled on the ground, still wrestling for control of the kinetic galvatron. I pulled my tiny, one-shot gun from the back waistband of my petticoat. All I needed was a few seconds of a clear shot at Ruthven's head.

Swarms of red light blinded me. Spiraling into a tighter and tighter vortex. The light generated a cold wind that drew me toward the center, compelling me to join the core of the light storm.

Rigby noticed the change and rolled free, flailing for balance, eyes wide with horror. He tried to rise to his knees. The lights pushed him back down.

But the necromancer had better tools at his behest. He chanted a fierce litany in an ancient language with the liquid syllables of Ish's native tongue. The blood on his shoulder thickened and clotted before my eyes. He gained strength with each word.

Rigby's hold on the weapon weakened.

Ruthven rolled to his feet in one graceful move worthy of the best opera dancer. He had his kinetic galvatron in hand and aimed it.

"No!" Drew and I screamed at the same moment. He leaped and took Ruthven down in a flying tackle.

The gonne rumbled and hissed, emitting a long shaft of green light. The red light in the room screeched in accompaniment.

The green light caught Rigby's hand as he tried to cover his eyes with his arm. His dominant left hand.

He screamed.

I kicked the real gun away from where Drew fought Ruthven to the ground, flat on his back, hands pinned by his head. The kinetic galvatron skidded across the floor, the purple crystal worked free of its slot and slid across the floor to stop at my feet.

I bent, painfully, to grab it and hide it in my cleavage.

The red lights continued to roil around and around concentrating on Ruthven.

And then I knew what Drew had accomplished while I dealt with Ruthven and Reva.

He'd broken the hundreds of Leyden jars, freeing the trapped souls. Hundreds of angry women concentrated their life's essence into a furious mass. As one, they formed a spear of red light that pulsed with green and yellow and blue. Together they plunged into Ruthven's open mouth, his eyes, his ears, up his nose. Like a swarm of bees they buzzed and whirred as they took possession of his body. His skin mottled back and forth with the bright jewel tones of his invaders. His teeth turned green while his hair took on the hue of fresh blood. Blue pinpoints of light sprouted like whiskers from his face.

Drew flung himself away from the necromancer, lest he be caught in the fury of Ruthven's victims.

I could not hear Ruthven's screams. The shouts and curses of his victims drowned him out with a fury akin to a stormy sea crashing against broken cliffs. In their last act of life they invaded his mind and yelled abuse at him using his own voice. He flailed and struck at his eyes with his own fingers, digging and plucking, driving him blind.

Driving him mad with hundreds of tortured voices bent on destruction inside him.

 **Chapter Thirty-Three**

I SHIVERED as the cold damp of the cave penetrated my bones. Wrapping my arms around myself offered little comfort, so I turned my back on the man who had threatened the stability of all Britain with his perversions. Then I bent and attacked my petticoat with a small knife. In seconds I'd freed several yards of cordage designed to stiffen and shape layers of delicate cloth.

I handed the silken rope to Drew, with my back still turned to Ruthven. "Restrain him lest he do himself more damage," I said curtly. I had to swallow hard to keep from crying.

Crying for lost Toby and Kit Doyle, for Violet! For damage to Reva, for all the deaths Ruthven had caused, for Drew's betrayal of all I thought he held sacred and moral, and for . . . for whatever Rigby was or did that I could no longer trust him.

"You never cease to amaze me, Magdala," Rigby said. His respect sounded grudging. He stepped away from me and entered the din of Ruthven's madness.

I responded by turning my attention to Toby. I owed him a respectful burial, alongside Kit Doyle. I owed him more, but there was little else I could do for him now.

"He won't live long," Drew said as he stuffed

something into Ruthven's mouth to keep him from biting off his own tongue. "Not even in restraints in Bethlehem Hospital."

"That's what happens when you transfer souls without the permission of the victim," I replied, remembering in detail what Stamata promised me.

A fate that might have been my own if Jimmy hadn't rescued me from Byron's last lover, so that I might rescue Reva, his sister.

Her exposure, both physical and mental, to the outside world and the eyes of strangers meant she was dead to the Romany community. But they still loved her and honored her. I owed it to them—I owed it to *her*—to take care of her now.

No one could replace Violet, but Reva would take her place at my side.

Keeping my eyes averted, I went to her. More resilient than I expected, she sat up on the table on her own and worked to drape the sheet around her. Holding her head high with a straight spine, and a determined thrust of her chin. Then her mouth opened and her dark eyes grew wide. She pointed at the other table.

Toby twisted and jerked. He blinked his eyes and turned his head, fixing his gaze upon me.

"He was dead," Reva whispered. "I watched the life leave his body. That man did not even give him the respect of transferring his soul to a jar. Your boy saved my little brother. He deserved more. He deserved better. That man killed him just because the boy was annoying," she sobbed. She wouldn't name Ruthven. He was dead to her and to name him might awaken his ghost to haunt her.

She jumped down from her table and hurried to Toby's side, brushing tangled hair off his brow and whispering soothing words.

Toby's throat worked as he tried to form sounds. That surprised me. Toby didn't speak much because he forgot proper words for things and what he said rarely matched the images in his head.

I went quickly to his side and held his hand. He blinked again and again as he focused upon me. Then he squeezed my hand.

"Toby?" I asked. In this bizarre cave with arcane equipment of death, anyone, or anything could reside inside my boy.

"J . . . Jeremy," he croaked dryly.

"Dr. Jeremy Badenough?" I gasped in wonder.

"At your service, Madame Magdala." He nodded in respect, not able to sit up on his own yet.

"Not Toby? And he is Toby," Reva protested.

"You were in one of those jars?" I blurted out.

"Yes," he breathed, then swallowed, trying to force moisture into his mouth to lubricate speaking. "Water?"

Drew approached with a flask and touched the mouth of it to Jeremy's lips. "Not water. But something to jolt you back."

Jeremy took a sip, then sighed in relief. "The water of life."

"Whiskey," I finished the thought for him.

"Rigby needs a doctor," Drew said quietly.

I glanced over his shoulder to see the priest sitting up, back against the funeral niches, cradling his crudely bandaged hand against his chest. His face twisted in agony, as pale as death. And he panted shallowly. Not good.

"Can you drive the train?" I asked Drew. I couldn't look him in the eye. Guilt formed a hard and heavy knot in my belly. I'd doubted and questioned him.

"I can," Jeremy piped up. He sounded quite chipper.

But then Reva held his other hand as she bent to kiss his brow. "My hero," she whispered. "You sacrificed yourself to save me."

"Jeremy or Toby?" I asked, just as quietly.

"Jeremy tried to save me. Toby was a hero before

that." Reva straightened still clutching her makeshift toga about her. "That one," she pointed to the writhing and choking Ruthven, "wanted to rape me to enhance my outrage. Toby was already dead. Jeremy broke free of his bonds and attacked Ruthven. He died for his efforts, and the others put his soul into a jar."

I stiffened.

"How . . . what atrocities did you commit while trying to gain Ruthven's confidence?" I asked Drew, finally raising my eyes to his.

He said nothing, merely turning to help Rigby stand and supporting him on the short trek to the idling steam engine.

An outlaw at heart. From highwayman to necromancer. What else?

Reva helped Jeremy off the table. He and I checked Ruthven's bonds as we lifted him to his feet. His ravings quieted to muttered foul words, whether his own or provided by those who possessed him, I did not know. Then we escorted him to the baggage car of the train that would shortly leave hell.

 Epilogue

"I HAVE ASKED His Grace the Archbishop to re-assign me to a parish," Rigby said quietly when I visited him in his quarters at the episcopal palace a day and a half later.

"Is that a good or a bad move?" I asked. I sat primly on the edge of a hard wooden chair a proper three feet from his bed. A simple monastic room, with minimal furniture and stark in lines. A prie-dieu in the corner beside a window supported his open prayer book. I could picture him crawling out of his bed with the crisp white linens and thin blanket to spend hours on his knees. He'd have to prop his damaged left hand on the slanted surface as a constant reminder of what he'd done. What he'd *accomplished*. And how he'd managed it.

I imagined he had more than a few sins to atone for in his quests to bring down necromancy for His Grace.

"For me, it is good news. It is time I left the field of clandestine work. The sinister side of me has been burned away." He glanced ruefully at his heavily bandaged hand resting within a substantial sling.

"Does it hurt much?" I had to know how much he'd sacrificed for his work.

"No more than my conscience."

Ouch.

"You had a right not to trust Sir Drew." He looked up at me then. I could not read his emotions.

"I doubt he will see it that way," I said on a deep sigh. My one regret in this mess was that I'd lost my love. He hadn't spoken to me since leaving the cave of white-washed death. Not one word on the long journey home, not even a note to say he'd arrived home safely or delivered Rigby to the tender mercies of the archbishop and his physician. Nothing.

This was worse than the loneliness when I didn't know where he'd gone or what he was doing.

"No. I doubt he understands himself well enough to realize what he was really doing," Rigby said. He shifted his gaze out the window to the inviting green leaves of a willow. "Fitzandrew entered into partnership with Lord Ruthven with the good intention of stopping his plot. And he ended it well by aiding you in destroying his weapon."

"But in the middle . . . while he sought to gain Ruthven's confidence?"

"Let me say, that if you hadn't come to rescue the girl, I doubt Sir Drew would have done anything to stop Ruthven. He appeared deep in the thrall of the power necromancy offers. Such a lure can make a man justify any action to gain it." Rigby dropped his head back into his pillow and kept his face turned away from me.

"He has long sought adventure skirting the laws of man and God. A normal and productive life was never enough for him." I had to look away and blink hard against new tears.

"Even his affair with you was risky. You skirt those same laws, but with an aim to correct wrongs in our society. He sought only to tear holes in the fabric of life as he tore through it."

"And you?" I asked. Did I truly want to know what

atrocities he had committed in trying to root out the enemies of his faith?

"When I have recovered my strength and have settled in to my new parish, I would like your permission to court Miss Lucy."

Whatever he had done in that cave of horrors was between him and his God. He'd work it out eventually. For good or ill.

"If my Lucy will have you, that is her decision. I presume the archbishop and his wife love you enough to make certain your parish can provide you with a decent living."

"His Grace has given me a large bonus for my years of work, which I have invested carefully. He also recovered part of my inheritance from my adopted parents. I can provide for a wife and several children."

"Then, my only proviso, as Lucy's protector, is that you tell her everything." I set my chin in determination.

"Everything?" he asked bleakly.

"Everything."

He drew in a deep gulp of air. Then nodded. "If that is my penance, I accept."

"Your penance is not mine to dole out. You have to figure that out for yourself."

"Will you take Sir Drew back if he does a similar penance?" He speared me with a penetrating gaze, determined to drag all my secrets from me.

"I don't know."

"What will you do in the meantime?" His face cleared of strong emotion. His boyish smile tugged at his lips and lit his eyes.

"I shall apologize to Ish and let him return to his safe and solid life in Oxford. He does not appreciate adventure as we do. I shall destroy the kinetic galvatron when Ish has finished examining it. I have taken Jeremy back to the Book View Café where he uses the guise of the simple, moon-faced boy sweeping my stoop as a means for gathering information. It is amazing how people ignore those less fortunate and presume that because Toby is simple of mind, he won't repeat their gossip. In private, he is looking forward to working with my book catalog—he is a most excellent librarian—and courting Reva. She looks upon him favorably."

"What will happen to Reva? She can't go home."

"No, she can't. By Romany law she is contaminated and dead to her family; though they still love her and honor her memory. I shall attend their funeral for her. So Jeremy and I shall teach her to read, as she wants, and she shall help me run the café because Lucy is soon to leave me for you." I breathed deeply. "The time has come to bring Maggie into the fold, to train her for something less nefarious than life as a pickpocket. My little family of ragamuffins is growing."

He smiled brightly. "And tonight?"

"Tonight I bake and cook a feast for after the coronation. Tomorrow, you are welcome to join us, if you have the strength. I shall close the café and take all of my helpers to view the celebration of the peaceful transfer of power from one monarch to another. And we will dance in the streets with thousands of others to celebrate the peaceful continuation of Britain as we know it."

Special bonus material!
Please enjoy

DANCING IN CINDERS

by Julia Verne St. John

Dancing in Cinders

March 1835

I THOUGHT ABOUT LIGHT and glass frequently
that ... interesting ... year. Watery spring sunlight
drifted through the rain-spotted windows of *Café du
Paris* on Charing Cross Road in London. The shaft of
yellow light from a beleaguered sun through thick mul-
lioned glass windows turned my *café au lait* to shimmers
of gold that enticed me to look deeper into its depths,
find truth in the whirlpool I made with my spoon.

Not now. I couldn't afford the time or distraction of
getting lost in the swirls and patterns of my coffee. Deliberately, I put down the spoon and sipped. The coffee master had to be French or Italian. One of the few things the
owners had done right was to hire him. I didn't trust any
Englishman to serve a decent cup of anything but tea. Or
maybe beer, though the Bavarians did that better.

And I didn't trust the ruggedly handsome fur trader
sitting at the center table, all by himself, yet he'd placed
his tall top hat—excellent beaver fur dyed coal black to

match his frock coat—by one place beside him, and his caped cloak—lined with a Hudson's Bay trade blanket for extra warmth—on the other, as if reserving those places for people he expected to join him. He'd been there an hour and he never looked up at new patrons entering with anything like expectation. Instead, he looked wary and keenly observant, shifting his attention from newspaper to patrons and back again. The weathered lines around his jaw and eyes, and the permanently sun-darkened skin told of a hard life. I needed to see him walk to know more. To know if he'd been hired by my lady's enemies to kidnap her.

He hadn't the look of the romantic glory-seeking followers of Lord Byron.

In the meantime I could imagine the intensity of the fur trader. While not beautiful, as so many dandies were in London these days, he was attractive in a raw sort of way.

And he appeared taller than me; his long legs stretched beneath the chair opposite him, and the tabletop brushed his first rib. Few men topped me in height. That made him more attractive by the minute.

Not today. For either of us.

This lean and hard man, practical and decisive, was obviously on home leave and hadn't been in London long enough for the coal-smoke filled air to soil his fresh-from-the-tailor linen and waistcoat.

Occasionally his fingers flexed as if they itched with emptiness, and he reached for the pocket of his cloak as he reassured himself that his weapon was loaded and close to hand. Smart man.

My hands felt the same way. I'd spent too many years protecting my young charge to be comfortable without a pistol in my pocket, a stiletto disguised as a decorative hatpin, and a *sgian dubh* tucked into the top of my boot.

Another time I might be interested in this man. I allowed my assessing gaze to linger a little too long on his thin-lipped grimace. He looked up just then and returned my stare with equal assessment and a regretful smile.

I sat with my back to a corner, as I did most afternoons at this time, the multipaned window to my left and a bookshelf filled with newspapers and magazines from Paris, Berlin, and Marseilles on my right. Those papers sadly needed updating; the news was a month old.

Another figure walked between me and the suspicious fur trader. I'd noted her when she arrived a few moments before and dismissed her the moment she ordered tea and marzipan for herself and a young maid loaded with shopping parcels. The girl's country seamstress might be skilled, but she hadn't visited London in over a year, probably three. Her pleated skirt didn't flare wide enough, and knotwork, in a vaguely Celtic pattern, adorned the area between knee and hem. That trim hadn't been in fashion for quite some time. The ribbon on her hand-decorated bonnet was clumsily finished and the rooster feathers adorning the crown might be colorful and attractive, but they were not proper ostrich or peacock.

"Madame Magdala?" the country girl asked shyly. Her hands shook slightly with nervousness so that the teacup rattled in its saucer. She'd recognized me as my alter-ego, in spite of my proper black dress. A sharp girl. The maid took a chair at an empty table three places to my right, toward the back of the café.

"Yes?" I drawled affecting the east European accent of my alternate personality.

"I ... I was wondering what you charge for a reading?"

She didn't look as if she could afford my usual fees. I was a novelty for friendly and casual looks into the future for the nobs and their courtesans who attended salons on the fringe of high society. Those fees padded my bank account quite nicely.

The money I earned as Madame Magdala was a necessity for me if I were to secure a safe future for me and Miss Augusta Ada Byron.

This country girl, though, looked as if she truly needed advice from me, Miss Elise the governess, and not some Gypsy fakery. Was she the reason the swirls in the coffee nearly compelled me?

"For you, my dear, nothing. Sit. Join me." I gestured expansively. The polite murmurings around the busy café stilled as all turned to gape at me. Madame Magdala was flamboyant and always the center of attention. Miss Elise, (I hated the honorary Mrs. Title granted to high-placed servants) governess to Miss Byron, was meek and invisible. Well, maybe not meek. I could defend my charge vigorously when I needed to.

"Vhat do you need, my child?" I asked the country girl.

"Aemelie Griffin, Madame." She held her gloved hand across the table in greeting.

I brushed her palm with my fingertips, polite but distant, not inviting intimacy.

"I . . . am in London with my cousin. For the Season. But I . . . I have no interest in the dandies my cousin thinks are appropriate for me and my station." She kept her eyes lowered and her words quiet.

"Ah," I sighed with appropriate romantic depth. "Another has caught your eye. Perhaps someone above your station?" I guessed she came from landed gentry—her muslin gown might be outdated but it was of good quality. If there was a title involved, it was minor or distant in her family tree.

"Lord William, Baron King," she said even more quietly.

My attention riveted upon her, forgetting those around me. Dangerous. But I had other plans for the eighth Baron King than this country mouse. The future I had witnessed had grand plans for Lord William.

"How did you meet Lord William?" I picked up my spoon without thinking and stirred my coffee into a deep whirlpool. I engaged every bit of my formidable willpower to keep from looking into the swirls just yet.

"He's our neighbor back home." She looked up, hope sparkling in her eyes and a half smile on her lips. "I've known him all of my life. But of late he spends more time in London than at the estate. He's making a name for himself in politics."

"I see. At home you are one of a very few pretty girls of the right class to attract his attention at assemblies and private gatherings. Here in London you are an insignificant shadow among many beautiful women bent upon marriage to the most eligible bachelor of the Season." In early March, the Season had not officially begun, but ladies flocked to the city with their debutantes in tow, scrambling for access to the best modistes, and lining up invitations to the balls, musicales, and garden parties. All to find husbands for the girls. Becoming the wife of a man wealthy enough to support her, was the *only* respectable occupation for a young lady, unless she waited too long and had to settle for the position of governess or paid lady's companion.

I had chosen my place primarily to protect those endangered by Lord Byron's depravity. Over the years I decided to avoid marriage. I'd not let any man gain control over me—by law or by love.

Miss Griffin's blushes drew my attention away from the spinning coffee and my own musings. Lord William was already much in demand.

"Yes." She heaved a tremendous sigh that lifted her bosom dramatically. "My father is the rector of the parish. His grandfather is the Earl of Bloomington." Ah, a younger son with little allowance but good connections.

The fur trader took notice of her quivering bosom.

Hmm. Perhaps he was no enemy, merely a man on home leave in search of a city wife. Did he have a country wife—perhaps a Red Indian country wife—he'd left in the wilderness until his return? Many traders did.

This girl deserved better. But I also needed her to open her eyes and seek a husband closer to her station in life. Sir William was not fated to love her. I knew that. A vision in my coffee had told me.

The time had come to look away from the tiny window lights that badly needed replacing with newer, thinner, clearer, and larger panes, and into the still whirling coffee. I might find truth there. I might find only coffee. I never knew. My clients always presumed I found, and spoke, a true vision. I made certain of that.

Keen observation told me more than my vague and symbolic visions.

My eyes tracked the circular motion of the golden liquid. My perception closed inward; darkness dominated the periphery. The patterns danced within the circles. Dancers waltzing the patterns of life.

The girl, Aemelie Griffin, danced around the edges with a tall and lean man full of intensity. A man strong enough to protect and love her in an uncertain world. Their steps took on a different cadence from the waltz, more a stomping country-dance, exuberant and joyful.

I couldn't help but smile at the truth of that image. For at the center of the dance, still following a graceful and romantic waltz, glided my girl, Miss Ada, with her own strong man with hints of gold in his hair—like a coronet. An earl's coronet.

But the coronet turned to flames encircling them, burning all in its path to cinders. The flames reached dangerously close to Miss Ada's glowing skirts.

"I have it on good authority that Lord William will attend Lady Hasselwhythe's salon tonight." I pitched my words so the fur trader could hear them clearly. Lady Hasselwhythe and I had an understanding. I vowed never to reveal her string of young lovers to her husband, and she issued me an open invitation to her salon.

Any evening, with whatever company I chose. "My card. Present it to the footman at the door. He will give you entrance."

"Oh, thank you, Madame. Bless you," the girl gushed. She clutched my hand tightly as she rose. I pressed the card on her as an invitation for her to leave. She practically danced out the door. Her maid followed tiredly.

I scooped up the ignored marzipan and ate it, letting the delicacy of sugar and almond paste restore some of my depleted humours. A vision always left me limp and listless for a time.

Then I held out a second card toward the fur trader.

"And will Lord William truly attend the salon?" he asked in a deep gravelly voice, as if he'd swallowed too many dusty winds.

"At some time in the evening, perhaps later than expected. But the young baron's first destination is a private musicale evening. You have Miss Aemelie Griffin to yourself for several hours. Convince her quickly that she is in love with you."

And then Miss Byron proceeded into the café and ordered hot *chocolat* before she even looked for me. She knew I'd be here. I usually was. I would never disappoint her. Her maid stepped behind our lady, also burdened with parcels. She flopped into a chair at the same table Miss Griffin's servant had just departed.

The fur trader gathered his hat and cloak, and left, dragging his right leg slightly. In that moment I doubted he'd return to his wilderness. If he did, he'd take a wife with him to a staid job in one of the fur factories rather than exploring the wilderness in search of beaver and otter. Either way, I suspected Miss Aemelie Griffin would be satisfied.

I almost envied her his long hard body and his keen focus.

"Tell me of your day, Miss Ada," I said in my normal accent, once again the modest governess.

"Miss Elise, I have had the most wonderful inspiration. I discovered five errors in Mr. Babbage's calculations and corrected them. I believe he can now proceed with the building of his Difference Engine without hindrance." She produced a thick notebook, loosely bound, and opened it to a page filled with arcane symbols and numbers. They could have been Romany scribblings for all I knew. Except I could read and speak a little Romany. Mathematical equations were more exotic and less understandable.

"That is good. Mr. Charles Babbage needs to succeed in building his calculation machine to satisfy his investors," I added.

"Yes, I know." Ada dismissed my concerns. "Can you imagine the huge advances in mathematics we can achieve when we have accurate logarithmic tables?"

"Did you attend your fitting for your evening gown for the musicale tonight?" I had more pressing needs for the girl.

"Um . . ."

"You forgot." I sighed in disappointment.

"No. I had the fitting, but I found the fabric very ornate and stiff. I'd prefer something lighter in silk chiffon and a more sober color . . ."

Daisy, the maid, nodded to confirm they had indeed visited the modiste.

"You sound like your mother."

Miss Ada closed her mouth with a snap.

"You helped me with the design of the fabric, Miss," I admonished her. "The protection it will grant you is necessary."

"I don't believe there are any followers of my father still alive." She pouted.

I maintained a firm silence rather than comment. We'd foiled too many plots against her after Lord Byron "died" in Greece ten years ago. I had experienced firsthand his depravity, his twisted philosophy, and his obsession with immortality. I knew the length his followers would go to in order to bring him back to life.

"Can you redesign the soul transference machine?" I asked her.

"Not without your help. You destroyed the original back in '16." The year without a summer. Lake Geneva. A house party at Villa Diodati. She didn't have to remind me. "You know how the machine all went together."

"And I will never, ever, willingly help build another." I clamped my teeth on that statement and deliberately looked away from my coffee cup that had begun to hum in the back of my mind. Instead, I signaled the coffee master that I needed a fresh cup. This one had gone cold.

"If we must attend the musicale, I suppose we should return home to change." Ada didn't look happy about that. "I presume you found the components for the miniature Leyden jar during your errands?"

"Yes," I replied with satisfaction and dismissed the coffee master with a gesture. "But I think I would like to consult your solicitor on the way. I have an interest in buying this property. I could do much with the ambiance, the space above and below stairs, and I'd serve better pastry." Lots and lots of lovely space above for living and entertaining. Even more space in the cellars for my special project. I'd checked.

"You are a wonderful cook, Miss Elise. But surely you will remain with me. You don't need a business. I will take care of you." Ada took my arm, holding me close to her side.

"But soon you will marry." I'd seen it in the dancing coffee. Dancing while the world burned to cinders ... "You will not need your old governess when you have a husband and children. You barely need me now."

"You are more than my governess. You are my greatest friend. And ... and I'd like you to stay with me forever, as my companion. Not that I believe I shall ever marry. I've never met a man more interesting than the mathematical challenges Mr. Babbage presents me. And I doubt that Mother will ever approve of any suitor. My father frightened her so badly she doesn't like men much at all."

We both knew the truth of that.

"Glass beads, Elise? Surely my wardrobe budget extends beyond glass beads!" Ada stamped her foot and glared at me as I put the finishing touches on her ensemble. She lifted the chain of crescent moon beads with disdain. Each bit of copper-colored glass bore the impression of an eight-pointed star—a Romany symbol of safe haven. "My father was a baron. My mother is the Baroness Wentworth in her own right. We have a position to maintain."

"Yes, you do. And you can't do that if you are dead or held captive by the enemy." I drew a copper wire from the pendant bead—a disk cunningly designed so that the brilliant red-gold starburst in the center drew the eye and the clear background disappeared—and touched it to the top of the miniature Leyden jar secreted in Miss Ada's scant cleavage. Fortunately, this year fashions called for frilled tuckers draped over the shoulder and nesting at the top of the bodice. Plenty of places to discreetly hide the components of my invention. Or weapons.

As the wires touched chemicals in the jar, electricity arced through the beads and down the copper wires woven into the white gauze overlay on the dress. The younger son of a lord who dabbled in these things promised me that as long as the circuit was complete the carbon fiber within the necklace would react with the glass and the copper.

I didn't understand it all. But I trusted Andrew

Fitzandrew to know what he was doing. Sir Drew always knew what he was doing. Delicious man.

Ada gasped as the glass beads glowed and the gown shimmered with scintillating sparks. "It . . . it is gorgeous, Elise." *Amazing how she took interest in her appearance once we started the dressing process. I trusted that she would also become interested in men once presented with one who had an adequate understanding of mathematics.*

"I have it on good authority that Princess Victoria will attend the musicale tonight."

"*Merde!*" Ada exploded. Her left hand went to the beads and threatened to rip them from her throat. "That means *her* mother will be there, and therefore *my* mother and her Furies will also be present."

"Your lady mother has high hopes to become a lady-in-waiting . . ." *She sought royal protection for her daughter.*

"And all London knows that will never happen. My father's scandals will prevent either of us ever being fully accepted in proper society."

"Ah, but one can always be a fashion setter and slide into society by a back door," I soothed her. *I'd already started the process for myself.*

"I know that half smile and lowered eyes, Elise. What are you planning?"

"I am only a simple governess. I have not the means nor the cunning to plan anything more elaborate than a lovely gown for my charge." *I could not meet her eyes.*

"And will Miss Elise fade into the wallpaper tonight while Madame Magdala stands at the center of the room demanding more attention than the soprano hired to entertain?" She smirked.

"I did not know that you knew . . ."

"Of course I know. Now what are you planning and how does it involve the *Café du Paris*?"

"The way light changes when passing through the windows of the café made me think about how the room will change if we replace those thick and wavy panes with larger, thinner, and clearer ones."

I didn't need to say anything more. Miss Ada's fertile imagination started thinking about light and the mathematics of light and how to apply them to some new invention.

I disconnected the wires on the gown's electricity and shooed her out into the evening fog. A real pea souper tonight with cold sea mist mixing with the coal smoke that permeated the air. We covered our faces with finely woven veils to keep as much of the poisonous air out of our lungs as possible. All the new inventions required power, power generated by steam, fueled by coal ... "We'll take a proper hansom cab with a real horse pulling it," I announced.

"But the carriages pulled by steam-powered horses are so much more efficient, and warmer," Ada protested, coming out of her obsession for a moment.

"A real horse can smell the presence of other vehicles and avoid crashing. A steam machine cannot," I huffed.

"Machines will always prove more efficient," she returned.

The horse got us to the private residence of the Countess of Kirkenwood in good time. We passed three steam carriages that had collided with each other, gas lamps, and pedestrians along the way.

∘⚙

"If I'd known you intended the necklace for another, I would not have given it quite so much tender, loving care," Sir Andrew Fitzandrew whispered from behind me. I felt more than saw the heat of his gaze on my lace-draped cleavage. Society might dictate that a mere governess needed to wear sober black. That didn't mean I had to remain meek in an ugly gown.

I'd noted Sir Drew's arrival and his position in Lady Kirkenwood's crowded ballroom the moment he arrived, just as we took seats for the performance. That he was the only person present taller than me helped in my observation. The countess had converted the space into an auditorium with straight lines of straighter chairs made barely comfortable with red velvet cushions. As chaperone to Miss Ada, I had to sit next to the girl in a prominent place in the third row, no matter how tight and uncomfortable. I couldn't see behind me to discover if Sir Drew had bothered to try and fit on one of the chairs, or stood against the wall instead.

Lord William King sat in the same row as we did. I'd made sure of that, so that Miss Ada could translate the Italian aria for him, if he required.

During the intermission, I stood near the wall beside the dowagers where I could watch the entire room and make certain that Lord William King made polite conversation with Ada and two other young couples, but did not become too forward.

"I needed all of your tender loving care to go into that necklace," I replied to Sir Drew. He stood a little too close for proper polite society. His body warmth filled my back and slid through many of my senses. Lovely man.

"She does glow quite nicely," Sir Drew admitted. "Brilliant idea, touch her gown and the too forward admirer suffers a shock. Aim a pistol at her and you can't be certain where she is or was or will be because of the afterimage. Lord William is entranced. But does he see the young woman beneath or merely the lovely shimmer that lingers behind every time she moves?"

Mr. Charles Babbage wandered into the ballroom, stout, clumsily dressed, red-faced, and stinking drunk. He clung to a sheaf of papers and headed straight for Miss Ada.

"Excuse me, Sir Andrew. A new guest has arrived. I

must attend." Curses in every one of the five languages I spoke—one cannot grow up in Switzerland knowing how to converse with any less.

"This is not the time to discuss business," I said sternly as I took Babbage's elbow with both hands and steered him back to the dowagers' wall.

"But I must . . ."

"Not now, Mr. Babbage. You will make a fool of yourself." I put all of Madame Magdala's force of personality and authority into my words and my grip on him, even though tonight I was supposed to be the invisible governess.

Sir Drew had turned away, so I did not have his company to help keep Babbage away from Ada. Besides, I needed a few words of my own with the inventor.

"How are you progressing with your Difference Engine?" I asked, standing squarely between him and the rest of the party.

"It is of no consequence. I have new plans, a new machine that is even better." He gestured widely, sending several pages skittering across the floor. "I must enlist Lord William King as an investor. This may be my only opportunity . . ."

"You do not have the opportunity tonight," I insisted. "No one will invest in your new machine until the first one is built and proven successful."

"But . . . my Analytical Machine is so much more important . . ."

"Not to men who want to see a return on their investment before giving you more money."

We argued for several more minutes. The man was more inflexible than my corset! He had brilliant ideas and some aptitude but no follow through. I felt sorry for his wife.

"Excuse me, just one moment," I begged, searching frantically for Sir Drew. He stood only five steps away, speaking flirtatiously with our hostess. He was an expert at flirting, as I knew all too well.

"Sir Drew," I said a little too loudly. Still holding Mr. Babbage by the elbow, I dragged him behind me. "Do you have a moment to . . . um explain the concept behind Miss Byron's unique necklace?" I didn't have time to wait for a reply. I had to intercept the newest guests.

"Lady Byron." I dipped a curtsy directly in front of my employer. "What a surprise to see you here. If you had informed Miss Ada of your plans, perhaps we could have shared a carriage."

Lady Byron's Furies, er . . . two companions, delicate Mrs. Carr, and fierce Miss Frend, tried to edge around me, barely acknowledging me with a nod. They had their sights set on Miss Ada and Lord William. From their frowns, I knew they disapproved of him. They disapproved of every male of the species. In the ten years I'd been with Miss Ada, I'd never heard a kind word about any man from these three. But they rarely graced our establishment with their presence. Lady Byron preferred adult company (but only of females) to that of children.

She also felt that by dividing the household she could keep Ada's location a secret from those who wished her harm.

"What are you about, Miss Elise?" Lady Byron hissed.

I suppressed the angry growl in the back of my throat. Tonight I had to present myself as a civilized human, not a tigress defending her cub in the wild jungles of India.

"About, Lady Byron?" I used my superior height to look down my long nose at her. Once, she'd been beautiful and vibrant. Lord Byron had destroyed that. "Why, I'm paying my respects as is proper. I'm sorry you missed the first aria. Madame Louisa has an amazing range and breath control." She also had an impressive bosom. Sir Drew was making note of it right now.

A quick glance showed me that Princess Victoria and

her mother, the Duchess of Kent, emerged from the refreshment room with a near complete entourage of ladies.

The Furies tugged at Lady Byron's sleeve to direct her attention toward the real purpose of their visit. All three hastened toward the guests of honor, dyed ostrich feathers in their gauzy turbans bobbing like the topknot of an officious rare bird.

I sighed in relief. Miss Ada and Lord William had progressed to finger brushing as he relieved her of an empty wineglass. Time to return to Mr. Babbage and *my* purpose tonight. Sir Drew would have to wait until later, presuming he didn't grow impatient with me and make a liaison with the soprano.

"The Difference Engine and its ability to calculate and print accurate logarithmic tables will be a tremendous boon to navigation . . ." Sir Drew said idly.

"I cannot make the Difference Engine work," Babbage finally admitted in a tone so quiet I had to strain to hear him.

"Miss Ada found the errors in the mathematics this afternoon. She can make it work," I jumped into the conversation as if I'd never left.

Babbage's eyes widened with hope. Sir Drew's mouth quirked up in an affectation of boredom. I'd have believed his expression if I didn't see the sparkle of amusement in his eyes.

"Then Miss Ada must go over my designs for the Analytical Machine this very evening," Babbage insisted, taking a step toward the lady with his sheaf of papers held before him like a talisman. (Somehow he'd gathered up the stray papers without toppling over.) He wobbled a bit as he stepped. Sir Drew easily guided him back to the wall.

"Not tonight." I checked over my shoulder. Our hostess rang a little crystal bell to gain the attention of her audience. Ada and Lord William made their way back to their chairs, looking expectantly toward the countess. Lady Byron and her Furies hovered on the fringes of the crowd around the princess and her mother. They'd be mightily disappointed when all the chairs in the first and second rows filled with higher ranking guests.

That would put them in the third row with Miss Ada. I couldn't have that.

"Mr. Babbage," I said firmly, gathering my courage. "Will you allow me to oversee the building of the Difference Engine, thus freeing you to design other projects?"

He dragged his gaze away from Ada and back to me.

"You have the funding. I have some knowledge of things mechanical." I also had access to some talented Romany traders who could make *anything* work. "Miss Ada has corrected the problems in the early design. Let me help you with this, and when it is done and working, your investors will throw money at you for a machine that stores and retrieves information—like the cards some libraries are adopting."

Oh, yes, I had plans for the little café Ada's solicitor negotiated to purchase. "The properties of light and refraction seem to be ideal for such a machine." I didn't know that for certain, but the distortion of images by the thick window panes of the café had given me an idea. The swirls of coffee seemed to confirm them when I looked after supper.

"Light? Prisms?" His gaze turned inward for a long moment.

I wanted to shake him back into his senses so I could take my proper place beside Ada and Lord William, edging out Lady Byron and the Furies. The way Lord William tilted his head toward my girl, listening attentively—probably to a dissertation on ratios, algebra, and abstract calculations well beyond me—I hoped the eighth Baron King would have the courtesy to call upon us tomorrow, and reserve the first dance at the first ball of the Season.

Babbage came out of his reverie and stared at the papers in his hand. "Light and prism. Yes. That is the solution. May I call upon Miss Ada tomorrow to go over my calculations?"

"Will you give me the supervision of the Difference Engine?"

Sir Drew frowned at me.

"Yes, yes, do with it what you can. I no longer have the time . . ." Mr. Charles Babbage wandered back out the way he'd come, still stinking of drink but no longer drunk.

As I turned to take my seat, Sir Drew offered me his arm in escort. That surprised me. Polite society expected him to take a mistress, but never to identify her in public. He endangered my reputation by such a gesture, and thus my ability to protect Miss Ada . . .

A commotion at the doorway, loud voices of protest and shuffling bodies, halted everyone in their tracks. The Countess Kirkenwood ceased her introduction of the next aria in mid-sentence. All eyes turned toward the towering white-and-gilt double doors at the entrance to the room as they slammed open, banging and reverberating against the walls. The sight of one hundred bodies whirling in protest at the disturbance nearly sent my vision spiraling into the darkness of a vision.

Sir Drew dug his fingers into the flesh of my forearm. That slight pain jolted my eyes back to reality. I had no time to lose myself. He knew Madame Magdala well enough to realize the consequences of losing me to a trance.

The sight of a slight young man with old-fashioned flowing locks, a silk shirt open at the collar with lavish sleeves barely contained by a loose black cloak with three caplets around the shoulders, high riding boots splattered with mud, and eyes wild and unfocused would have dragged me out of the vision just as easily. The intruder dressed in a style of nearly twenty years ago, more romantic than practical.

The exact same fashion favored by Lord Byron.

I think I groaned. Couldn't these idiots at least keep up with the times?

The interloper carried a flintlock pistol in one hand and a clay pot, stoppered with cork and a braided wick, in the other. I'd seen those vessels before. Filled with gunpowder and sharp bits of metal, Lord Byron had favored them for making loud noises and wide craters.

The painted clay looked vaguely Greek. A poor imitation. Of course it looked Greek. The disillusioned young men who worshipped Byron and his poetry had to imitate all of his preferences and his vices.

How many lives would he willingly take in his quest to resurrect Lord Byron?

"Give me the girl!" the interloper demanded, waving his gun toward every young lady in the crowd.

Princess Victoria screamed. Her mother screamed louder, and shriller. A bevy of men hastened to stand between their future queen and the madman. Lord William among them.

My girl stood alone and unprotected in her shimmering dress.

The madman zeroed in on her. In five long strides he closed the distance and held the gun to her temple.

"No." I tried to scream, but no sound emerged. Electricity created the glowing afterimages. The electricity relied on the flow of sparks jumping from one bead to the next. The Byron imitator could use those sparks to ignite his jug of Greek death.

A new screech pierced the air. Lady Byron. I knew it of old. More strident and attention gathering than the princess, or her mother. She fainted, followed by more yelling and chaos from her Furies.

They were of no consequence in this business. I

stalked toward Miss Ada with determination, eyes burning with hatred and fear.

The gun turned on me.

"You! You caused the death of my lord!"

Single-minded bastard. I hadn't heard that accusation before.

"You destroyed the machine that would have kept him alive." Oh, that.

As long as he kept the weapon trained on me and away from my girl. But he had his gun arm wrapped around her neck, tightening in a crushing reflex. The other arm still cradled the little clay pot, the more dangerous weapon.

I sensed movement at the edges of the room while the madman looked only at me. "We need this woman to save my lord before his soul withers to nothing!"

"His soul was a withered mass of ugliness long before he died," I snarled.

"He was a genius. His poetry lifted so many to the heavens. He saved my soul," the man countered.

Sir Drew and Lord William edged closer now that they knew the princess was safe. Safe only as long as the idiot did not ignite the wick in his bomb.

"His actions damaged more people," I said. As long as I could keep him talking, we could close in on him.

"Don't come any closer, or I will blow up all of you!"

I paused.

So did Sir Drew.

But Lord William, bless his brave heart and gallant soul, was to the man's off side and obscured from view by Miss Ada's elaborate gauze turban complete with bobbing feathers.

Never had the fashion looked less ridiculous than at that moment.

"I'm taking the girl. She's the only one who can rebuild the machine." The wild-eyed fanatic urged his captive forward. She dug in her heels.

His hand slipped to her sleeve. A spark jumped from the dress. He jerked back, shaking his shocked hand in disbelief.

He still held the Greek jug.

"She can't rebuild the transference engine without me, and I refuse to ever allow such a machine to be built again," I said through gritted teeth.

"Then I'll take you both. I'll do whatever I have to in order to revive Lord Byron." He pushed again, his arm tightening around Ada's throat—carefully away from the dress—while the gun pointed right between my eyes.

Something stirred in Ada's eyes. Gone the blind panic of a moment ago. Gone the meekness hammered into her by her mother. What emerged was the strong woman I had raised with skills to defend herself.

She stomped on her captor's foot with her soft shoes. The thin soles with only an inch of heel barely changed the man's attention. But the elbow to his gut did.

He doubled over, coughing, carrying Miss Ada with him. Her skirts brushed his face as they tumbled to the ground.

He screamed as much in outrage from the electrical shock as pain.

The gun exploded.

I felt a whoosh of air past my ear before I heard the flash of gunpowder.

More cautious guests hit the floor, arms over their vulnerable heads.

Every detail jumped into perfect clarity.

Sir Drew and Lord William rushed forward. Not before the electricity in the glass necklace sparked repeatedly in random directions. One bit of fire landed on the wick.

With visions of the entire house burning to cinders flashing before my eyes, I lunged for the clay pot. Sir Drew grabbed the necklace, breaking the filaments that bound the strands together as well as the chain of sparks leaping from one to the other. Lord William wrenched the gun away from the madman.

The sizzling wick had nearly reached the lip of the pot. Too close for me to grab.

But I had my trusty hatpin. I stabbed the wick and flicked it free as the flamelet tried to sink into the pot. Angrily I ground the spark to ash beneath my heel.

Only then did I breathe.

"It's not fair!" wailed the young man. Suddenly he looked very young and vulnerable with one arm pinned high against his back by Sir Drew. "It's not fair that *she* should live and the poet king cannot. We have to find a way to restore him to a body. The world dies more each day without his genius." He lapsed into sobs that demanded pity.

I had none for him or his kind. "While I live, I will fight every one of you fanatics to the death to prevent the insanity of Lord Byron from returning. He was a murdering necromancer, for heaven's sake," I hissed, making certain the young man heard me, but no one outside our immediate quartet.

My focus expanded, barely noting the screaming guests and fainting ladies. I saw only that my girl was safe, shuddering with huge sobs. She reached for me instinctively. I'd been her primary companion for ten years. More a mother to her than the lady who claimed the title.

Lady Byron beat me in the race to hold the girl upright while Sir Drew and Lord William wrestled the wild-eyed poet to the ground. As if in slow motion other gentlemen joined them in restraining the sobbing lout. Heavily built men in house livery appeared to remove the garbage and turn him over to the authorities.

I had no choice but to follow Lady Byron, her Furies, and my Miss Ada. Lord William and Sir Drew remained behind.

✿

"No one is to be admitted, Carrick!" Lady Byron informed the butler as the doorbell rang for the fifth time the next morning. I was surprised she'd left her bed. Probably sensing that the world would come to her today in search of gossip about the night before. She'd thrown herself upon the lounge in the second parlor with a damp cloth over her eyes. I'd seen nothing of the Furies.

Miss Ada had roused herself, her adventures forgotten, in the face of some new mathematical challenge or scientific paper to write. She still bore a few bruises on her throat where the glass beads had pressed tightly before Drew broke the strand. She ignored them easily.

But I had been watching the front of the house for one particular caller. I yanked the door open wide two hand widths before Carrick could reach for the latch. "Welcome, Lord William."

We exchanged pleasantries in the front hall. I took his hat and thrust it at Carrick before the senior servant could protest.

"I've come to return Miss Ada's necklace." He held out the strand of beads, all jumbled together, some still on their string, others not. The pendant bead still had a bit of copper wire protruding from the bottom of one ray of the starburst.

"Thank you, my lord," Miss Ada said from the stairway. She descended gracefully, despite a furious Mrs. Carr protesting behind her. She embodied the reason we called Lady Byron's companions Furies. They were rarely less than furious in the presence of a man.

"Carrick, please bring tea to the front parlor," I ordered as I herded the young people in that direction.

"What is the meaning of this?" Lady Byron demanded. She charged into the hallway with tendrils of hair dangling free of her coiffure, her gauze turban slightly askew and mouth pinched as she fought her headache.

I'd have a headache also if I'd consumed two bottles

of wine and three snifters of brandy to "calm my nerves," after the events at the musicale. Nothing like a short shot of whiskey to do the job without the morning after problems.

"My lady," I said softly, mindful of the low murmurs in the room behind me. I leaned against the closed doors to make certain my girl and her swain had at least a few moments of privacy. "There are rumors from Kensington Palace that Lord William finds high favor with the Duchess of Kent, *and* Princess Victoria." I couldn't add that I knew an earl's coronet was in the man's future. I knew that from my visions, but Princess Victoria did not yet know she would grant the title when she assumed the throne. "Would you rather be lady-in-waiting to the queen's mother, or to the queen herself? If Lord William courts your daughter as ardently as he fought for her life last night . . ." I let the assumption linger in the air between us.

The lady bit her lip in indecision. She took a step toward the front parlor and retreated, twice. Then she stood in indecision before summoning her companions into the second parlor.

Two months later I stood on the threshold of *my* new café. The old sign had been replaced by my new one only this morning. Proudly I turned the key in the lock and entered. It was late in the afternoon. The previous owners— my new employees—lingered while they cleared and cleaned at the end of a busy day.

My mind already planned changes. Big and small: move this table, replace the magazine rack with a larger bookcase, and most certainly update the windows to allow more light inside. Then I'd slowly move my things into the flat abovestairs. I couldn't leave Miss Ada until she married Lord William later in the summer. Oh, yes, that betrothal had happened within days of his returning her glass necklace.

The happy couple gave up looking longingly into each other's eyes long enough to follow me inside. Sir Drew lingered behind, frowning at the sign in full disapproval. Mr. Charles Babbage stumbled in after them. He surveyed the space, much as I did.

"This is where you want your machine?" he asked, a little disapprovingly.

"The space is too limited except for the operation console. That will be here, in the center of the café, in full view of the patrons. The rest can fill the cellars, the walls, the attics, and part of the building next door." I waved my hands expansively.

"This will take time," Miss Ada added. She, too, walked the space available. "How many books do you intend to store?"

"As many as we can acquire. Periodicals and newspapers from all over the world as well. The new dirigibles can bring them from Hong Kong, New Delhi, and New York, as well as Paris, Athens, and Cairo." I smiled in satisfaction, already envisioning rows and rows and rows of books.

"Why do you need up-to-date information from all over the world?" Lord William asked. He trailed behind his ladylove, more interested in her than my plans.

"Need I remind you of a wild-eyed poet the night of the musicale?"

All of my co-conspirators froze in place.

"He did not act alone. There are others. We must look for patterns; watch the movements of those who seek to shift souls into and out of bodies, natural or mechanical. We must never allow Lord Byron's followers to succeed."

Miss Ada nodded agreement.

"So you need my Analytical Engine to find and retrieve books and pamphlets and such, based on key data entered. Hmm . . ." Mr. Babbage stroked his chin in deep thought. Not much else mattered to him but the designing of his new invention.

"You don't have to do this," Sir Drew hissed in my ear. "Please, let me take care of you."

"Until you find someone younger and prettier, or your wife rises from her sickbed." I shook off his restraining hand.

Just then I noticed two figures walking past my café, the tall fur trader—who had lost a lot of his limp—and Miss Aemelie Griffin. Arm in arm, they paused to read the closed sign on the door. They looked so very disappointed I couldn't help but open the door for them.

"Welcome to Madame Magdala's Book View Café. Can I get you a cup of coffee?" I asked, the eastern European accent falling lightly from my lips. "And perhaps a bit of pastry. Or something to read?"

Acknowledgments

An author may write a book, but many others spend hours assisting with research and ideas, support and shoulders to cry on when characters will not behave and follow the original plot.

The Bookview Café, a publishing cooperative, graciously gave me permission to continue the adventures of Madame Magdala, a character I created for *Shadow Dancer*, my story in the *Shadow Conspiracy* anthology edited by Phyllis Irene Radford and Laura Ann Gilman, Bookview Café 2009. Christopher Doyle, who appears in these pages as Kit Doyle, delved into esoteric places to find a proper name from northern India for Ish. Facebook friends went beyond the call of duty to make math fun and hand me jokes: Tim O'Halloran, Amy Wood, and Paul Sanford. Bob Brown helped design the electric dress. ElizaBeth Gilligan came through with much knowledge of the Romany. And then there's Sara Mueller and Joyce Reynolds Ward who were always ready to brainstorm and critique the work over boar tacos.

Tim Karr, my beloved husband of many years, dragged me to every steam train and antique tractor show to help me understand how the engines really work. He also took hundreds of photos to remind me.

Agent Mike Kabongo of the Onyxhawke Agency and editor Sheila Gilbert at DAW were responsible for pushing me through to the end of this project.

Many thanks to all of you. I owe you more than you can imagine.